Praise for *Perilous Prophecy*
Winner of the Prism Award for Best Fantasy Novel

"The mythology is compelling, the emotional journeys are moving, and the treatment of diverse religious backgrounds is beautifully done: all who work toward good are seen as having common cause, no matter the external differences. I only wish [the book] had been longer."

—*Fantasy Literature*

"[Hieber's] work is pure magic. I love and enjoy the haunting beauty that she's created. You really must find the time to read these books if you haven't had the chance yet."

—*P.S. I Love Books*

"Leanna's exquisite language, a hallmark of her writing, guides the reader across continents and through dimensions. An engrossing, heartbreaking, uplifting story of disparate people drawn together for a cause bigger than they can conceive."

—*True-Blood.net*

"Hieber's writing is beautiful as always. She has the ability to describe in a way that captivates, making the setting just as interesting as the action or dialogue."

—*Pop Culture Breakdown*

TOR BOOKS BY
LEANNA RENEE HIEBER

The Eterna Files
Strangely Beautiful
Eterna and Omega
Perilous Prophecy

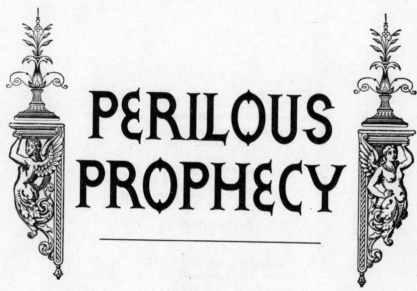

PERILOUS PROPHECY

LEANNA RENEE HIEBER

TOR

A Tom Doherty Associates Book
New York

PERILOUS PROPHECY

Copyright © 2017 by Leanna Renee Hieber

All rights reserved.

A Tor Book
Published by Tom Doherty Associates
175 Fifth Avenue
New York, NY 10010

www.tor-forge.com

Tor® is a registered trademark of Macmillan Publishing Group, LLC.

The Library of Congress Cataloging-in-Publication Data is available upon request.

ISBN 978-0-7653-7744-9 (hardcover)
ISBN 978-1-4668-5588-5 (ebook)

Our books may be purchased in bulk for promotional, educational, or business use.
Please contact your local bookseller or the Macmillan Corporate and Premium
Sales Department at 1-800-221-7945, extension 5442, or by email at
MacmillanSpecialMarkets@macmillan.com.

This novel was originally published in a substantially different form
under the title *The Perilous Prophecy of Guard and Goddess*
by Dorchester Books in 2011.

First Edition: June 2017

Printed in the United States of America

0 9 8 7 6 5 4 3 2 1

PERILOUS PROPHECY

PROLOGUE

The goddess stood on the Liminal edge, the boundary of the Whisper-world, a precarious place where guardian angels are appointed and fates are sealed, a space where beautiful or terrible things are set in motion, depending on what is required.

It was time to choose the new Guard. She'd seen the previous Guard onto the field, saw to it that their spirits were happy and at peace. They now rested with their fellows while she stood at a new beginning. This moment was always an important one. A critical one. Yet the past overtook her, wrapping its claws around her throat.

Ah, light! Running across the grass, she laughed. The sound brought spring. Nearby, the Muses frolicked, rejoicing in the sudden newness of life. Her beloved would be here, too, beautiful, winged, and warm. Not cold and horrible like the one who had stolen her away.

In centuries to come, she would curse the day she had been so careless. She would curse the day she failed to look behind her to the cave opening, where burning eyes watched.

The call of a great bird sounded, and a warm wind surrounded her. Strong arms cradled her, and laughter greened the trees. The Muses rushed into the field, delighted. It was a reunion of dearest friends.

Her beloved kissed her deeply, the spring breeze entwining his black hair with her own prismatic tresses. Trailing the line of her body with his fingertips, he pressed against her, aching, desperate. Winged and eternal, the Keeper of Peace, the Balance, the true husband of her heart. Phoenix.

He drew back and stared at the woman who should not have become another god's bride.

His body burst into flame.

She should have foreseen the danger, but she had not. Nor had she heard the growl from the distant shadows, seen the watcher's eyes grow hard.

Phoenix's form exploded, his feathers scorched and smoldering. From him came an unforgettable, ungodly shriek of agony. She screamed, too, a noise that rent the heavens.

Her terror made the rain come, dousing Phoenix and muddying the ground with water and blood. But it was too late. Hysterical, she cradled the charred and reeking body of her true love. The Muses watched in horror.

The wind picked up. It lifted a huge feather with gentle hands, consoling, murmuring sweet sympathies; it knew the depth of their love, as did all that was divine. The feather moved as if with a life of its own, seeming to float of its own volition. Five Muses ran toward it. Four ran away.

Her true love's corpse crumbled to dust. Backing slowly from the body, she felt madness overtake her. Wailing, she beat her fists into the ground until her hands bled.

"This is far from the end!" she shrieked. Gathering up his ashes, she cradled them in her skirts, pieces of bone, feather, and hair; her tears moistened the wretched fragments. "The world will not release you. I do not release you. It will not end this way. We will return."

She turned to face the cave where the murderer lurked. Behind him stood a host of the restless dead, cackling and shrieking, bloodlust rising in their tortured hearts. These were the wretched dead that she could not reach, could never reach; they were hopeless cases that needed higher, more powerful salvation than her grace and light. These were the dead who tormented the living.

"Come. Home," Darkness growled.

"You are not home," she spat.

His red eyes narrowed. Her stomach heaved and she doubled over, helpless. A sickening, rotten pulp flew from her lips, and Darkness snickered. Damn him for tricking her all those years ago. If she'd never eaten those seeds, sickly sweet and insidious, he'd never have gained an advantage.

She stared at him in fury, rising unsteadily to her feet. He might have power over her body, as the Whisper-world had truly infected her, but he couldn't control her entirely.

The dead rushed out into the field, floating over the earth, gallivanting in their ghoulish fashion, their bones disjointed and their forms horrendous.

"Frolic, friends," Darkness gurgled. "Feed. Me. Misery."

But, no. From the still-burning ashes of Phoenix came new flame. The ashes in her hands and skirts stirred, and the bloodred color of the fire shifted to a cerulean blue. From its glow emanated a force that was peaceful and full of music.

The low-burning azure flame took on first the shape of a feather, then a veritable pillar of fire, and the goddess gave a choked cry at the sight. Phoenix was not bested, nor was he alone. Here were the Muses who had stood by him, gossamer and glimmering angels, five beloved companions who were the best of friends. They stared down the restless dead with unforgiving eyes.

"You will feed Darkness nothing" came a ghostly whisper that nonetheless rumbled like thunder, and the undead paused. "Henceforth know to fear me. My friends and I shall turn you back, all of you who terrorize the living. My murderer will pay. We will starve his restless bones until they are dust. Restless dead, meet the guardians of the living. From this day forward we wield righteous justice. We can no longer leave the Balance to the Earth herself. Her children need aid against the likes of Darkness, who seek to enlarge their empire of misery. Tremble in our path, you who seek to grow shadow."

The host hesitated, unsettled. From deep within the cave, lightning flashed. Darkness seethed.

All light vanished from the sky. In return, blue fire covered the ground like a flood. Two worlds were shifting, creaking, opposing each other in earnest, and only one could be the winner. But the victor would not be proclaimed that day. The barrier pins between life and death shimmered, and the Whisper-world acknowledged that battle was right. Balance would be maintained despite the violence that had been done. Darkness could not reign triumphant. A Guard was necessary.

Darkness gazed about the field and growled.

She whom many called Persephone approached her husband slowly. Those red eyes retreated into the cave, widening in apprehension as a great light began to emanate from her: white like a dove. Persephone gazed upon the new force that had gathered, at the five friends who had in that moment pledged to fight an eternity at her lover's side. She blew the fiery ghost of her lover a kiss and bowed her head to the attendant Muses, knowing now was not the day of their triumph, knowing many days of sadness lay ahead.

She turned back to Darkness and narrowed her eyes. "In time dawn will come, and you'll bow to our light," she declared. Clutching the ash, feathers, and bone of her beloved, she lifted her diaphanous robes and stepped back into her Whisper-world prison.

THAT HAD BEEN LONG, LONG AGO, BUT THE GUARD STILL FOUGHT the good fight.

"It's time, my love," called a whisper at Persephone's cheek.

Blinking back tears, she stared into a floating orb of blue fire; all that remained of her one true love. "You are a ghost. Dust and vapor," she murmured.

"Yes, darling, I know," he replied, all too accustomed to this exchange. "But it's time. Time for a new Guard."

"Yes," she echoed, her voice hollow. She did not want to go through this again. And again. For such as her, fate was a wheel that turned too slowly. "Where do you and the Muses wish to fly this time?"

"Cairo, I believe. Let them confer."

The ghost of great Phoenix hovered beside her at the Liminal edge and directed her attention beyond. Here, upon this unique threshold, a window upon a great proscenium with curtain lifted onto the world, anything could happen.

At the crest of the proscenium arch, a vast clock of mortal time ticked musically, the movements of its intricate metal hands and barrel of numbers denoting the year, ever changing but slow and subtle. This place had been born near the dawn of humanity, back when the purgatorial Whisper-world first separated from the mortal one, leaving a single, flexible portal between. The Whisper-world was a dank, gray empire born from the misery of humankind, Darkness its incarnate lord—but the Liminal edge was always vested in the needs of the living.

Because of that, the place favored the work of the Guard, so from this precipice of possibility, the Guard were chosen time and again by Phoenix and his Muse attendants.

The Muses in their timeless forms, iridescent and beautiful, vaguely humanoid shapes floating luminous as one might imagine angels, each a whirling wind of song and stars, joined the two divinities. They flew across the Liminal border in a dizzying, sparkling display of light and beauty, and Persephone smiled. She could not help but smile whenever she looked upon such good friends, and her oft-labored breathing eased. But there were only four of them.

"The Heart was overeager," the Muse of Intuition cooed, its iridescent form neither male nor female. "Heart found a perfect soul in Ahmed Basri and has already gone ahead. The rest of us must catch up."

"Great One, Our Lady," acknowledged the Muse called Memory, nodding a shining head first at Phoenix, then Persephone. "We come wearied from war and yearn for less burdened soil."

The cerulean fire of Phoenix shifted to entwine his Muse friends in a wide embrace, a binding circle. His voice held regret. "Show me, friends, one ounce of soil turned by mortal hands that is not somehow burdened. I will gladly send us there."

Intuition spoke: "Would that such soil existed. But, no, Heart has fallen for Ahmed and his visions and was off to Cairo in a shot. I daresay Cairo's a good choice, with its grave-robbing and such. There's great unrest around the tombs of that ancient civilization, which long ago worshipped you, Great One," it informed Phoenix. "We've found powerful mortals who match our need. And their myriad backgrounds will make our Grand Work . . . quite a challenge."

The four Muses chuckled. Truth be told, they enjoyed unsettling mortal lives. There was a bit of playfulness in each that enabled them to hold on to humor and heart, lest they fall to Darkness's traps.

"I've already touched my chosen," Intuition continued. "He would have died in a fire this morning if not for me. We are known for cursing mortal lives, perhaps, but so should we be known for saving them."

The fiery form of Phoenix gestured with an armlike appendage. "Precede me, friends, and I shall follow in a moment to seize my own host."

"The Power and the Light," the four Muses murmured in reply.

As Persephone watched her friends leave, tumbling into a blue sky spread vast before them, she remembered how they'd all once lived less troubled lives. She remembered bitterly how she'd sworn to be again with her beloved in the flesh—but that had not yet happened. And now they were off once again to fight the good fight, leaving her behind. This was their chosen task, one that might last for all eternity. She knew that it was necessary, but she wondered when her own time would come.

The Liminal, ever mercurial, ever mysterious, perhaps sensed her mood. Above, on the Liminal's proscenium arch, the clock that gently ticked away mortal life whirred, and its intricate metal arms spun. The numbers on the barrel shifted, and the wide window suddenly revealed a scene from the past. Persephone and Phoenix saw no longer the sparkling Muses careening toward their chosen ones in Egypt, but a gaslit street at dusk, homes and town houses full of Romanesque details with candles burning welcome in windows.

Outside one town house, German-speaking servants readied two carriages. Phoenix did not need Persephone's language gifts to translate, for the Liminal made all comprehensible. A well-to-do family turned to gaze fondly at the house before entering the carriages, one of which was loaded with their trunks and other belongings. The mother and father ushered their dark-haired daughter into one of the fine conveyances, but two persons lingered on the pavement.

The elder, an exceedingly severe woman in an elegant black dress, her black hair streaked with silver and wound tight upon her head, clamped one hand firmly upon the shoulder of a young boy who looked older than his age in his fine, dark suit. His black hair hung loose around his face, his dark eyes shone uncannily sharp.

"Once we're in London, child, you'll see. A great future will unfold," the woman promised in a thick accent. "Alexi," she said sharply when the boy did not respond.

"Yes, *Babyshka*?" He looked up at the woman he'd called grandmother, his face impassive, his voice strong.

"What symbol crowns the alchemical pyramid?" she demanded.

"The firebird," he replied.

"Exactly. And what will you do with him?"

"I shall harness him in my hand."

"So you shall," she promised. "There is more to our folklore than mere stories, my dear child. There are two worlds, the mundane and the mystical, and I've called them both down upon your head."

The woman brushed a lock of hair from his face, then cupped his cheek in a gesture more authoritative than kind. "You'd best do something with them."

The boy looked at her, unflinching, in unspoken agreement.

"Who is *that*?" Persephone breathed. The Liminal window had changed texture with the time shift, so she could see her own form reflected as if on a pane of glass. Every color of her was shifting subtly, as if her body were a prism held to the light and turned by a gentle hand.

"I'm not sure," Phoenix murmured warily.

The older woman spoke again: "Someday, my boy, you'll light the darkness with your fire, and all the world will bow before it. I'd stake my life on that." She helped the boy into the carriage, then turned and stared directly into the Liminal, though that was of course impossible. She stared as if she could see Phoenix and Persephone, as if she was *daring* them. Then she held out an arm, deigning to allow a footman to help her into the carriage.

As Persephone gasped, the scene faded to black, and the timepiece of the Liminal stirred, whirred away from the boy's childhood scene to present the current mortal year of 1867.

Persephone felt her excitement rise. Her multicolored form cycled through its hues more quickly, as it always did when her emotions were high.

"Phoenix, my love. That boy . . . I've never seen a mortal so like *you*, an elegant young king of wisdom. Why, his grandmother even called you down to his hand. Surely that's a sign. He'll be your Leader!"

"No. He's too young," Phoenix protested, his fiery form floating upward to the Liminal clock and doing the math of the elapsed years. "It doesn't add up. We take our mortals as late teens. Doing the Grand Work at his age would break him. Besides, we've already chosen Cairo, and the Taking has begun. He will be in London, and there can only be one Guard at a time."

Persephone stared at the Liminal window. The Germany of years prior had faded, replaced by a metropolis of towers and domed temples. The morning call from muezzins lifted prayer into the bright sky from the slender spines of pearlescent minarets. She squinted at the brightness, her eyes having not quite adjusted from the shadows she hated, though she rejoiced at the feeling of the sun upon her face.

"Soon you've an annunciation to make with the Muses and their new Guard," Phoenix urged gently. "And I must find my Leader—one of appropriate age. I believe I know just the one, and she has little inkling how her mortal life is about to change." He wreathed phantom tendrils of flame around his love—the limited interaction they were allowed. "But first, I must know how you fare."

How did she fare? She worsened every year. The corner of her diaphanous robe was stained with blood and pomegranate juice, a sickly, rotting combination she'd been coughing up for centuries.

"The pain comes and goes," she murmured, giving a valiant smile and suppressing the rattle in her lungs. "I always feel better when I meet my new Guard."

Stepping to the threshold, as if she were a bird ready to fly from a branch, she added, "But you must find out about that boy." Then she stepped through the portal and disappeared in a blaze of light.

After a moment, Phoenix set off behind her.

CHAPTER
ONE

Cairo, 1867

EIGHTEEN-YEAR-OLD BEATRICE SMITH STARED INTO JEAN'S deep blue eyes and really, truly wanted to be in love. Wholly in love. It was a fitting time for it: The breeze was warm, the Egyptian sun was bright, and the ties of her bonnet were undone. She had stolen a few moments away from the ever-present eye of the housekeeper—who, Beatrice knew, had been hired by her father not only to clean their rooms but to keep watch over his daughter. For the moment, Beatrice was gloriously without scrutiny, on her own and able to make her own decisions.

"Will you ever go back to England?" Jean asked, his French accent as delightful as the lock of his sandy-brown hair as it bounced in the breeze. "Do you even remember England? I'll bet you don't remember it like I remember Paris."

Beatrice looked out over the city. They'd hidden themselves above it all, sitting on the anterior ledge of a tower at the Church of Abu Serga. Old Cairo's minarets pierced the uneven skyline, spires calling to heaven, cupolas and spherical forms above intermittent brick complexes, graceful curves among rectangular blocks, a feast of shapes and varying heights. Along the stones far below strode both the wealthy and poor, robed and suited, veiled and open-faced; bronze and pale, the native and the foreigner.

"I remember a little," Beatrice replied, finding it hard to think of any place that wasn't Cairo. "I remember how different the colors are. Perhaps the distance of memory mutes England's hues, but it seemed a gloomier palette. As for going back"—she shrugged—"there's so much work here, I doubt Father's thought one whit about Oxford. He hopes to find out everything about the pyramids before everyone else. I'd like to help him."

Jean grinned. "Ah, yes, that's right. He's too busy grave robbing."

"No, Jean." Beatrice scowled. Jean was always teasing, but he should know better than to jest about a most passionate subject. "Father isn't like that."

"What's wrong with it if he were? Valuable stuff, antiquities—and I'm sure your museums will do a much better job of preserving them than the natives."

"You can't think like that, Jean. That's the whole trouble," Beatrice scolded, easily sliding into the role of lecturer or professor. "Just because a way of life died doesn't mean you can go tromping around their graveyards and taking souvenirs. Father's interested in the culture, in learning about the hieroglyphs, about elaborate burials, about their rituals and their daily life. Civilization began in Nile soil. It's fascinating.

"Father's not just here to take things. He's a gentleman, you know. Though I daresay most Englishmen are less refined . . ." She paused, sighed, and said, "Then there are the tourists. They'll come to ogle Father's discoveries once they learn of them. In fact, they've already begun. Have you seen the guidebooks? Entitled people with money to throw away, thinking they can learn everything about a faraway place and its people in a few unthinking moments," she finished sharply.

"You've heard too many of his lectures." Jean elbowed her, yanking at a bonnet tie.

Beatrice readjusted her ribbons. "Just think if someone were to go into your Notre Dame and overturn the vaults just because they were curious. There'd be hell to pay—"

"The recently dead are different than the *ancient*, Bea," Jean interrupted. "Your father might be standing in the way of a great discovery."

"He's trying to stand in the way of *looters*, Jean, that's very different. I daresay your father wouldn't mind a nice trundle of loot," she muttered. She'd been attracted to Jean because he was carefree and jovial. But if he didn't have a serious bone in his body, how could she ever talk to him about what was meaningful?

Jean held up his hands, the cuffs of his white linen suit ruffling in the breeze. "My family remains firmly rooted in the good, clean, honest work of banking. Father wants nothing to do with cursed mummy gold. But in a few years, none of this will matter. I plan on stealing you away to Paris as soon as I've the chance, and I'll make you Mrs. Jean Pettande before your father can say Book of the Dead. God willing."

Beatrice blushed and cocked her head, then gave him the first challenge of their young relationship. "What if I don't believe in God?"

Jean gave an amused scowl. "You're too young to be an atheist."

"And *you're* too young to know the truth. You grew up surrounded by Parisians. I grew up here. How can Coptics and Arabs, Sufis, Sunnis, Jews, and everyone else who lives here all believe different things and all be right?"

Jean shrugged. "Someone's got to be right."

"Who, though?"

Jean grinned. His ruddy cheeks dimpled. "Might as well be me."

Beatrice snorted, not sure whether she was amused or disgusted. "Why, Jean, I do believe you've succinctly stated the very heart of conquest."

He grinned. *"Oui."* His dive to place a kiss on her neck made her giggle. "But unlike Napoleon, all I'm interested in conquering is you."

Shifting his precarious position on the ledge, he pulled her into a real kiss. Then, as a thought obviously occurred to him, he pulled back and raised an eyebrow. "If you don't believe in God, why do you care about anyone's mortal remains, like those musty old Egyptians?" He gave a mock sneeze, and she glared at him.

"I don't believe in the Book of the Dead and I'm hardly convinced about our Bible, but that doesn't mean I want to steal bodies and put them out for a show. I respect the tactile. What I *see*. What I'm not sure about are all the things I can't see: gods, demons, ghosts, curses—"

"You know, you really are too opinionated for your own good. I'm going to lock you away in a Parisian flat," Jean said. "That's what you really need." He scrambled to his feet, a risky action on the narrow ledge.

"Jean, be careful," Beatrice snapped. She was annoyed by his words, even though he was joking. But was he joking? It would serve him right if he hurt himself, she thought in a moment of unkindness.

"Do you hear that, Cairo, Beatrice Smith shall be Mrs. Jean Pettande, stolen away like an antiquity, never to be seen again!" he shouted, holding on to a gritty, sand-bitten window frame with one hand and flailing about with the other. "I'll protect her like her father protects the ancients!"

"Stop!" Beatrice said, growing angry. "Stop talking like that. I don't want to be stolen away or protected, I love Cairo."

She did—more, even, than she loved Jean. The city was beautiful, complex and fascinating, its cultures, its histories and people . . . She found some young locals attractive, which went very much against general British sentiment. Considering the societal abyss that prevented her from ever really getting to know any of them, such attractions were foolish. Someone like Jean, foreign as he was, was still European: safe, accessible. He was someone she was *supposed* to care for. This was what women her age did: They were courted; married; and raised families. A limited existence. Jean's brash tone of conquest rode Beatrice's sensibilities roughly, souring her sunny, lovely day.

"Oh, Bea, your father may have let you read books and taught you ridiculous rituals of useless dead people, but you don't seem to grasp your place in this world. Look at you right now; you're just where a girl's supposed to be." He giggled, shifting his weight as she glared at him. "At my heel, as I stand above and survey our kingdom!"

There came a cry from downstairs, followed by a gust of wind, a powerful blow focused like a presence. Sand blew about, peppering her exposed skin; Beatrice's blood chilled. Far below, women and priests cried out phrases she recognized as scriptural exclamations, and she pursed her lips, passing off any superstitious fancy.

Suddenly she couldn't see Jean . . . and she couldn't quite feel her own body.

All within her gaze went blue. Beatrice's hands pressed hard against the tall window frame, holding her in place as a great force collided with her body. There came a burst of angelic music and blinding light, a thrilling jolt through her blood. A firm voice said: "You'll not hear my voice again. You'll only feel my fire. But you, Beatrice Smith, have been chosen for the Grand Work. You are now more than human, and you will fight on the side of angels for a better world. You are the Leader of the Guard."

Blinking images, of a circular room and a bird, fluttered before her. The wind swept all around and through her. Beatrice was too shocked to utter a sound. At last the moment faded and her senses returned to the present.

Just in time—or just too late. . . . Beatrice squinted past her blowing bonnet strings to see Jean's wide eyes and the top of his mussed brown hair vanish from view. He had fallen from the ledge upon which he'd danced only moments before. There were screams. It was a long way down, and Beatrice should not have looked, but she did.

So much red against so much white. She wasn't sure she believed in God, but now, maybe, she was convinced of something otherworldly. What had spoken within her? Whose voice had graced that terrible moment of pain and euphoria?

Tears streamed down her face. People ran to Jean's body, though they were careful to keep out of the widening pool of blood. Beatrice ducked back, avoiding the upward gazes, gasping, wishing to see no more.

Coldness poured over her, one overwhelming sensation after the next. An icy draft? Something transparent appeared, gray and shimmering.

Jean. It was Jean! He floated before her, grayscale in his linen suit, his luminous face wearing an expression of confusion. He opened and closed his mouth as if speaking, yet she heard nothing. A gasp tore from Beatrice's throat. She was staring at a ghost. She didn't believe in such things; she'd just said so. She was being proven woefully, horrifically wrong. He was holding his hand out for her, as if everything would be all right.

Beatrice reached for him, an unreleased scream threatening to tear her in two. Jean stared at her sadly. Seeming to realize something, he shook his gray head, disappointed. Then he blew her a kiss and his image faded from view.

Sound finally tore from her lips. Beatrice fell to her knees on the cool stone floor, retching until she felt warmth on her hand like a ray of sunlight. Turning, she found a woman of unparalleled beauty had appeared suddenly beside her: glowing, majestic, full of colors. A glowing, floating woman whose hair was black, then brown, now blond; her skin was pale, then olive, now dark—

Her sanity had been shattered. That, or this was a wretchedly cruel dream with an avalanche of events and sensations.

"I'm sorry," said the woman, tears falling from her ever-changing face. She blinked blue, then brown, eyes. "I'm so sorry. I lost my lover, too. He was murdered. He burned to death before my eyes." Tears, as silver as mercury, rolled like beads down her cheeks and dripped to the floor.

"Who are you?" Beatrice asked, choking, wiping her mouth.

"What are you?" She knew that sounded rude, but clearly she'd gone mad. She didn't need manners when she'd gone mad.

"I'm whatever you want to call me, and I have a job for you," the magnificent creature said, her voice breathy and yet echoing, the sound of something heavenly.

Beatrice stared at her diaphanous layers and shifting colors, trying to sound brave but knowing she didn't. "Wh-what do you want with me?"

"I want you to know that death is not the end. I'll even show you it isn't."

Beatrice was suddenly full of fear and guilt. "I was saying I didn't believe in God, but . . . I don't know. Please don't tell me Jean was punished for my blasphem—"

"I'm not handing out punishments," the woman interrupted. "I am here to help set you on a path. You have been chosen for the Grand Work."

"I've been chosen as a nutter," Beatrice murmured. "And you can't be real." She rose shakily to her feet. All she wanted to do was weep, alone.

"Just outside," the woman said, "in a place that's neither here nor there, at the edge of time, between two worlds, your new friends are waiting for you."

Beatrice stared, her mind struggling with the realization that she had changed. There was something inside her now, something warm and full of power. The sensation was making her dizzy, but it wanted her to be strong. Resolute. A leader.

"If you say so," she whispered, dazed, moving awkwardly to the stairs. She descended, her bonnet askew, her blond locks mussed, her eyes full of tears.

At the foot of the staircase, on the landing, looking similarly dazed, stood four young people. They were all about her age, and they were looking up at her. Waiting.

CHAPTER
TWO

IBRAHIM WASIL STARED AT THE SMOLDERING FOUNDATION OF his home. He'd watched it burn for several hours, hanging back from the crowd, his keen ears picking up all the murmuring about the dead bodies rumored to be inside. His, they thought, and the body of the man who had acted like his father. Not his true father. Only Allah knew where his real parents were or if they had ever felt guilty for abandoning him as a baby on the stoop of an Englishman's home.

"Like Moses," his friend Isaac had once said when they were children, playing in a university courtyard. Isaac was a Jew, but the Fatimid Caliphate had had a relative tolerance for other religious groups, and while that ancient empire was long fallen, some of its basic principles remained in Masir, in al-Qahira, in this city the Europeans called Cairo.

There were tensions, of course, between faiths, races, classes, and intentions. The pale skin of colonial interest could never entirely be trusted, whether it be French or British. However, one kind and gracious example of pale skin had raised him unquestioningly as his own, yet with respect for his birthright: James Tipton had made sure that Ibrahim was heir to his rightful Arabic language and faith and proud of the name Tipton had given him, the name of a prophet. Tipton had also taught Ibrahim the Queen's English and escorted him to Christian services as well as Muslim calls to prayer. A professor of religion at the University of Cairo,

Ibrahim's father had encouraged him to be whatever he wished and had given him a place to call home while he determined what that might be.

Ibrahim wasn't sure who or what he prayed to as he stared at the ashes of the only home he'd ever known, the tomb of the one true good man he'd ever known.

He'd begun the day as a creature of two worlds, English and Arabian. Now, alone at the age of eighteen, orphaned for a second time, he wasn't sure which world would take him, or if he would have to choose. James Tipton had managed to effortlessly create a loving mix of faith, culture, and sensibility. Others Ibrahim had met, both English and Arabian, made it seem one had cling to specific viewpoints and reject all the rest. Some of his own people rejected outright the honest intentions of James and others at the university and had accused Ibrahim of abandoning his true self by living among them. For a boy who never for a moment forgot he'd been abandoned on a doorstep, this was a deeply painful accusation.

Uprooted, he could be anything now, anyone. He could choose to be a ghost, he realized. The crowd assumed him dead, after all. Was that the answer? To be a ghost? Wondering and wandering? Something had pushed him out of bed, into the market, early this morning, an unusual desire for ripe, glorious pomegranates. That strange, pressing urge, he realized, had saved his life. Would that it had saved the life of the man who'd provided a home for him.

A sudden, violent gust knocked him forward, and a furor rose within him as if a bird loosed from a cage flapped madly at his insides. The pomegranates he had held through all the hours he had watched his home burn fell to the ground, rolling away and bleeding onto the sandy stone.

As if this day had not held changes enough, Ibrahim now suffered yet another. Thinking he had become like the dead, he now saw them.

Ghosts stared back from every few feet; grayscale and luminous, spirits from Cairo and the specters of nomads, ghosts of all faiths and races, eras and classes. He felt an overwhelming wish to follow each and every one, to understand why they had been driven to Cairo's streets, eternally wandering in and out of shops and homes.

He heard a strange new voice, speaking in a language he'd never before heard and yet, miraculously, understood: "Hello, my torch-bearer, Intuition. I saw the measure of the man you could be and had to save you from your fate. I'm sorry for your loss, but you gain new family and a new future today. I have plucked you from an early death to learn a story and fight the good fight. In the beginning were two lovers, beings of light who fought wrath and woe. We are their continued struggle, and it is in their name I welcome you to the Guard."

Ibrahim heard these confounding words both within himself and all around him. Before he could begin to process them, his gaze fell upon the transparent ghost of James Tipton.

With a puzzled expression on his grayscale face, the man floated over his home, staring at its cremated remains, then surveying the gathered crowd. When his gaze fell on the young man he'd lovingly and unquestioningly called son, he smiled his small, consistent smile, as if in seeing Ibrahim safe, Tipton had determined that all was well.

His adoptive father waved, and Ibrahim bit back tears. His senses could not be trusted, and he would not show such womanly frailty, yet he was nearly overwhelmed. The bird kept beating in his chest. Something urged him to move forward, to seek out a new destiny. He had the uncanny sensation that he was now tied to other beings than himself and that he would never be alone again. But was that what he wanted? The sensation was both terri-fying and wonderful. Was this comfort or madness?

A blinding light bloomed beside him and he turned to behold a luminous woman, the flawless epitome of many types of beauty, made from shifting colors.

"You are not Allah," he said, uncertain.

"Correct, I am not," she replied.

"Or one of the saints. Or prophets. You are an angel, then?" Ibrahim pressed his eyes closed, wondering if she would vanish when he opened them, if his mind had been entirely torn asunder by the day. She was still there, in all her colors.

"An angel if you like, it doesn't really matter. Come, Ibrahim," the woman entreated. "I'm sorry for your loss. Let me show you where you belong."

She held out a shimmering hand. Ibrahim looked at it, then back at the burning rubble. James Tipton had vanished. Ibrahim hoped that his Christian saints would hold him close. He was a good man. Surely Allah would take him. The two faiths, having come from the same roots, weren't dissimilar when one stripped away mankind's trappings. Something greater would take care of his father.

"Do not be afraid," the woman said. "I'm here to take you home."

Ibrahim gulped. She lowered her hand, giving no sign of offense that he had not touched her. Glancing at the pomegranates lying bruised and dribbling onto the stones, she frowned and kicked the fruit aside, then began to walk away.

"Come," she bade him, and he did, following her through the city.

As they headed to a destination unknown, Ibrahim felt moved to ask only one question. He knew that whatever had spoken to him—the thing that was now within him—was inherently good, just like the man who'd raised him. His senses had grown sharper, and he'd never felt so alive. The world was at his fingertips.

Ibrahim had never been a social creature. He liked books, grand architecture, and quiet spaces. His brain was nearly bursting with strains of poetry, texts in their entirety, and scholarly pursuits, yet he was suddenly made happy by the certainty that he was on his way to meet friends.

"My mind is changing," he murmured. "Why?"

"You'll see" was the only answer the multicolored angel would give.

CHAPTER
THREE

PART OF AHMED BASRI'S CONSCIOUSNESS KNEW THAT HE WAS dreaming, yet the hazy knowledge that he lay in bed was little comfort. He was witnessing something terrible that he could not wholly understand. It was a war. A horrific war. There were monstrous metal machines, roaring screams like angels plummeting from heaven. Or demons. Baffling abominations on an unknown shore under a colorless sky. This gray, muddy struggle had no kinship to anything he'd experienced in the golden warmth of Cairo.

He had always held joy in his soul, since the very day he learned what it meant to do so, and these scenes of foreign terror shook him to the core. This was a warning, surely; why else would such portents be shown to anyone? And the dead. So many dead. Too many. Fear began to seep into Ahmed's buoyant heart like water into a punctured boat.

"The dead have no place to go," he heard himself murmur, though he was not yet awake. "Help them," he urged. "Help the dead pass."

Thus he exhorted the soldiers around him as the noise of those horrific mechanical beasts filled his ears. No one responded. They were too busy dying and becoming transparent shades, luminous yet sad. The air was gray—but not because it was a cloudy day in whatever country this was—France? He thought he heard French. Cairo had been overtaken by the French in the previous century; a bit of the language lived on in the city. But it wasn't a cloud causing these thick, gray swirls. The air was gray because it was filled with the dead. The dead choked the sky.

Ahmed feared for the joy in his soul. Who could see such horrors and retain hope or love? Who could gift happiness to others when such perils were in store?

He fought back and was rewarded. Words sounded, in a language he'd never before heard but somehow understood:

"Yes, Beloved. Foster your joy," murmured a song of wind and stars, a divine voice. "For you are the Heart. You are a visionary, meant for great things. And you will attain them. In the beginning there were two lovers. These beings fought a greedy shadow that sought to spread misery across the land. We carry on their ancient quest to light the darkness. This is the last you will hear me speak, but I welcome you to the Guard."

A gust of wind whipped through his small room, making chaos of the modest flat that his parents kept immaculately tidy. He shot up in bed, awake. The morning sun fell warm and assuring upon Ahmed's face, and something climbed into his soul like a man slides a silken tunic over his body. Music and light filled him to the brim.

Had his vision called this herald, or had this herald caused that vision? He did not know, though they seemed linked. Neither was how he might expect mystical revelations to come, nor did they use the words of his Sufi teachings. But Ahmed had always known there was more to the divine than any man might grasp. He was sure that whatever he now carried within him was inherently good.

Yet wasn't he too young for such a gift as this? He had not studied long with his teacher and it seemed premature for him to receive such spiritual grandeur. He reeled from equal parts of desire to accept this intrusion as divine and a longing to reject it and reclaim familiarity and some sense of himself. But no further guidance came to him. His questions remained unanswered.

The pale window curtains, whipping about in the unusually

forceful breeze, drew his attention. When he looked out, he saw ghosts. Spirits and specters of all sorts mingled in the busy Cairo streets. Floating amid the thronging life was death, their gray forms a stark contrast to the golden hue of his city. He resolved to go out to them.

"Mother, I'm going for a walk," he called as he passed the apartment's main room, where she sat hemming a robe, lit brightly by the sun. He recognized her as beautiful, her layered, thin robes splayed around her like the petals of an open flower. He recognized her as someone he loved. Yet it was as if he were suddenly looking at her through an inverted spyglass. She was as distanced as he was changed, and today would forever separate them.

She nodded, her black eyes glistening with the soft peace she'd always had, and he knew he would always cherish that about her, though now from a distance. Whatever had taken up residence inside him was changing how he interacted with all he met: the dead and the living.

Feeling quite calm despite these realizations, Ahmed was delighted when he was bade join new friends. Like faraway strains of music he felt their distinct heartbeats, feathers against his ears, pleasantly drowning out the bustling sounds of the city. Five other souls, he heard. With himself, six.

The terror of his vision faded, replaced by his usual joy and an entirely new sense of power and wonder. His heart seemed to grow a new chamber, expanding to heretofore unknown proportions. Cast from the nest, he walked out into the world to test his wings. Whom would he meet? And should he tell someone about the vision of war that had first woken him to this new glory?

CHAPTER
FOUR

BEATRICE FELT THAT HER MIND AND BODY WERE SUDDENLY, drastically, different. They were still distinctly her own, but at the same time, they were more. *She* was more. And so were the four people standing before her.

In a side portico of Abu Serga, Beatrice stared at each in turn, first at a young man in robes that struck her as Sufi; her father had educated her on local cultural dress. Beside him stood a round-cheeked, buxom girl dressed in something quite French, her face white as a sheet. A tall British boy with strawberry-blond hair stood close to this girl's left—he had to be British with those at once hand-some and utterly ungainly features—and next to him was a stunning young woman with golden skin.

This last was someone Beatrice recognized. While Abu Serga's Coptic service was a world away from the Church of England, Beatrice's father had satisfied himself that it was Christian, and they had attended services here regularly. Beatrice had seen the girl here but had never spoken to her; though they worshipped in the same place, to Beatrice, their worlds had felt so very different as to be a barrier between them.

The quintet stared at each other, looking, Beatrice thought, as if they'd seen not one but a thousand ghosts. She almost laughed at that. Perhaps they had.

After a long, assessing moment, Beatrice finally asked, "What's going on?"

"Haven't the foggiest." The red-blond boy shrugged and scratched his head. His accent confirmed his British origins; from the north, likely.

In Arabic, the youth in the dark Sufi robes said that he was suddenly seeing ghosts. He grinned as if excited.

Beatrice replied, her Arabic nearly perfect, "I saw a ghost, too." She choked on her next words, forcing them out. "I just lost my . . . my beloved. He fell from the ledge"—she gestured upward—"and died."

The golden-skinned girl stepped forward. "I'm so sorry," she said in faltering English. After a moment: "I'm Verena. Verena Gayed."

"Verena . . . like the saint," Beatrice murmured, clearing her throat and straightening her body. Unraveling would not do. The girl smiled proudly and nodded.

"George," the Brit murmured, taking the cue for introductions.

"I am Belle, and this is all very strange," said the girl beside him in a thick French accent, looking nervously at George. The boy blushed, and all of him was suddenly as red as parts of his hair.

The young man in Sufi robes smiled beatifically. "I am Ahmed. My eyes are open now to wondrous things." His radiant expression faded. "I've seen terrible things, too, though, and I hope to gain their meaning." After a moment he said, "We are missing one. We are supposed to be six, aren't we?"

That was true. Beatrice felt a sense of these young people gathered from all walks of the city. She could feel them like echoes of her own heartbeat, and there was one more distant than the rest, though it was getting closer.

"Come," Ahmed said. "Let us greet the sixth."

He led them out the front door of the church and down a lane that led to a mosque. Beatrice's mind was filled with a thousand questions and concerns: Why were they all following Ahmed without objection? But her worries fled when she sensed the strong persona they found standing upon a stone-inlaid star when the lane opened into a plaza.

"I'm here," said a rich voice in Arabic.

The newcomer was a tall, golden-skinned youth in a long, fine tunic; Beatrice's heart told her he was the missing sixth of their coterie. His gleaming black hair, neatly trimmed, curled around his ears beneath a beige cap. He was, she admitted to herself, distressingly handsome, and his wide black eyes immediately pierced her to the core. There was an aura of prismatic light all around him.

"My name is Ibrahim Wasil," he said. "I was led toward you by an angel."

That angel now stepped out from behind him, all light and color, the same creature who had comforted Beatrice earlier.

"Hello, my beloveds," she said, her quiet voice a compelling music.

Beatrice wanted to scream. Nothing made sense. The world was spinning too quickly; the new things happening inside her were not tenable, not when her heart was broken. She needed a moment to—

"Leader," the multicolored angel prompted, staring at her. "Your fire, please."

Beatrice stared back. What on earth did the woman mean?

"Oh, look!" Verena exclaimed, staring at Beatrice's hands.

Beatrice looked down to find that her hands were glowing blue. Cerulean fire wreathed them, fire apparently harmless to her skin. It was cool, energizing, tingling, and full of song. The voice in her mind had said she would carry fire, but for what purpose? What did it do?

The moment she needed to clear her mind was apparently not to be granted. Instead, a wind whipped up, and Beatrice's blood froze in recognition. This was the violent wind that had sent Jean to his death.

No. Jean had been precariously balanced and foolish. The

wind could not be blamed for his death. Suddenly he, and the love Beatrice had felt for him, seemed very far away. A whole lifetime apart.

She stretched out her hand, moving her fingers in amazement as azure flame danced about their tips.

The angel gestured, insistent. "Leader, send forth your fire to open the sacred space."

Beatrice set her jaw. If she was being called a leader and held fire in her hand, she might as well do as this supernatural being instructed; any heretofore unknown powers were about as sensible as every other odd thing happening all at once. She cast her arm forward, and a door appeared where there had been none before.

The company jumped. The tall portal hovered in midair, bordered by hieroglyphs written in shimmering blue fire. Light beckoned them downward, inviting. Stairs appeared.

Beatrice had cast fire from her hand and opened an impossible two-dimensional door into another world. A part of her trembling body wanted to faint, but she was too fascinated to dare lose consciousness. Had she not, in some way, asked for this? Had she not always hoped her destiny would be grander than that of an everyday Englishwoman?

"Your sacred space is neither here nor there," the angel spoke up. "It is eternal, and it exists only for the Guard. Its time and dimension are relative. So come. Join me."

Ahmed was the first into the void. He practically charged. Beatrice threw a hand forward as if to halt him, then gasped as an arc of flame leaped to life around the rest of them, licking harmlessly at the hems of their garments.

"We've all gone bloody, stark, raving mad," George murmured. Beatrice was glad someone else had been brave enough to say it.

"Come!" called Ahmed's voice from below. "It's beautiful!" he added in English.

Beatrice turned to the prismatic woman. "How do we know it is safe? If I am Leader, am I not now responsible for these persons' welfare?"

"You are" came the reply, "and it pleases me to hear you say it. This place exists to keep you safe."

Beatrice waited, but the angel did not continue. "That isn't an answer," she protested.

"I'm afraid you'll have to grow accustomed to that." The multi-colored woman loosed a strangely bitter laugh.

Though her words caused them uneasiness, the group moved to the threshold. It hummed with harmonic, audible energy. They were glancing in perplexity at one another when Ahmed appeared, running up the stairs.

"Come!" he insisted. "It's truly grand!"

It was hard to say no to Ahmed's enthusiasm or to his ineffably contagious smile. Giving a communal shrug, the more reticent members of the party descended at his heels.

At the bottom of the stairs, the six found themselves in a circular stone room lined with pillars and illuminated by the light shining through a great stained-glass bird hanging far above, a fiery mosaic halo constructed around its feathers. Beatrice, Ahmed, George, Belle, Ibrahim, and Verena stared up at it, gaping. Beyond the pillars lurked a thick darkness that seemed to pulse and shift the way stars shimmer in a nighttime sky.

The colorful angel had followed them down and stood beaming at the foot of the stairs. "What are you?" Beatrice demanded of her. Verena and Belle looked over as if her tone had been too sharp. Beatrice closed her eyes, fighting a wave of anxiety, and when she spoke, her voice held a more even tone. "Please tell us."

The creature eyed them singly, staring as if examining each of their souls. "Given your collective backgrounds, you may feel most comfortable thinking of me as an angel. I'm not human, though

I feel as you feel and care as you care. I even bleed like you bleed, almost. I've been called many things, but names are immaterial. The Guards that have come before you call me their Lady, out of affection. But of all my names, Persephone is my favorite."

Their young eyes blinked away many seconds of silence. George coughed in discomfort, his cheeks again red. Everything the six thought they knew was now being redefined. Moreover, though she had not said so, none of them could quite get past the feeling of being near a goddess.

"Why have you called us?" Ibrahim asked, in Arabic.

"For the Grand Work" was the woman's reply—words Beatrice heard both in Arabic and in English. She wondered if Belle heard French.

While compelled by this divine figure, Beatrice was also confused and upset by her. She felt Ibrahim's cool and intense gaze alternating between Persephone and herself—a gaze fraught with both distrust and attraction. Beatrice resisted the urge to look back.

Ahmed spoke up. "What is that?" he asked. "What is your commission?"

His words resonated off the walls, and now Beatrice heard Arabic, French, and English, nearly simultaneously. It was as if the room knew them or was learning them. This place was alive with all of their hearts, souls, and languages.

The goddess threw forward a hand, her lovely face grimacing as if the act hurt her dearly. It was not without effect, however, and a black square became a rectangle and then a doorway. Another doorway in the air. Portals within portals: Was this an endless iteration?

"Look. Learn," the goddess said. "But never go in."

Beyond the doorway were long corridors, each dark and dank. Endlessly gray. Whispers and murmurs, though nothing intelligible. Shades. Hundreds—no, *thousands*—of shades, each floating

listlessly down the endless corridors. Death. It was death, and so
much of it.

From deep down one corridor, a moving shadow drew closer.
Tall and vaguely human in form, it glided with unearthly grace.
It wore dread, rancor, and decay like a cloak. Red, burning eyes
glowed in its tenebrous face, two terrible lamps that Beatrice was
sure would cause madness if stared at for long.

Hundreds of red eyes opened in the floor of the corridor, as if
something had just awakened to their presence, followed by hissing and a terrible dread growling.

"What is that?" Beatrice exclaimed. Glancing at her companions, she found them paled, color draining from their faces, and
shivering with fright.

"That is Darkness; he is known as such," replied Persephone
with venom in her voice before twisting her arm and closing her
hand into a powerful fist, and with a ripping sound the portal
snapped shut. Beatrice and her companions could breathe normally
once more.

"He and his desires are what you fight. Fear him and his domain, but do not fear your Grand Work. Here, on Earth, you have
power. You are the mortal arbiters between life and death. You
have gifts, each of you, to help."

She turned to Beatrice. "You, Beatrice Smith, are the Leader.
As you know."

Beatrice's nostrils flared. Her posture straightened the way her
mother—rest in peace—had always required. She set her jaw. While
she wasn't sure about Persephone, she was certain that, because she
was a woman, if she didn't accept the title of leader with authority
and confidence, the rest would share a lack of faith. She set all fear
of madness aside and accepted the mantle of power.

Persephone turned to Verena. "You are the Healer. Some of the
spirits you will face are truly dangerous. They will manifest violence

upon those they've subjected to their possession. For them, you will need Verena's hand."

Verena lifted her hand in amazement. It glowed with a faint warm light that limned her golden skin and glinted in her dark eyes, heightening her already prominent beauty and illuminating the fear in her expression. Beatrice couldn't blame her. Only one hour ago they had been normal mortals going about their daily lives. Now they were the agents of gods.

Persephone turned to Ahmed, who was staring at Verena in awe. "Ahmed. The Heart." The Sufi smiled widely, his expression as radiant as the Healer's hand. The other five found themselves smiling as well. Ahmed's joy, like his smile, remained contagious.

"How do you know our names?" Ibrahim asked, his tone careful.

"Because you are my beloveds. The Muses, my eldest friends, chose you to join with my love to fight hungry Darkness, who would blanket the Earth with his miserable, restless dead. I will help you in return." She gazed kindly at Ibrahim. "You, Ibrahim, are Intuition. You will be the first to feel the Pull, the exact point of each spiritual disturbance. You are your Leader's right hand. Your clarion voice, and your strength, will be critical in the fight."

Ibrahim turned toward Beatrice, his face blank. He was withholding both judgment and, she couldn't help but feel, acceptance.

"You, George, are the Artist. Evil won't acknowledge the importance of art. Make it."

George opened his mouth, blushed again, and closed it.

"Belle." Persephone turned to the round-cheeked girl, speaking now in French, though all seemed able to understand. "You are the Memory. Our mentalist. You will alter the recollections of those affected by malevolent spirits. You will turn the innocent away from poltergeists and terrors they ought not see, wipe their minds with but a wish. You shall find that you can see each past with but a touch, and that your will can work wonders upon others. You allow your fellows to move more easily through this world. Take care with this gift."

The young Frenchwoman nodded, a host of varied emotions playing over her face.

"How long are we in your service?" Ibrahim asked cautiously.

"You're not in my service. You are in the service of mortality, in the service of all life triumphant over death. You are soldiers of this world against the onslaught of the next, and you will be soldiers until the Muses decide to release you." The divinity's tone was matter-of-fact, as if she'd said these words many times before.

"What if we refuse service?" Beatrice asked out of curiosity. Out of the corner of her eye, she noticed that Ibrahim's lips twitched, either disturbed or heartened by her boldness; she couldn't guess which.

Persephone smiled. "Would you rather answer to *him*?" With a violent gesture, she ripped open the portal again. Those terrible eyes, the weighty dread, the utter, soul-sapping misery, incapacitating despair, and helplessness of that realm. Nightmare walked there. Nightmare was born there . . . *No!* No, she did not want to answer to that.

"That's enough," Beatrice said, seeing how her companions—save Ibrahim—quailed.

Persephone closed the portal with a fluid gesture, satisfaction on her face. "Then go forth. You'll know when you're needed. And you can return to this sacred space—known only to you, made only for you—to renew your flagging spirits. Bless you for your work. This world needs you. Otherwise Darkness will take over, city by city, land by land. If his minions are not checked . . . Believe me, none of us want that fate."

Ibrahim glanced uncomfortably at Beatrice, but his words were directed to them all. "There is an oath upon my lips; I feel a burning need to speak it. I assume it cannot be undone. It may bind us eternally to these forces within. I do not know if we have a choice in this destiny, or what that destiny entails, so I'll not say this oath if any here object."

"You are wise, Intuition," Persephone murmured after the walls had finished translating his words. "Sensible and measured, you should rightly ask such questions of those who serve with you. And of those who command you. Your minds and hearts shall be sorely taxed, and so you must understand why." She made her way to the center of the sacred space, onto a spot where a great feather carved in the floor reflected her colors. "Let me show you how the Great Vendetta began."

She opened her palms wide. Suddenly the six saw through her eyes, and felt with her heart, more powerfully than all human hearts combined. She showed them her history, channeling it from her soul into theirs. Darkness was guilty of vile, unforgivable deeds indeed, and they could help keep him in his place. They would join this sacred fight.

When the vision faded, Beatrice and her companions wept.

Persephone wept as well, her tears liquid silver that fell and merged with the blue fire that threaded the floor. Flame and sorrow seeped into the stones, making the place more luminous and full of resolve. This sacred space was built by tears, perhaps. Beatrice could imagine nothing else.

The goddess walked among them once more. "Fire, light, and love shall fight against shadow, despair, and eternal restlessness. We can never eliminate the enemy wholly, for misery clings stubbornly to the human soul. But we can keep the Balance, perhaps even tip it to just this side of the light. To let Darkness tip the scales is to lose every last mortal mind. So take to your duty, please, and wield the powers we have given you. Do so for all of your kind."

"Say the oath of the Guard, Mr. Wasil. Please," Beatrice murmured. "I doubt any of us has the capability to walk away."

Ibrahim cleared his throat. His words were choked. "Wasil-Tipton. Ibrahim Wasil-*Tipton*."

Beatrice cocked her head. "I'm sorry?"

"James Tipton was not my birth father, but he took me in and raised me well. Before I came here, I was wondering who I should be. Now I know. I shall take his name, for he was a good and honorable man. As I make an oath to fight on the side of angels, I do so in the name of a man of faith who died today." Ibrahim turned to the goddess, and his face was that of one who had seen great loss. "He, too, died in fire. Unfairly."

"But you, my beloved, were spared," the goddess said.

The others were nodding in empathy, and she turned to them. "All of you were chosen for a reason your Muses know more than I. Some of you would not have lived had you not been chosen. Some of you would have lived much different lives." She glanced at Beatrice, her face grave. "Some of you asked for there to be more, and I hope you remember that. For what the Grand Work demands of you, you must give. But now I must go. As deeply as I regret it, the Whisper-world of Darkness has its hooks in me, and to struggle is to prolong my agony."

Ahmed spoke, using a mixture of Arabic and a new tongue that they all recognized as intrinsically their own, a language of friends, the language of the Guard. "And you—why do *you* not choose a human host and join the fight? If the Muses did so, couldn't you? Would you not then be free?"

A pained look crossed the divinity's face. "Ah! You, great Heart, you feel mine. You feel how I ache to love again, to be held again. But for me to come here . . . it would not be the same as the Muses. I've never been mortal, and I'm terrified of it."

Her sad face brightened in a disconcerting reversal and she continued, "We have fought Darkness for so long, and always in the same way, but . . . we have begun a new age. A gilded one. It may be time to move against Darkness at last. Who can tell?

There have been odd shifts in the Liminal space from where I joined you.

"Be well, beloveds," she continued sweetly. "Call upon the Power and the Light to aid you. I shall return; yet until then, you must fight on your own."

She opened her palm. The inky maw of that shadowed, whispering world opened once more; murmurs of pain from thousands of years sent shivers down Beatrice's spine. Goodness, did she really live in that hellish pit? It was clear she did not want to return to it.

Persephone turned her head and coughed as demurely as she could, but a spot of red dribbled from the corner of her lip. Blood? Was she ill? The goddess turned again, suddenly earnest, her face that of an excited child as she addressed her newfound friends. Yes, it was blood on her lip. That drop fell to the stone floor, where it vanished, but when she took a deep breath, the Guard heard her lungs rattle.

"You'll forgive me, won't you? You'll allow me a moment of beauty before I go back?" she begged, then gave an odd, off-balance laugh. "I shouldn't, time ticks and so does Darkness. But to walk the streets among you dear human beings, to feel the pulse of the Earth, how its vibrancy sustains me . . . How I love you mortals and the marvels you create! I'll go and look upon something grand, something awe inspiring, before I turn my face to shadow once more."

She adjusted the layers of shining garments over her body and vanished.

CHAPTER
FIVE

CLEARING HIS THROAT, IBRAHIM BEGAN THEIR NEWLY DISCOVERED oath in the sacred space. Much like a call to prayer, it was clarion and regal: "In darkness; a door. In bound souls; a circle of fire. Immortal force in mortal hearts. Six to calm the restless dead. Six to shield the restless living."

"The Power and the Light," Beatrice murmured.

"The Power and the Light!" her new fellows chorused.

No, Beatrice, she urged herself. *Say it like a Leader.*

"The Power and the Light!" she cried, and felt the whole of her body surge with pleasure and power, as if the phoenix above warmed her with the hearth in its wings. There came a formidable result: Cerulean fire rose around them, leaping from the floor to burst high into the air. Chords of heavenly music tuned by stars roared in their ears, and the hearts of the six burned hot and intense; there was no other moment in the world but this, no other force, no other reason for living.

It was a delirious, beautiful sensibility that Beatrice didn't want to end. It was a moment that defined and defied existence, as close as she would come to heaven without dying. In this fire, by this light, they had become demigods. They would walk this land of Isis and Osiris, among the sands of ancients, banner bearers of the culture's ancient gods. They were being reborn here, and with them, Phoenix. Once more an old mythology was being made new. In their image. In their blood. In their hearts. For all that she was still Beatrice Smith, she was also far *more*. They all were.

They bathed in the sort of warm light that banishes the darkest nights of the soul, and only guardians of time could know how long they stood drinking in this ambrosia. When at last the symphony of stars hushed to a whisper, when the column of celestial light faded and the sacred space became hazy blue-gray again, when the stained-glass bird was only dimly luminescent, not ablaze like a sun, they all stared at one another.

"That was right bloody incredible," George exclaimed.

Ahmed laughed, which gave all of them permission to join in. There was really nothing else to be done. In indescribable wonder, a strange family had been born.

Belle addressed them, her voice tremulous but clear, bringing them back to reality. "We'll need to go to our families one by one. We're not likely companions, so we need to make introductions. Moreover, we need to be able to come and go as we please. My gift urges me to make us transparent to those we love: We must become ghosts in our own lives so that the Grand Work is never undermined by the particulars of mortal life. It . . . it will not be easy."

As each offered the location of his or her home, Beatrice began sorting out an order in which to visit.

Ibrahim was the last to speak. "I've nowhere to go," he said in softly accented English. "As I told you before. My house burned down this morning, and the man who raised me died in the fire. I have no one else."

Beatrice felt her face grow hot with embarrassment. "Of course, I'm sorry." They were fellows in loss. Fresh loss.

When he stepped away from the group, deflecting all pity, Beatrice couldn't help moving forward and speaking for his ears alone. "I lost the man courting me this morning. This very morning. We are brother and sister in loss, Ibrahim Wasil-Tipton," she stated.

Ibrahim stared at her. "We are not related," he replied coolly. She could tell he did not intend to be rude; he was simply stating fact. "We cannot truly know how each other feels. Despite what's happened here, hearts are too private, too individual. Do not assume."

Beatrice was stung. She straightened her shoulders and turned to walk away, almost colliding with Ahmed, who had approached them from behind.

"Ibrahim, our family has a spare room. I know they would gladly take you in, and Belle's powers can assure it. What say you, brother?"

Ibrahim nodded. "Thank you," he murmured.

Beatrice bristled at the warmth in Ibrahim's eyes. Ahmed, with that shining, engaging face that could warm the coldest stone, he could call Ibrahim brother and she could not. Why? Perhaps because she was a woman and not of his people. She was of the invaders' ilk, and female; even supernatural circumstances could not change that. Why, then, of all people, did he have to be her second-in-command? Why was she Leader? Such a pairing seemed ill suited.

The group was quiet as they traversed the city that afternoon, making dutiful stops. First came the stately rooms where Belle had been raised as an only child, and the dazed, comely matron who was her mother.

"*Bonjour, Maman—et au revoir,*" the French girl said softly, tears streaming down her face. The others stood in the doorway, watching. Belle shook badly until Verena stepped forward, placing a hand on her shoulder. Then Belle spoke with mounting confidence. There was an aura of light about her. Magic was at hand.

"These are my friends, and I have a new purpose. I shall come and go as I please. As will these friends. We here obey new masters, not those of our respective households. We will do the Grand Work without question. You will not stop us."

"Of course, daughter," Mrs. Montmare agreed, her eyes fluttering under the weight of magic being worked. "None shall stand in your way."

In Ahmed's family's simple, tidy flat, the conversation was much the same, though Ahmed added the introduction of Ibrahim. He was greeted with polite distance and an invitation to stay. Ibrahim's face was emotionless, but he bowed and thanked the elder Basris with what Beatrice recognized as genuine sincerity.

Ahmed's father was not at home, having gone to the mosque for a meeting with his Sufi teacher that Ahmed should also have attended. Now each of the Guard had a new faith and claim upon them in addition to their old beliefs, and each would have to find his or her own ways of balancing that claim with the others.

En route to George's home, which was farther south, Beatrice, still feeling a bit disjointed and rebuffed, determined that as Leader it was her duty to rise above any personal affront. In order to coordinate her new battalion, she needed to know the various needs of each member.

"Mr. Wasil-Tipton," she began. "Do you imagine there will be services for your father? Would you like us to arrange something? Is there a way we may be of help?"

The group paused, not wanting to seem insensitive. Who could be sure what Ibrahim was thinking, other than perhaps Ahmed with his new talents? His face was like a mask.

"I appreciate the sentiment," Ibrahim replied. "The university will likely have a memorial. But truly, with this odd destiny, I don't believe I shall go. If I'm thought dead, it is better I remain so. All of you, look what we're doing here. You're all becoming ghosts to your families. So shall I be to the world."

They all reflected on his words. This single day had aged them all by years.

They began again down the street. As they did, Verena hurried to catch the tall Beatrice, whose long strides made it difficult. "And your . . . companion? What of him? Can we do something for you? For him?"

Beatrice felt all eyes upon her. She choked back a wave of tears, grief just under the surface but recently supplanted by fear, power, wonder—at leadership, at their new language—and myriad other sensations. "No, I . . . I'm sure Jean's family will take care of . . . I don't want to see the body again. I witnessed his ghost move on. That will suffice. No one knew we were together today, and I daresay he was prone enough to trouble that his death mightn't be a complete surprise. Now, enough on that. George, how much farther?"

"Another few streets," George replied. "Just south of the square here."

It did not take long for Ibrahim's stride, similarly long-legged, to bring him abreast of her. "I should have asked after you in turn," he said. "I am sorry."

Beatrice shrugged. "We've all had a trying day to say the least. We must forgive any unintended slights."

He evaluated her expression, seemed satisfied that she meant her words, and fell back to walk beside Ahmed.

Glancing back, Beatrice saw the Sufi take one look at him, murmur an Arabic benediction about grief, and place a hand over Ibrahim's heart. She was surprised by Ibrahim's reaction.

"That's wondrous," the young man breathed. "Offer it to Miss Smith, too."

When Ahmed stepped forward, Beatrice accepted his gift. The young man's jolt of heart-bound power enveloped her grief and lifted it free from her body. Beatrice could almost see it, could sense Ahmed gazing at it, as one might examine a captured dove. Then Ahmed set it free with open hands.

"Thank you," Beatrice breathed.

"My pleasure," Ahmed replied, and they all knew that was true.

A fine residential complex housed the Tyler household; as they neared, George told them he had a brother, Bob. Meeting Bob, who was rather sour, Beatrice was glad George had been chosen. She also wondered if some distinct quality, of either leadership or independence, was more present in only children.

"None shall stand in your way," echoed George's parents and brother, as had Ahmed's and Belle's mothers.

In the cluttered and book-filled Smith home, Beatrice continued the formula, trembling as she spoke to her father.

"These are my friends and we are called to a great purpose," she said, trying to keep her voice level and strong. "We shall come and go as we please. All will be well."

Her dazed father simply nodded and returned to his desk, a wide wooden surface ever piled with papyrus, beads, and shards of clay.

"Do you hear me, Father?" she asked, moving forward to clasp his hand. In that touch was the phoenix fire, to make her declaration permanent.

"None shall stand in your way," said Leonard Smith softly.

Though the response was what she wanted, what she needed, it was unsettling, because she had always intuited her father *would* stand in her way, would oppose her desire for a career, would in time find her help at grave sites and in academia unladylike and demand she turn in her passions in exchange for trapped domesticity. While she had no doubt he loved her, she assumed that love was conditional. Now, apparently, her only conditions were those of the Grand Work.

Her heart ached. The closeness she and her father had known when she was little would never be regained. Perhaps it had fled years before, and she was only now seeing the distance.

WITHIN THE ENDLESS LAYERS OF SHADOW THAT MADE UP THE Whisper-world, Darkness's minions flocked around his throne. In a foul mood, he'd drawn dread curtains to sit entirely wreathed

in blackness, his robes thick around him, no outside light penetrating. Red eyes blinked slowly, two deadly rubies glinting in the
darkness.

Outside paced his dog, one pair then two hundred bloodred
eyes glimmering to life; their shifting numbers glowed more with
fire than intelligence. The guardian creature drooled and whined,
shifted its protean form, became a roiling mist, then again became a hundred-headed hound. Bored, Darkness tore open the
curtain and tossed the creature bones from the river. The mass
of vaguely canine heads pounced. Countless teeth gnawed the
offering, those infinite fangs now and then gleaming in a bit of
reflected light.

"Just let me follow her," Luce the Gorgon growled from the
mouth of a nearby corridor. His most powerful asset was always
at the ready, folding her arms over the swaths of gray fabric wrapped
around her lithe body and head. Onyx snakes writhed, hissing
and snapping, beneath her thin veil. "Let me prove myself to you."

"Leave. Me. Alone" was Darkness's reply, a low murmur in his
usual halting cadence, thick and wet, the sound of storms.

"It isn't going to get any better. It's been centuries," Luce said
in a conversational tone that seemed out of place in such bleak
surroundings. "You'll not break her until you find whatever it is
she's hiding. I think she's got something she'd like you not to know
about. Some private treasure."

"She'll hate me. All the more. If I begin rooting around,"
Darkness replied. Robes shifted. Bones clicked against each other
as Darkness adjusted his position.

"She'll never *not* hate you," Luce replied. "She always has."

The shadows moved, a whiplike thrash at nothing in particular
that hit some sad, passing spirit who wailed in pain. Luce could
hear Darkness's teeth grind.

"*I* don't hate you." She sashayed up to where the shadows were
thickest and knelt before him, running her hands up into the

impenetrable blackness. "I adore you," she murmured, fumbling blindly at his robes. When visible, they were bright crimson, the only color in this gray wasteland. Other than *her* wretched colors. Persephone.

"I. Am aware. Of your sentiments," Darkness replied, and the shadows kicked her away.

Luce scowled. "You're a fool."

"You. Are brash. For a servant."

"How else can I lift myself in your esteem?" the Gorgon asked. "It isn't like the olden days. We're all falling apart, us great ones. We're splintering. We're weakening. Humanity slips farther from our command. She's beyond hope, all mewling and retching. This may be her last century before she's nothing but pulp. Remember when she bled herself all over these stones in that pathetic attempt to break free? That was just decades ago—"

Darkness whipped his robes and shadows again, this time casting Luce backward upon the stone. "Of course. I remember."

"Well, it could have consequences!" Luce exclaimed, unruffled, picking herself up and glaring at his tall, potent form, at the red fires of his eyes. "Her pathetic attempt opened huge holes in your kingdom. Who knows what, in her desperation, her powers might do? You must admit that she was never meant for this place, would stop at nothing to destroy it if she knew how. She's nothing but a hindrance—"

"*Stand. Down,*" Darkness roared. Luce cringed, expecting to be struck. Instead, Darkness beat his chest, rattled his own bones, turning his despair inward. The water of the nearby river crested and its murmuring voices wailed and wept. "She is beloved of the dead!" he wailed. "And why shouldn't light couple with shadow! We are two sides, day and night! Together since time began!"

"*Separated* since time began," Luce insisted calmly. "Day departs. Night takes over. They cannot sit side by side. You are of one kind, she is of another. Her light hurts you. Your darkness decays her.

Isn't it obvious it's a poor match after all these years? *I* am of your kind. I am trying to help you!"

"You torture me with your words," Darkness muttered.

Luce dared again to kneel at his feet. "My liege. You've lost your strength. I hardly recognize the master I came to serve. You might want to start listening to me rather than wallowing in self-pity like all the spirits you command. Leave *them* to miserable uselessness. You're meant for something greater. You need to remind them all that you're the lord of the land; that light, in the end bows to shadow. All life ends in the pitch depths."

Darkness growled and Luce smiled to herself, delighted at the sound.

"If," the shadows rumbled, "I have my way. It ends. With me."

CHAPTER
SIX

BEATRICE LAST, THE SIX MEMBERS OF THE GUARD WERE FULLY detached from the watchful eyes of their families. Now, as the sun dipped behind Cairo's minaret-spiked skyline, Beatrice felt an odd rustling in her blood, a burning sensation that had her itching to move.

There was no time to question, to run; there was only time to think what must be done. The new sensation felt like a sandstorm under her skin, a gathering of disparate elements into a whirling vortex. A pin on an inner map.

"What is this?" George exclaimed, clutching at his heart. "Tell me you all feel something, else I'm dying before you at the tender age of eighteen."

Belle laughed nervously.

Ibrahim shook his head and spoke with a quiet confidence Beatrice admired. "The Balance between worlds is like a tapestry. When a thread pulls, we feel it. When a member of the restless dead tears free from that fabric, we must smooth it down once more. West," he instructed. "We move west. The Work begins."

They followed their Intuition past a bustling market square teeming with people, glittering with wares and fabrics, reeking of scents, and at last they found a young man in loose pants and tunic floating in an alley, entirely supine but airborne. The hem of his beige tunic gaped down from his back like a fluttering flag. His body was luminous.

Belle shrieked. Beatrice moved in front of her, placing herself in the specter's line of sight, and thus was the first to enter the alley. It wasn't that she wanted to see this abomination any more than Belle, but her instinct told her that this was her proving ground, and she must rise to its challenge.

Ahmed held out his hand to Belle, a gesture urging her not to worry, and smiled. The French girl's shoulders immediately eased, as did everyone else's. Ahmed's joy was potent magic.

"You each have a gift," Beatrice instructed, trying to use the sort of voice that made people turn and listen. Surprisingly, her companions did. "And we each have an instinct. Use it. Now."

She whirled toward the floating boy and flung out her hands, phoenix fire instantly ready, even eager, to be wielded. It flowed from her hands, seemingly knowing what to do, enveloping the youngster's hovering form like a bubble of water, and the boy's possessor became visible.

Reaching up and out from the innocent light brown face of the boy, like peeling up a layer of foreign skin, yawned a transparent, silver-white skeletal face, a terrible maw unhinging as deep-set sockets with no eyes were superimposed over the terrified open eyes of the child in the air. The boy's thin body was shaking as he floated.

Ibrahim reached into the new, vast library in his mind. He chose scripture from the Quran and spoke it bravely, directing his words at the demon above. Displeased, the offending spirit strained and thrashed inside the youth, tearing at the dusty linen of his long tunic and frayed vest, turning the boy's honey brown skin a pallid gray, threatening to transform him into a ghost before their very eyes.

Verena gasped. From the look on her face, the entwined beings horrified her, yet the living victim's obvious pain drew her forward. She reached out to touch him; his racked body went limp at the contact. Her hand was bathed in soft light, and its application was mercy.

George reacted next. Taking charcoal from his pocket, he took to the nearby stone wall of the adjacent building, and in a few swift strokes he etched the outline of a great dove. Beatrice squinted before realizing that the dove was not only a picture but a word. The body of the bird curved down and continued into Arabic script that read *Peace*.

"That is brilliant," Ahmed breathed. George beamed, his fair skin pinking, his cheeks dimpled, making him somewhat the cherub.

None of them knew precisely what they were doing. Nonetheless, instinct proved true, and Beatrice was proud in a way she had never felt: of herself, and of these strangers who were suddenly family.

The possessed boy's gaze snapped to the dove, to *Peace*, and the sight kept his eyes from rolling and his mouth from foaming. She could tell they were making progress. As well, Beatrice noticed that if she moved her hands closer together, her binding blue fire constricted the creature within him, and she could more clearly see the spirit's form around and within the boy's body. The spirit hated its shackles.

Belle came close and touched the boy's ankle, then hissed in pain at what she felt. Ahmed was swift at her side, bestowing joy, reminding them all to breathe deeply. He gave a soft laugh to buffer their hearts. Possession infected the air and the mind with heavy negativity.

"What did you learn, Belle?" Beatrice asked.

"It cried out from the towers and saw dumb sheep below. A muezzin, he was, once. But at some point he turned and sang for evil. Sang not to lure men to prayer but to depravity. Humanity, dumb sheep . . . He wanted to scare them, to turn them all. It *wants*. It hungers for so much more than this life can give . . ." She shuddered and Ahmed's attention was again needed.

"He sang from the towers calling others to prayer," Ibrahim murmured. "And yet the creature never learned how to pray for himself. How sad." After a moment he cleared his throat and recited:

I desire fire from Your burning sorrow,
and I want to take cover under the dust of Your threshold.
I am in a death struggle with my ailments
and from Your presence, I ask
a moment of happiness.

Ahmed had tears in his eyes when Ibrahim finished. "Ah, Rumi! Well chosen, friend!"

The other just bowed his head in reply.

Beatrice, gazing at Ibrahim and listening to his recitation of the beloved Sufi poet, had let her fire slip. The beast within the boy wrestled more violently, flailing against the sense and beauty of the poetry. She scowled and squeezed her fists and her fire constricted in reaction. The boy gurgled in pain, suffering with his possessor, but Verena placed a lit hand on his throat and his choking eased.

Belle had moved to the mouth of the alley and was turning away the denizens of Cairo. At first appalled to see a boy floating in midair, after encountering Belle, they moved on as if nothing unusual had disturbed their day.

"Cantus," Beatrice said, her mind full of song. Her powers commanded the conclusion of this rite.

"Which?" Ahmed asked, surprised by the question. It was indeed surprising to find a new language upon their lips, a songbook as well. Their work came replete with hymns, and their fluid

teamwork suggested they'd toiled together for centuries. Whatever guided them had.

"Quietus," Beatrice replied, with no choice but to trust her newfound instincts. This poor young man was not the only one possessed. They all were. Of course, the Guard was possessed by the
powers of lit Balance, and she far preferred those to the glimpse
the goddess had given them of the alternative.

Belle returned to the circle; Verena stepped forward as the young
boy's body seized up with pain; Beatrice wound her fire tighter
around his limbs. They all began the cantus: a soft melody with
words formed from the root of the first human language. They sang
of a return to the simple raw materials of life, encouraged all
things to abandon earthly trappings and return to the bosom of
creation. Something older and wiser had formed these words, which
felt eerily familiar, like a long-forgotten mother's lullaby.

It wasn't merely their voices that provided music, either; the very
air was full of song. The fire was, too, and the wind that wrapped
around their skirts, robes, and linens.

The muezzin's spirit exited the human body it had tried to wear,
violently ripping free and causing the boy to fall to the ground.
Verena and Ibrahim dove to catch his head so that it would not
strike the stones. The malevolent spirit floated above, transparent
and skeletal, having lost whatever humanity it might once have
possessed, rags hanging from its bones.

The majority of the spirits Beatrice had seen coursing the streets
were more like transparent people, appearing as they would in life,
not rotting or skeletal. Perhaps, she mused, the more intact a spirit,
the less harmful. The more it wore a raw, rotting existence, the more
cause for alarm.

She flung her arm forward, whipping cords of blue fire about
the specter's wrists and ankles. It struggled like a puppet trying
to free itself of strings; the creature's jaw sagged and snapped

furiously, and Beatrice assumed it was speaking. She wondered if he was saying something important or just spewing vile, impotent threats. Why were they not gifted with the ability to hear as well as see the dead? She prayed the instigators of the Grand Work knew what they were about.

She tried to pull her fire tighter, unsure what should happen next. Would the spirit disappear, break apart? Turn to dust or mist? How would they know when they had won?

The ghost threw its head back as if to wail. Loose bricks in the alley trembled. The creature broke from its phoenix-fire bonds and spun upward, floating high to a turret, to a mosque's minaret where it played muezzin again to whatever would listen. Still they could hear nothing.

Ibrahim watched thoughtfully. "I shudder to think what sorts of calls to prayer it offers today for the dead."

"Damn," Beatrice muttered. "Quietus was not strong enough, perhaps."

"The boy is alive," Verena replied. "The cantus was good enough. But I need time with him. I feel that, with practice, I will become quicker, stronger, but—"

"None of us are experts yet," Belle said. "You did a brilliant job."

Verena smiled and glanced at Ahmed who, when he beamed back, had her practically glowing with pride.

"Wait with me a moment," the Healer bade them. "I'd like to make his skin seamless once more." She gave a slow and steady pass with her subtly lit hand over the boy's body. Her work was painstaking, for there were tiny fissures in his skin where the possessor had tried to crack him open like a shell. She had to pass her hand over him twice.

"I doubt we've seen the last of that one," Ibrahim stated, staring up where the spirit had finally disappeared.

"Why?"

Ibrahim shrugged. "Because my Intuition says we won't. And my gift is yet to be proven wrong."

Beatrice laughed. "The Work is hardly a day old; there's plenty of time left for that." Truth be told, she didn't mind his confidence in his powers. It more evenly distributed the massive weight of their destiny. She didn't want to have to act confident alone. She wasn't sure she could pull it off uninterrupted.

"What do other cities do without a Guard?" George asked, sinking to his knees as everyone took a seat around the fallen boy, waiting for Verena to finish.

"The Grand Work must move about the world, city to city, as the angel said," Ibrahim stated. "It is about balance, and the fabric of spirits is a blanket cast wide over the earth. I imagine that we are sent where the disturbances are worst."

Whether her second-in-command respected her or not, Beatrice couldn't help but be glad he was around. He said eloquent, sensible things that made their strange new world more digestible. And he was exceedingly pleasant to look at, which would nicely offset staring down ghostly skeletons and spectral horrors.

"I wonder where the Guard was before us," Ahmed murmured. "I want to say in a war, but I may think that because of my vision."

No one had an answer for that.

"Well, my unlikely new friends," Beatrice said, "the lesson of the day seems most certainly 'Be careful what you wish for.' I'd been thinking I wanted more mystery and adventure in my life. I seem to have called down entirely more than I bargained for."

"And yet you led the charge, *Leader*," Ahmed stated, then gestured to their recovering subject. "We saved a life and a fine young mind today. The first battle in the Grand Work is already won."

Beatrice was not the only one heartened. Ahmed opened his arms to them all; his smile was still pure contagion. Embattling skeletal hatred, an insanity that drives souls to suicide and madness, had lingering effects, and mortals could not help but be rattled by it. Ahmed's joy moved like a bright lamp among them, rallying his fellows to appreciate the wonders they had wrought.

The boy stirred. His eyes fluttered open. He stared up at the dove on the stone that read *Peace*.

Belle moved close. "It was all a terrible dream," she murmured in French-accented Arabic. The boy's eyes clouded, as if the memory of the event was being removed, then he sat up, blinked, rose slowly to his feet, and wandered off toward whatever business he had abandoned when overtaken. The Guard watched him go, six silent companions.

"I'm starving," George stated suddenly. He grinned. "Belle, persuade some fine café to feed us, else we'll make sure they're haunted forever."

They all stood and brushed themselves off. As they did, Beatrice noticed a tiny excitement in her fellows' expressions, as if they were all thinking the same thing: Without their families or any attachments, wasn't this great responsibility a great adventure?

CHAPTER
SEVEN

P<small>ERSEPHONE</small> <small>SIGHED AS THE PORTAL SHUT BEHIND HER, SEALING</small> her again in a world of shadow. This damnable purgatory would yet drive her mad, with its wailings and whispers, eternal regrets voiced in endless repetition. And its king. She heard his tread. Nearby. There was no avoiding him. A footstep, a scrape. A footstep, a scrape. Flesh, then bone. Tick . . . tock. Life. Death. Each in the blink of an eye.

"My Lady" came the sad voice of a rotting woman in clothing that may have been Puritan. Or perhaps she'd been a nun; it was austere and black and absorbed all of Persephone's shifting radiance. The spirit collapsed at her feet, kissing the pale posies that, in an endless cycle, bloomed then rotted as she walked. Persephone felt tears wash her feet and water the dead and fallen petals.

"What is your name, spirit?" she asked, bending to touch the wretch upon the cheek and lift it to its feet.

"Maria."

"Why do you weep?"

"I cannot quit the darkness, it will not quit me. There is such a void in my soul."

"Maria," Persephone commanded, "look at me."

The gray, shuddering spirit did so. Her eyes were cataract-covered sockets.

"Maria. *Choose* to nullify that void. Misery only wins if you let it."

"Show me light, my Lady, show me hope!"

The spirit's cries were hungry and desperate, and Persephone had to hush them. If the ghost went on like that, half of purgatory would flock here and devour her whole with their endless need. She closed her eyes. Her light cost her nothing in the mortal world, but here, it caused great pain. This place had begun to eat away at her insides; her divine form had been rotting for centuries, soured from within and corrupting her budding life and infinite youth. She felt her bosom burn, and when she opened her eyes, she saw the shifting rainbow of her life force clear the cataracts from Maria's eyes.

"Bless you, my Lady," the spirit cried out in celebration.

She ran past Persephone, singing, and hurried down a corridor that brightened from a deep blackness to a pale gray. Maria was being drawn toward the Liminal, and from there the Liminal would send her onward—to the Great Beyond, if the spirit was cured enough. If not, perhaps she would be return to haunt the earth, spending another round as an observer. Or maybe she would be recycled into another human life, given another try to get it right. Persephone wasn't ever quite sure what happened to any soul she managed to free, for she had never made those rounds herself. Her own cycle was more limited.

The use of her light made Persephone cough, a sickly sound that rattled more as the years went by. Now and then she brought up blood and seeds and spat them upon the wet floor of the Whisperworld.

She heard noise. A fleshy clap, then the click of bones. The slap of palms, the click of bones. He was here. Clapping.

"They so adore the one who hates them" came his voice, as if from across a cavern.

Persephone turned and squinted down the long corridor behind her; the shadows were tall and regal, and the red eyes of the shadow king burned within. She sighed. This conversation was always the same. Darkness both adored and abhorred when she did such deeds as this. He loved that his subjects welcomed her as queen and begged for her attention, but loathed that she set so many to rest or onward toward vibrant missions.

"I have never hated them," she said. "You always think you know my heart. And you always fail."

"I know one thing," he rasped.

"And that is?"

"You hate me."

"I didn't used to. I pitied you, as it wasn't your fault mankind made you from its wastes," she stated, her voice flat, the script true yet spoken by rote. "Then you killed my love. Made him a ghost so that his arms will never again hold me. I will forever hate you for that."

"Promenade with me."

Persephone knew if she didn't, he'd follow her until she did. When she humored him, he allowed her some freedom.

"Shall you set more of my minions free?" he asked.

She coughed again; this time fewer seeds, more blood. "I wish I could."

"I'll tell them you are indisposed."

King and queen together walked the corridors and caverns, along the riverbank lined with skulls and trellises made of bone, crafted with care and fastidiously maintained by the Groundskeeper. Darkness's subjects fell at their feet, and many cried out for Persephone's touch, for her time, for a glance. Darkness batted them away with great sweeps of his robe. Its fabric in the ghostly light was visible as crimson. All light was ghostly in this place save hers.

She wept because she could not help those who begged her; her constitution was too weak. Quicksilver tears fell from her face and rolled away along the stones as tiny metallic beads that disappeared into the crevasses and muck of mortal sorrow. Sometimes those tears made talismans and magic. Sometimes they fell, useless, to the ground.

She tried to avoid looking at the floor of the Whisper-world. While her step birthed flowers that soon died, the tread of Darkness brought forth insects that went scuttling into cracks and seams. The countless tiny movements never ceased to disturb her.

"I want to do so much more," Persephone murmured. "Every year I can do less and less. This place rots me."

"Mmm," Darkness replied.

Once, she'd used so much of her light trying to set souls to rest that her heart was actually wounded in the process; she'd been almost destroyed by the following seizure. The episode had been so frightening to the entire Whisper-world that Darkness had instructed Luce the Gorgon to magically ascertain where the Guard was, then he hurled her body into their care. Shutting himself back up in the Whisper-world, he had left her there, in old Ireland, until she was well enough for him to reclaim her. She remembered her convalescence with some wistfulness.

The Guard healer then, in time, came here. All members of the Guard did, though they rarely knew the Whisper-world would eventually be their fate. Because of his actions, this particular man had been granted a certain amnesty. His spirit knew the ways of the Whisper-world like few others. He kept well out of the way and tried his best to have the Whisper-world forget him, lest Darkness turn spiteful. Darkness had a limited memory, for good or ill. He rarely walked the full breadth of his domain, and there were ways to stay safe if you did not draw his wrath.

Persephone never would forget him. Good Aodhan, brave Healer. He was one of her favorites. She always did what she could for him.

Realizing they were passing the grand dais, where the river became a moat surrounding vast stone pillars wound thickly with dead ivy, crumbling ruins that always been ruins, Persephone withdrew her hand. One pass was plenty, and Darkness would not dare press his suit.

She could use her light to scald him if he did; she'd done so before. Yes, she could hurt Darkness, but she was not powerful enough to overtake him in his own domain. For that she would need help.

She would need an army just to fight the minions who would flock to him. While many spirits sought her help, many more would rather see her bleed. If she battled Darkness, she might set an army of the best of life against an army of the worst of it. But she was not a creature of war; love and peace were her calling, and thus, plans of battle were lost on her.

"Good night," she murmured. "I continue my walk alone."

Darkness's Raphaelite face—and then his skull—scowled. He stalked to his throne, sat, and whipped his robes into place. The layers settled in a pattern, the shape of a great crimson rose. It remained the only color, save for hers, in this dreary place: an enormous red rose frozen in the heart of darkness. Beneath the petals, mere bones. That was Darkness's tempting lie.

Persephone turned away and strolled as if wandering aimlessly, but in truth heading in the same direction Maria had run. The Liminal always helped her find her way in this labyrinth, sending a spark down a darkened path that would lead her to who and what she sought.

She took roundabout corridors, glancing behind to see if any of Darkness's minions followed. The Gorgon worried her most—their mutual hatred ran deep. Relations always worsened when Persephone was weak, as she had been after her seizure and after an episode earlier in the nineteenth century; the shark smelled blood in the great river of souls.

The goddess knew she was playing a dangerous game, hiding all of the Guard's spirits in one place, but the deception had sufficed for centuries. Though what was that span to eternity?

Darkness would never let these spirits pass to the Great Beyond, to the place that was their just reward. Someday that sweet release might yet be earned, but her hour had not yet come. In the meantime, she preserved and protected her army.

Ducking into a crevasse in the dark, wet rock, she felt the damp of death press in upon her and fought its cloying tendrils. Sorrow stifled her nonetheless; fluid welled up in her mouth. She spat pomegranate juice, red and sour, onto the gray stones.

"Light, I say," she murmured, raising her glowing hand before her face and ignoring the taste of fruit in her mouth, refusing to let it corrode her spirit. This was one of Darkness's many tricks to keep her here. If she didn't focus, if she didn't keep her mind on her mission, she'd start to drift, eat seeds, drink red juice, and finally lose her core of light and mortal joy once and for all. Darkness desperately hoped for that, though neither of them knew what would happen next if it came to pass.

No. She'd made a promise to her beloved never to give in. Never.

Moving ahead, her bright, ghost-white hand was a lantern in the gloom. To all else, and in her reflection, she was all colors at once, shifting, prismatic, iridescent. But to her own eye, when gazing down at her own flesh and hair, she was entirely colorless: a bright, luminous white; an eerie, blank pearlescent canvas.

Holding her breath, Persephone came to where the crevasse widened into a cave and an underground creek became a pool before her. She plunged into dark, cold water and swam, feeling her thin garments float around her limbs. The murmurs of the dead roared in her ears like the crashing of ocean waves. It wasn't long to the other side, but she hated this journey. It always felt like eternity, and she'd had a good taste of that already.

Ahead there was a large stone, beneath it was a faint glow of light, a barrier that had been made responsive to her presence. She dove under and felt light shine bright from the other side, dancing on the other side of her eyelids. The cries of the dead were now drowned out by only the sound of water.

Nearing shore, she pushed her head out of the black water, gasped for breath, and kept her eyes shut until they could adjust. The light here on this side was bright and blinding, as close as she could imagine to heaven in this place.

Finally opening her eyes when her hand grazed sand and tufts of grass, she gazed upon the denizens of this fabricated Elysium, drinking in the sight of a host of transparent forms from every human epoch and culture, all staring down at her from the crest of a rise and holding out their hands for their great Lady.

Here, she was reminded once more, was the beautiful, luminous army that she needed. But how and when she could best use them was uncertain; she didn't dare risk them if she couldn't be sure . . .

Thousands of Guards stood there. Her white hands fumbled at the riverbank in her eagerness to get to them. Their welcome buoyed her to shore, as if their hearts literally lifted her up, and she placed her bare feet on solid, warm grass.

It was a miracle, this expanse of open green on a perfect day. The Guard's choice for their solace was an Elysian field where she did her best to keep them happy and protected. It sapped a degree of her remaining power. Still, here they all were, or nearly all of them. Some had chosen to remain on Earth, to wander or watch over mortal loved ones; a few had managed to slip away uncounted, and the very first Guard had long gone on to peace. But thousands remained.

"Dear Lady," she heard them murmur, in many different languages, bobbing, floating, or kneeling before her.

"Hello, darlings," she said, and the echo of her voice splintered into countless different tongues.

"We've a new set," she stated. "Cairo this time. Did the others make it here all right?"

A broad, rugged-featured man in a plain tunic and sash, his long hair a mane down his back, stepped forward. "Yes, my Lady, they're just being shown around and made comfortable," he said in old Gaelic.

Aodhan directed Persephone's attention down the slope, to a group of six spirits. The women in wide skirts and fine hats, the men in uniforms and mustaches, they bent over a bubbling spring, dipped their hands in glistening water, and smiled at one another. In American-accented voices, they said that this field was better than their proposed Central Park in their dear New York. If that was ever fully completed, they agreed with a laugh, they'd have to haunt it.

"Thank you, Aodhan," the goddess replied in Gaelic. "You know it always does my heart good to see you, my savior." He'd been the one to literally restart her heart and clean up the blood that had poured from her mouth. Her appearance had shaken his Guard for weeks.

"Of course, my Lady." His grayscale face darkened in a blush, and he gestured her to precede him.

"How long ago was that, when I nearly died in your arms?"

"You're immortal," Aodhan assured her, "you can't die."

"Well, it hurt. Terribly," she said. "But how long? You see, Aodhan, time is so different for me. When I'm with mortals I've this desperate sense of time, as if everything moves in a blur, vanishing like hourglass sand, but here . . . it's all hazy, odd, disjointed. I don't know if Darkness has kept me here a hundred years or a thousand. Or more. I'm not faring well," she added, a cough encroaching. "Pardon me."

Her lungs rattled; a disgusting, alarming noise.

"That was mortal centuries ago, my Lady," Aodhan replied. He placed a hand over her sternum. His healing powers had been long since passed along to a successor, but there were faint traces left, and he bestowed what little succor he could. Her seeming death rattle quieted slightly.

"Thank you," she murmured. A tremendous guilt washed over her, one that had been building for some time and was becoming unbearable.

"My darlings, I should let you go," she murmured to her champions. "I should find a way to get you to your reward."

Their faces were a wash of bright spirits. Aodhan said with a gentle smile, "You say that every time."

"I am a too fond parent, scared of the evils of the world," she mused. "If I'm made of sentiment and of hope, just as my captor is made of misery, then why do I falter?"

"Because you were never meant to be trapped. None of us were," Aodhan replied. "And you're not sure how to free yourself. Or us."

She looked at the grass blowing gently in a magical breeze. "So Hope must trap her children with her?"

"For our own safety," Aodhan said, but she could tell he was tired. They all had to be. Very, very tired.

Aodhan understood. When he had repaired her heart, he'd been taken into her memories, shared that pain of hers that no touch of his healing hand could cure. No magic in the world could restore what Darkness had taken from her.

"One day it will change," she insisted, knowing that sometimes even these dead needed to be reminded of what they were fighting for.

The Guards were listening, intent. She opened her mouth to continue, but stopped short at a warm caress as a disembodied hand made of blue flame pressed its fingers to her lips. Signaling.

"Go." Aodhan smiled. "Spend time at your true husband's grave."

Tears welled in her eyes as she turned away. Far down the gentle slope was a ring of birch trees, their bark pale and elegant. As she neared, their leaves rustled and their limbs bent as if reaching toward her. Encircling the trees was a ring of heather and a faint haze of blue light. She felt Phoenix's power humming around her and within her. What pieces she'd managed to recover of her lover lay beneath this soil. Part of his fire was ever tied to those remains, and to her, a modest portion of power separate from the Grand Work, with a will of its own.

She nearly fell into the ring of flowers, pressing her body to the earth and running her fingers through the heather as if it were her lover's hair. The leaves rustled and the flowers enlarged, filling her nostrils with a sweet and living smell, obliterating the lingering stench of her lover's burned flesh, which never entirely left her consciousness save when she visited here.

Persephone rolled onto her back. Two tiny wisps of blue flame hovered just over her face, as if he were atop her and the flames were the sparkling love in his eyes. She tried to imagine him, to exactly recall every strong feature and tiny, gorgeous detail of wisdom, of power and light made incarnate. But it had been so long. Her lungs grew heavy and she turned her head with a helpless, ugly cough.

"We should be looking for a body *you* might take over," the fire murmured. "Perhaps you should join the next Guard. You sound worse by the day. No matter what you tell me."

"I'm scared," she whispered.

"I know."

The breeze caressed her intimately. Tendrils of air spread palms down her body, her diaphanous layers of clothing no barrier to his spirit. A pressure curled down along her flowing locks, over her arms, dragged up her thighs, thrilling her to her core. She gasped, the flowers the only witness to this passion as she writhed against their bed.

"I need you," she whispered. "Now more than ever. What did you find out about that boy? That Alexi?"

"His family has been in London, looking to move to a new

home," Phoenix's ghost replied. He added, "London always was one of your favorite cities."

She chuckled. Flowers bloomed beneath her shoulders at the sound. "I remember when you flew me over the Thames, before there were bridges . . ."

He purred in fond recollection. She gasped at a particularly brazen, if ghostly, caress, and gave herself over to the acute sensation. It was some comfort, even though it was only an echo of all they had once known.

Rising to her knees, she stroked the sturdy heather all around her, a flower she'd planted here because it reminded her that life could thrive and be beautiful in difficult climes. Against its purple glory, the colorless skin of her hand appeared less youthful than ever. Hope was withering.

Overwhelmed, she smoothed the layers of thin fabric that floated about her body. Kissing the ground, she bid farewell to her beloved's grave and fled up the slope, leaving this echo of what should have been her marriage bed. The many incarnations of the Guard strolled along the green crest, arm in arm, group with group, beside tree and flower, appreciating the blue sky and one another's company. They seemed at peace, happy. If they weren't, she wondered whether any of them would say.

Approaching the boundary waters again, already dreading the cold, black misery they contained, behind her Persephone heard the Guards saying good-bye in their many languages. Their words seemed to reach her across a chasm, distant, fleeting. She was praised using many different names, terms as diverse as the varied beliefs of the world.

Blowing kisses, she fell backward into the water and shot herself down under the barrier stone and across to the other bank in a graceful few strokes, jumping up and into the gray shadow, shaking off the river that clung to her and made her garments heavy with sorrow.

Only later would she recall that, as she moved into the crevasse that would take her back into the Whisper-world's unmitigated clutches, she had faintly heard the sound of hissing. She was faltering indeed to have been so careless, to not hide more carefully where she had been. It was foolish not to have more zealously guarded her treasure, for it was all that she had left to live for.

CHAPTER
EIGHT

IBRAHIM SETTLED IN AT AHMED'S HOME, AND THE TWO YOUNG men marveled at the ease with which they floated in and out of the consciousness of the Basri family. Ahmed was the only child, clearly adored; but since the magic of the Guard had claimed them, he was adored at a distance, as if through a veil.

The shift clearly saddened Ahmed. That joyous, expressive face was so easy for Ibrahim to read. When even a hint of the Grand Work passed between them, the glow of the Heart would obliterate all else, and it seemed the whole house lit with him, even after the sun set. In general, things seemed to be going well. Thus Ibrahim was surprised to be awakened by his friend in the middle of the night.

"The war in the ground!" Ahmed cried, launching up from his cot, moisture dotting his brow.

"What?" Ibrahim sat up across the room, rubbing his eyes. His sleep had been heavy, his body still adjusting to its new powers and sensibilities. The Grand Work was more than mere mortals could digest in one fell swoop.

"A vision," Ahmed murmured, shaking his head. He got up and walked into the main room. Ibrahim followed. Ahmed l[i]t tin lamp whose mirror brightened the candle flame and [c]ornate metal pattern onto the richly colored rug, the[r] carved wooden chair below a bookshelf filled with S[crolls] and tracts.

"Would you like to speak about it?" Ibrahim asked.

"I see a war. A strange war with metal dragons and guns like I've never known, horrible guns dispensing death like falling rain."

"Why do you say it is a vision rather than a simple nightmare? What have we to do with such sights?"

"Because it was about the dead. They've nowhere to go. There are simply too many. It's terrible. I should tell the angel when next she descends."

Ibrahim nodded, then suddenly clutched his heart as a flash of pain swept over him. Though still a new sensation, it was immediately recognizable. This was his Intuition at work. This was the Pull. The sensation was raw, as if something were spreading across his nerves; his circulatory system shifted to match the haphazard streets of Cairo, and all he could think was: Giza.

He knew, too, the location of each of his compatriots. Most strongly he felt Beatrice. He felt them all rise from chairs or beds and pinpoint the same location his own senses decreed. He scowled.

"What is it?" asked Ahmed, rising.

"Of course," Ibrahim replied, grabbing a pair of long coats from the rack near the door and tossing one to his friend. Shrugging into the other, he strode out into the courtyard, Ahmed at his heels.

Ibrahim felt the night air bite his skin even through the coat and the simple linen tunic he wore underneath.

Ahmed prompted, "Of course?"

"Of course there's trouble at the pyramids."

"Wherever great spiritual energy has amassed, there shall we be directed. Ibrahim glanced at him, awaiting some further explanatory, but his friend just shrugged, adding, "Full duty will come in time."

He pursed his lips. "Lovely. My new companion, with his good nights, will counter every concern

"I'll try," Ahmed agreed with a winning smile.

Ibrahim couldn't help but laugh, until a new thought made him scowl. "I say, it's the foreigners meddling with our dead that's causing the trouble."

"Believe in curses, then, do you?" Ahmed asked.

"No, I believe in human stupidity, disrespect, greed, and obsession with conquest. Things that never fail to cause harm."

Ahmed put a hand on his shoulder. "All fair and understood. However, I suggest you add something of joy to your list of beliefs, brother. It is necessary for a life well lived." Using his gift, he shared with Ibrahim some of that component.

As they traveled southwest through Cairo from their position near the citadel, a wind at their feet gave them an uncanny speed, as if they'd been given Mercury's shoes.

"I suppose the angel could have stirred and roused the dead," Ibrahim muttered after a long silence. "She was keen to see our 'mortal wonders.' I wouldn't have expected tourism out of a divinity."

"She's a creature of peace, not unrest; surely her intentions were solely to admire," Ahmed countered. "If anything, her presence might have inadvertently stirred a yearning for life again. She does have a way about her, does she not?"

Ibrahim shrugged. It didn't seem proper to be moved by a being he could hardly comprehend. But it was true; she was a raw and captivating force of nature that could not be dismissed.

Their augmented movement brought them, some half hour later, to Cairo's outskirts, with the vast sands of Giza beyond. It was such an abrupt shift from streets to unruly, ever-shifting sands. The Pull drew them not into the desert but to a café and shop that catered to foreign tourists seeking the pyramids.

In front of the nearby stables stood Belle, with the reins of six docile camels in her hand. George rounded the corner at a run, his half cloak, vest, and undone shirtsleeves flapping against his gangly form. The sight of the Frenchwoman, in a fashionable pink dress, with six wide-eyed camels looming at her back made him howl with delight.

"Bloody genius!" George exclaimed. "How did you—?"

Belle tapped her temple and smiled sheepishly. "I've learned I can get my way in absolutely anything. Terribly dangerous, this gift of mine." Her French accent was heavy but she was all the more charming for it.

Beatrice was standing a few paces off, near where the road widened. Her simple black riding outfit, well suited for travel, looked elegant on her tall frame, and her dark blond hair was pinned beneath a sensible hat.

Verena was the first to move forward and claim one of the camels, her dark robes rustling in the night breeze. Ahmed offered his help to ease her up to the fabric saddle, which she gracefully accepted. George ducked, narrowly avoiding a veritable grenade of camel spittle, then giggled, reaching up to scratch the beast's muzzle.

Noticing that Beatrice was staring into the distance, mouth agape, Ibrahim followed her line of sight and gasped.

"Allah, God, Yahweh, and Osiris have mercy," he muttered.

The rest of the Guard shifted until they could see what had drawn their Leader's attention—a sight that surpassed the wildest and most morbid of imaginings.

Kilometers ahead stood the necropolis . . . and the great pyramid and its smaller cousins were *erupting* with ghosts, the restless dead like luminous silver lava that coursed down their perfect slopes. What the half moon did not illuminate, these spirits made bright.

"Do we have to deal with *all* that?" Verena breathed, staring at the ghostly volcanoes.

"I hope not," Beatrice replied. She set her jaw, then mounted a camel with ease.

Ibrahim furrowed his brow, impressed. He followed suit, grumbling when he could not match Beatrice's grace, instead having a bit of difficulty gaining a firm perch against the hump. The camel glanced back in irritation.

A few paces into the journey, Belle said, *"Mon Dieu,"* tears glistening in her eyes. "One spirit is fine. But that . . . *that's* a bit much. That is absolutely terrifying." She added *frightening* in Arabic, just in case anyone failed to catch her faltering English. Several others added similar thoughts.

Neither Beatrice nor Ibrahim joined in the chorus. She looked over at him; seeing his reflection in her pale eyes, he felt suddenly older. So they faced the absurd terror of floating haunts and the biddings of angels. She didn't seem any more elated about it than he was, but she didn't seem frightened, either. Instead she appeared sturdy, elegant, and composed.

She stared at him as if they were peers, which was unsettling because she was Western and a woman. Then again, these were uncommon circumstances. He sat straighter in his saddle.

Beatrice asked, "Well, now that we know everyone's petrified, what are we to do about this little circus?" She held up her hand. Blue fire hovered in a ball.

"I've been practicing," she continued, staring at the flame, which she cast out, then brought back close again like some kind of toy. "It's fascinating. I keep thinking I've lost my mind, but if I have, then so have all of you. I hope you've all been thinking? Practicing?"

She spoke, Ibrahim had to admit, with the stern and unaffected air of capable command. He was pleased to see the firmness of her gaze as she studied each of their companions; it was critical that their leader not appear daunted.

She chuckled when they all nodded or shrugged. "Lovely. Like lambs to the spiritual slaughter." Then she spurred her camel on. "It's all right," she said casually, as if speaking to the animal. "I'm still not convinced I believe in ghosts. Perhaps that is a healthy separation. Psychological detachment may equal greater efficiency."

"Will we have to go *in*?" Belle breathed, her fear mounting. She stared at the enormous monuments and their attendant clouds of spirits.

"No," Ahmed replied. "Look. We won't have to go far at all. They're coming to us."

It was true. While the bulk of spiritual activity clustered in bright gray light around the great pyramid, a platoon of spirits marched directly toward their small band. They were floating above the sand a meter off the ground, in neat rows, bare-chested and clad in pale loincloths.

"Servants. Buried with the royals—some say alive," Ahmed remarked quietly. "I can't imagine they were happy about it."

"Who would be?" George murmured. "I mean God save the Queen and all but I'd rather not be buried with her when the dear lady goes."

Beatrice smirked and Belle giggled. The sound of laughter was welcome against such a spectral host.

Ibrahim closed his eyes. Information was at hand. He now owned a sensibility that was foreign to the way he was used to his mind working, but the knowledge felt clarion and true and he wished to the heavens he could explain it.

"No. These aren't servants, these are those who *designed* the great pyramids. The engineers. Their noble's remains were disturbed and they're looking to settle a score, recover grave goods or perhaps the body itself—or visit a haunting upon the offenders," he said. He'd spoken in Arabic, then translated a few words to English, but Beatrice was already nodding, understanding him from the first. He added, purely for her benefit, "There are many offenders when it comes to the ancient dead here."

Beatrice held up her hands. "Not my father. I know the sites well. He's lauded by all Egyptian colleagues at the university and within antiquities for his reverence and respect."

"Tell that to these gents," George murmured.

The platoon of restless dead was upon the company quickly, a wave of ice-cold air preceding them. From Beatrice's lips flew a command spoken in the Guard tongue now native to all.

The six slipped off their camels. Belle took charge of the creatures, still appearing shocked by her sudden facility with them and surprised when they listened, and guided them a few paces back. Thankfully, the camels seemed unconcerned by the dead.

The Guard formed a circle in the sand, their young faces illuminated by the moon, the light of the spirits, and by a great blue fire that coursed around them and rose into the air like a water spout, whipped by the wind. Sand tumbled over the hems of their dresses, robes, and boots. Notes of music caressed the air, an angelic choir tuneful and vibrant. Clouds cleared from the sky above them and the stars seemed to burn brighter in affirmation. A few slow tears rolled down Ahmed's smooth face, bright with serenity. Ibrahim wished that he felt so at peace.

With a deep breath and a forceful exhalation, Beatrice opened her hands. A net of blue fire leaped up, surrounding the spirits that had formed a circle above them. The skeletal spirits were speaking, their loosely attached jaws flapping rapidly and angrily, but the Guard heard nothing.

Ibrahim felt the oppressive weight of death and the surety of his own mortality. Dread flooded his veins, and the empty eyes of one of the ghosts drew him forward a step, sending an icy chill seeping into his bones. His mind was flooded with images. Every time in his life when he had said something hurtful or done something hateful flashed before his eyes, and he knew he was a wretched being, meant only for decay.

Then his mind washed clean; the oppressive fog lifted from his brain. Belle had brushed his temple with her finger. He nodded his thanks, and she smiled demurely, her round cheeks dimpling.

The Guard's separate gifts worked increasingly in concert. George pulled out a walking stick, and began darting about in the sand. Ibrahim wanted to watch him—there was something compelling about what he was doing—but he could sense Beatrice's energy straining as she worked the fire to keep the spirits contained. Finding a surprising text upon his lips, he recited the Book of the Dead, though the ancient Egyptian vernacular had previously been unfamiliar. Some of the spirits became captivated, nodding, suddenly rethinking their mission. It seemed that while the Guard could not hear the wails of the dead, the ghosts could hear the living quite clearly.

Other skeletal forms strained against the confining fire, thus straining against Beatrice. Ibrahim felt her energy falter and was alarmed that he felt so attuned to her. The metaphysical bond was both intimate and unsettling. Seductive.

Beatrice growled in frustration. A few spirits broke free and lunged at her, their incorporeal hands creating a distinct pressure around her throat. Another somehow sent a rock hurtling at her face; the impact left her cheek weeping blood in a thin scarlet line.

She growled a command. The spirits unhanded her as if scalded and backed toward their still-contained fellows.

Verena glided near. Her glowing hand touched Beatrice's injury, and the blood vanished. Ahmed countered the black clouds of misery that the spirits shed by moving to his fellows and placing a finger on their heart; each of them was then able to breathe more easily despite the stifling press of death. Ibrahim offered a new Book of the Dead text to keep the ghosts engaged rather than violent.

Beatrice gritted her teeth. "Now for a cantus to quiet them into submission."

"I've got something I'd like to share," George exclaimed,

running forward. "Excuse me," he called jauntily to the spirits floating above. "Oh, ghosties of the great monuments, do come and look at my exhibition, it may move you," he declared.

Some spirits moved to hover above the elaborate grooves that he'd wrought in the sand. They placed hands over their mouths and reached for the others; then, in a rushing burst of gray light, they all went scurrying back toward the pyramids, where they vanished into the sand, one by one.

The Guard stared after them, catching their breath. George looked rather pleased with himself. Beatrice cast blue light over George's creation, illuminating the source of the spirits' defeat. Using his walking stick and some creative footwork, he'd drawn in the sand a beautifully rendered image of a great bird with outstretched wings, flame wreathing up from its claws and tail feathers.

"I haven't a bloody clue what I meant while doing it, but looking at it now I think it's quite nice—don't you?" he asked with a grin, running a hand through his hair.

"A phoenix," Beatrice murmured. "Why, that's lovely, George." The English youth blushed, staring down at his work.

"And quite meaningful to them," Ahmed added thoughtfully. "Transformative power. Rebirth. The Egyptians worshipped Phoenix; he was a god to them. They must have thought we were his votaries and dared not test us further."

"We *are* his votaries," Beatrice reminded them all, blue fire shimmering along her fingers like liquid jewelry.

"The air!" Belle exclaimed with satisfaction. They'd begun to feel the Balance as if it were temperature. She went to her camel and hopped up with a facility that defied the restrictions usually caused by women's garments.

"And yet . . ." Beatrice scowled, gesturing to the still active overflow of spirits cascading down the sides of the pyramids.

"No, I understand," Verena said quietly, watching the display. "We're here to protect mortals, not to police every ghost. We'll never

be able to look at these monuments again without seeing the tumult, but we're not called to that melee. Not yet. Not unless it
comes for humanity. Tonight troops came charging toward the
Giza populace, so we had to stand in the way. A mortal barricade
for mortal hearts."

"Well said," Beatrice commented, "very true."

Everyone nodded slowly. Ahmed reached toward Verena as if
he wanted to take her hand. She stared at his hand, then him, and
smiled, but did not move. Beatrice's expression became a scowl.

The feast of unrest here saddened Ibrahim. He wondered if
the Book of the Dead had helped any of the pyramids' souls find
peace or if it had only served to confuse them. He was certain the
unrest had more to do with mortal meddling than any flaws of
faith. He was so lost in thought that it took him some moments
to realize that the others had remounted their camels and were
heading back to Giza. He hurried to catch up.

They hadn't gone far, so their return did not take long. Beatrice
was the first to arrive back at the tourist depot. After a limber
dismount, she tied the animal to a stable post and turned to her
fellows.

"Well, my troops," she declared. "Good work, it would seem.
Until we next feel the call to arms."

The rest stared after her, blinking as she walked away, still
unsure what sort of protocol they should follow at the end of meetings such as this. Eventually they took her action as dismissal.
There was little else to do at this time of night but return to the
central city.

Ibrahim watched his fellows sort themselves into couples in a
way that seemed understandable, Ahmed asking Verena in which
part of the Coptic *hara* she resided, Belle and George exchanging
halting French and English sentences and smiles. A few Giza residents stumbled past and stared, surprised at the seemingly upstanding and well-kept youths who shouldn't have been wandering

the streets at such an hour. Before they could ask questions, Belle waved a hand and they turned, dazed, and wandered away.

Beatrice vanished around a corner, and Ibrahim practically ran after her.

"Do not misinterpret this," he called in smooth English. "It isn't that I require your company, it simply isn't the wisest idea for a young woman to walk alone at such an hour." Her black traveling skirts swished about her as she strode forward and then bounced to a halt. She turned, one eyebrow raised.

"While in any other circumstance I would entirely agree," she began, "I somehow think I'll be all right." She gazed down at her palm, in which she held a ball of blue fire.

"I'd suggest you not entertain any unrealistic sense of security," he cautioned. "Don't tempt fate. Your fire works on ghosts, not human criminals. Don't think you're a god."

Beatrice made a face. "I know I'm not a god. But I would like to be left alone. This Grand Work madness came at a most unwelcome time. I must remember that I'm in mourning."

"As am I. And I respect that. But as your"—he swallowed—"second-in-command, I should see to it that you are escorted home. I can walk several paces behind you if you'd rather."

Beatrice's face softened. "Thank you, Ibrahim," she said in Arabic after a quiet moment. "You are a gentleman. Walk with me, then. But please forgive my silence. While I know I ought to be asking all the things new friends should, I've no stomach for niceties at present. We'll have all the time in the world for cordiality—or so it would seem."

Ibrahim nodded, intrigued by her cool tone. Intuition told him it hid something. She was forcing herself to be distant.

They kept to shadows and silence as the city thickened around them, veering toward the Citadel. Glancing at the passing ghosts, seeing that they seemed uninterested in him, Ibrahim wondered if he and she really were allowed to speak freely, like friends and comrades. If so, what on earth should they say? Where would they begin? The Grand Work was redefining their identities, and he could hardly remember how the world looked and felt before, though he knew that at the core they each had been chosen for who they were. They were not changed but . . . heightened.

Despite that, they were no less alone.

THE WHISPER-WORLD ECHOED WITH THE GORGON'S TRIUMPHANT cry. "I've found where she keeps them all!" Luce crowed as she ran to tell her master, dancing around those shadows lit by red eyes.

Darkness launched to his feet. Down from the massive stone throne he stepped, casting open the veil of darkness and standing, a luminous and bone-white skeleton. "Where? Where is she? Is she there?"

He was suddenly a beautiful man. In the next moment a skeleton.

"No, she's out cavorting with mortals, as usual," Luce sneered, daring to slide her black-robed arm into his, which was flesh, then bone. "While she's away, you ought to make your move. Gather your most miserable minions, the ones without hope, all those who have refused redemption. Bring them. We've a field to burn."

CHAPTER
NINE

PUTTING THE GAPING MAWS OF THE RESTLESS GIZA GHOSTS
behind her, Beatrice bid Ibrahim thanks and a quiet good night at
the front door of their building, and he bowed his head and disappeared around the corner.

Climbing the stairs with a quiet tread, she unlocked the front
door of her father's apartments and went directly to the study,
where she assumed she would find him. He was always up until all
hours, poring over glyphs and pieces of pottery. She kissed him on
the head without a word, receiving no smile or acknowledgment in
return, then glided silently to her room. Rest was imperative.

She tried to ignore the pain of her dear father having hardly
noticed her, for that was the way of things now. Her cohorts across
the city were surely feeling the same, passing phantoms in their own
homes.

Beatrice stared at the ceiling as a vague horror crept over her.
She should be truly in mourning, not having to remind herself of
it. She should be helping her father make discoveries. She should
be creating a name for herself in Egyptology. And yet, here she
was, her purpose in academia supplanted by something she couldn't
accurately describe, even to herself. Her family had been replaced
by five strangers and an angel.

Instead of finding Jean's image on her eyelids when she closed
them, she saw the disturbingly handsome face of her second-in-
command. As firmly rooted as if meant to be. As if *they* were meant

to be. But how could such different people be fated to unite? It was nonsense. Ibrahim was a stranger. Where was this odd sensibility coming from?

Keeping sharp and defensive was all she could do to keep boundaries. She couldn't let a stranger, one so cool and detached toward her, know that she was drawn to him. He was her second-in-command, and he likely resented her for it. Men always did.

"I couldn't help that I was chosen as Leader," she murmured. Then she was overwhelmed by contrition. "Surely he doesn't feel this weak contrivance of emotion. He can't feel any of what I do. I'm projecting my grief onto Ibrahim, feeling a strange attraction . . . No, the man hates me. This is absurd."

"It isn't" came a voice at her bedside. The light of the room shifted colors.

"Good Lord! Couldn't you knock or offer a bit of warning?"

The goddess sat at the end of her bed and smirked. "I thought you didn't believe in the Lord."

"I don't know what I believe. But recent events have at least renewed my faith in cursing," Beatrice replied.

Persephone chuckled. "It isn't absurd to find yourself drawn to your second-in-command. It's only natural. Leaders and seconds have loved each other for ages, no matter who they are, men, women, no matter where they come from or how they may identify. All the Muses are interested in is the soul, not the body. Shouldn't that be the way? Of course; it isn't a *mandate* for partnerships to arise, they simply often do." She leaned close. "He's dreadfully handsome, isn't he?"

"You were eavesdropping," Beatrice hissed, blushing. That would teach her to sort through her emotions aloud.

"No," Persephone argued. "I just wanted to say good-bye before I return to the Whisper-world. I never know how long I'll be gone in terms of your time. It may be a month or a day to you, I've no idea, but being away from the living always feels like an eternity to me. When I feel a pull to my Guard I try to make my rounds to those most influential. You've done well. Take care. Keep faith."

The goddess vanished, leaving Beatrice still blushing and awkward. But at least she had some sense of why she was feeling such a pull toward Ibrahim. There was a Guard precedent.

She couldn't be blamed, then. And, of course she wouldn't act on it, considering his indifference. She did have her pride, after all. A whole hell of a lot of it.

SEVERAL STREETS AWAY, AHMED WOKE WITH ANOTHER CRY. Ibrahim stirred groggily, rubbing at his eyes and fighting a sense of déjà vu as he sat up.

"The nightmare again?"

At the foot of his friend's bed sat the angel, Persephone. Ibrahim found that calling her an angel still felt more natural to him than calling her a goddess. Not everything he believed had to be overturned at once.

Ahmed breathed heavily. He saw Persephone, turned to Ibrahim and offered a valiant smile.

"What is it?" the divinity asked.

Ahmed addressed her. "Visions came to me at the same time as the Grand Work. They showed a war in the ground, where the dead have no place to go. Why do I keep seeing it unless it's a warning? I tell you, this is important. The dead have nowhere to go . . . Surely that means something to you, my Lady."

She considered before shaking her shifting-colored head. "Alas," she admitted, "such a vision is unfamiliar to me."

"It is of a time I cannot yet fathom. There are machines, terrible constructions of metal. It all seems fantastical and impossible. The dead, oh, so many dead! They speak to me. They tell me not to close every door. Do you know what door?"

"I recall that the Heart was desperate to go to you, was so very eager to choose you, Ahmed. Perhaps this was why. It knew it gained both a joyous heart and a visionary. It sensed that you could help our cause."

"Perhaps," Ahmed said, shaking off the nightmare and regaining hope.

"Or it is all too human madness," Ibrahim muttered.

The angel turned as if to admonish him, but instead replied, "Visionaries or madmen. There seems a hair's breadth distinction at times."

"But you'll be alert, should this suddenly mean something?" Ahmed begged. "If this torture was for no good purpose . . ."

"Of course I'll take your vision to heart!"

The Sufi nodded, satisfied. Ibrahim noticed that his eyes had dark circles underneath. How long had Ahmed been suffering these dreams?

Persephone bit her lip. "May I offer you something?" she asked. "I wish to counter your pain with something beautiful."

Ahmed nodded, eager. Ibrahim watched her a bit more closely.

"While I'm hardly omnipotent, I can deeply feel the human heart—of my Guards in particular. I can affect a journey of release should you choose to accept it. A living daydream of something beautiful. A journey into a favorite, perfect place, if only for a moment. Think on that and we'll travel there. Close your eyes and think of something heavenly."

Ahmed did. Persephone touched his temple with her fingertip. He shivered—in delight, Ibrahim hoped.

She turned. "Would you like to come?" she asked.

He stared at her a moment. She cycled through a few different shades. Finally he moved toward her. She gestured him closer. Reaching out a fingertip, she touched his temple . . .

The world changed. They stood on a wide rooftop, a vast stone courtyard. The Nile delta stretched out below, lush, verdant, the source of all life. There was music, incredible music, as if a thousand muezzins called out in Arabic, in pure, powerful tones from a hundred unseen towers.

Ahmed was transformed. His long, layered tunic was all white and a tall camel-hair cap perched upon his head. The Sufi's eyes were closed in rapture, and there was a huge smile upon his face as he listened to the sung prayers.

Persephone stood at a respectful distance, eyeing Ahmed with unquestionable love. In this moment she did not shift. She was entirely without color, her hair and skin from head to toe, her diaphanous robes; all was solid white as if to match Ahmed's robes.

The Sufi began to turn, his left foot the pivot, his arms up as if welcoming the world; one hand was turned toward heaven, the other to Earth. His white skirt spun out around him, low at first, higher as his spinning grew and the hymn swelled. From what Ahmed had described to Ibrahim about his faith, Ibrahim recognized this as part of a worship ceremony. This was Ahmed's personal, private joy: Sufi whirling. And the beauty of it, of the singing and of the simple meditative movement and worship of a mysterious divinity, brought Ibrahim close to tears.

Ahmed opened his eyes to fix his friend and their mysterious angel with a meaningful gaze. In one gesture, he encouraged them both to imitate his form. To join in his affirmation. Which they did. How could they not?

It did not matter how much time passed. Eventually, the music quieted. The bright expanse of the perfect day darkened, Ahmed turned to Persephone, and suddenly they were all back in his small Cairo room.

"Thank you for that," Ahmed said, his voice thick with emotion. He turned to Ibrahim and added, "Such as that was a glimpse of the unseen world, as close as we'll get to the afterlife while we yet live."

Persephone smiled, her colors bright, refreshed.

Ibrahim chuckled, enjoying the memory. "You may make a believer of me yet."

Ahmed shrugged. "I don't worry for your soul."

Such a pronouncement was good to hear. Ibrahim smiled.

Persephone's colors darkened. "I must go back."

Ahmed frowned. "Again? It is not yet the season, is it?"

The goddess's smile was fond. "There are many different seasons across this planet. We abandoned the old schedule long ago. It's better that way. I am leashed but come and go as I please, and if I return regularly, he tends not to watch so closely. But I'm sensing things are about to change. We're on the cusp of a new dawn, and I want to be both places as much as I can—so I can react quickly." She blew both Ibrahim and Ahmed kisses, her eyes sad. "You be sure to enjoy this world. The next one comes soon enough."

Ahmed nodded. "Be sure to think on my vision, my Lady, should you find it useful."

Persephone sighed. "I never take what a Guard says for granted. And if there comes a time to use your wisdom, I shan't forget. But as for now, I see nothing."

She cast her arm forward, and a black portal ripped into the room. Ibrahim and Ahmed watched in awkward silence as the beautiful creature steeled herself and straightened her shoulders. Did her hands tremble? She drew a deep breath and stepped inside. With a snapping sound the portal closed. They were again alone in the room.

"It is terrible to see a divine being of such gentleness move frightened into a dark night," Ahmed stated.

Ibrahim nodded. The sight was indeed deeply distressing, and Instinct rustled his blood, shuddered against his bones. There were many dark nights ahead for all of them, not just Ahmed. If these mounting shadows were hard for a divinity, what would they be like for mortals?

CHAPTER
TEN

WHAT PERSEPHONE HAD SAID TO IBRAHIM AND AHMED WAS true: She had some freedom, but it was best if her feet often touched the ground of the Whisper-world. If she didn't go back voluntarily, the maw would eventually open, she'd feel wrenching pain, and shadowy claws would drag her back by force.

Gliding through the darkened corridors, she saw that the regent was not on his throne. Relieved, she turned toward her resting place, a platform a few paces nearer to the river. A pair of red eyes blinked at her from the floor. The dog.

It wasn't a dog, exactly, but what else could one call this gruesome guardian? It sometimes appeared in a dog's shape, save that it had far too many heads, too many tongues salivating for violence. Persephone had a fondness for animals, but this was not an animal. It was a swarm of shadow and teeth. And it, like its master, liked her to know it was watching.

But she was not without recourse, and she was unafraid to strike back. She struck the air with her delicate hand: A cracking sound reverberated through surrounding corridors as a burst of dazzling white light snapping out from her body like a whip. The creature turned its hundred tails. Uttering vague, canine noises it fled, shadows breaking apart like rats scurrying away.

Alas, wielding her light here always had consequences, and Persephone's bosom seared with pain. She choked, pomegranate juice upon her lips, that eternal bile that had bound her here so long ago. She spat, and the stones sizzled with the heat of her blood and residual light.

Gasping, she sank down upon the bed Darkness provided her. Though she rarely spoke to him, nor he to her, it seemed to keep him satisfied when she lay upon her bier near the throne, just as it did when she took his hand for a promenade through his kingdom.

An old wound ripped open within her, something far worse than the usual repercussions from her powers. She shot up from her bed, assuming Darkness had returned and was torturing her with another of his nightmares. But his chair remained empty.

Somewhere Darkness was stoking the fire of eternal anger. Persephone picked her battles, always had, but now a battle was picking her. She had an inkling that, in one eternal night, everything would be different, like the day he'd killed Phoenix.

Seeking the source of her discomfort, she ran, but the stone corridors confounded her. He'd changed them again, a maddening and confounding habit. She lifted one hand before her to light her path. The haggard spirits in her way ducked clear, knowing not to trifle with this luminous fury.

Was Darkness moving against her Guard? It was time for a fight. It had long been time for a fight. Darkness hadn't bargained for a fiery bride when he'd kidnapped youth, beauty, love, and hope; all elemental aspects of one prismatic being. He'd thought these meek mortal properties were easily controlled. He was mistaken, though she was often too scared to see anyone hurt.

She could feel the field burning even before she saw the flames. The crevasse that had hidden the entrance was blown open, the barrier stone rubble that made a jagged stone bridge, the water that served as a moat to the field was half drained.

The flames rose high, the fog of misery thick, the sky she had crafted for them had gone unnaturally dark. An unearthly sound tore from her body, and her rage lifted her into the air, great gusts of wind whipping all around. The smoke flashed with shifting colors as she floated forward. Age-old anger burst open deep wounds, and her ancient terror made a rain come and douse the flames, but it was too late; her gorgeous field was blackened.

A battle raged by the birch trees, where the Guard's many spirits fought an equal number of infernal dead. Blue fire trickled between them but was spread thin. Though the bulk of the Power and Light was in Cairo, being channeled by Beatrice Smith, a portion would always be tied to Phoenix's remains, and that portion fought fearlessly.

There was a hole in her paradise, a cracked archway in what looked like an expanse of rolling hill. Her Guard were being tormented by the most vile of Darkness's minions, and they did not have the advantage of their old powers. They were surrounded, being driven in clusters, picked at, brawling.

Darkness was nowhere to be seen. This place, even with its once blue sky now a charred purple twilight, was too bright for him.

"Halt!" Persephone cried in that language known only to the Guard and the dead. The battle paused as if the combative arms were uniformly lifted by strings.

The Guard stared at her and nodded, but the infernals just grinned. A battle cry from somewhere deep below rumbled the blackened earth beneath her feet, an ugly cry from Darkness's hollow throat. It sounded louder from the water, from that rising tide toward which her friends were being pushed. Darkness wanted to suck his foes down into the whirling depths of the river.

The battle resumed, with the dead forcing her champions toward the shore. The screams of her Guard had Persephone tearing out her hair.

Aodhan broke from the battle to draw her away from the breach. "Take the remains of your beloved and go. Leave this place. Don't let what's left of him fall into Darkness's hands; he'll just scatter the ashes in the river, or worse," the Celt told her. "You're going to have to use all your energy, all your heart, to get yourself and him away from here. You can fight a battle for us another day."

"Where is he taking you?" Persephone sobbed.

"I've hung back out of his sight, gone back and forth to see the first battalion imprisoned. In a tower. Far behind his throne, in the shadows of the shadows. He's corralling everyone there. Gather your lover and make a plan for tomorrow, for today is already lost."

Persephone's tears had formed into tiny, sharp tacks that she threw at the feet of her foes. The dog had come, leaping and yelping, its one then a hundred forms nipping at Guard flesh; it had squealed as its dread pads were pierced by her quicksilver thorns.

As much as rage bade her fight, she knew Aodhan was correct. Persephone blazed light and tore ahead, casting back restless spirits as she ran to the circle of heather, to the trees that grew from her love's resting place. The eternal flame of phoenix fire lashed out at offending spirits, then flowed around her, sustaining her light.

Falling to her knees, she tore into the soft earth, desperation giving her fingers strength. She could hear Darkness screaming, but he could not come within paces of her here. Especially not lit like she was. Her breath was ragged in her throat, her bosom burned, and she knew her impenetrable aura would last only moments longer.

She unearthed a vessel carved with a feather and lit by blue light. Phoenix's physical remains.

"My Lady," Aodhan breathed, suddenly at her side. "We have safe passage for you, *there*. Come quickly while the bulwark holds."

She glanced up to see the Guard spirits again fighting back those gray, sagging, miserable wretches from the bowels of the Whisper-world, creatures that hardly had human form remaining, flanking an opening through a gray stone arch.

"Aodhan, tell them I'll come for them. Please. Tell them I'll come."

"They know, my Lady."

"But you must remind them; they'll forget. Rally them. They'll despair in this place—"

Aodhan held up a hand. "Just don't be long."

Persephone nodded. "And you, stay clear of him. Do not be captured, no matter what. Follow behind me. Haunt the Earth, bide your time. Come to the Liminal with me. I have no choice but to beg its help."

Aodhan cocked his head as if suddenly hearing a noise. "Something's coming, my Lady." He smiled, his eyes far away. "Some strange and beautiful things are coming, my Lady. But you must make them happen."

Persephone nodded, clutched the vessel of her lover's remains tightly to her, and ran. Aodhan followed, pausing at the burning edge of the field, which was torn open like a wound, to aid a comrade at the jagged threshold. The woman, from a Chinese Guard formed centuries prior, screamed rallying cries for their *Fenghuang*.

Where to go? The Liminal would tell her. Persephone concentrated all her remaining energy, nearly broken by burning pain, her breathing labored. Her light flew out in an arc, shifted stone and cleared a path directly to that magical place whence angels were appointed. She quickly made her way to it, being sure to close the pathways behind her. She would not be followed.

"Dear Liminal," she gasped at the vast frame that seemed to her most like a proscenium, but with the power to enact any play and every player. Its glassy surface bore no picture, though it crackled and sparked, sensing what was happening in the field. If Persephone wasn't mistaken, murky traces of blue passed over its surface like roiling clouds, perhaps showing a loyalty to phoenix fire.

"I beg your help," she continued. "I know your allegiance is not to our kind but to the mortal world, but the Grand Work is for mortal good, as well you know. Darkness has taken the field; surely you feel the suffering he creates. I dare not leave our great source of power within these walls. I fear Darkness would pervert my dear heart's remains, destroy what little I have left of my beloved. Please. Show me where to go, where to take him. I'm not even half as strong as I once was. Help me set a new course."

The Liminal sparkled. It whirled, it shifted, and Persephone found herself lurching forward and through. Her bare feet touched smooth marble. She had landed in a grand, dim, open foyer. It was unfinished. Moonlight filtered through dusty pale curtains and gave the vast room an eerie glow.

The perimeter of the foyer was lined with pillars; a pair of halls led out through an arch on either side. The space seemed incomplete, with only one wall painted and the stone unpolished. There was a mosaic seal at her feet, but it, too, was unfinished, though Persephone could make out the word FRIENDS and the image of a dove of peace.

"Friends," Persephone echoed. "I could not have asked for a better word of comfort."

What was this place? She licked her finger and put it up to the air, testing the winds of time.

"I'm in your day, my dear Guard. This is 1867. But where, then, are you?"

She moved across the great foyer, bare feet padding across the silent, empty space, and stared out the window at gaslit carriages and paupers upon cobblestone streets.

"Why, it's London."

Her heart quickened. Somewhere in this great city was a young man who had inexplicably captured her interest, a boy who her instincts said would be important. Who could mean *everything*.

But none of that now. She had her Guard spirits and the remains of Phoenix to think about, so she returned to the incomplete mosaic. In her arms, the vessel glowed.

"Bury me here. This feels right," the essence of Phoenix whispered, like a kiss glancing off her ear.

"But you're so far from Beatrice," Persephone protested, "from your Guard."

"Beatrice owns part of my fire, not all; you know that."

"Still, won't you be spread too thin? You're not used to resting in mortal soil. The Whisper-world has access to all places, it sits beside all cities, lands, fields—"

"We have to test this. Darkness did not offer us much choice. Let us explore this place. The Liminal sent you *here*."

Persephone took to the halls, finding the rooms marked with numbers and stocked with an inordinate number of boxes that were filled with books. Schoolbooks.

"Yes. Of course a god of wisdom should rest in a school," she murmured. She held her beloved's vessel as if it were a fragile baby. "But what happened? Why is this place so empty and abandoned?"

The school was beautifully appointed on every floor, Romanesque in style with a courtyard and four halls that formed a fortresslike square. Gazing out the windows, she saw that no grand lane showcased its entrance; it was surrounded by alleys and narrow streets.

Persephone descended to the wide, welcoming foyer, passing below a vaulted ceiling. It was entirely dark here, the windows on the first level having been boarded up. Her own shifting color provided all the light she needed, however, and across the room, the word HEADMASTER on an office door caught her eye.

"Perhaps *you'll* tell me your secrets," she murmured, opening the door.

In the small office, stacked with books and strewn with papers, Persephone set the urn upon the desk and sat in the high-backed chair. She flipped through the letters and ledgers scattered atop the desk, which dealt with curricula for men and women, supplies and other details, and employment referrals. All the missives appeared to be quite friendly. Truly. The word "friend" was everywhere.

It dawned on her.

"Of course. *Friends.* You're a Quaker institution, aren't you?" she exclaimed. "I've always liked them; they've the right idea about things."

Her eye fell upon a stack of papers crumpled on one side, as if held in a hand that had closed into a fist. Foreclosure? The bankers had withdrawn funds. A parliamentary outcry. Boycotts. Finally, a government move to close the institution before it even opened.

"Ah, yes," Persephone murmured sadly. "The Friends have long been persecuted. Well, we'll see about that."

Returning to the hall where she had first landed, to the loose tiles of the central mosaic, she lifted a loose plate of plaster, revealing floorboards beneath.

"Here, my love? Is this indeed what you wish?"

A tendril of fire kissed her cheek, offering assent, so she placed the vessel between two floorboards and laid the plaster atop, smoothing the loose tiles down to make an even surface.

A crackling noise from behind made her turn. She gasped. The wide, stagelike portal of the Liminal edge had opened again, lightning threading across its glassy surface. The Whisper-world was hazily visible on the other side, a great wind emanating from its frame. Aodhan stood there, smiling, though his gaze was distant, his eyes unfocused. She rejoiced that he was safe, if only for the moment, and thanked the Liminal for letting her know.

When she turned back to the transplanted grave of her beloved, she gasped again. The mosaic had been entirely transformed. Now it was complete and cerulean fire coursed along its outer edge. The dove had become an eagle, grasping a fiery torch in its great glittering golden claws. The seal bore a new message:

AS THE PROMETHEAN FIRE WHICH BANISHED DARKNESS, SO KNOWLEDGE BEARS THE POWER AND THE LIGHT

Phoenix fire had a new home. He, and the power of the Guard, was safe in this abandoned place. A place she would make vibrant with life and opportunity.

But it was a long, long way from Cairo.

CHAPTER
ELEVEN

In a matter of weeks the Grand Work was becoming a habit, uncomfortable as some aspects were. Its six practitioners had begun to develop routines; they were growing accustomed to their powers and to one another.

The gentlemen often congregated at the edge of a small café in central Cairo. The powerful cloud of hookah smoke that lingered there made them feel as if they were somehow shielded from the outside world.

There, in the heart of the old city, it could be keenly felt that epochs had come and gone; the old streets were encumbered with mosques and other great buildings, the countless grand squares, laid out in massive asymmetry, were all filled with great antiquity. A modernization—or as some might call it, a "Westernization"—had begun around great al-Qahira, but here, surrounded by buildings centuries older, the Grand Work felt itself in good, ancient company.

It was only a matter of time before the men began talking more pointedly about the women. On this night, when the stars were bright and the smoke particularly sweet, Ahmed went so far as to recite a poem he'd written about Verena:

Your hand is that which bestows life.
Your face is worthy of a jewel mine.
Great forces brought People of the Book

Together in ways that sing glory
And I shall sing your glory always.
Your heart is a dove of peace.
Your whole being enslaves me.

Ahmed's kind, affable face was hopeful as he finished. "Well?"

"It's not Rumi," Ibrahim replied, knowing the beloved Sufi poet was Ahmed's favorite. Ahmed's face fell. "But I think she'll love it," Ibrahim added and chuckled when his friend beamed. "If we encounter a lovelorn spirit, perhaps I'll recite it."

The poet gave a thoughtful sigh. "Since the Grand Work has disrupted my ability to study with my father and our teacher, I find that writing helps alleviate my guilt." He shook his head. "I may have gone to *khanqa* like Sufi before me, but I've a different commission now. Still, I sometimes feel I should be farther along on the path of faith than I am."

"If it's any consolation, I think you're the closest thing we have to godly," Ibrahim offered.

Chuckling, the Sufi shook his head in modest denial before launching into a new recitation, again a piece of his own creation:

O Grand Work, we wield you with our minds and hands,
You chose we special few as servants of your Peace
When those who do not know you would yearn for you
Bound to earth, you tether us to Heaven

In the midst of this rapturous ode, George entered the café. Seeing the reverie Ahmed had put himself in, and Ibrahim's raised eyebrow, the red-blond youth said nothing. When he finished, George applauded. Ahmed bowed his head. Ibrahim's cocked eyebrow remained.

"You know, Ibrahim," George said, pulling up a chair next to him, "Your name, 'Wasil,' is like the English word 'wassail,' which means to drink heartily in good company. To be merry, festive, and hospitable. I think there's a secret, jolly, festive, drunken Englishman inside you somewhere."

Ibrahim blinked. "If so, please gather our friends and exorcise him."

George paused, frowning until he glimpsed the smirk growing on Ibrahim's blank face. Then he laughed heartily, clapping Ibrahim too hard on the back and nearly spilling his Turkish tea. "That, my friend, is dry English wit."

Ibrahim replied, "While I did learn much from the man who raised me, please don't think you English invented everything."

"Fair enough!" George held up his hands.

"You Westerners, in all your conquering and claiming, think you created civilization. It began here, you know," Ibrahim added.

"And I love this land for that. Truly, I do." George grinned and changed the subject. "I've filled my brother's room entirely with art. He hates art, but Belle has him praising it and asking for more. It's wonderful!"

Ahmed returned his smile and Ibrahim enjoyed a quiet chuckle.

George continued, a picture of rapturous youth alongside the similarly cheerful Ahmed. "Here I am, doing the one thing, the only thing in the world I've ever wanted to do—paint—and I suddenly have my family's blessing. They're merchants. All they know is trade on the pound, franc, and the para; they know nothing of spirit. They were going to disown me! I tell you, the Grand Work hasn't just saved other souls but mine, too."

"But has it saved your heart?" Ahmed asked. "It has mine. I just read Ibrahim a verse I composed for Verena."

George's fair skin flushed. "Well . . . There's Belle, of course. Her parents couldn't have chosen a better name. Beautiful in all ways." He said no more, but his expression spoke volumes.

Ahmed turned to Ibrahim, a mischievous sparkle in his wide, dark eyes. "That leaves you our auspicious leader. Unless you'd like to duel me for the fair Verena and compete in composing Rubaiyat verses? George's heart is wide open to me. Yours? Inscrutable."

"I feel the Pull," Ibrahim hissed, getting to his feet. It had hit him like a wave of heat from a fire. "A disturbance in the Copt *hara*, not far from the Smith and Gayed households."

George raised an eyebrow. "Did we make him so uncomfortable that he uses our Grand Work to change the subject?" He gave Ahmed a coy grin, but a moment later the two both groaned, thrown forward by the pain of the Pull. Ahmed rose, tossing coins on the table as the English youth muttered, "That was too convenient."

Already headed out into the dark city street, Ibrahim glared at his friends over his shoulder. "You were being worse than matchmaker women. Come. We've work to do."

It wasn't long before they turned a corner to find fabric, litters, chariots, and palm fans floating everywhere down the avenue. Mortals in the employ of a European tour company, likely Cook's, were squealing, horrified, for everything they'd gathered for a paid reenactment of an ancient parade was being lifted away by unseen hands.

The ghosts of those who would have actually participated in such a rite—or a ritual somewhat similar; one could not count on Cook for historical authenticity so much as providing what Westerners assumed and wanted to see—fussed over them like locusts. The avenue was a mess of floating props and a chorus of mortal screams.

George opened his pack to pull out a small paper-wrapped rectangle. "Well, this is a right bloody mess," he grunted, ripping the paper to reveal a small canvas in a wooden frame.

Beatrice was already present and had her hands full, literally. Cords of blue fire were attached to the legs of litters and to the wheels of chariots in an attempt to rein in the items and those spirits running about with them. It looked as if she were holding handfuls of absurd kites. Ibrahim almost wanted to laugh along with Ahmed, who was doing so freely, but watching Beatrice he was stilled. Struck.

She wore an elegant taffeta evening gown, likely having come from some sort of university function she'd attended with her father. The plunging neckline of the rich plum-colored dress showed far too much skin. Western fashion. In the struggle, her hairpins had come undone and a few dark blond waves fell down past her shoulders. Her piercing blue eyes, which sparkled in any light, were ferocious sapphires, reflecting blue fire. Ibrahim felt the button at his collar poke into his throat.

"Could you enlighten us, please, sir Intuition? Or do you plan to stand there staring?" Beatrice called.

Ibrahim cleared his throat, loosened his collar, touched his temple, and suddenly spouted a set of old city rules about where public assembly was appropriate and when. A few cowed spirits vanished, even in death terrified by the prospect of law enforcement.

Belle was busy directing traffic and removing the considerable crowd of gawking bystanders. Verena was attending the bruises and scrapes caused by the melee. George shrugged and hung his picture, a winged and glorious form that compelled the viewer to dream of angels, in front of a plaque commemorating some military victory no one remembered.

"Lookie!" he cried. The spirits slowly did, one by one lowering their resistance enough for Beatrice to give them a swat of blue fire that caused their flight. At last they had all relinquished their purloined goods and fled.

George gathered up the wreckage. Ibrahim helped with the heavier items, so that the street was soon passable. Slowly but surely the lane was emptied.

Beatrice stepped up onto the walk, off the cobblestones, and leaned against a stone archway intricately carved with geometric arabesques. She breathed heavily, patting the sweat on her brow with a delicate handkerchief embroidered with butterflies. Ibrahim, knowing she had been chosen as a warrior, young, female and all, was intrigued to see she had not discarded what she'd been before. He found such antitheses fascinating. They had even factored into several recent reveries.

Ahmed moved close to Beatrice and bestowed his gift, staring into her eyes. The smile she gave him, wide and clearly heartfelt, changed her still-fierce expression into something relieved, befitting undone tresses and glimmering eyes. The effect was as beautiful as the painting of Athena that Ibrahim's father so treasured, a woman in armor who smiled gently, considering a bouquet of flowers. To his surprise, Ibrahim found himself wanting Beatrice to turn her consideration upon him.

She was always sharp and full of business when interacting with him, exactly as he was with her. It was best that way, of course. He had neither the heart nor the effusive power of Ahmed. He could not summon such a smile from a creature like this; it wouldn't be proper for either of them.

Why did that thought cause a sudden sorrow?

THERE WAS A PARTICULAR WEIGHT TO IBRAHIM'S GAZE TONIGHT that Beatrice had never before experienced. The way it touched her, as if it were a lasso, gently but firmly reeling her in—she could not ignore it. She tried.

"Good work, friends," she said. Everyone nodded, wiping their brows and shuffling their feet.

The thought of them going their separate ways, six separate heartbeats spread out throughout the great city, gave Beatrice a sudden pang. Life no longer made sense without the company of these friends. While at first she'd needed solitude and distance to think, she now needed them to survive. Whether or not it was a natural progression, it was the truth.

"Come," she said, "the night is cool, refreshing and finally peaceful. Take some tea or coffee with me; my home lies just up the street."

"Tell me you've liquor," George said.

"I'm sure my father has a cabinet full," Beatrice said with a smirk. "Whatever poison suits you."

"Huzzah!" the English youth cried. He held out his arm for Belle, who took it without hesitation. Ahmed gestured for Verena to walk beside him at a close but respectful distance. Beatrice strode toward home, needing no man's arm.

Mr. Smith was asleep in the tall chair of his study, and Belle made a shushing sound in his direction to make sure that remained the case. The Guard took to the main room, making themselves comfortable on poufs and a divan, or, in the case of George, after gulping the brandy Beatrice handed him, lying flat on the floor.

"So. Tired," he groaned.

"I daresay our leader did most of the work tonight," Ibrahim commented.

Beatrice stiffened at hearing this, preparing tea at a standing tray, but her lips curved into a small smile, and a sensation of pride and pleasure gripped her stomach.

"Art is exhausting!" George insisted, splaying his body out further.

Belle and Verena chatted so quietly that Beatrice couldn't determine the subject, but the French girl blushed, and her gaze flickered to George. Beatrice had to admit he was quite a sight, in formfitting breeches and with undone shirtsleeves, his body supine, facedown upon a pillow.

Ibrahim went to the bookshelves that took up the entire north wall, his impassive face as engaged as she'd ever seen as he studied the spines of the volumes that filled each shelf. Beatrice moved to his side, offering him a cup of tea.

He took it with a polite nod and pointed to a row of Jane Austen's titles. "I assume those are yours?"

Beatrice blushed. "Well . . ."

"They're not bad. But I like Dickens better."

She was about to express surprise that he should have read popular English writers, but she remembered the English name he honored . . . and that showing surprise that any intelligent person had read something not native to them was rather condescending. Instead she offered, "I've noticed most men do."

"I'll look at his *A Christmas Carol* quite differently now, I suppose, working with ghosts and all."

"I look at everything differently now."

Ibrahim nodded. "*Pride and Prejudice*?"

"What?"

"Your favorite?"

Beatrice shrugged, then nodded. "I suppose I'd say so."

"I've noticed most women do."

Beatrice raised an eyebrow. "You've asked them, have you?"

Ibrahim smirked. "No, not a one. It's simply the best known, so one assumes." He gazed at the wall. "James had countless books and papers. All kinds, from all cultures. They were my best friends. Counting the characters, I had thousands of friends. It isn't often a man can say he has thousands of friends, can he?" His eyes were warm despite the melancholy in his tone. "All those friends died in a fire."

Beatrice bit her lip, her sympathies going out to him. He took the offered tea and exited onto the arched, pillared balcony, which was decorated with intricate arabesques of birds. She keenly understood loss, considering her mother so long ago, though she felt guilty that she did not miss her, or Jean, more. The loss of her mother already seemed a lifetime away, and Jean had joined that distance. If the loss had been her father, things would be different.

Oh, how she, a precocious and lonely child deemed too intelligent for her own good, understood how one's friends could be in books. Oh, how she understood being raised by only a father, with no maternal warmth in the home. She wanted to extend more than courtesy to Ibrahim, and staring at the vast bookshelf, she knew there was something she could offer.

Joining him on the balcony, she said, "Please, take some of these volumes with you, whichever you like. Old friends, perhaps . . . or make new ones."

She hated how her voice sounded more like that of the lonely child she once was than the woman she wished to be. But the fact remained she *was* young, despite how the Grand Work had aged them. Yes. Still young. And still lonely, despite her new friends.

Ibrahim stared at her a moment, his dark eyes like gleaming onyx, entrancing in the moonlight. "Thank you," he said. "I would enjoy that."

He turned to stare out at the city. "My house was there," he stated, pointing east, his eyes narrowed. "I would like to think the whole of the city my home. Alas, our thoughts, like ghosts, haunt one mere building, unimportant in the grand scheme . . . and yet, everything to that person."

Beatrice wanted desperately to say something clever, something as effortlessly poetic as he. But her throat was dry.

He sipped his tea, then grimaced. "I wax melancholy, unfit for company."

She shrugged. "I know loss well. You lost your home and your guardian. We were thrust suddenly into bearing the weight of the city's very sanity on our shoulders, by unthinkable means. Do you think I have no capability to empathize? We're quite the pair."

"We are not a pair," Ibrahim replied.

Beatrice blinked. Goodness. Did he have any idea how cold he sounded? "Of course we aren't," she replied. Her sharp tone made her seem too defensive. "I didn't mean it in a . . . in a coupled sense. Wouldn't dream of it."

Ibrahim exhaled. After a moment he said, "It would seem fate has placed my life at the mercy of the English. I'm in no way objecting to that circumstance; however, it does leave me at a loss, at times, as to touchstones for my soul." He added quietly, turning away. "Thank you for the tea. And very much for the books."

He moved back in toward the bookshelf. Beatrice was left to stare up at the stars and then back at the place in the distance where James Tipton had died.

CHAPTER
TWELVE

PERSEPHONE PACED THE THIRD FLOOR OF WHAT SHE HAD DECIDED
to boldly name Athens Academy, trying to calm her desperate,
careening thoughts. How could she free the spirits of her Guard?
Not only did she have to unlock the prison gates Darkness had
fashioned, she had to find some way to give them the advantage in
battle. She needed an army.

They needed to be somehow reminded of what they once were.
As long as they could access the phoenix fire, they could work
together, echoes of past greatness. They could win a great victory
over Darkness. Perhaps they could do so here in Athens.

"Could that be so, love?" she asked, gazing down at the seal in
the floor. "Shall these bricks prove the conduit?"

"Bring the precipice here," the Power and the Light murmured
in her ear. "Bring the depths of the Whisper-world to me and let
me bathe it in fire. It's time for a war. On our terms. With the army
we have gathered. There are enough Guard spirits to best him and
his agents of misery."

"But, my love, the danger! The whole point was always to keep
the Whisper-world safely shut away." Persephone's heart pounded
wildly. "To bring it *upon* the mortals . . . It undoes the very purpose
of the Guard, does it not?"

"Limit the fight to Athens alone, contain it. I shall bless these
bricks with fire, and from here we'll end the vendetta. Darkness
can't help but be drawn in when worlds collide."

"Knitting the worlds," Persephone mused. "Do I dare?"

"Reckless as you were, you must remember how it was done," Phoenix said. "I hope this time you will be more careful."

Persephone looked down, and a silver tear splashed onto the brass seal.

"Not that you have to relive those moments, darling," her beloved cautioned, but it was too late. She was lost to the memory of a painful, vital revelation.

IT WAS A TIME, EARLIER IN THIS SAME CENTURY, WHEN THE dread press of the Whisper-world so choked her soul of light that ending her existence seemed the only choice. Her form was not human, nor did her body operate on human principles, and so she doubted she could throw herself on some funeral bier like Juliet did over her Romeo.

She had plucked a hearty rose briar that had been born and died at her feet, the thorn strong and sharp. She dug it into her own skin, winced, wept, and bled. Bled and bled. That blood had poured onto the dank Whisper-world stones, gathering in eddies, surging in rivulets toward the Whisper-world barriers, where it began to dissolve the stones. Her blood wanted out. It wanted free of this place. She had collapsed.

Her beloved had felt the shift in her, caught the scent of her draining life force. The part of his fire in the Leader of the Guard had immediately reacted, abandoning its human host to rush unencumbered to her, streaks of blue fire flashing through the Whisper-world's darkness. When Phoenix's flame touched the pools of her blood, light began to shine through from beyond. The two of them were creating tiny windows, merging the two worlds.

At those holes gathered the restless dead, both inside the Whisper-world and on Earth. They stared into each other's worlds, stared down upon the struggling body of that goddess of shifting colors. Small flowers grew and died at her feet and fingertips; she evoked a thousand tiny cycles as she wept for a life she could never regain.

The dead—even those she'd have deemed hopeless—cupped their hands and gathered her blood, trying to return it to her. They gathered around her and lifted her body, cradled her, stroked her face. Even the spirits of murderers and fiends lent aid, struck by the plight of a falling angel.

"We need and love you," crooned the spirits on the mortal side, staring in from flowering fields or busy streets. Those standing in dank black corners within the Whisper-world mourned, "Don't fall. Don't give up. Not like this . . ."

Traces of phoenix fire raced over her body, his ghost doing what he could to rouse her. "My love," he whispered. "Why this? Isn't there another way to find release? Why this instead of becoming mortal? Why this instead of attempting a new form?"

Persephone's eyelids drooped, and she fumbled for words. "I . . . I'm scared. Being divine has been . . . hard. I doubt mortality is any easier. And I'm tired." She gave a slow shake of her head, then noticed the shadows around her faltering form had lengthened. *Him.*

"Go," she begged Phoenix. "He's coming; hide."

The ghost of her beloved knew to pick his battles. His cerulean fire retreated and dimmed, but he watched from a distance as the assembled crowd of spirits whirled to face the tall, regal shadows and bowed to their master.

"She wants out," they said.

Darkness stood like an ebon tower, red eyes in a black silhouette. Sometimes he was beautiful. At that moment he was not. He growled. His shadows bent like a huge claw, clutched Persephone's wilting body, and threw her toward one of the windows her blood had opened. Phoenix's ghost encased her in an embrace of fire as she hurtled forth.

A familiar, dark maw opened at the last moment, saving her

from being cast out into some deserted space: the portal used by the Guard. The dark rectangular door led to the Guard's sacred space, and Persephone landed in its center, Phoenix's ghost slowing her fall with an embrace of fire.

She heard Darkness grunt. "I'll drag her back again once she's recovered. We've done this before . . ." He was already working furiously to seal the shadows behind her, hissing at the light that discomfited him as much as the flowers that grew in her wake. All life was extinguished in his realm, life and light. Only decay remained.

She was scooped into the strong arms of the Leader, Dmitri Sergeyevna. At the time, the beginning of the nineteenth century, the Grand Work had been operating in Russia.

The Guard gasped to see their herald, their Lady, so humbled. She looked up with tears in her eyes, blood pouring from her arms, robes splayed around her, at a tall, black-haired stable boy-turned-demigod.

"I don't know how much longer I can hold on," she murmured to him, allowing him to hold her, to rock her, to say everything would be all right. Their Healer was soon at her side, his glowing hands offering a tingling release as her flesh was once again made whole.

Dmitri and his Guard, like every Guard before, were aware of the vendetta for which they fought. They believed it, and each Guard had seen how much their Lady struggled to maintain Light. As Russians, they embraced the firebird and easily made him their own.

"My Lady," Dmitri murmured, his voice rich and low against her ear, very much like the voice of Phoenix himself. "Don't let the shadows take you. We wish we could shelter you here with us always. Could you not take pains to join us?"

"It is good to be with friends," Persephone replied, not answering that question but instead relaxing further into his embrace.

He stroked her hair and held her tight, and for a moment she almost believed that she was again with her beloved. In the light of the Russian Guard's sacred space she was healed. More important, because her blood had opened such porous portals between mortal and spirit world, she'd inadvertently gained knowledge that altered the game.

"I'LL BLEED THE WORLDS TOGETHER!" SHE DECLARED, DRAGGING her mind again to the present, her feet bare and cool upon the marble floor of the Athens foyer. It occurred to her that the scene she'd relived hadn't been very long ago in mortal time. She wasn't terribly adept at tracking mortal years, but she believed her mounting desperation and volatility had been entirely contained within their nineteenth century. She had apparently reached a breaking point in this age.

Padding slowly about the grand space, gazing through its windows at the darkening London sky, she felt her determination grow. Speaking to the seal, this time she stated it more firmly: "I'll knit the worlds with my blood."

A sparking tendril of blue fire offered agreement, and her words became a vow.

She heard a tearing sound. Behind her was the Liminal edge, open and lit. The vast metal hands of its overhead clock shook and shuddered, meaning the vision it projected was not certain; this future was not set in stone.

The vision took place on a dark night in the very room in which she stood. A tall, striking man dressed all in black swept a young woman across the floor in a delicate waltz. The pair was alone, and the moonlight magical.

Persephone gasped. The woman . . .

"It's *me*."

It wasn't her, exactly; she was watching a young mortal. But the woman looked very much like her—like what she saw when she looked at herself. Flesh entirely devoid of color. Pearlescent hair, blanched skin, eerie, ice-cap eyes with faint slivers of blue— it was as if she were watching a younger self in a mirror, her hand upon the shoulder of a magnetically beautiful man who looked very familiar.

"And it's *him*!" Persephone breathed. "That boy. Grown. It's Alexi."

The vision's subjects did not speak, only stared at each other, enraptured. The young woman's lips parted in a silent sigh. Her opalescent eyes drank in her dance partner, her gaze a glorious surrender.

If Persephone was not mistaken, the man was equally smitten. His stoic expression was betrayed by the way his dark eyes glittered; his sculpted lips curved slightly whenever she sighed. This was the start of something wonderful.

Persephone whispered in delight, "An unchaperoned waltz by moonlight? Scandalous for the mores of your age!"

Yet who could have denied them this simple dance, this pair holding each other at a decorous if fond distance, this luminous girl lit by moonlight, this ghostly, eerie goddess—

"I'll be *you*," Persephone cried.

The vision bled into another, where the two dancers waltzed once more. Alexi was again in all black, the same as when she'd first glimpsed him, as a young man. This time, however, the strangely beautiful girl wore a finer dress. Something else about her was older, too; not years but experience.

Their waltzing bodies stood close. No longer decorous, this was the dance of two lovers. A silver ring glimmered on the girl's finger, a silver band on his, too.

"Oh, Alexi, how your wife will stare at you," Persephone breathed.

His face was transformed by adoration. Yet there remained a hint of wild desperation along with the new softness. *Why?* she wondered. He had her, so what was to fear?

A third vision appeared, a blaze of blue fire. The two were now bent over the Athens seal; there was a key and an explosion. The foyer was suddenly awash with ghosts. Not just any ghosts, either. Ghosts of the Guard. Persephone recognized them all. Here were all the Guard that had ever been, from every city, every age. All were taking up arms at this academy and—

Persephone gasped. "My army! It's true, we must bring the army here."

Why was the Liminal showing her this? Seeing the way the hands of its clock trembled, this future couldn't be certain. If Persephone knew the Liminal, it was showing her a future it wanted— for these two mortals, for her, for what she could become . . . But this was no *fait accompli.*

She saw the girl again, a mirror of herself, and for the first time in eons Persephone saw herself reflected in another's eyes . . . and beloved.

Alexi held the girl. Blue fire erupted around and through him, cascaded over the bricks and left Athens awash. So he was the Leader of the Guard after all in this vision, despite Phoenix's earlier concern. What would happen to Beatrice? Alexi was a glorious conduit, Persephone admitted. This was where the battle would come to pass, and he looked ready. Where else should they fight but at the source of their power, where she had buried her Phoenix?

"I'll pledge the whole of my fading light to this future," she vowed.

Her declaration made the Liminal crackle. Persephone felt a wind sucking inward, into the Whisper-world, beckoning her to return. To begin. The visions had faded.

Indeed, there was no time to waste. She had work to do. Painful work. But rather than bleeding herself recklessly, as she had the first time, she would wield her magic carefully, methodically. And to keep herself from despair, she would think of people who made her smile. She would remember the comfort she'd felt in Dmitri's embrace, recall the vision of a grown boy whom she only knew as Alexi, twirling her embodiment around this very foyer. If she could hold on to these signs of hope, all would fall into place. Finally, she had something worth fighting for.

But, could she do what the vision wanted? Could she take the form of a colorless mortal girl with the mind and heart of a goddess? Yes, she would come into that black-haired boy's life with all her power and glory, with all her collected knowledge and wisdom, and she would make things right. Gloriously right.

"Hold on to Light, my love," Phoenix's ghost called out, a trail of fire coursing out from the seal, out and around her body. It was warm and tender. "Face the shadows knowing the house of Darkness will come crashing down. As long as you hold to your core principle, the hope you are made of, Darkness cannot overtake you. You must now plant seeds that will sprout and flower."

"I'll begin anon," Persephone murmured, moving to the Liminal edge. She paused only a moment before stepping through.

CHAPTER
THIRTEEN

BEATRICE HAD BEEN IN PAIN FOR DAYS. IT WAS NOT THE PULL. IT was not the increasingly exquisite agony of being so near and yet so far from Ibrahim. This was something else. It was good that she generally wore gloves as a lady must, for they lessened the sting. It felt as if patches of her skin were peeling away.

She was startled by a luminous and colorful appearance in her boudoir. The newcomer appeared worried. The goddess was awful at hiding emotion. Beatrice imagined this artlessness was something her ancient lover found attractive, but she found it troubling. It didn't seem proper, to so blatantly wear one's heart on one's sleeve. That was something one trained out of a child.

"What is it?" Beatrice asked.

"The game has altered."

"Game?" Beatrice echoed. "Please don't say our lives are a game to you, that we are your mortal pawns. I don't suppose you could tell me why parts of me feel on fire. It tests my ability to be polite."

"By 'game' I mean the struggle in which we are *all* caught up," the goddess exclaimed. "The king of the Whisper-world has captured every Guard spirit that ever was, save for the original set. They were so long ago, before we thought to build the field . . ."

Beatrice blinked.

"There's a field," Persephone explained, clearly wistful. "Gorgeous, built by consensus. You can't spend eternity surrounded by gloom. But it's gone, washed away by Darkness. I was forced to move the remains of Phoenix from their rightful resting place to untried ground. This is an unprecedented action for an unprecedented time. Unless we take a stand, you'll never be free of hell. Something entirely new must be undertaken for your eternal safety—yours, and that of every Guard."

"Hell." Beatrice set her jaw. "That's lovely."

The goddess gestured. "Pack your bags. You're leaving for London."

"Why?"

"Because that's where the remains of Phoenix burn on, transferred from the Whisper-world to mortal soil. That's likely why you're in pain. I'm sorry to hear that, but a Leader's never been so far from the hearth of their fire."

Beatrice shook her head. "Why London?"

"Why not?"

"Why not here, where we, your chosen Guard, were planted?"

"Because in the coming years the Power must be in London. That simply is so. The source of the Grand Work now lies near the banks of the Thames, and you must go to it."

Beatrice fought a wave of anger. She was already tired of having her life uprooted by the whims of the eternal. "By whose omnipotent authority has this been done?"

Persephone lifted prismatic hands. "I never said I was omnipotent. I had to move my beloved to a safer location. Why London? Because I was told that's the place to bring the war!" Her hands began to shake, and she wrung them. "The Fates decide. The Liminal decided. And it is because someone is already there, someone who will prove critical."

Beatrice tried to sort through this new information. "Persephone, you cannot expect to overturn mortal lives whenever you wish. For us to simply pack bags, leave home, blindly follow danger . . . All without answers! We live in a gilded age of *science*. 'The Fates decide' is naught but an incitement to riot."

Persephone gave her a hard and unflinching look—the first
Beatrice had ever seen from her. "All creatures must adapt and
change tactics to survive. Even I know that. Shall you tell your
fellows about London or shall I?"

Beatrice sighed. It wasn't that she didn't want to help the goddess, to do her duty, but the burden had grown so in the weeks she
had now carried it. . . .

"I'll call the meeting, but this is your doing," Beatrice said
pointedly. "You must tell them. And what the hell is the Liminal?"

Persephone glanced at her. "The place from which all blessings
flow. And curses, I suppose. It depends on the soul doing the
asking." She took a deep breath. "I'll make the announcement, not
to worry."

The prismatic creature vanished, leaving Beatrice swimming
in mounting anxiety. Interpersonal dynamics and itchy skin paled
in comparison to moving six unlikely companions across the world.
She doused her irritated hands in cool water for the thousandth
time and cursed supernatural whim.

It was not pleasant, but Persephone returned to shadow.
She had to, though he wouldn't have noticed yet that she was
missing. Time was indeed different in the Whisper-world. But
Darkness would eventually require her presence. She would have
to act as if he had won, as if he had cowed her at last. And he would
believe it.

He would be unbearable, lording over her in his perceived triumph. Not until she discovered how to claim that colorless mortal
body of her visions could she manage a prolonged absence.

Persephone knew vaguely where the seals were, the pins that
held the worlds apart. Those seals, formed of stone and spirit, had
existed since the Whisper-world had separated from the mortal,
back when civilizations were new. Though the seals were set deep
in the Whisper-world's murk, those attuned to the mortal world

could sense warmer, fresher air in their vicinity. The flowers she created took longer to die near the seals; they fully bloomed before curling and giving way to putrefaction.

But this was not the only marker. In case anyone might gain hope at these crossroads, Darkness had made sure to deter them with a font of despair, rerouting the more horrid underground currents of the Whisper-world to surround the pins with the acrid vapors of suicide and slaughter. They burned Persephone's nostrils.

Stepping into shallow water that nipped at her toes with tiny teeth, the goddess allowed a sliver of her light to illuminate the alcove of gray stone before her. A thin golden ring was visible, glimmering against the wall, its circumference a few feet wide.

Persephone plucked a particularly sharp briar from the flowers that grew at her feet and watched the rose harden into death. Using the thorn to prick her thumb, she hissed as her blood, thinner in these dark depths, flowed freely. She placed droplets upon each of the stones, ran it in a circle around the golden band. Only when met by phoenix fire would it open the world. Through blood and fire her army would be free. In time.

In the distance came the sound of hissing. Persephone hurried away. The last thing she wanted was to be seen by a spy. Sour pomegranate juice was always at the back of her throat in these dread corridors, so to mask her activity, Persephone spat. The Gorgon would assume she'd had one of her frequent spells of sickness and be none the wiser.

She glided back to the great stone dais, wincing as she ignored the weeping pleas of the Whisper-world's denizens, unable to spare any light. Her power must be saved for a ghostly girl and the man she loved. Those ice-pale eyes confirmed that Alexi was the one she'd been waiting for. Suddenly she was no longer afraid of becoming mortal. Not if her beloved could be there in that magnificent, incarnate form.

Stopping at the moat's edge, she scowled at the bold bulb of crimson. It was always jarring to see that distressingly beautiful red rose at the dais. Persephone assumed he rested in such a manner to mock all the dead flowers at her feet.

The petals peeled back one by one to reveal a naked man. He was beautiful; then he was a skeleton. Then again flesh. He stood, and those crimson robes hovered around him in glorious folds, as if he were imitating a painting of Christ; the color scarlet representing a certain carnality, reminding the viewer that the depicted was a *mortal* savior. But Christ had been a human of light. Darkness was inhuman shadow, ticking away life and light, second by second, flesh into bone and back again, savior of nothing.

"Back. So. Soon? I thought you'd run off and punish me." His voice was like wet gravel.

"I came to check on my beloveds."

"Wasting away, as should all who exist here." He wagged a skeletal finger. "Exceptions are not fair."

There had always been an unlit stone tower behind the dais, a column of moist slate growing like a vast tree trunk with no leaves or life. Persephone hadn't thought much of it, never dreamed it would become a prison. Now Darkness gestured to it, and Persephone moved closer, spying a door sealed with a long hanging chain and a thick padlock. A hefty, dull silver key with a slender ring stood in the lock. Persephone moved to snatch it.

Darkness batted her away. "Ah, ah, ah."

He alternately clucked his tongue, then clicked his jaw. Removing the key, he glanced down at his breastbone. When it was bone, he slid the ring about his sternum. It was visible when he was bone, then hidden under flesh when he was man.

"It's fitting, you know, this." He gestured to the key as it flashed into sight. "You cry your silver tears here on my stones. Sometimes I collect them, make them into useful things. You have imprisoned your friends yourself. This very key, made from your tears."

Persephone balled her fists at his cruel taunt. It took every ounce of control not to slap him with a burst of light, to level declamations and threats, to use every last bit of her power to crack open the prison gates and flee with them all. But such an act would be fruitless. If she did that, she'd tear herself in two, and Darkness would simply round the Guard up again. There was no escape. Not this way.

Shaking her head, she said, "Pity and hatred. It's all you'll ever know from me. It's a shame. You could know love."

"I have others who bow to me, who love me," Darkness countered.

"But do you love them in return? What do you know of love's equality?"

"I love you."

Persephone laughed hollowly. "Hardly. You can't fathom the quality. You seek to *possess* me. You act as a petulant child, as a prison guard and torturer, nothing more. The ingredients you are made of are absent love. And that deficit will one day destroy you."

She fled, hearing Darkness grind his teeth behind her, and concealed herself in a side corridor, waiting to see if he would follow. He did not. A small light flickered, like a firefly, a short distance ahead. When she followed, it led her to the Liminal edge. Apparently it was ready to assist her once again.

A GUARD MEETING WAS CALLED. BEATRICE AND HER FELLOWS descended to their sacred space, where the goddess awaited them.

"I've a mission for you, friends," she said, anxiety in her eternally youthful voice, "on a distant shore. For some of you it will be a homecoming of sorts." She looked at George and Beatrice. "For the rest, an adventure. The source of your power has been relocated due to . . . an emergency."

"You're asking us to abandon our homes?" Ibrahim asked. "To leave Cairo?"

Persephone sighed. "You understand the basic principle of the Grand Work, do you not?" she asked. "That Darkness feeds upon mortal misery and sends his restless dead to collect it. You—the Guard—have been starving him for ages. Eventually, however, you six must all die. You are mortal, if what you host is not.

"I must tell you that this is now your fight more than ever. Darkness has taken the spirits of every Guard that ever was and locked them away." She opened her arms to show them.

Her gesture lifted a window onto endlessly miserable Whisper-world. At the center of this lifeless purgatory sat a vast, huge tower, from which the sounds of weeping could be heard. "All the Guard that have ever been are trapped in that prison," the goddess declared.

An exhilarated but mad look in her eyes, she continued, almost ranting. "You fight for me and my beloved, and all of your kind. Oh, my darlings, this age of yours! Such books will be written, such love stories, such letters and poetry . . . Mine is a tale for the ages and I need you to make it beautiful. Tell not only my trials but my triumph! For I will triumph over Darkness at last. I've begun my greatest task. We shall prevail."

The Guard stared at her, frightened both by Persephone's sudden madness and the fate that awaited them.

The goddess spoke again, more evenly. "You'll go to London by sea. No one will question you, not when Belle casts her magic. Pack your things; there's a ship leaving in the morning. I'll see you soon."

The reply she received was silence.

"If nothing else, do it for your Leader. While she has not complained, stoic as she may be, I know that she is in pain. The remains of Phoenix have, for the first time, been moved into the mortal world. Into safety far away. But that separation wounds Beatrice in the meantime. To *London*, my loves. To London. That will solve all." And then she was gone.

The Guard stood staring after the goddess long after her shifting colors had vanished into the shadows. They then turned to Beatrice, concerned, and she grimaced, sure they were all left with the same thought.

"An adventure!" George cried, surprising her.

Ibrahim looked at Ahmed and Verena, then addressed the Europeans. "We're not posing as your help."

"I wouldn't dream of asking," Beatrice snapped. Were their worlds truly so impossible to bridge?

Verena moved close. "I'm sorry for your pain," she whispered, placing a glowing hand upon Beatrice's closed fist.

"Thank you." The physical pain eased slightly. The rest would remain.

THE ODDEST PART OF WHAT FOLLOWED WAS WATCHING BELLE go to each of their families and tell them that their children were going away. To school, it was explained. The families nodded and wandered off, indifferent. The only emotion provided was by the Guard themselves in support of one another. They stepped up, pressing a shoulder or offering a nod of encouragement.

Ibrahim quietly excused himself from this excursion. Beatrice wanted to know where he went wandering instead, what his lonely soul might be feeling, but they were not linked in a way to share such things.

Late that evening, Mr. Smith called to Beatrice in the sitting room. "Bea, a nice boy is here to see you!"

Beatrice rose from the divan, smoothed her skirts and wondered who had come to call. It had to be a Guard, but which? Weren't they all spending last moments with their families? She glanced at the trunk she'd just spent hours packing. It sat like a millstone in the center of the room, a weighty crate representing the terrifying unknown.

A "nice boy"? Surely it was George. Her father hadn't been

terribly fond of Jean, and Beatrice had assumed he'd rather she be courted by an Englishman. She wondered what on earth he'd say if he ever actually noticed she spent time with two Egyptian men. Her father worked with the locals, respected their artifacts, and had learned—and taught Beatrice—both Arabic and much of the meanings of their ancient symbols, but his daughter keeping company with their boys? Her study of society had led her to believe that the British were oft masters of hypocrisy.

"Oh!" she blurted when she discovered her visitor, who was waiting for her in the sitting room.

"Disappointed?" Ibrahim asked, sounding almost amused.

"No. Just surprised," she replied. Her sense of hospitality, a quality evidently inherited from her mother despite her early passing due to cholera, led Beatrice to say, "I could make some tea?"

Ibrahim looked at the tea service and shook his head. "No, thank you."

"Please, sit." Beatrice gestured to the fine divan, taking a wooden chair opposite.

Ibrahim sat but did not relax. His back remained straight, his movements showed simple grace, to the point and full of purpose. It was a quality Beatrice admired and wished she had, knowing she fussed and fidgeted too much. To her chagrin, she now found herself fluffing the lace at the edge of her blouse sleeves.

He studied her briefly before speaking. "While my gifts are still expanding within me, and I cannot credit myself with an expert conclusion regarding their meaning, my Intuition is that this trip to London is dangerous. I feel it in my bones. I cannot in good faith allow it to go forward without voicing concern."

Beatrice took a moment to allow his words to register, then argued, "My discomfort aside, all travel has its dangers. We've a mandate from a higher power that expects us elsewhere. I'm as leery of the journey as you, but do we have a choice?"

"Of course we have a choice," Ibrahim said. "Let the Grand

Work choose others to take up our mantle. Others in England. Why us? There are plenty of people in the world to create an odd, ragtag band. They only need six."

"But we were already chosen. Truly, Ibrahim, I question the Grand Work every minute of every day, yet I can't deny that it has changed me. If the power that grants it is elsewhere, do I have any choice but to follow? Do I brook further pain, further risk to the world, by staying apart from it?"

"But it won't be safe. I feel it. I feel some tragedy will come to one of our number, that the goddess, well meaning as she may be—"

"Infuriating as she may be," Beatrice added.

"She may be playing loosely with our safety, her eyes on some larger future goal. She told us of our fate after we die, with hardly any concern for how we may take such news."

Beatrice sighed. "What do you suggest?"

"For us not to go. I'll be more than happy to state my reasons. I was granted a gift. It is warning me. I am only honoring the Grand Work by stating my concerns to you."

"I don't doubt it."

"Good. Then you'll understand why I won't be on that ship in the morning."

"The goddess may have something to say about that."

"Should she, I'll tell her exactly what I've told you. As Leader, if you're interested in protecting your comrades, we should not board that ship."

Beatrice shook her head. "We'll talk about it at the docks tomorrow. I'm happy to relay your concerns, or you're welcome to speak your mind yourself, declare what you think should be done. I've no taste for a dictatorship. However, while I respect your gifts, other reasons lead me to board that boat. I am weak and in pain. I believe that is because the tether to my power now stretches across an ocean."

"Could it be a psychological reaction?"

Beatrice set her jaw, fists clenching. "What are you saying? I'm a credit to my sex. My father and every one of his colleagues at the university would attest to that. I'd like to think I've proven myself thus far."

"I'm not calling into question the quality of your mind or talents. Or your father and his colleagues at the university . . ." Ibrahim swallowed hard and looked away.

Beatrice recalled that Mr. Tipton had worked at that university. She hadn't meant to bring up a painful subject. Truthfully, she didn't want to leave any more than Ibrahim did, but her body felt magnetized toward the West, and she couldn't ignore the sinking sense that failing to take the steamer wasn't an option.

"I suppose trust is entirely subjective and a personal choice," Ibrahim said softly. "My preference is not to board that ship. And because my gifts have labeled Verena as particularly vulnerable, I will share my thoughts with her—which may influence her choice as well."

Beatrice sighed. "I'll inform the group of your concerns, but you'd best be prepared to speak to the goddess if she shows up wondering."

"Indeed," Ibrahim said. Rising, he added, "I know my way. We need not stand on ceremony."

Nothing in Beatrice's life could have prepared her for this circumstance. She commended herself for dealing fairly and calmly with her second-in-command, for letting him go his own way as a benevolent leader. And while she credited him with being respectful despite disagreement, she still had to calm her racing heart. Her discomfiture had nothing to do with the politics of the situation. It was infinitely more personal. Which made it infinitely less agreeable.

CHAPTER
FOURTEEN

THE NEXT MORNING, BEATRICE AWOKE AT FIRST LIGHT AND dressed in a sturdy skirt and blouse designed for traveling. While there was mutiny afoot, she wanted to be prepared for any eventuality, and if boarding that ship meant her hands would stop burning, she'd take the trip alone if she had to.

Wrestling with sentiment, Beatrice went into her father's room, kissed his forehead as he slept, and left her home. She stood for a moment looking at the fine building that housed several English families in relative space and luxury in this densely packed city, at its arches and ornate finery, and wondered if she'd ever see it again. She straightened her spine and hardened her heart.

The Grand Work rearranged priorities, keeping many emotions distant, like storm clouds on the horizon. Perhaps that was what Leaders did, looked at everyone's pain from afar. Especially their own. At some point, surely all that sentiment would come crashing in, and she hoped it would not prove stronger for having been put off.

She flagged down a young man she knew to be a neighborhood errand runner. In moments her trunk was packed into a rickshaw and she was jostling onward to her destination, unsure what fate awaited her.

Other rickshaws with familiar passengers converged at the docks of Alexandria as if a great hand were bringing them all together. George was assisting Belle out of her transport while Ahmed was already standing at the dock, contemplating the vessel in which they would voyage to England.

At least, Beatrice hoped they would. She didn't remember much of London from her childhood, just that it was gray and crowded. At this, a pang stung her heart. Cairo was golden.

Glancing about as her hired help carried her luggage onto the platform, Beatrice noted that Ibrahim and Verena were nowhere to be found. She gave the young man a larger bill than was necessary, feeling nostalgic already for her old neighborhood. He beamed, bobbed his head, and disappeared.

At the head of the dock stood a man in a fine suit who was clearly there to assist English and French tourists. Belle strode toward him with George at her side. Beatrice watched the man's eyes cloud; then she overheard assurances about first-class luxury and such. After George elbowed her, Belle pressed for champagne. Success was soon confirmed by George's ridiculously large grin.

Before George and Belle directed ferrymen to take their trunks aboard, Beatrice halted them with a word in the Guard language. She was soon encircled by her three comrades.

"Friends, we've dissention in the ranks. But it's not without its just cause. I would let Ibrahim tell you himself, but—"

"And so I shall."

Beatrice turned. Ibrahim came forward in a finely embroidered tunic and linen coat, his dark eyes confident if hard. Paces behind him stood Verena, shifting on her feet like a frightened little girl and not a woman of eighteen. Perhaps Ibrahim had told her she was destined for danger.

"Friends . . ."

He spoke the word as if he were still getting used to the idea, even after the many weeks they'd spent on the Grand Work, which rode Beatrice a bit roughly. There was no other word appropriate for people thrust into such strange affiliation, even if they were not those you would choose for yourself. She took a moment to wonder: If George or Ahmed had spoken thusly, would she have thought twice? Perhaps she expected more courtesy and camaraderie out of her second. Again she considered that the Muses must have made a mistake.

"I'll not be taking this vessel with you. Neither will Verena. My gift of Intuition has warned me that there is danger ahead for the most vulnerable among us. Thus I cannot condone this journey. My foremost commitment is to the protection of our comrade."

Ahmed stared at Verena, his joyful expression becoming anxious. Beatrice could feel a wave of discord wash through her fellows like strains of music gone terribly off-key.

"But . . . but the Work will always have its dangers. Is this any different than before?" George asked the question while Belle nodded.

"I fear the danger shall worsen. Cairo is our home soil, the place we were chosen. To uproot ourselves is to run the risk of being tossed to the wind, of becoming groundless, no better than those spirits out there."

Ibrahim gestured to the sea. It was true; there they were, ghosts like sails without a boat, rigs with no tethers, gray bodies billowing in the breeze, buffeted and hapless. It was a sobering image. Then came the unsettling realization that there were many more spirits at dockside than when Beatrice had first arrived. As if they were gathering.

Was it a farewell committee of the dead? Or was it a cresting tide of conflict that Beatrice felt very truly in her blood, a distinct, uncomfortable sensation that something was not right?

There came a ripple in the air and a burst of light.

"What's this?" the goddess said, her feet touching down on the dock. Where they did, Beatrice marveled, delicate ferns sprouted up. "Why are you here when you ought to be on that boat? Isn't it nearing departure?"

Sure enough, a clanging bell made them all jump. Beatrice glanced around to see that their baggage had been stowed; Belle's lingering magic must have influenced all around her.

Ibrahim and Verena hung back. The Egyptian girl's face was pinched in a grimace; it was clear that she was torn. If Ibrahim felt the same conflict, it did not show. They had brought no luggage.

Because the goddess had made herself visible, Belle had to make sure the busy docks were dealt with, and so she found herself circling the group like an officer on patrol, waving her hand at anyone who gaped at this prismatic creature of unparalleled beauty and magic. Belle's gift sent the dockworkers, ferrymen, and passengers drifting to other destinations.

"My Lady." Ibrahim turned to the goddess. "Intuition warns me there is great danger for us in London. It is my duty to inform the group if we are walking into a trap. While I'd not dare accuse you of duplicity, I fear there are perhaps unintended consequences to this sudden journey that even you may not be able to foresee."

He spoke with such cool intelligence that it seemed a crime to disagree, thought Beatrice.

The goddess managed. "Danger is always courted by the Grand Work."

"See?" George said.

"But what sort of man would I be if I, sensing danger, sent my comrades directly into it?" Ibrahim countered.

"I commend you for your caution, Ibrahim, I truly do, but the danger is in staying behind when the pendulum of power has so radically swung elsewhere. When the balance is so terribly skewed against you, the danger here outweighs whatever you feel awaits you."

"How can you so easily override what is felt in my veins?" Ibrahim asked. "Am I not afforded more proof than words?"

"I'm sorry, you're right," the goddess murmured. Waves too tall for the weather rose to slap the docked ship. "I showed you the dread of the Whisper-world only. When you asked me why, before, I should have shown you the *whole* of the picture. I forget that we ask so much while offering so little." She closed her eyes, and a wave of pain crossed her face. Flinging an arm forward, she cut a vast rectangle in the air.

Something caught Beatrice's eye. At the distressing sight of what she could only assume were a few drops of the goddess's blood dripping down her arm, Verena darted forward, her hand glowing. Persephone opened her eyes and held out a hand, halting Verena and offering a soft, gracious look of thanks for her effort. But it would appear this blood was not meant to dry or fade.

Behind her, a gray rectangle had appeared, as if a gaping wound had been cut into the fabric of reality. On the other side was that wet, gray world they'd glimpsed from their sacred space on that first day, a world of corridors, rushing water, and countless restless dead. They wandered, devoid of any color, existing in monochromatic misery.

Beatrice felt the warm Cairo sun through the muslin of her blouse, yet her heart felt the terrible cold of this other world. Two temperatures she endured, one that was warm upon her skin and another that was internal and yet no less real. The Guard could only gape.

"Again, the Whisper-world," Persephone said. "It is not down but sideways. It is always just to the left or right of your soul. It was made and fed by mortal misery. If you six should part, it will tear a small hole in the mortal world and a bit of hell will break loose. The longer you are separated, the larger the hole. When the Guard was formed, the Whisper-world reacted. You and it are inextricably tied."

Some of the ghosts turned to look at the living through the portal. Looking into their hollow-eyed, harrowed faces was like staring at assured doom; it was a contagion of the soul, a festering wound for which there was no cure. Just looking at the Whisper-world was suffocating, let alone stepping across into it or letting it pour out unchecked into . . .

Ahmed moved among his comrades, bestowing his gift with a slight touch upon the temple. A jolt of fresh air into struggling lungs, and each of them revived.

The gray dead approached the threshold opened by Perse-phone. Beatrice wondered with alarm if they could step across, so many of them that the Grand Work would be entirely overrun and outmatched. The spirits on the living side approached it, too, blanched white and floating like vertical clouds above the water. Dead looked at dead, all of them in some hazy state of re-membrance.

"The unseen Balance all around you," the goddess declared.

Belle was trying to deter foot traffic and muttering that if they'd had any sense in their heads, they'd have had this confer-ence in private. Looking down at the sound of water slapping more violently against the dock, she squealed. The white caps had taken the shapes of horses' heads with sharp teeth. The thrown-open Whisper-world was turning nature sour and vicious. The delicate ferns that had grown at the goddess's feet were now rotten and moldy.

George dragged Belle toward him as Verena rushed to Ibrahim's side, completing the circle of friends. This small gesture caused a ripple through Beatrice—and, she assumed, through the rest of them—an affirmation that the circle was not meant to break. Ever.

"My friend," Verena murmured, staring at Ibrahim. There were tears in her eyes. "Do not endanger everything for my sake. You yourself said there's nothing about your gift that makes this cer-tain. I'll take my chances . . . if you'll help protect me." She turned to the others. "I don't mean to be trouble."

"I'm not going to let you end up a sacrifice," Ibrahim hissed. "While I comprehend the value of the Grand Work, I am not convinced being at the whim of gods remains in our best interest . . ."

Beatrice looked at them, wondering, there was something about the way the two of them stared at each other . . . Surely Ibrahim fought for Verena out of love; the woman was unquestionably beautiful, as the men could not help but see.

Verena turned to Ahmed, who stepped closer to her. She did not wield her loveliness like a weapon, but it invited protection nonetheless. Beatrice wondered which man she cared for more. Then she chided herself for indulging in personal drama when the world of the dead was gaping open and oozing mortal despair into a perfectly nice Cairo morning. A love triangle should hardly take precedence.

"It's your choice—to weaken the barrier between these parallel places or to fight the good fight as commissioned," Persephone called out, her eyes now the same gray as the terrible place behind her, that place that had so long ago laid claim to her. Beatrice wondered anxiously if the Whisper-world's pull was affecting the goddess and if she'd be able to close the gate she'd opened.

"I'm not refusing to fight, I'm refusing to place my comrades in harm's way," Ibrahim insisted.

"You're mortal. You'll always be in harm's way," the goddess breathed. "It is not the fault of the Grand Work, Ibrahim Wasil-Tipton, and you know that better than anyone."

The goddess and Ibrahim shared a sad, knowing look that made Beatrice wonder what Persephone knew about him and his fate. The boarding bell tolled again, and the divine one wrung her hands.

"Don't you understand that the Grand Work has reached a new height? There waits a worthy army to put back in its place this growing cancer, this mounting Whisper-world press. I'm fighting for a way to make things right, but you must trust me. You cannot stay here, and you cannot be divided."

Beatrice noticed that the people nearby, Egyptians and tourists alike, workers and the leisure class, were pressing their hands over their hearts and glancing around as if seeking the source of a sudden pain. Belle was doing her best to remove their memories, but if they weren't careful, these mortals might drop dead right here, feeding the Whisper-world with yet more souls.

"All aboard!" the steamer's captain cried.

"Ibrahim," Beatrice pleaded. Verena bit her lip, tears in her eyes.

The goddess moved forward, her step still creating life, but it was sparse. Thorny green budding sprouts stabbed her feet, which shed droplets of blood on the struggling plants. The flowers faded behind her as if they were mirages. She took Verena's hand and kissed it.

"That is a kiss of life," Persephone breathed. "I do not give it lightly, as it requires strength I ought to conserve. I cannot promise danger will not come; that would be lying to you. But you'll not die on my watch. That I vow."

Ibrahim gave a shuddering sigh. "I suppose it is the best offer we have," he said. He waited for Verena to meet his gaze and give consent. Beatrice doubted, with a jealousy that shamed her, that he would ever offer her the same gentle patience.

Verena nodded and addressed the goddess. "Please close up that terrible world. The example was not lost on us." Even Ahmed was visibly rattled.

The goddess whirled to the portal and threw her arm out, her hand shaking, blood droplets spattering the hem of Beatrice's skirts, and the maw snapped shut. The thick air thinned, the water receded, the sky opened to a clear blue, and the sun shone once more upon their harrowed faces.

"Don't worry," Belle assured Ibrahim and Verena. "I'll make sure you've everything you need once we are on board."

After the group shared one communal breath, Beatrice was the first to step onto the gangway. She was not eager for the journey, but she was Leader, and the pull toward England was undeniable. She would set an example. While her compatriots, especially Ibrahim, did an impressive job of hiding their fear, she wanted to show them no futher hesitation.

She took a position at the rail, where she was joined by the other five—and the goddess. Feeling a sudden chill, Beatrice turned to see a skeletal spirit in torn robes, its jaw hanging open like a gruesome puppet, drawn to taunt the goddess. It bobbed before her, looking much like the ghost they'd first fought, that muezzin of malevolence.

Persephone batted at the annoyance with her still bloody hand, which Verena again took into hers to heal and cleanse and this time the divinity let her. "Shh, you wretch," the goddess hissed at the spirit, and Beatrice wondered what it was saying to make her grimace so.

The spirit hung its head, chastened, but instead of sinking or slithering away, it moved to the boat's prow and hung there. Beatrice could swear that it was smiling. But it was a skull. It couldn't smile. There was something about the ghost that filled Beatrice with unusual dread, as if it had been waiting for them or searching for a new world to terrorize. It turned to the sea and opened its bony arms.

"It seems we have brought some stowaways," Belle muttered, gesturing to the specter.

"That's bound to happen," Persephone remarked. "The Grand Work is a magnet for spiritual forces. It's inevitable that you trail the dead, and they you."

"What a joyful life we've earned," Beatrice muttered.

"It *is*, isn't it?" Ahmed exclaimed, inverting her sarcasm into truth. He put his hands on Beatrice's and Belle's shoulders and they felt a breeze in their veins as if he had loosed a dove in their hearts, the flapping of its wings a flurry of peace. His eyes were on

Verena, and she grinned. No matter what lay ahead, no one could refuse the Heart.

THE VESSEL PITCHED. SO DID BEATRICE'S STOMACH. SHE PRAYED for swift currents to bring the trip to completion. The sea was rougher than usual, she heard crewmen say in inelegant tones as they clomped past her door. She wondered if that was because the ship carried an entourage of death and restlessness to London.

Every rocking motion of the vessel brought another curse, and more bile, to her lips. She clutched the sides of her narrow bed with white knuckles, unaware of where the rest of her company was aboard the vessel, too queasy to take note of the multiple pulses tied to her own. Frankly, she didn't care; she was unfit for company and too embarrassed to ask for help.

They'd settled in without incident. Belle's powers were so frightfully useful. It was true that they were an unlikely traveling set, the six of them, and they'd raised more than a few eyebrows when seen together above deck. But one little smile and wave from the Frenchwoman and they were making themselves at home in first class. Beatrice was surprised by the luxury. Cairo had become quite the destination, she supposed. This brought her thoughts of her father with a small pang, and she wondered if more traveling Brits would help or hinder his work.

Beatrice fixed her gaze upon the dark porthole above her bed and tried not to move; the stiller she could be, the less disruption to her reeling body.

"Let's go to London. It will be an adventure," she muttered.

Suddenly she missed the life she could have lived, a haunted life that never again could be. In times of discomfort, one always wishes for alternatives.

She wondered if her mother had been this ill when they had traveled to Cairo, when Beatrice was four. She did not recall the journey, but remembered her mother hadn't fared it well.

When the new life of the Guard had first begun, Beatrice had looked for the spirit of her mother everywhere. Now, realizing that only the restless dead remained on Earth, she was grateful to have never seen her mother's ghost. It gave her a small amount of comfort to think her mother had somehow found peace. From what her father sometimes murmured, usually after he'd had a drink or two, Mum hadn't much liked Cairo. So perhaps she was better off, but Beatrice would have loved a mother's touch upon her forehead at that moment, gently telling her to hold on and have faith.

She felt a tweak at her temple—there were ghostly happenings afoot, perhaps the work of those who had followed the Guard aboard. Damn them. There was Work to be done and she couldn't sit up straight.

There was a knock at her cabin door.

"I am indisposed!" Beatrice called, then snapped her mouth shut and willed back a wave of nausea.

"Leader, your services are required aft. There is some sort of . . . siren" came a deep and concerned voice.

"You'll have to fight her without me, Ibrahim."

The door swung wide.

"I thought I locked that," Beatrice muttered, turning away from her Intuition, who stood in the doorway like an elegant statue; a stern yet beautiful work of sculpted art guarding ancient treasures. She didn't want him to see her like this, so helpless. It would only feed his disdain.

"It appears the sea does not agree with you," he said. "I'll summon Verena."

"This is no work of a phantasm," Beatrice said, and hissed as she felt another wave of nausea. She hoisted herself over the nearby basin. "She will be of no help. Please leave."

She was surprised when he did, and she returned to her bed to lie flat again. Moments later, to her chagrin, Verena appeared in dark, rustling robes, giving Beatrice a friendly smile. "You're quite green," she stated.

Beatrice moaned. When the Healer placed a glowing hand on her stomach, she shuddered once, then went still. Verena's glowing fingertips traced a line up her arm toward her neck and then her temple, as if gauging her pulse. After a moment, Beatrice heaved a long sigh and sat up.

It was as if Verena had detached the symptoms from her mind, her light some kind of block against the effects of her roiling stomach that matched the pitch of the seas. Beatrice would take it and hope it lasted.

"I'm much better, surprisingly. Thank you, Verena," she stated. Ibrahim had been right to fetch her. "What did I hear we have out there? A siren?" She made a face and stood up. "Honestly, is there such a thing?"

Going aft and glimpsing the glowing specter, she couldn't help but come to the same conclusion. The ghostly woman's form was lithe and long; she trailed phantom fabric far above the deck and her hair whipped behind her in a snaky halo. Her mouth was a wide O, and while the Guard could hear no sound, the panes of glass in the door to the captain's cabin began to fissure and splinter.

The Guard formed a circle below the floating form, which seemed even more luminous against the moonlit mist. Beatrice glanced around. Belle must have cleared the deck of all persons, for it was just them, the rough sea, an encroaching storm, and this unhappy wraith.

"Bind," Beatrice commanded. A trickle of blue fire leaped from her hands and lit a ring of light around the group like a match dropped upon a line of oil. The spirit's face snapped down to stare at them.

"She's shrieking. So sad," Belle said. "Drowned, drowned she was. Taken by the sea."

"Can you hear her?" George asked, always in awe of her talent.

"No, no. It's just what I sense. My powers could gather more sense of her if I had something to touch. Ibrahim, what do *you* feel?"

Ibrahim closed his eyes and concentrated. "I don't believe she is malevolent," he admitted. "She is merely displaced, having drowned, as Belle said. Perhaps she is warning us. Perhaps she doesn't want us to perish in a storm as she did."

"Or she wants us to follow her to yonder rocks," George muttered.

"Perhaps," Beatrice replied. "And so we ought to try to quiet her."

Ibrahim opened his mouth, prepared to give a benediction and begin the process of importuning the ghost to peace when his brow furrowed and he stared at Beatrice's hands. She lifted them, showing everyone the flickering, faltering flame. "Yes. The fire is hard to muster for long, given the current distance." She hissed. "And it's terribly uncomfortable." It was downright agonizing, but she couldn't let her fellows know how bad it was. That was leadership's curse.

"Where's our goddess when we need her?" Ibrahim asked grumpily. "Wasn't she just with us?"

"Our Lady comes and goes when and how she will," Ahmed said. "She's likely resting. Didn't you see how the Whisper-world affected her?"

Like Ibrahim, Beatrice felt bereft, but offered no comment.

Great light bloomed as Persephone appeared. Her bare feet balanced on the ship's masthead, the shifting-colored beauty smiled at them from on high. "Sometimes you need only ask," she said, and turned her attention to the sea.

"Thank you for the help, m'lady," Beatrice murmured, glancing to her dim hands, which held hardly the light she would need for a fight.

"I only wish I could do more, beloveds," the goddess murmured, her gentle voice rising above the waves. "I wish I could fight at your side each and every time."

The air calmed, the clouds cleared away, and while the sea did not grow immediately still, the boat ceased its frightful rocking and adopted a more gentle sway.

"How the spirits obey you," Ahmed wondered. "Would that we had such swift facility."

"You do," Persephone assured. "It is you who improve me. I need you as my warriors—to remind me of my duty, to bring out the best in me, to rally me to my own cause. And I cannot always be in this mortal world," Persephone said before turning to the troubled siren still wailing above the Guard. "Peace, friend. *Peace.*"

As the spirit ascended, like a star rising into the sky, calmed by the goddess's gentle powers, Beatrice ran to the rail and vomited over the side, Verena's cure evidently a temporary salve.

Verena went to her, placed a hand on her shoulder. "Come on, dear, let's get you back below. I wish my gifts were constant, or that my hand could utterly smooth the sea."

As she took Beatrice's hand, a few crewmen scrambled past them to the prow. A few crossed themselves, others murmured that they were being watched over by angels. Belle and George remained on deck, Belle doing her best to keep the damage to a minimum.

"Angels and devils both," Ibrahim muttered.

Beatrice longed to ask her second what and how he was feeling, if his instinct was roiling here like her stomach. But he was her business associate and not her friend. He would tell her only if it became necessary. She let herself be led below, steeling herself for the rest of the voyage.

CHAPTER
FIFTEEN

THE NEXT DAY, A LOUD RAP AT BEATRICE'S DOOR MADE HER aching head reel. This was followed by Ibrahim's smooth voice. "Miss Smith, I have come to pay you a visit, if you are of a mind to admit me."

Thankfully, she had been well enough that morning to dress and had dressed nicely, though a glance in the mirror showed dark circles under her eyes. She scowled. Why should she care what Ibrahim thought of her appearance?

"Yes, Mr. Wasil-Tipton, how may I help you?" she asked, moving carefully to the door and bracing her hand hard upon the frame to mask the shaking of her limbs.

"As second-in-command, I thought I should confer with you."

"About what? Is there a decision at hand? Do you bring another doomsday account?"

"No," he said simply as she opened the door.

"Then why are you here?" Her tone was sharper than she intended.

Ibrahim blinked. "I . . . I came to tell you that I appreciate the way in which you allowed my viewpoint to be presented to our fellows, and to our Lady."

"Noted. You are welcome," she replied and moved to sit upon her bed, her head swimming. Fainting in front of him would be beyond humiliating. He'd have to catch her in his arms . . . Not to mention it was terribly improper for him even to be in her room in the first place.

He looked closely at her. She was sure it was just her miserable imagination, but it seemed he was masking a laugh.

"Please go," she growled. "Stop enjoying my humiliation."

Instead, Ibrahim came closer. "Lay back," he said.

Beatrice felt a shiver rush down her spine, this one not originating in her quivering stomach as she eased down onto the bed.

Ibrahim dipped the waiting cloth into the basin of cool water on the bed stand, then placed it gently on her forehead. It was the first time there had been any contact between them. Granted, there was a cool cloth between his fingers and her skin, but Beatrice felt the exchange nonetheless. She tried not to have her pleasure become visible as he stared down at her, his face impossibly noble. He looked too much a prince to have been left on a doorstep. How could anyone abandon such beauty?

Perhaps it was the gentleness in her gaze that allowed his firm expression to soften, his dark eyes to warm. The two of them said nothing, but Ibrahim kept his hand on her forehead and the compress.

Beatrice closed her eyes. "I want to go home," she murmured.

"That's something we can agree on," Ibrahim replied. "Breathe deep. Try to rest."

He rose and was about to leave the room when he paused. "I cannot presume to understand your recent physical state, as your powers differ from mine, but I was quite overtaken by the physical effects of the Grand Work, and if the force you've been cloven to has been ripped away, I cannot imagine the discomfort. I cannot imagine it helps seasickness, either. You are somewhat composed, considering."

Beatrice eyed him. "Are you attempting to give me a compliment, Mr. Wasil-Tipton? You might practice a bit more."

The corners of his lips twitched, and his dark eyes sparked. Then he shrugged. "It isn't my fault if you women have a need for praise but no appreciation of subtlety. Good day."

"Good day," Beatrice replied.

She gave a bemused chuckle as the door closed behind him, telling herself that it was only because she hadn't been touched in so long that his small gesture had been so pleasant. Had seasickness upended more than her stomach? She gave a moment's pause to considering Ibrahim's hand and what it might feel like were there no fabric between it and her. Another distinct shiver unrelated to the sea coursed down her spine.

Beatrice cut the thought from her mind. Touches were meaningless, and she would do fine without them. She was a woman self-assured, set apart from such romantic nonsense.

WHEN BEATRICE AT LONG LAST WENT ABOVEDECKS, SHE FOUND the other ladies of the Guard appreciating the bright sun from deck chairs, soaking up as much as they could before the clouds of the British Isles were drawn over them. Thankfully, the sea was presently calm, and her battered nerves were in a better state of cooperation.

The three women chatted happily, shifting between languages with a fluidity that went without comment, facilitated by occasional words in the Guard's communal language and the uncanny aid of Belle's mental tricks. As they shared a second pot of tea, they noticed a bright light appear in a wicker chair beside them.

"May I sit with you? The company of bosom friends is something I've always craved," murmured Persephone, smiling shyly. As powerful and ancient as she might be, she often seemed young and preciously awkward.

Belle and Verena looked at Beatrice, who shrugged and rose to play hostess. The teapot was suddenly fresh and full, when no human had been near. A fourth cup was waiting at the ready. Such, apparently, was the benefit of taking tea with a divinity.

"You were talking of love?" Despite her shifting colors, it was clear Persephone blushed.

"Are you certain you're not Aphrodite?" Beatrice asked, handing her a filled cup balanced on a delicate saucer.

The goddess chuckled. "Would that I were."

Belle asked, "Do you know them, other deities of old? Is everything we've come to believe in our respective faiths a lie? Were the Greek myths right all along?"

Persephone gave an odd laugh. "Is there a conflict between what I knew and what you might believe, you mean? Not necessarily. I know . . . *forces*. I do not call them by the names you do. We've our own titles, if ever such words are spoken. Of all my names, I like this best, and use it because it came from mortals, whom I adore.

"I drift in my sphere and other forces drift in theirs. Sometimes paths cross because they are destined. Something far greater than I turns the prism that changes my colors, and it alone knows every mystery."

"When did you and Phoenix meet?" Verena asked, her face aglow. Beatrice guessed she was a true romantic. The quiet ones often were.

Persephone blinked, then smiled warmly. "I first spied him in a field full of sunflowers. He was touching the seeds and arranging them into iterations. A divine mathematician."

"When?" Belle pressed.

"My sense of time and yours differ. I know it was a simpler age, back when we were made new from you beautiful mortals, freshly congealed from all your hopes and dreams, sprung from your needs and desires and fueled by your energy. Beautiful beings were birthed from your souls—and terrible beings, too. But Phoenix . . . was *always* beautiful."

"Show me, please," Verena breathed, adding passionately in Arabic, "I seek windows into souls. That is how I can see my own more clearly and heal more precisely. Give me a window. Do you think or live in any way like us?"

Persephone sighed.

"I'm filled with mortal emotions. In fact, I am able to hold more within me than your mortal bodies ever could. But I imagine falling in love is the same for us both." The goddess bit her lip and smiled. "If you wish to indulge me, who am I to decline?" She lifted her prismatic palms.

It was as before in the sacred space: Her vision overtook them.

Suddenly the women were in that very field of sunflowers; their blooms of a brighter yellow than Beatrice had ever known existed. In the distance was the sea, vast and sapphire, the sound of its waves an intoxicating lull.

Phoenix surpassed beauty. The women collectively gasped. He towered above the flowers, yet bent to them with grace and fascination, a vision wholly angelic. His great wings were pure energy, incorporeal and delicate, transparent feathers made of light. His long black hair made a striking contrast to the rest. He was without clothes; his luminescent body lean and powerful.

His wings artfully hid his nether regions from view, which was just as well for the propriety of the moment. Verena in her robes, Beatrice and Belle in their European traveling fashions, they stood invisible amid the flowers of this ancient field and watched Persephone approach. Her shifting colors infused his lit wings, like beams through a stained-glass window.

His dark eyes drank her in as a greeting.

"Patterns," he said, his voice distinct, low, and rich. He held up a sunflower and pointed to its dark center. His finger traced the ridges, and the seeds ordered themselves at his command. "Everything can be arranged into one. Perfected. Life—one beautiful equation."

The goddess gasped, delighted, and the sunflowers grew taller, their petals opening wider. "Can I be arranged into a pattern?"

"I know nothing of your properties," he replied. "Not yet." He took a step closer. "Would you give me leave to ascertain?"

"I give you leave," she whispered.

He took a long moment to parse her with his gaze. Finally he said, "Your heart is constant, for it is your heart that so illuminates you. Your colors are ever-changing, painting the world with every emotion. You would never bore me. I find that . . . of wondrous value."

She took a step closer. "My palette is vast but my heart unchanging. None yet has won it. There must be a reason I was drawn to this field today . . ."

"Ah," he said. "My equation was missing a variable. You could be that variable, should you desire such a place. I am a constant." A light danced in his eyes as he touched her cheek. Wildflowers of every kind sprang up at her feet. The field was swiftly awash in every color of the cosmos. Phoenix looked around, greatly pleased. "Action, reaction. Good."

"Action," she breathed, and turned her face into his hand to kiss his palm.

"Reaction," he countered, and his wings enfolded her.

The field was suddenly filled with music. The rhythms of their pulses were perfectly complementary. In the distance, shimmering, glimmering forms of indescribable beauty danced upon a hilltop.

"The Muses approve," Phoenix stated. "They sing for us."

He raised his palm in the air, and Persephone pressed her hand to it.

"You are a being of light," she said, "so why hair of onyx hue? Your eyes, too. Such contrast. You are light but not *all* light. Tell me what you're made of."

His voice was rich thunder, a promised storm. "I am tethered to this world, to its mortals and the birth pangs of their civilizations.

They begin to understand darkness. As day must pass into night, so we must learn to love darkness, to own it and still remain true to the light. Dark and light are not synonymous with evil and good. The palette is complex. I am Balance. I am the between, with feet for the ground, wings for the air. And you, you are all the colors I've awaited. May I hold you?"

"For empirical evidence or for pleasure?" she countered.

"Both."

"Please do."

He seized her in powerful arms, and suddenly she was airborne, lifted up by his great wings, the music of the Muses swelling in response. Her shimmering robes buffeted him as he slowly coursed over the field with her, a flight of both leisure and delight. It was revealed that the flowering field grew atop a sheer cliff, and out they flew out over that crystal sea that arched its waves toward them, magnetized by their pull. The drama of the vista was as breath-taking as their airborne, graceful forms.

He watched her intently as they soared, ascribing meaning to each of her shifting hues. Midair, he held her tight with one arm and traced the outline of her face with his fingertips.

"Of your colors I am most drawn to the blue—your willing-ness to see solutions to everything." He touched the hollow of her throat. "You render the mathematician an alchemist. You have wrought change in me."

She placed her hand on his cheek, examining it. Their caresses were each an exquisite experiment. "The colors you see in me, I do not see them. I see none on my skin."

"The blank whiteness of light contains *every* color. You do see them, all, all at once."

She wrapped her limbs more fully around him. "You are the solution to everything. Your white wings hold constant all my variables."

"While you light the world with your rainbow. What a balance we make indeed. Do you declare constancy?" he asked, a rumbling, hopeful murmur.

"Give me your vow, and I will."

He planted a firm and claiming kiss upon her, descending. They once again touched the sunflowers, then fell to their knees. A ring of birch trees sprouted around them, stretching in an instant to a great height, sheltering the gods' impassioned embrace. The field became a verdant space of leaf and blossom, sun and shade. The whole of the land shimmered as the flowers continued to grow, diversify, and magnify. It was a celebration of a glorious union.

The Muses danced, the music swelled—and suddenly the women were again on the deck of their ship, all of them blushing. The vision had been inescapable and all-consuming.

Two such powerful forces of nature coming together had created a wave of heat and emotion beyond any mortal experience, and Beatrice thought poor, sensitive Verena might faint. She herself was feeling quite hot and fanned herself with her hand.

The goddess had vanished. Perhaps she was living in her memories, unable to bear to part from them. Beatrice could not blame her; that was a memory worth living in indefinitely.

Belle sighed. "How poetic and beautiful!"

Beatrice raised an eyebrow, fighting to reclaim her usual outward equanimity. "Well, yes. But, truly, the gods are such shameless flirts."

Verena giggled into her teacup.

Privately, Beatrice was still overcome, hoping there was some pairing for her that was just as meant to be. At the thought of such a partner, her stomach tightened, and she recalled a cool cloth upon her forehead, the gentle press of a golden-skinned hand.

Her sigh became a scowl. The gods had been scandalous and artless. Phoenix's claim had been sudden, presumptuous and bold. Gods, she supposed, might act thus without censure. Mortals could never speak with such freedom, certainly not if they valued propriety. Mortals must dance, play games and say fine words, within the rigors of societal constraint. Gaining a true partner was never so simple a path. For most mortals, love was as much misery as it was joy. She wondered if the goddess understood that. It would prove to hurt them all if she didn't.

IN THE DAYS TO COME, NUMEROUS POTS OF TEA WERE PREPARED, George consumed a good deal of champagne, and the Guard listened in on the frivolous conversations of wealthy travelers. Beatrice caught Ibrahim rolling his eyes at ignorant comments made about Egyptians, as if one trip to a foreign country afforded the English all the evidence they needed to concoct theories and assess values of cultures not their own.

Ibrahim assured Beatrice when she appeared concerned. "I am well aware that not all Englishmen are insufferable prigs. Just a great number of the ones who travel."

Prigs? Beatrice snickered, caught off guard by a word she wouldn't have expected him to use. But then again, he had been raised by an Englishman—about which she deeply wanted to know more. Frankly, Ibrahim spoke with such simple grace she found she liked to hear him talk about anything at all. But she could not question him; she merely waited for him to choose to reveal himself, and there was no further conversation between them that day.

George had taken to drawing caricatures of everyone on board, and he came away with a healthy roll of bills in his pockets. He kept offering to pay for their meals and wine, until Belle insisted that it was money honestly earned and that the Guard would not judge him for his own indulgences.

Beatrice could hardly eat more than plain biscuits, even fortified by Verena's healing hand. She tried to pretend to her compatriots that she was the picture of health and hadn't a care in the world, but she was sure her pallor betrayed her. Thankfully, no one offered her pity or any special consideration.

Ahmed had found someone on board who had bought a *kissar*, an instrument in the lyre family. With great cheer he insisted that it not be displayed on a wall as the Englishman intended but instead be loved and played. The fellow could not refuse, and soon Ahmed was singing and entertaining the entire vessel.

His gift was transcendent. Power flowed from his voice, his eyes; the poetry of Turks and Arabs and great Sufi leaders washed over all the travelers and made their hearts soar. It was heavenly. Aside from Verena's occasional helping hand, Ahmed's music was the only thing that made Beatrice able to forget her seasickness. It made Belle and George take hands, and Beatrice realized with unquestionable surety that their touch was a vow.

Verena seemed drunk with awe. She stared at Ahmed, and with the same surety Beatrice realized another choice had been made. It all seemed so natural, this pairing off. Yet Beatrice and Ibrahim were utterly unable to look at each other.

At least Beatrice didn't feel she could look at him. Not without betraying something. Her heart was lonely. The pulses of her friends, beating in her own blood, made it all the more evident. She did wish to love again; she was young and it seemed a crime not to. But every sentence, movement or glance, reminded her that she and Ibrahim were stoic, stubborn creatures of different worlds floating on an ocean as vast as the gulf between them.

When the music ended, there were the dead. Always the dead. Beatrice felt her coterie's hearts plummet as dread of their tasks crept in. Ghosts were seen on the water in vague clusters, likely hovering over sunken ships that lay on the ocean floor.

The spirits that had followed them onboard in Cairo were more concerning. Had they been so eager in life to get to England? Their presence on the ship defied the laws of spirits, Beatrice believed. As far as she knew, spirits were tied to people, to land, to hearths and homes. The dead weren't adventurers. Of course, as the goddess intimated, perhaps things were changing.

Persephone had been absent since their tea party. Beatrice imagined her wandering those terrible gray corridors of the Whisperworld, a prisoner, remembering love in a time of flowers. That saddened her. The creature deserved a verdant field and an angel to hold her close. But it would seem that life, for divinities as well as mortals, did not always afford them what they wanted.

When George alerted them that their journey was nearly over, her body rejoiced at the idea of solid ground and the pain in her hands began to ease. She could finally remove her gloves a moment and flex her aching fingertips.

A cityscape grew in their vision until it became an undeniable leviathan. The bosom of the great empire was beautiful and terrifying, a sprawling, huge, sooty creature. It loomed, a mammoth collection of interlocked beasts; sporadic fires of industry spouting from the smokestack noses of countless sleeping dragons. The waterways of the Southampton port were covered with a crouched horde, any of which could wake at any moment and in one lick swallow their large boat whole.

Beatrice studied the light in the sky, seeing how it changed, how it thickened and grew gray. Perhaps the walls between the Whisperworld and the mortal world would prove thinner in England. There certainly were plenty of spirits about, and grayscale was the communal palette.

The pit of her stomach that had been reserved for seasickness and the occasional pain at being near to Ibrahim with nothing to be said or done about it was now overtaken by dread. While she hadn't ever taken a census, she could say for a certainty there were *far* more spirits here than in Cairo. Clearly the Guard had their work cut out for them.

The dead were waiting.

CHAPTER
SIXTEEN

A FEW OF THE MANY BARRIER PINS KEEPING THE WORLDS separate were now spattered with blood—and tears, for good measure. The pain seared deeper the more Persephone cut. The flesh of her arms and thighs was scarred and not healing as quickly as she wished. But she hid the traces, wound her robes tight, and acted like nothing was out of the ordinary.

"You do realize I'll do anything for you," Darkness blurted during another of their obligatory promenades. His jaw chattered, making his earnest tone something absurd.

"You mean *to* me," she clarified with an edge. "You'll do anything *to* me."

"I'd rip the worlds apart if you abandoned this place entirely."

Persephone felt her pulse quicken. Was he sensing something worrisome about her mood that he dared such a threat? She had to play the game as much as she could bear. She couldn't have him tightening the leash now, increasing the illness in her blood to the point where she'd be bedridden with the rot of the Whisper-world. He always seemed satisfied to see her weakening. She had to seem too dispirited to be inventive.

"I can't escape," she stated, putting a plaintive note into her voice. "I've tried everything possible to get away. I've tried to die. The Whisper-world has so deeply infected me, I am forever bound to return. You have, at last, won."

Darkness made a sound like a delighted child's noise. Persephone quit his dais, not wishing him to make her repeat the lie, leaving him to his glee. Following paths to the Liminal, she slipped through the gate to the mortal world, where she found herself, as she often did, in the sacred space. The Guard were absent.

Bitterness, bile, and anger surfaced within her. If this emotional backlash had happened in the Whisper-world, her feelings would have manifested into veritable shackles, but now she merely echoed Darkness's words. "He'd rip the worlds apart. Dear God, he'll undo the barrier pins himself in order to find me."

Yet wasn't that the point, the very aim she worked toward? Yes, but it needed to be done to the Guard's mortal advantage. On the seal above, her vision had revealed a veritable army of spirits crashing down on Athens—surely that indicated the worlds would merge. But glimpses weren't a plan, and one did not just flirt with opening such barriers. It would be the end of mortal life as they knew it if things were not tightly controlled.

Hopelessness accosted her, fear of the vagaries of what she was attempting, and she let tears come as they would. It was safer to shed them here, lest the shadows lap them up to use against her and those she loved.

Falling to the stone floor, her tears rolled into a peculiar pattern. Her sorrow shaped lines and curves that drew phoenix fire. A portion of his flame coursed through the room in immediate empathic response, rising above and engulfing the tear-drawn symbols.

Persephone watched, fascinated. The droplets drew together, hundreds of tiny beads running toward one another and into a small hole at the center of the mosaic. The mercurylike tears filled that hole and began to stack upon themselves, forming something rounded at the top, oddly notched and gleaming silver.

A key? It was another key. But what was it to?

As the liquid and flame continued to shift, Persephone realized the image on the floor was a map: the floor plan of Athens! Beside them, another map, of sloping curves and meandering paths: the Whisper-world.

At some point, she knew, these places would join. Here was a way for the Guard to prepare; this was a map of the merge. Phoenix was lighting their way.

"Oh, beloved," she murmured. "Isn't it beautiful how magic can still be new to us? That there are gifts around every corner, despite our suffering? Isn't it wonderful that I can still be amazed?"

She bent to kiss the stones of the floor. The sacred space had been created when the Guard itself was born. Much like how the Whisper-world had separated from the mortal at the dawn of civilization, so had the sacred space split at the inception of the Guard, separating itself from both worlds similarly to the Liminal edge. Thus it had its own properties, could sometimes fashion the unexpected to serve the Power and the Light. Or, she supposed, it could serve another power. She wondered if a future Guard would inadvertently call upon the wrong side of the light.

"You may choose the wrong path, beloveds, but I cannot hold your hands forever," she admitted ruefully. "You must make the right choices yourselves."

Beyond the stone pillars lay shimmering darkness, a place between space and time that was unfriendly for mortal and divinity alike. She knew that every Guard who put a hand into that darkness came away scarred, and she prayed that those shadows would ever stay static, that nothing would come from the other side. She hoped that the dog would stay at heel, the Gorgon would never grow curious, and that Darkness would only fight when provoked. The time of their final battle was the advantage she sought.

Thinking of her vision, of Alexi and the girl bent over the Athens seal to free Guard spirits, Persephone laid hold of the key made of her tears. When she lifted it from the floor, the map vanished. Keeping her robes about her, she ascended to that upper seal and examined its fine tiles. There indeed was another keyhole. But when she tried the key, it did not fit. A different lock for a different key.

Her heart sank at the thought of keys. The most necessary key was the one Darkness had imprisoned within him. It would have to be stolen. She, whomever she would become, would have to obtain it. She would have to become the seventh member in a Guard of six, a mortal bringing them the final piece of an age-old puzzle.

But how was this all to take place?

"Ah, Beatrice." Suddenly, an unprecedented idea filled her head. Two Guards. Was that possible? She would need the help.

Persephone blinked, feeling something shift within her heart, and clapped her hands. "Oh! They're here!"

ONCE THEY DISEMBARKED FROM THEIR TRAIN, THE WHOLE OF London sprawled before them, brimming with life and sound. Beatrice and her Guard stood just outside the grand King's Cross arches, taking in the myriad sights. London was more populous than Cairo, but there was a similar bustle and old-world chaos.

A ripping sound and a burst of colored light heralded the goddess. Lovely as ever she appeared, though there were disturbing dark circles under her iridescent eyes. Her layered gown was spattered with what appeared at first to be blood but then shimmered like red silk when she stepped into their world. The Guard looked nervously at one another.

"Welcome to London!" Persephone cried, visibly excited, beckoning them like an eager child as passersby darted around her, her colors lighting them preternaturally. Thankfully for Belle, the goddess had arranged her diaphanous gown in such a manner that her magic shielded her from view by the populace, visible only to her Guard.

The divinity tapped the temples of two cargo hands, who stopped what they were doing and moved away. "There, your bags and trunks are taken care of. Come! Let's see the city!"

Wide-eyed, the goddess led them down a multitude of lanes and avenues, practically crowing with delight. Beatrice and her fellows took in London more warily, but none could deny the joy of adventure once they were in the thick of it.

This city was in some part theirs, though its citizens would never know. The sentiment bolstered Beatrice as she tried not to be overwhelmed by its size and density, its sounds and smells, its extreme wealth and staggering poverty.

Like every ancient city, London was host to many different styles of architecture—and to residents whose families originated in every country and culture England had pierced with its flag. Beatrice noticed that Ahmed's and Ibrahim's shoulders eased a bit when they saw they were hardly the only persons of color walking London's streets, though the latter's brow remained furrowed.

Perhaps he felt a burst of homesickness. She couldn't blame him. London was a vast stage with countless sets and an infinite cast, asymmetrical and busy like Cairo, but where Cairo's rouge was vermillion dust, London's was soot. The wash of gold traded for the press of gray would take some getting used to.

A great, weighty pain burned in her bosom, and the Pull—or something vaguely like it—dragged her in the direction the goddess was heading. Was the great soul inhabiting her so magnetized to its missing parts?

"Separation from phoenix fire has quite taken a toll on me, but it being close, my body yearns more than ever," Beatrice whispered to Verena, who, in reply, put a slightly glowing hand upon her back. It felt lovely, countering her pain and the irritation that still inflamed her skin.

In the Bloomsbury district they turned down a street that was more like an alley and came upon an oddly grand portico entrance to a Romanesque fortress of red sandstone. The lintel read FRIENDS.

"That's nice!" Ahmed exclaimed. "Friends!"

Everyone smiled.

"What is this place?" George asked.

Persephone grinned, obviously pleased with herself. "We are going to open this school. It shall be full of friends, indeed, and it shall be called Athens Academy!"

"Why not the School of Friends?" Ahmed frowned.

"Because England is not terribly tolerant of the Society of Friends, or as some would call them—"

"Quakers," Ibrahim finished. "James, my . . . father spoke reverently of his Quaker colleagues in America."

"Indeed. This school was closed because it sought to employ teachers both male and female and from diverse races and backgrounds, to educate both men and women equally, and to allow students access to all subjects," Persephone stated.

"Why should it be any other way?" Beatrice said.

The goddess nodded. "So I assume I'll have your unconditional support in seeing it open once more, under a title that shall draw less scrutiny. The classicists of this age won't mind a bit of Greek homage, for its students will never know that the Phoenix of their myths lives beneath its very eaves."

"Ah," Beatrice breathed. "That's why, standing here, I at last don't feel so broken."

"Yes. My apologies," Persephone said. "A lesser person would have fractured under the strain. You are Leader indeed, Beatrice Smith." She touched Beatrice's cheek with sisterly fondness, then turned to the rest of the company.

"Unless you wish to settle elsewhere, you can take to the upstairs rooms here or to the unfinished parts of the hall that will be used as dormitories. Do wander this rapturous city. But first, before we settle in, we need to locate some Friends to make good on this building's valiant mission. Ibrahim, my Intuition, would you be so kind as to show me to some Quakers?"

CHAPTER
SEVENTEEN

The wind had picked up and carried something strange upon it.

Alexi Rychman was a practical young man; his parents encouraged the quality. His grandmother, however, was not. Not entirely. He knew that of his whole family she cherished him most. His sister loved him dearly, but his grandmother gave him the sense that he was the most important person in the world. His parents found this appalling, but it was an honor young Alexi took very seriously.

His grandmother encouraged hard work and pressed him to excel at school, but also supported his fascination with alchemy. She was an ardent Spiritualist and oft spoke with otherworldly airs. If Alexi believed in such things—which he didn't—he would have thought she was secretly a witch.

Now, echoes of her mysticism had fourteen-year-old Alexi staring out from the flat where he was secretly apprenticed to a brilliant alchemist. Gazing down onto London, he felt the winds of fate were blowing. There was something in the air. A chill. A frisson of possibility.

"Oh don't be silly," he scoffed at himself and returned to mixing his powders.

CHAPTER
EIGHTEEN

An unlikely set of seven companions threw open the doors of an unmarked building Ibrahim had promised was a Quaker meeting house. Inside, a group of twenty middle-aged persons sat in the silence Quakers often kept at meetings, waiting for the Holy Spirit to move them to speak.

Several children were dispersed about the attendees, all with heads bent. The adults were dressed in modest fashions of the day: wide skirts, full-sleeved blouses cinched to slender waists, fine coats and well-kept waistcoats. Nothing ostentatious. The children were the same, well presented and not out of fashion but uniformly utilitarian. One woman was on her feet but not speaking.

At the sound of the doors thrown wide, everyone turned.

"Hello, friends!" cried Persephone. She was a prismatic, shifting, indescribable creature, and it was clear from their expressions she was like nothing their mortal eyes had ever seen. The entire room gaped.

"This is . . . She's a . . . member of Parliament," Belle stated, her French accent more pronounced when she spoke loudly, holding out her hands, bestowing her magic, "here to make a decree."

"I'd vote for her," George added with a grin.

"You'll henceforth remember her—and all of us—as belonging to the Prime Minister's . . ." Belle turned to George. "What do you call it?"

"A cabinet," George said.

"Cabernet," Belle repeated.

"Not wine, Belle. Cab*inet*." Beatrice rolled her eyes. "This is absurd."

"Cab-*i*-net." Belle blushed.

The goddess continued with her proclamation. "I am here to tell you that your closed academy shall live once more. The building in Bloomsbury, abandoned due to injustices and prejudices, shall reopen as Athens and you shall staff it." There were murmurs among the crowd of excitement and joy, like a dream was coming true. "But we must keep quiet about our venture, friends. We live in intolerant times. Who led the Friends Academy before its closure?"

A man stood, tall, sharp-featured, with blue eyes and a regal appearance. "I did, your honor. My name is Richard Thompson, and I wanted my niece to have the same chance that fellows at Oxford have." He gestured beside him to a young girl in her early teens. Tall and spindly in a sensible dress, she stood and blushed, locks of brown hair falling stubbornly from their coif and into her wide blue eyes. "Rebecca here is absolutely brilliant, and I wanted her to have every opportunity."

"And so she shall!" the goddess declared. "You shall see these fine fellow . . . ministers of mine around the institution. But remember! Athens Academy must be London's best-kept secret. I daresay Parliament will shut it down again if they hear a word. So, carry on! Truth, equality, simplicity, and peace be with you all!"

The goddess whirled toward the door with a flourish and exited, leaving the thunderstruck congregants behind. Her Guard trailed in her wake, not wanting to be caught answering any questions they'd be hard pressed to answer.

"Don't worry about the practicalities," the goddess exclaimed, measuring their worried expressions. "*They'll* run the school, as they were quite ready to do before. As for the bankers' loans, well, let me take care of that. That whole world is delightfully intricate, but I can be *very* persuasive when I want to be!" Her prismatic eyes glittered with the delight of purpose and action.

As they darted again in the direction of Bloomsbury, Ibrahim caught up to the goddess and pointed back toward the simple brick building from whence they had come. "That girl. That Thompson girl."

The goddess nodded. "An Intuition if I ever saw one. See? You can spot your own, can't you?"

"But . . ." Ibrahim furrowed his brow. "Are my powers split in two?"

"Two Guards at one time?" the goddess exclaimed. "That's never been attempted. Yet . . . we're at a new dawning, so who knows what's possible? Thrilling!"

They'd never seen her so invigorated. She seemed a bit feverish, in fact. But when one's heart is exuberant, one becomes more compelling, and the goddess even more so, her luminous magnetism something none of them could deny.

They traveled to the school. Ascending the steps below the bold FRIENDS—a sight that again made Ahmed smile, though that took very little—the goddess moved through the foyer as if leading a tour.

She pointed to the left, down a colonnaded hall. "Sacred space, accessible there through the chapel." She pointed toward an upper floor. "Above you'll find the grave of Phoenix. Make yourselves at home. Stay safe. I must be off." Then she flung her hand wide, a portal opened up, and she disappeared without another word.

WHILE SOME OF THE GUARD CHOSE ROOMS WITHIN ATHENS'S halls, George and Belle decided to wander the city, as they had been wont to do all through their last days in Cairo. Making their way through a twisting set of winding alleys, they stumbled at last upon a cozy bit of treasure. The garden-level pub seemed thoroughly warm and inviting save for an unfortunate placard out front declaring it THE BEAST and decorated with a cracked, time-worn painting of a hellish-looking dog. With naught but a nod, George and Belle descended the stairs and took a bay window seat that looked out past the wrought-iron rails of the stairs and out to the winding cobbles beyond.

The place was nearly deserted and likely had been for some time, they determined, for the help waited upon them as if they were royalty. While the pair had dressed smartly, their trappings alone did not warrant such fawning attention. At one point their hostess muttered something about hard times and wishing someone would come along and take the place off her hands.

"I'm . . . getting a funny feeling," Belle said, rubbing her temple.

"Me, too. I think I've found home," George stated. "I can't live in a *school*. A pub, on the other hand? Brilliant." Ever the artist, he was already measuring wall space and redecorating.

The hostess's husband came out to greet them, and it wasn't long before Belle's powers of persuasion came into play and it was suggested that George buy the property, which consisted of the downstairs pub and a few upstairs rooms. The price they settled on was quite reasonable—and as Belle's family had long maintained comfortable wealth and a precedent of spending it lavishly on their daughter's random desires, and George had made a handsome profit drawing on the boat, neither she nor George were concerned about the cost.

"The first thing we must do," she insisted once the deal had been struck, "is change that horrid sign." Her eyes lit up. "I've got it!"

When she whispered it in his ear, George gave a great laugh. "*La Belle et La Bête*? Beauty and the Beast. We shall tame the beast indeed, and this shall be a place of respite for all our friends. And a home for us."

This was a wholly agreeable thought, and they passed several more pleasant hours dining and drinking and daring to hold hands. The sun had completely set before they stopped staring into each other's eyes. They had begun a new life together, and the realization was glorious.

THEIR FIRST EXPERIENCE OF THE PULL IN LONDON WAS QUITE odd, foreign, not at all like the way it had felt in Cairo. The feeling wrenched Beatrice's heart as she descended the school stairs, and she dreaded to think this would always be how it felt here. Tears stung the corner of her eyes as her body all but dragged her toward the river.

That the change troubled the whole of the Guard was clear from the expressions on everyone's faces. They gathered on the Embankment and stared at the mass of spirits that rolled across the Thames like whitecaps upon the ocean. London had more open, restless dead than the constraints of Cairo's ancient tombs.

Beatrice noticed that Ibrahim's face was grimmest of all. Surely he sensed her staring at him, for he snapped his head around to look at her, then glanced back at the spirits. His eyes darkened. "Which of that undulating mass are we meant to corral?"

"All?" Verena gulped.

There was an army suddenly. Troop after troop, a wafting battalion in grayscale lines, a sea of floating forms that stared down at the Guard from a great height. This ghastly welcoming committee dove upon the Guard all at once. There was no time to take hands or gather their great fire.

"Why, this is the most coordinated effort I've seen yet," Beatrice said as she and her companions dodged the spirits. Righting herself and smoothing her skirts, Beatrice lifted her hands, and blue fire leaped indignantly forth, as strong as it had once been in Cairo.

"Perhaps they've begun to unionize," muttered George.

At this, Ahmed giggled. Beatrice could have blessed him for that sound, which reminded them all that they could choose to feel the freezing weight of death or instead find their position somewhat absurd. That simple shift in point of view made it easier to fight.

What followed was a haphazard battle, unfocused and unsatisfying. Belle was exhausted and had trouble rounding up and dismissing the passersby. Beatrice didn't know which of the many spirits should be first upon which to turn her fire, so there was chaos for a time. Ibrahim declaimed verses loudly, as if addressing Parliament, whose lavish new houses were being built just down the riverbank. Ahmed and the rest kept up as best they could, but all of them flagged. In the end, the crowd of specters was dispersed and attended, but the Guard's energy was spent.

As a reward, however, Belle and George suggested their friends come to the new café they'd just made plans to purchase, and the group agreed to the requisite journey. During the slow walk, Beatrice mused on the state of spectral affairs.

"We made a bit of a difference today, but we'll never put to rest *all* of London. The city is simply too haunted, and we but scratch the surface. Maintain balance? It feels more of a struggle here than ever."

"It's all this gray," Ibrahim murmured. "Are you sure this is England? Perhaps it is an extension of our goddess's prison, of the Whisper-world itself!"

"There's sun!" George countered unconvincingly. Ibrahim raised an eyebrow at his colleague, who mitigated: "Sometimes."

"We'll address it when next we see our Lady," Beatrice said. "Perhaps the Balance has indeed changed."

"I wonder that a Guard may be less powerful when supplanted from their homes," said Ibrahim. "If, historically, we are tied to great cities and their residents, I can't imagine there's ever been an *immigrant* Guard."

"That may very well be true," Beatrice allowed. "Alas, we are thrown into an 'unprecedented time.' I'm sure that will have its consequences."

THEY HAD TO WAIT A WEEK TO GET ANY SATISFACTION. IN THE midst of a meeting in the sacred space, Beatrice called upon the Power and the Light. A portal formed, and Persephone staggered out, a gaping wound in her upper arm.

Everyone gasped. George, closest to her, dove and caught her falling body. He eased her to the floor and Verena was immediately at her side.

"Hello, friends," she breathed. There came a deep, knocking rattle from her lungs.

"What on earth?" Beatrice knelt beside her.

"Knitting the worlds," Persephone mumbled, her eyelids fluttering. "Preparing for a fight. It'll take time, surely, but once everything is ready I can take *her* body. We'll start anew."

The Guard all looked at one another. They had no idea what she was talking about.

"You're bleeding," Belle said.

"Yes, it's part of the process," the divinity replied. "What to do . . . ? I came here to do something. Ah, yes." She stared sadly at all of them. "My memory seems to be going. It comes and goes so much this century. Can you help me up?"

George and Verena did so, Verena steadying the goddess with a glowing hand. None of the others said a word.

"Part of the preparation is in maintaining this building," Persephone remarked. "A shield for safekeeping. Beatrice, will you come with me? I need to kindle a bit of fire and could use your help. The rest of you can stay where you are."

Up several flights of stairs they ascended, the goddess, gliding otherworldly, her step birthing flowers, scented and lovely, that faded into ghostly traces of perfume as she passed. Beatrice felt each heavy tread of her own inelegant boot. While her carriage could never compare to Persephone's, she straightened herself and felt the rejuvenating rush of phoenix fire in her veins. She'd never prove a goddess, but she would prove herself a wise choice for power.

In the third-floor foyer, atop the seal of Athens with its great golden eagle, the goddess placed her hand upon Beatrice's shoulder, drawing out her fire.

"I give my breath and my light to these stones," Persephone vowed. "I declare these stones safe haven."

There was a reaction in the air, sparkling and shimmering, a gauzy layer of light ascending like thin fabric cast high in a wind. A shield in the air. The goddess looked up, pleased, before her lovely face shifted with pain.

She turned her head and coughed, an ugly, terrible sound. Deep crimson fluid burst from her lips, smelling of copper, dried flowers, and distinctly of soured pomegranate. Landing on the flowing, diaphanous sleeve of her robe, the matter transformed and became smooth, gorgeous crimson silk.

Beatrice stared with horrified fascination. "Wondrous, how terrible things can be made lovely," she murmured.

The goddess smiled and was suddenly radiant, the circles under her rainbow eyes less dark and deep. "I do believe that's what I'm here to do. A certain alchemy—strange into beautiful.

"This world heals me. But it can't heal me entirely. I don't suppose it would shock you to learn I'm falling apart, Beatrice. I think you all can see that now. It seems I need to take a body and live, as the Muses live in the Guard. This will come to pass, and here in London. But I don't know when. The timing is off, I'm *off* . . . We need to bring things together. Have patience with me, will you?"

Beatrice considered the goddess a moment, taken aback by the vulnerability of this great unpredictable force and trying to summon the right response. "I'll try. But patience is not my strong point."

"It never is, for Leaders," Persephone mused.

"I thought you said we were all individuals."

"You are, but all Leaders share certain distinct qualities. You are of a kind, and all would love or hate one another if you were all trapped in the same room. Oh!" Her face fell. "You *are* all in a room together. All the Guard that ever were, now in prison. Darkness made a key for his dungeon. Made it from my tears." Her eyes narrowed, her beautiful face turned a terrible scowl.

"Terrible, terrible." In the next instant, she smiled and clapped her hands. "But let's take a look at the new sky we just fashioned as a protection! I've never done this in the mortal world; let's see how it turned out!"

Beatrice shook her head, not understanding most of what Persephone said and reeling from the shifts of the goddess's mood. The only thing consistent in Persephone's chimerical nature was that every action was underpinned with a sense of her love.

Outside, they found the sky changed indeed, gaining a layered, shimmering quality. The thick clouds were quick to cover the changes, blanketing all London in gray.

The goddess seemed satisfied, however. "My spell took! I'm rather pleased. Now. Back to the pitch and the murk. Be well," she called, threw her hand forward, her arm shuddering with effort, creating a black rectangle in the air, and she was again gone, leaving Beatrice full of dread in her wake.

CHAPTER
NINETEEN

THERE WAS NO LONGER ANY QUESTION; THE GRAND WORK WAS more difficult away from home. This was doubly frustrating for Beatrice, who had felt such pain in Cairo when the phoenix fire was ripped from the Whisper-world and transplanted. She'd assumed when she got to London she'd be twice the Leader for being near its source. Would that were so.

The work continued. Exorcisms in squalid rooms, chasing poltergeists down narrow streets, battling veritable spirit gangs that clogged alleys and arteries of the city, all of it took more time, energy, repetition, and brute force than it had in Cairo. Weeks felt like years.

There was a certain comfort in having most of her Guard at the ready there in the newly renamed Promethe Hall, in the upstairs sets of fine wood-paneled apartments. Never mind that Ibrahim had his quarters just down the hall or that they all parted whenever the work was through.

The academy was a bustling place, workers finishing up with spare yet elegant final touches. Now and then Beatrice spied the Quaker headmaster, Richard Thompson, and his niece, Rebecca, striding about the place with pride, joy, and admirable efficiency.

While Belle's gifts had made the Guard rather invisible to the goings-on around them, there was one exception.

Whenever Beatrice found herself in the path of Rebecca Thompson, the girl stared at her, narrowing her eyes as if struggling to place her. A powerful mind churned behind those young blue-gray eyes, and Beatrice wondered about what the goddess and Ibrahim had said. Did Intuitions know their own? Would there be a changing of the Guard here in London? What did that mean for Beatrice and her company?

With the Pull almost always in play, at times Beatrice would go out alone to do the Grand Work, if the disturbance was faint enough. Usually the correction would be simple, the admonishment of a spirit with a smack of blue fire.

Tonight, something wasn't right, and Beatrice knew it. So did Ibrahim, apparently, for he appeared at her side as she headed for Athens's great front doors. Without a second glance or a word of greeting between them, they had a cab brought round and set out in pursuit of the Pull.

"Highgate," Beatrice said to the driver. Then, to Ibrahim, "Shall I call the others? It isn't much."

Ibrahim blinked. "It may not be much, but we're not very good these days."

"Not here we aren't. You're right, we need all the help we can muster."

She closed her eyes and felt Ibrahim doing the same, reaching out. She allowed the Pull to take over her body and felt it ripple, the sensation unifying all six. The others would follow the call if her message could find its way through the thick London fog.

"How long can we—?"

Ibrahim finished her thought. "I daresay, if it's always this difficult on this shore, the Grand Work will kill us."

It was uncanny. For one who seemed so indifferent to her, he had an odd way of knowing her thoughts. She pretended to stare out the window, hiding her agitation, as questions of intimacy flooded her mind. Suddenly she wasn't worried about how long their little coterie could withstand the forces of the Whisper-world; she wondered if he had been granted psychic abilities that he hadn't told her about. He was so quick to finish her sentences; was he as quick to know her secrets? That she often thought of him in quiet, private hours, when she lay in lacy robes mere meters away from his rooms?

She was a fool. Unknown horrors were afoot, and she was worried that a man who cared nothing for her might have some preternatural sense that she felt quite differently toward him? Absurd.

Straightening her posture, Beatrice recalled herself to the conversation. "The Work will kill us, you say? That's grim of you. We're not in tip-top form here in London, but we're not utterly outclassed."

"Don't you feel a great storm coming? Increasing havoc of the gods wreaked upon their pawns below?"

"Oh, I always feel a great storm coming." Beatrice chuckled. "It's my doom. I'm falling back into melancholic patterns of my childhood. Once a Hamlet, always a Hamlet."

"This is hardly about woman's frailty, Miss Smith," he argued. "Or Shakespearean hubris."

Beatrice grimaced at his words and tone, her eyes wide and her nostrils flared. "Must you have *no* humor in you whatsoever?"

"I'm talking of grave danger. My Intuition continues to feel it as it has since Cairo. You remember my trepidations. They have not lessened. You might make light of me, but you don't feel what I do. I lie with worry pressing like a demon down upon my chest, compressing the air in my lungs—"

"But *what* you intuit remains unclear! I do not deal in abstractions, Mr. Wasil-Tipton. Corporeal or incorporeal, I deal in what stares me down face-to-face. Until you give me more than 'a feeling in your bones of inclement weather,' I cannot sit entertaining your apocalypse-mongering.

"And *you!*" She turned her fury out the window to the mad-eyed ghost of a highwayman who rode alongside their carriage, brandishing a phantom knife he once used to relieve travelers of their purses or lives. "Find another maiden to frighten; you'll not get a rise out of me." She blasted the specter with blue fire, and his ghost horse reared and charged away. For a moment she regretted the action, but the carriage driver seemed not to notice anything amiss.

She hopped down from the conveyance when it jolted to a stop outside a great gate and, lifting her skirts, ran into the middle of Highgate Cemetery, tripping past eerily lit mausoleums, obelisks, and angels, a place lit in part by marble reflecting moonlight upon surrounding sandstone. However, the true lamps of the necropolis were the cluster of luminous gray dead who swayed and flapped their sagging mouths at a crossroads of cemetery paths.

"I'm sure these poor souls would agree with my sentiments, were we able to hear them," Ibrahim said mildly, catching up. Then he admonished the ghosts with a Buddhist proverb about detachment, addressing in particular those spirits clinging too tightly to specific monuments. They were likely attached to their bodies in the same way.

Beatrice ignored him, knowing her anger and frustration came from helplessness. Instead she worked her fire to best advantage. It was not enough.

The rest soon arrived. The ritual remained bogged down; they had a bit of trouble corralling their energy and focusing it, and it was as if they chanted their cantus from a faraway canyon where an echo muddied the effect. Still, while it was not perfect, they were able to get the task accomplished.

When the ghostly crowd had been thinned to a few floating specters who were scattered or who would prove quiet enough not to attract mortal attention when living family members came to grieve and lay flowers, Beatrice gestured her companions back to their carriages.

Mopping her brow with a kerchief, she resumed her conversation with Ibrahim, saying, "I will grant you, I agree that a Guard likely fights best in the city it calls home, not transplanted elsewhere. One always fights harder for one's home, does one not?"

"You'd consider Cairo your home, then?" He sounded surprised. "The city first in your heart, though it is not of your people?"

"Indeed. A golden home of richest beauty," she said earnestly, staring at him.

Ibrahim's generally inexpressive face showed subtle pride and distinct pleasure, making him even more handsome.

Staring out the window, not long after their carriage left from Highgate, Beatrice espied a grand estate, set back from the road a distance, its uppermost eaves silhouetted against the moonlit sky. It seemed uninhabited, with no lanterns lit at the gate or blazing at the doorstep. No curtains were drawn and the shutters were open, windows revealing a wide emptiness within. No. Not entirely empty. Something lent illumination. Beatrice called sharply to the driver, who halted at the edge of the estate's gravel walk.

"What is it?" Ibrahim asked.

"That house is calling us," Beatrice replied. "Something's inside; look at the light." She hopped down from the carriage and walked quickly toward building, seeing eerie, changing colors emanating from within.

PERSEPHONE HAD BEEN AT THE MESSY BUSINESS OF PINS AGAIN and now stumbled, dizzy and bleeding, into the mortal world, landing on the floor of an empty house. The regal structure appeared to have just been finished or renovated. Out the front windows she saw an impressive heath. Behind, a small grove of trees and a stable.

With no idea where she was, she assumed the Liminal had brought her here for a reason. To heal, surely, but for some other reason, too. The sky looked like England. The air tasted so. She allowed herself a moment of pleasure. This country had become as much a home as any place ever, because it was where hope lived.

Her head and heart heavy, she lay on the floor and allowed the miasma of Whisper-world despair to drain away. The strain of leaving her blood in such deep, dark places felt ugly and hopeless. Only faith in her visions kept her from entirely losing her mind to shadow, and the best way to cleanse the tainted air in her lungs was through weeping. She felt warmth course down her cheeks; quicksilver pooled in her palm.

Her tears formed a ring. A small, delicate silver ring in the shape of a feather, its quill meeting its tip.

"Oh," she murmured. "That's quite nice . . ."

Then she curled up on the floor to recover.

"WAIT HERE," IBRAHIM INSTRUCTED THE DRIVER.

He caught up to Beatrice at the door as she lifted the heavy knocker and let it fall. No answer. Trying the lock, she found it open and stepped through. The inside of the home proved empty, but there was light down the hall.

The two made their way toward it. At the end of the corridor they found Persephone lying huddled upon the parlor floor, her eyes pouring strange, reflective tears. It was her ever-changing light that filled the room with different colors.

"My Lady." Beatrice stepped closer.

The goddess looked up, startled, then relaxed again. "Hello, Beatrice, Ibrahim, how good of you to come," she said in a small voice.

"What . . . what are you doing here?"

"I don't rightly know. But I feel this is a special house. I'd like to live here. I want to be here. I care so very much about the mortal world and what happens here. I keep seeing a mortal in my visions, someone who is not a member of my Guard. I don't know who he is. I've seen him, I know his first name, but he's not here. There are so many things I don't know. Don't mind me; pouring my warm blood onto cold stones is so very taxing. I need to rest."

She curled up and closed her eyes, loosing an ugly, rattling cough into her arm. Apart from the maturity of her body, she looked like a helpless, gorgeous child.

"My Lady." Beatrice bent and reached out as if to press comfortingly upon her shoulder. The goddess held up a hand to halt her. "Please. I . . . I simply need to rest. I can only heal in this world. Do not worry. Please go."

Not knowing what else to do, Beatrice walked away. Ibrahim silently followed, closing the door behind them. He hadn't said a single word, so when she turned to him, she was shocked to find tears in his eyes.

He cleared his throat. "To see an angel so distracted and broken . . . It shakes a man to the core. If a being so lost is what protects the afterlife of mortals, the Guard in particular, then what have we to look forward to?"

Beatrice set her jaw. "She's right. She needs to take her next step, do something different, take another form. She needs to do it before she has no mind or energy left. I just hope she knows *how*."

PERSEPHONE HAD NO SENSE OF HOW LONG SHE'D BEEN ON THE floor of this beautiful dwelling, empty, waiting. When she roused and found herself still there, she begged for a sign. Since the Liminal had been taking unprecedented interest in and care of her of late, she hoped it might answer. If not the Liminal, then perhaps her own visionary gifts might channel help . . .

Her eyes clouded as a vision filled her. The night was suddenly day, and there was a man at the door, looking out at the garden. Tall and sharp-featured, with a mop of black hair and a black frock coat, she knew him: the man her mysterious Alexi would become.

So this grand house was—or would be—his? His eyes were dark, but they sparkled fondly, a contrast to his set jaw and pursed lips. This brooding man had found joy in something.

He stepped onto the veranda. Persephone saw herself in the garden. Well, not herself. Bright white, colorless, eerie; that self she saw only with her own eyes. But that mirrored self was smiling. She was deliriously happy as she ran to him.

The vision made her weep: Alexi embracing a porcelain crea-ture that the world would undoubtedly deem strange and suspect. But to him she clearly was perfection, as he drew back to kiss her passionately. Persephone's body ached with a fire her ghostly beloved could not quench, a need that had not been tended for millennia. She wanted to be touched again, kissed again. Like *that*.

Alexi scooped up the girl and carried her into the house, and Persephone wanted to be her more than anything in the world. The vision faded. The house lay empty about her.

"Laws of the mortal world, as your laws are different than that which governs me," Persephone prayed, "be with me now. Show me the ways in which I may serve you, you, my dark-haired destiny. You are Phoenix and he is you. I *see* you. I *see* me. Come to me."

Still in pain and exhausted, she curled tighter into a ball, clutch-ing the ring made from her tears.

The next thing she knew, she was roused to a bright day by carriages clattering outside. She glided to the window to see a family arriving, their carriages laden with trunks and parcels. A tall, dis-tinguished man with dark features disembarked from the first car-riage and helped a similarly striking woman down. They looked familiar . . .

A black-haired youth descended from the second carriage, an adolescent garbed in dark clothes suited to someone much older. He turned before the goddess could see and assisted a young lady exiting the vehicle. Surely she was the daughter of the fine couple from the first carriage; their striking grace and compelling airs were all of a piece.

The girl of eighteen stared up at the estate, the expression on her thin face shifting from stern to enthralled. Hiking up her layered gray skirts, she darted toward the front stoop, her boots clipped upon the flagstones. The boy turned to follow.

A sound tore from Persephone's throat, a gasp of gratefulness, joy, and hope. Birds in the garden began to sing.

"It's *you*," she breathed. Her heart was in her throat. He had come to her, just as she had begged last night. "Dear one, it's you . . ."

Of course, it would not do for the family to arrive to find her. Not in her present form. She glided swiftly up the banister to watch from above and shifted her robes to make herself invisible.

"Alexi," the girl called as the two ran into the house and began quickly exploring the downstairs rooms, "there's a grand study on this side; Father will be so pleased. There are so many shelves! Father can't use them all for his books alone, so surely there's room for your collection, too. And your desk."

"I should hope so," Alexi replied. Neither he nor his sister spoke with even the light German accent of their parents, meaning they'd been in England for some time; the goddess remembered the Liminal showing their move years prior. Why hadn't Persephone found him before now?

She watched as he poked his head into each downstairs room and glanced out the bay window below the stairs, moving with purpose and determination. He was a born Leader. Persephone desperately wanted his dark eyes to find hers, for him to know her for who she was, to love her as she loved him, but she would not interfere. Not until she could be certain the time was right.

The young man turned to address the man at the door. "Quite satisfactory, Father. A good choice of property, indeed." His quiet mother gave a slight smile and slid her arm into her husband's.

"As it shall be yours one day, I suppose it ought to meet with your approval, young master," his father said. "I hope it stands up to your keen inspection."

Alexi turned to the stairs. "You'd best be at my heels to pick a room, Alexandra, else I'll choose a closet for you."

The girl shrieked with an excited giggle, darting up the stairs. "Wait for me!" She paused at the top to look down. "Oh, Alexi!

Just look at the foyer, why, it's large enough to dance in. I'll teach you to waltz."

Alexi stared at her with disdain. "I'm going to be an academic. What need have I for dancing?"

"You will thank me for it one day, you mark my words," Alexandra declared. When Alexi shrugged and turned away, she chased him down the hall.

Persephone moved out of sight, gliding onto a balcony, where she let the sun blend her body with the sky. She watched fondly as brother and sister moved through the rooms and stared out the windows. Her breath caught when Alexi's dark eyes once gazed right through her. Perhaps it was wistfulness that made her see longing in those intelligent eyes, a particular longing for the future. A new life was indeed about to begin for the Rychman family, whether they knew it or not. She would keep the others ignorant, but perhaps Alexi could know . . .

A loud beating of wings drew Alexi's attention to the ravens alighting on the tree beside her. A squawk sounded at Persephone's ear; one large, regal raven stared at her, its black eyes oddly sentient. Persephone reached out her hand.

"Hello, herald," she murmured as the bird leaned toward her fingertips. "Shall you help us? We've much to do to knit a new family together."

The bird gave a rasping cry.

The wind picked up, and a patch of plumage on the raven's breast burned a sudden, shocking blue. The surprising sight sent a rush of powerful, intoxicating hope through Persephone's slender body. Suddenly she was more certain than ever that sometime very soon Alexi Rychman would indeed become Leader.

Persephone entered the house again, taking care to remain unseen, and drifted back to the parlor, where she found a familiar figure: Alexi's grandmother.

The woman cocked her head to the side as if sensing something.

She then spoke in rapid Russian. "When will you make him a Leader? I've demanded your attention."

Persephone felt her heart leap into her throat as she realized the woman was addressing her directly.

The powerful old woman continued, "I know who you are. He told me about the light changes, the floral scent with a sour undercurrent. Something jarring. Pomegranate, yes? I know you are here even if I cannot see you."

The goddess hesitated only for a moment, then slid her robe from her head and became visible.

"Hello," she said. "This is most unexpected."

Alexi's grandmother's almost smiled—a corner of her mouth twisted in amusement. "Yes, you are likely only known to a select few. A special six."

Persephone gasped. Alexi hadn't been taken yet, so he couldn't know any of this. He couldn't have told anyone anything. How did this uninitiated commoner know the secrets of—

"It was Dmitri Sergeyevna, in Moscow, who told me about you. He was a brilliant Leader, was he not? Did he not save your life, once?" Persephone gaped at her. "I know. The Guard is not supposed to share the Grand Work with any uninitiated, and I was *not* a member of that Moscow Guard.

"But I loved Dmitri more than life itself. I could not have him. Not by your decree but by that of my country. I, Katarina Novodevichy, was born high class; Dmitri Sergeyevna, a stable boy. But the Grand Work made that stable boy into a king, and I will forever worship you for it."

Katarina's eyes misted, and for a moment she was far away. "Dmitri and I loved each other since childhood. The night before I was forced to marry the aristocrat I never loved, I presented myself to him. I prayed for a child to come from that sacred night together, a testament to true love foiled by imprisoning society. And a child did. Irina, Alexi's mother. My husband never knew, and neither did Dmitri.

"It was best that way; it would have killed him to be away from her, and he had his Work. Irina was and remains a gentle but frightened creature; she inherited none of her father's strength. But now I have a grandson. Such a boy—he is magnificent and you know it. So, when will it happen? The Phoenix is now his birthright."

Persephone stood, stunned. "Soon," she finally said. "I believe it will happen soon."

"Good. Then I can rest in peace. I live only for the moment my grandson inherits his glory, and then these weary bones can rest. Dmitri will come for me, and our spirits will not pass on but instead travel the world in eternal adventure, together at last. I've seen to it Alexi will be well provided for, but it's up to you to make sure my firebird ascends his throne."

She walked away, leaving Persephone to contemplate the wonderful webs that certain mortals could spin. Apparently even gods could be drawn into them.

IBRAHIM WAS PULLED FROM A DISTURBING TREATISE ON INDUS-trialization as Ahmed shot up from the chair in which he'd been dozing. The library in the Apollo wing of Athens was where Ibrahim was most comfortable, surrounded by books, and the colleagues took near constant refuge there.

"The dream again? The war in the ground?"

"No." Ahmed shook his head. "I could hardly see anything, but the word 'betrayal' kept echoing in my mind, over and over again, like some thunderous bell. I fear there is a veritable battalion of betrayals ahead, and I don't know what that means. Do the bells of dread toll for us or for the goddess? What does Intuition tell you?"

"My feelings are muddy, though they concur with your visions. But for which of us, I cannot say."

"Then it must not be about us. It's about the future." Ahmed paused. "Often those with gifts see more of others than themselves. All we can do is share our prophecies and dreams. The great mysteries must use us as they will."

Ibrahim shook his head, baffled by Ahmed's genuine acceptance of their state. "You see such horrors, and yet you remain the most joyful soul I've ever known. How can you welcome such visions and remain so unscarred?"

Ahmed shrugged. "One must meet Darkness with joy. It lessens his power. That is the simplest element of my Heart-shaped gift, which I do not question. I lead a simpler existence for that. You could make the same choice."

Ibrahim chuckled.

"What?" Ahmed asked. "What is it? Did I say something amusing?"

"I'm just . . . I am not built as you." Ibrahim shook his head. "But I am very glad to know you, Ahmed. The world is better because you are in it."

Ahmed's smile was radiant. "True friendship is life's greatest commission. That, and true love. You have allowed yourself the former, and I am honored—blessed by it, even. But now you must allow yourself the latter. You don't have far to look."

Ibrahim quickly turned the tables. This was disquieting territory. "Your commission, surely, is Verena. It's obvious. You're sickening together."

Ahmed looked taken aback, but when Ibrahim offered a slight smile, he gave a joyous laugh. "Yes, she is heaven!"

Then they mused, as they often did, on beautiful women. Ahmed waxed rhapsodic on Verena, but Ibrahim spoke in vague terms, theorizing about hypothetical females, lest Ahmed force him into speaking about someone he was far too frightened to admit he adored.

PERSEPHONE FINISHED PLACING HER BLOOD ON YET ANOTHER seal. She knew better than to linger, so she went right to the Liminal edge, certain it would whisk her away to safely heal. After the last journey, she trusted it like never before. At that gorgeous proscenium, she found she had company.

"Aodhan. I didn't expect to see you here. Are you keeping safe?"

"I don't stray far from the Liminal. Darkness and his minions don't like it here, I've noticed."

"They don't understand this place. They fear it, and we must keep them fearing it."

Aodhan nodded, dazed. "I keep staring into this void, and sometimes I glimpse an image. I think it wants to tell me something . . ."

"Ask it." Persephone gestured, the motion casting the light of her colors ahead of her like ripples through a still stream. "Ask the Liminal what it wants you to see. It listens closely to those who were mortal."

Obedient, Aodhan said, "Tell me. Show me what you need me to see."

Apparently a request was all that was needed. A scene leaped to life; the clock above the proscenium remained still, meaning mortal time remained unchanged.

"Where is that?" Aodhan breathed, staring at a massive, sprawling, sparkling, shifting city.

"Welcome to London," Persephone replied, glancing at the Liminal clock for confirmation. "It is the current mortal year, 1867."

From her experience, it looked like morning on the crowded docks of the Thames. An overfilled boat tumbled passengers out onto the landing, and the Liminal focused upon a specific disembarking family. From their clothing, they appeared without much means. The father's face was hard, the mother's aglow with excitement and fear. Their daughter glanced around in unabashed wonder.

"Oh," Aodhan breathed, staring. The adolescent, her hair in a golden braid down her back, was broad-shouldered and sturdy, with fair skin and an engaging face. When she smiled, she was radiant. "Why, she's so much like my Brigid," he murmured, a tear rolling down his phantom cheek.

"Who was Brigid?" Persephone asked.

"A lass from the village. She wasn't Guard. I . . . I saw her nearly every market day, from when I was a wee lad into my old age. She was such a good woman, a right saint. I was too afraid that she'd think the Grand Work was witchcraft to ever say more than a few words to her. But, oh, how she'd talk to me. And how her eyes would smile. *That* smile." He pointed at the young woman whose eyes were still drinking in London. "She never married, Brigid. She never did. I wonder . . ."

The girl seemed to stare right at him, her rich green-hazel eyes sparkling. Both Aodhan and Persephone caught their breath. For the goddess, it was much like her encounter with Katarina Novodevichy and Alexi. Was this girl, too, fated for something special?

Aodhan exhaled, a soft, amazed sound. His hand lifted, glowing with a Healer's light.

"The circle is complete" came a distinct whisper. "They are now assembled. It is time."

Persephone's shifting color drained until she was as ghostly as Aodhan.

"I know that voice," Aodhan said.

"It's the Muse—your Muse, the Healer." Persephone choked. Her hues returned as she began to wring her hands, unsure whether to be excited or worried.

"But it never speaks . . ." Aodhan said slowly. "Only in death do they speak, or during . . ."

"The changing of the Guard. It's happening again, now, in London."

"But didn't you recently take a set in Cairo?"

"Yes, and transported them to London to help prepare—"

"We cannot ask our current hosts to relinquish their beloved Cairo" came the Muse's breathy explanation. "Their hesitancy shows in their Work and the Balance suffers for it as they do. We require those who call *London* home, in their hearts and until their end of days, and you, Our Lady, you don't have much time . . ."

Floating into view was the hazy, incredible form of the healing Muse, all starlight and music, glimmer and spirit. When the being floated across the Liminal threshold, the great wind that always signaled a new taking began to blow. It turned toward Persephone. "Are you coming, my Lady?"

Persephone swallowed. "Of course."

Aodhan stammered. "B-but this is—"

"Unprecedented," Persephone and the Healer Muse chorused.

"What of this girl?" Aodhan asked the Muse, reaching out a desperate, glowing hand toward those bustling docks beyond. "What do you intend for her?"

"She will be a Healer like you," the glorious form replied. "She will need your help. She is too young, but she will do. They are all too young, but they all must do." The Muse turned to Persephone. "Especially your new pet, my Lady."

It laughed, a tinkling sound. "Come. I'm the first to go. Your Phoenix will be reeling, but we will soon begin and he'll have no choice but to follow."

CHAPTER
TWENTY

THE DAY BEGAN MUCH LIKE THE DAY THEY WERE POSSESSED, the day they were made the Guard. An uneasy day where the wind was restless. Beatrice knew what the odd wind was, but she couldn't be sure what it was up to. They had already been found, she and her companions. What was that force looking for now?

It wasn't the Pull that drew her to Westminster Bridge. Not exactly. It was pain. What had begun like a familiar beating of wings in her veins had become a bird struggling, panicking to get out. Their Muses were rebelling.

Ibrahim and Verena stood at the crest of the bridge, having felt the Pull before her.

"The lack of our native soul is taking its toll, surely. Just like Ibrahim said," Verena suggested quietly, mournfully. She stared at Beatrice, puzzled. "And yet for you this *is* your native soil. Do you feel the pain I feel in my veins?"

Beatrice stared at her, then at silent Ibrahim, who appeared nauseated with worry. "I don't denounce my heritage, but Cairo is my home," she replied. "Yes, there is a fire inside me, a pain I've never felt. The sensation of our possession but in reverse."

Verena whimpered. "Are our gifts faltering? Perhaps none of this was meant to be."

"It's what I was afraid it would be," Ibrahim said.

Beatrice shrugged. "None of this has proven predictable. Even our Lady couldn't be sure what event would beget what. All we know is that something is about to change."

"Where, then, is she? Where is our Lady?" Verena asked.

The others of the Guard appeared, drawn by the same call. Verena's uneasy query was answered. Light swept over them. The goddess had arrived.

"Something is about to happen," she said, looking overwhelmed and excited.

"Why, thank you," Ibrahim muttered. "I'd never have guessed."

"We are in an unprecedented age," Persephone went on. "A prophecy is at hand!"

There was an explosion of light, familiar, warm—their Lady's light. Then they realized it was a different light, one they'd never actually seen, though it had once overtaken them, unawares. The six stared at the glow, absorbing the sight of what had possessed them, what had only moments ago been inside them, shimmering iridescence, now . . . outside, having peeled away.

Beatrice felt the phoenix fire rip from her veins and stumbled forward onto Ibrahim's outstretched arm. She saw her companions wince or recoil as the Muses, vaguely humanoid forms, were torn free from their bodies.

The sparkling, effervescent beings stared down at their former hosts. Their energies seemed kind, loving, and pleased, but they were moving on. So soon. Too soon? The six could do nothing to stop them. The spirits and their accompanying mass of winged blue fire tore off through London.

"Unprecedented," Persephone murmured, staring longingly after them. "I'm sorry, I must go," she cried, with a last look at the six mortals who had been left behind, before she vanished.

Belle began to cry. "I do not understand."

"It would seem we were useless. The spirits are finding better candidates," Ibrahim stated, his voice hard, his expression conflicted.

"Now what?" George asked. A mad smirk toyed at his mouth.

Perhaps, Beatrice agreed, it *was* best to laugh. Was it not best to be rid of this burden that was so hard to grasp? Yet was something still expected of them? And what of their lives? What would fill the resulting void?

WHEN THE UNPRECEDENTED HAPPENED, HE WAS STUDYING IN Mr. Absolom's secret laboratory, working on what he hoped would become a revelation of multiple alchemical chain reactions. The revelation he received was of a far different nature.

Alexi Rychman had been a lonely child, prone to obsessive reading and study. At age seven, his timid mother proclaimed him too intent and intelligent for her comfort. After that, he spoke rarely to his parents, instead reserving his limited energy for socialization to his sister and grandmother.

It was his apprenticeship with Mr. Absolom that had drawn his family to London from Germany eight years earlier, and he felt his parents resented him for it. But it was Katarina Novodevichy whose wealth provided for the family's comfort, so it was she who made decisions. In gratitude and out of love, Alexi strived to live up to her expectations and felt he had succeeded by all estimations.

As he supposed many intelligent children did, he found numbers, powders, charts, and books more agreeable than people. In the few moments when he cast detachment aside, he would smile at his grandmother, and she would grow misty-eyed and say something in Russian about the grandfather he never knew, claiming that there was hope for him yet. Katarina had always been his champion—in fact, Alexi's earliest memory was of her staring at him with an intent look, murmuring that he would grow up to be very powerful.

On this fateful day, something very powerful indeed was making itself known. Alexi heard a rush of wings, felt a strong breeze, and for just a moment thought that perhaps his alchemical powders were indeed blazing the trail to a new discovery.

"Hello, Leader" came a firm voice, speaking in a strange language he somehow understood. Looking up from his work, Alexi realized with a start that he was surrounded by blue fire. "This is the only time you will hear my voice, so listen close. You are a chosen one. *The* chosen one. What tops the alchemical pyramid? Me.

"The Grand Work begins, and the vendetta shall end with you. Treat her well, and make us proud." These cryptic words were accompanied by an incredible sensation of power, joy, wisdom, and freedom. An ancient, righteous fury told him he was now a defense against evil, a mortal angel in a grand tradition . . .

Terror struck him, and Alexi jumped back, running his hands down his black suit as if brushing off the intruder. In the next instant, something dulled his fear of this overtaking energy: the sudden knowledge that at the heart of it, whatever now held him in thrall was inherently good.

He had to get to Westminster Bridge. There could be no delay.

The sight of his laboratory table struck him with regret. What about the great work he'd been studying? Would alchemy be supplanted by this Grand Work? Was he no longer his own man? Was his love of science to be sacrificed on the altar of this new duty?

Alexi left Absolom's offices on Baker Street, his wide eyes filled with phantasmal sights. The dead were everywhere, floating along the busy streets, hovering in bustling doorways. As he passed, walking slowly to a new life, they bowed to him as if he were royalty. A force urged him forward like a bridled horse to Westminster— though a secondary desire burgeoned in Bloomsbury. Something important awaited him there, too: In his blood a treasure map burned and mysteries called to him in voices that he could not deny.

His heartbeat echoed with five others. The word "Leader" echoed in his ears like a betrothal promise. Alexi knew, with startling certainty, that by the time he reached Westminster Bridge and connected with those other hearts, he would have left boy-hood behind and donned the mantle of a man.

HIDDEN FROM EVEN THE MOST SKILLED MORTAL EYE, PERSE-phone kept to the shadows, watching as the fire overtook him.

His intent young face displayed a new gravity as well as the wonder and terror she recognized from her visions. She felt his heart throb and thrum with new force. Such was always the case, but never before had so much been on the line, and never before had she had such personal investment in the Leader.

As she followed him out into the packed, dirty, gorgeous streets of London, she knew there had never been a better time to weave the fabrics of the two worlds together. Gazing about the manic city, she felt a thrill of anticipation. Theater bills announced the appear-ances of mediums and magicians; bookstands teemed with tracts on Spiritualism and séances. Lecture halls were filled with after-life postulation. Paintings, sculptures, prints, and cards depicting mythological creatures and gods like Persephone herself were fawned upon by the educated and the mere titillated alike.

It was right that she claimed this world as her own. This gilded age understood sumptuous, glorious beauty, the rites and righ-teousness of spring. It also understood the dark, purgatorial whis-pers that defined the other part of her existence. Here and now, even as a mortal, she could be a child of two worlds. This grim and glorious age was her chance to live, love, and die as mortals did. It was an era tailor-made for her and for the Grand Work.

Provided she could follow through with the task, the exact de-tails of which yet eluded her.

At Westminster, the blue-breasted raven was hovering over five of the six chosen mortals, examining them. They gathered in a circle on the embankment, waiting for their Leader. The five were nervous, excited and . . . too young . . . but time wasn't on anyone's side at the moment. As Alexi approached, the sharp girl from the Quaker meetinghouse, the tall and spindly brunette, drank him in as if he were ambrosia. Ibrahim had rightly pinned her as Intuition.

Ibrahim. Beatrice, Persephone thought. Where were her other Guard? She'd left them there at this very bridge where they had been called; why weren't they here to see this torch carried?

Alexi spoke in a mature voice. "Good day. My name is Alexi Rychman, and this has turned into the strangest day of my life."

He and Rebecca Thompson gazed at each other, he the Leader, she his second-in-command. Rebecca blushed. Persephone's heart sank, for this Intuition would live heartbroken; she was not the companion of Alexi's future.

"Hello, Alexi," she said. "I'm Rebecca, and I feel the same."

"Elijah," spoke up a thin, blue-eyed blond boy garbed in striped satin finery that bordered on the absurd. He was the Memory, and he and the Artist regarded each other with subtle curiosity.

"Josephine," said the Artist in a soft French accent. Her lovely, youthful face was framed by two shocks of white hair. Persephone wondered if the Taking had caused them. Sometimes the process had such effects: Eyes changed color, mortals grew more beautiful, more intelligent, more fearsome, whatever traits heightened their powers.

Alexi had been compelling from the first, but as Leader his presence was inescapable. Persephone nearly revealed herself, over-eager to address them. But she had to pick her best moment.

"Michael," chimed in a sturdy boy with a grin that rivaled Ahmed's. The Heart, a strapping, broad-shouldered youth with ruddy cheeks and the contagious smile that distinguished Hearts from all others, he stared at Rebecca as if dazzled by her prim grace. His oceanic blue eyes were full of wonder.

"Lucretia Marie O'Shannon Connor," said a dusky blond girl in an Irish accent. She stared at the cobblestones, her hair falling to hide what was a fair but frightened face. Her plain dress spoke of modest means. This was the Healer, the one Aodhan had seen. "I suppose you could call me Jane if that's easier," she murmured with a shrug.

The flaxen-haired Elijah laughed. "I'll say."

Alexi's voice was firm. "And here I thought all my life I'd be a scientist. It seems forces at large have other plans. I don't suppose any of you has the slightest idea what we're supposed to *do*?"

Everyone shook their heads.

Give it time, Persephone wanted to urge. *Trust your instincts.* But that was for them to know, not to be told. She walked a fine line with every Guard; they had to learn to trust their own burgeoning talent in order to truly own their Muses' gifts.

Alexi continued. "Then let me ask a mad question. Does anyone, all of a sudden, see ghosts?"

"Yes!" everyone chorused. Their relief was palpable.

"Can you hear them speak?"

"No" came the universal reply.

"Neither can I, thank God, or we'd never have another moment's peace." Alexi glanced around, sighing. Persephone had witnessed many a Taking, and the scripts were always similar, the mortals struggling to comprehend so many foreign sensations colliding at once.

The raven above fixed its black eyes upon her, seeing, as animals did, past the robes that hid the goddess. Rebecca pointed to the bird, which began to fly away, and the group followed it toward Bloomsbury. It was good that this Guard had a familiar to join them; they'd need all the help they could muster.

The city engulfed them. On they walked, toward Athens Academy, Persephone trailing behind. The empty building would open to students within the year, but for now it was theirs. The sacred space awaited them.

Persephone was fraught with worry for Beatrice and *her* Guard. Had they returned to their rooms at Athens, feeling strangely hollow? It was unprecedented to have one Guard replaced with another in this manner, and she was certain there would be great confusion if they met. Perhaps bitterness. No, this was for the best. The two groups needed to steer clear of each other.

To make sure of that, she would have to release Beatrice's Guard from service, get them back to their lives. But Beatrice had become an integral part of her equation. Persephone frowned. The tasks before her were many, and she had no idea how to delegate.

Alexi had already begun to master the phoenix fire. He was proficient enough to open the sacred space, and it was there that the goddess would reveal herself and name each of their individual powers. Like she always did. But this time was different. This time was Prophecy. This time would be the last.

Opening a portal between the worlds, she stood upon its threshold to reveal herself to them, framed by the darkness of the Whisper-world. The jaws of the Guard dropped in wonder.

"My beloveds," she began, "I've not much time, but I must inaugurate you as I have done since your circle began the Grand Work in ancient times. There has never been a more crucial age than this one—this century, this city. Your world is filled with new ideas, new science, new ideas on God and the body . . . and most important, spirits. There's never been such talk of spirits."

She turned to Alexi, willing him to know her heart. She was terribly nervous. "Alexi, you are Leader here. Inside you lives what's left of my true love, the first phoenix born of ancient times. His great power was splintered, not destroyed. It is your tool. You control the element and are born again within it. My love lives in you, worthy Alexi, and you will fight Darkness by bearing the eternal flame of our vendetta."

She proceeded through the annunciation, giving each their titles, instructions, and duties. Then she thought of Darkness's threat to rip the worlds apart for her. It was time to change the usual script.

"Hold fast, for the struggle will worsen," she warned. "Darkness will seek to destroy the barrier between worlds. To fight this, Prophecy must be fulfilled. A seventh member must join you. She will come as your peer to create a new dawn."

Persephone glanced behind her, wincing, feeling the Whisperworld lurch in her blood, demanding that she step back into the darkness. But the threshold was different than it had ever been; it sparkled with a very familiar light. The Liminal was present.

As if sensing her discomfort, Alexi rushed forward. Normally she would have welcomed his aid, but now she stilled him with a hand. "You must understand," she said, "once the seventh joins you, it will mean war."

"Who are you?" Alexi asked.

The yearning in his voice made her ache—and smile. Her next words weren't delivered as planned. "I hope you will know her when she comes, Alexi, my love. I hope she will know you, too."

She. For some reason, the goddess could not say "I."

Something was disrupting her speech, allowing Prophecy to take on a life of its own. The interference was troubling, for Persephone desperately wanted to offer Alexi Rychman promises of love and happiness and knowledge that whatever sacrifices he made for the Grand Work would not be in vain.

It was the Liminal, she realized. In its infinite wisdom, it wanted Prophecy played out entirely by mortals. All would be left to chance, will, and mortal hearts.

"Await her," she continued, hearing herself speak words she did not intend to utter. "But beware. She'll not come with answers but be lost, confused. I have put protections in place, but she will be threatened and seeking refuge. There shall be tricks, betrayals, and second guesses. Caution, beloved. Mortal hearts make mistakes. Choose your seventh carefully, for if you choose the false prophet, the end of your world shall follow."

All she could promise was hope. Not herself. Not the girl she had seen. Just hope. And she had to hope, as well, hope that he would fall in love with her like a normal mortal man would.

She immediately regretted what she'd begun to cherish. This could lead to such madness and pain. She'd been running after phantom visions, forcing them to come true. But Pandora's box was open and Hope was the only thing left inside.

"A sign!" the Heart insisted, sturdy, amiable Michael. "Surely there will be a sign. When will she come? How will we know what to fight against?"

"You'll be led to fight the machinations of Darkness by instinct. But you shall not always be fighting," she assured them, knowing there was yet time. "You are also as you were. Your mortal lives and thoughts remain unchanged, though augmented by spirits."

She thought a moment, wondering what she could promise them. What had been consistent in her visions?

"Look for a door. Something like this"—she gestured to indicate the portal—"should be your gauge. But don't go in." She gave the Whisper-world a baleful glance. "You wouldn't want to come here. You'll see this threshold together, all of you. I cannot say precisely when your seventh will come. I'm powerful, but only the great cosmos is omnipotent. But she will be placed in your path. And once she is, you won't have much time before a terrible storm arrives."

In the distance Persephone heard barking. The dog. He had sniffed a threshold held open too long and now moved to guard it.

She heard Alexi ask her name. Guards always asked her name. They had a right, but one name was such a limiting thing. "It hardly matters. We've had so many names through the years, all of us."

Yet, to mortals, a name was so important. Staring at Alexi, at his worried, amazed face, she was compelled to offer one final caution. If she couldn't give him certainty, at least she could give him this: "Please be careful. Listen to your instincts and stay together. A war is coming, but it isn't what you think. Hell isn't down, it's around us, pressing inward. Your seventh must be there when it comes, or she will have died in vain."

"Died?" Alexi cried.

"One must die to live again," she said. Then she blew him a kiss as the portal snapped shut. She could keep it open no longer, not with the Whisper-world monsters on their way.

Trapped again in shadows, the goddess sighed and slid to the ground, her back against the stone wall, her head in her hands. Moisture kissed her skin with dread. She'd not thought of death until the word left her lips. She supposed it was her turn to be a phoenix and rise from ashes.

CHAPTER
TWENTY-ONE

STILLED BY SURPRISE AND PAIN, BEATRICE WATCHED THE GLIM-mering, iridescent forms of the phoenix fire and its attendant Muses as they swept from her and her Guard and scattered into the sky in a burst of angelic music. The Muses spread out across the city; the flame congealed into a large ball over the Thames. Like a growing azure sun, it suddenly burst into a wide-winged, glorious birdlike form.

Finding her voice, she shouted up at the great avian vision, "What? No parting words for your unwitting servants?"

The immense cerulean bird immediately descended, and a rumbling voice of thunder and stars, wind and sage calm, poured forth. "We are sorry. We forget mortal courtesy. You justly deserve every accolade, but our commission draws us onward. You have served valiantly and are rewarded with an early end to your duty. Go in peace."

The departing Muses darted to and fro, visible in the sky, before making dizzying dives toward what Beatrice assumed were new hosts. She wondered if her fellows felt as she did: hollow, wounded, and confused, like a child suddenly left alone in a crowd.

Though their powers had left them, their ability to see the dead had not. In fact, the dead seemed more present than ever, as if they, too, sensed the great shift.

Ibrahim moved toward Beatrice and reached for her, as if she could steady him. She yearned to take his outstretched hand, rare as such an offer was. Before she could move, she felt a sudden chill that rippled through her like a seizure.

The rest of Cairo's Guard obviously felt it, too. Ibrahim whirled, his eyes wide and his bronze skin pallid.

"Careful, we're vulnerable. Oh, no, this is the moment!" he wailed. "The moment of warning!"

A skeletal form appeared in their midst, clad in a rotting robe— the spirit that had followed them from Egypt. Its jaw sagging in a constant scream or some dreadful song, it had been waiting for an opportunity all along.

Ibrahim tried to intercede. "Verena!" he cried, throwing himself before her as if to stop a bullet or sword, but the transparent spirit passed right through him, seeking a more delicate, vulnerable target, as had been foreseen.

The phantasm hurled itself atop Verena, who cried out and collapsed. Her warm golden face instantly turned a glowing gray. She had become a darkly luminous case, endangered.

Ahmed caught her just before she dashed her head on the cobbles. With surprising strength, he lifted her and turned to the others. "We must get her to a doctor," he said in Arabic.

George shook his head. "No English doctor can treat this."

"To the academy, then," Ibrahim growled. "To the infirmary. If Muses are off to find a new Guard, they sure as hell better bring them back to us—and we can tell them a thing or two then."

Seeing that Ahmed would have trouble walking with his burden—he was sure to trip over Verena's dangling skirts—Ibrahim, a taller man, lifted Verena into his own arms, saying, "Allow me."

Beatrice noticed how the muscles of his neck strained and his knuckles went white. Verena was shaking violently in his hold and Ibrahim was holding on to her for dear life. The odd entourage set off at a quick pace.

"They're looking at us," George remarked. The Londoners around there were indeed staring at their motley cadre.

"I'm sorry, I can't turn them away," Belle said mournfully, holding up her powerless hands. She kept her tears silent, knowing they were of no aid. George grabbed one hand and dragged her along.

Beatrice fought back fury. Somewhere in this city, right now, was a new Guard who could help them. For all she knew, they might be crossing paths right now, missing one another by a few streets.

At last they reached Athens. The school was still boarded up, not scheduled to open for another few months. As they climbed the stairs, they felt pressed back, as if a great hand kept them at a distance. The air before the door was threaded by lightning and held a dim blue shimmer.

"What the hell is that?" George barked.

Beatrice's stomach fell and her anger soared. "The goddess put a protective barrier over the academy, presumably to keep out the wrong sorts."

Ibrahim growled. "We are no longer the Guard, and in our arms we have *exactly* the wrong sort."

The two of them shared a look of helpless fury. If they had struggled with the Grand Work before, they'd never felt so grievously wronged.

With Athens off limits, a chapel down the street seemed the safest bet. Their coterie ducked into the shadowed nave, grateful for empty pews bereft of inquisitive priests. Ibrahim laid Verena on one with a velvet cushion.

Verena's body lurched and her lungs rattled, the mysterious and horrible fluids that seemed inherent to possession welling from her eyes and down her nose. Ahmed, unflinching, wiped it all away with the sleeve of his tunic. Beatrice tore the hem of her skirt to provide more fabric, and Belle did the same, then walked away, her face showing the pain she felt, seeing her friend in such a state.

Beatrice sat and held Verena's shaking feet. Ahmed took her head in his lap, and Ibrahim knelt upon a padded cushion meant for prostration, trying to make sure she didn't fall off the pew. It seemed oddly fitting in that moment.

"Can you say anything to keep it at bay?" Beatrice asked, feeling useless. There was no power in her fingertips but they itched to cast out demons. She wondered if this phantom feeling of sensation was what amputees suffered, this awful yet certain feeling of something that was no longer there.

Ibrahim could not stop staring at Verena. "I . . . I've nothing. My library is gone," he said, looking as helpless as Beatrice felt.

Ahmed launched into a recitation of Rumi, hoping to ease her pain or at least distract her from it. No one could tell if it was working.

Ibrahim jumped up. "I'll go to the Athens library. If I do not have a library here"—he tapped his temple—"I shall re-create it. I'm harmless to the barrier on my own; I won't be shut out." He ran out.

Ahmed kept reciting poetry, offering verses he had written for Verena. She said nothing, only shuddered and wept noxious fluid, and Ahmed wept with her.

Soon Ibrahim returned, carrying an armload of tomes on faith and beauty. He took over for Ahmed, whose voice was growing increasingly faint. Ibrahim's was sure and clear, and the passages he chose were intelligent and to the point. Beatrice had never found herself admiring him more.

This might not cast out the demon, but it clearly kept the horrific thing from progressing in its evil work; they were not seeing in Verena the full extent of damage they had seen in others during their short time of service.

Beatrice turned to George, nodding to the still weeping Belle. "Take her elsewhere. She doesn't have to see this; there's nothing she can do. It's all right; we'll wait for the others."

"No," Belle said quietly. "The . . . *new ones*. I want to see them, too. I'm praying for them to come with every prayer I have."

"Then sit and try to calm yourself," Beatrice said firmly. "There is no sense in you suffering in addition."

Belle nodded and crossed to a baptismal alcove opposite, where she sat stiff vigil near a tomb. George flanked her, a silent sentinel much like the statue of the saint that bore his name, the patron of England who stood in grim marble triumph at the entrance to this place of worship.

Beatrice squeezed Verena's hand. "The goddess gave you a kiss of life, remember? Don't you dare forget it. That must count for something," she said. But truthfully, she felt they could only count on one another. Mortals were best looking out for themselves. But if Beatrice wasn't mistaken, at the reminder of Persephone's kiss, Verena's cold hand flickered a small ray of light.

EVERYTHING IN ALEXI'S BODY SCREAMED FOR HIM TO REMAIN with his new friends; everything in his heart screamed for the love of that unnamed goddess. His senses were reeling, and he wanted to go home. So he did.

He entered to find madness at his family estate. His sister lay broken in a heap on the floor, breathing shallowly and looking dazed, and his grandmother was wheezing like she was about to die of fright. The house looked like a storm had cut a swath through it, glass broken, vases overturned, doors unhinged.

Rushing to hold his grandmother, asking what had happened, all she offered were mad notions of demons and great winds tearing through the house; intimations of witchcraft.

"There's something different about you," she said, staring at him intently. Eyes widening, she exclaimed in Russian: "The firebird—that's it. A darkness comes, my boy. You must light the darkness with your fire." That cryptic instruction became her last words. She did not breathe again.

Alexi crumpled to the floor, staring at those most precious to him. The help came, made wailing noises, and at length went about sending for a doctor for Alexandra. They also shouted that a bed should be made up for the departed Katarina.

"What's happened?" whispered his elder sister. Though she was unable to move and the extent of her injuries was unclear, her mind seemed undamaged. She stared at Alexi, clearly trying to figure out what was different about him.

He wanted to answer with the only reply he had—"We're haunted, we're bloody cursed!"—but before he could, his head seared as if someone had split his skull. Gasping, he recoiled, and Alexandra put her hand to her mouth and did not say another word.

The staff returned; some took Alexandra off to her bed. Others were carrying off Katarina's dead body as Alexi struggled to his feet and backed away.

"I'm so sorry, I must go," he said, already knowing that he'd never forget the helpless, frightened look on his sister's pallid face.

The Pull had him, and it dragged him, with claws on his heart, back toward Bloomsbury. He should not, it seemed, have left his fellows. Everything and everyone he and the rest of the Guard once loved was now haunted and cursed, but he had no time to grieve. He was the firebird. He was Leader, so he'd better rise to the challenge. If he did not, his curse would surely worsen.

VERENA MADE A SOUND LIKE A GROWL OR A DOG'S BARK AS THE creature inside struggled to claim her completely. Belle wept softly against the baptismal font, George's white-knuckled hand on her shoulder, trying to be comforting. Time inched by. Ibrahim moved on to another tome.

"Should we move her?" Ahmed asked. "Try for a doctor?"

"They'll come," Beatrice stated, glancing at Ibrahim, who nodded.

"If I read whatever ghost of Intuition remains correctly," he added, "they'll come."

As if responding to his assurance, there came a sound, and the door was flung open. Beatrice held her breath. A young man, tall and black-haired, striking featured and dressed in fine but austere clothes, made his entrance.

A distinct wind picked up, filling her mind with a strange music that Beatrice knew well. The newcomer charged forward, blue fire trailing from his outstretched hands.

The new Guard.

Dear God, they were young, even the Leader. Fourteen, fifteen, perhaps? But his spirit was strong, Beatrice could feel the timelessness about him. Blue fire poured from his hands, and his fellows stared at him in awe and fear.

It will take getting used to, she wanted to say, but she couldn't even hail the newcomers, so entranced was she by their Leader. Beatrice wondered for a moment if she had ever looked so full of power, so *unbelievable* as this young man did now. Perhaps the Grand Work would always amaze, no matter who wielded it.

"Luminous," the Leader murmured, "I believe we call this a luminous case. A possession with intent to harm." The five youngsters gathered around, terrified acolytes.

Beatrice opened her mouth to say, *Yes, luminous! Help us, you hapless fools, then run for your lives! Damn this Work, it's nothing but a curse!* But no words escaped her.

She glanced at her fellows, who were all also staring at the other six, Guard to Guard, though no one said so. Ahmed and Ibrahim stepped back from Verena, clearing the way. Even as he moved, Ibrahim's attention was fixed on the spindly brunette at the new Leader's side. She was assessing the situation with a sharp, undaunted gaze. The Thompson girl was Intuition indeed.

A thin, blond boy in fine, if foppish, clothes stepped close and stared with apprehension at each of Beatrice's assembled company. "And I make them forget we're here . . . *how*?" he asked.

"I wasn't given a guidebook, Lord Withersby. Use your hands," the Leader retorted.

Beatrice smirked despite herself as the young lord waved a hand in front of her. Her thoughts and memories remained unchanged, but since the Cairo Guard were frozen and unable to participate, that was a moot point. Perhaps it was best, after all, that they stood there, staring. Beatrice had received no help when leading the Grand Work for the first time, so why should anyone else?

A dark-blond woman in a plain dress, blushing, knelt by Verena's bedside. "I'm so sorry for yer pain," she murmured in a soft Irish brogue. "My name is Jane, and I'll try an' help you like Alexi said." She rallied herself with a meek smile and held up her hand, which glowed with a flickering white luminescence.

Though it was pale and untrained, Verena seemed to recognize the light. Her pained expression eased, as did the tears coursing from her eyes.

Jane put her healing hand on Verena's forehead, and Verena's body was racked with a new seizure—the London Guard had hardly come to their first charge as experts. The work was progressing, however, and Alexi urged his power outward, commanding the phoenix fire to contain and extract the offending spirit. Beatrice prayed he could finish the job.

She wanted to tell him to stay steady, that results were not immediate. She couldn't know what he was thinking, of course. Nor could she really help. No one could tell you about the Grand Work—you had to feel it. You had to own it for yourself.

Beatrice was suddenly sure this was why none of them could offer instruction, encouragement, or reprimand; that would only get in the way. The goddess had said there were never two Guards. A Guard was always on its own. Some force beyond them had stilled their tongues to make sure of it.

The Intuition glided forward, a surprising air of elegant, refined grace about her for one so young. The Grand Work had aged them years in a less than single day, severed their innocence and youth. Beatrice remembered the very same happening to her.

"Lord Withersby," the Intuition began crisply, "if you and your touch might offer us some clue about the offender, I might be able to wield my newfound library to best effect."

The blond boy, the Memory, said, "Indeed, Miss Thompson, indeed." He stepped closer to Verena, angling past Jane and bending over her to speak softly to the suffering one. "My, you *are* beautiful, miss! Whatever brought you to England, this land of dreary gray, when you are a queen of a golden kingdom?"

"Miss Belledoux," Alexi called, "as you've not had time to produce a studio full of fine work, what do your Artistic instincts tell you about how you might be of service?"

The gorgeous brunette who had been studying Withersby snapped to attention. She thought a moment, then smiled and darted to procure a golden icon of a dove from the baptismal alcove; she kissed it softly and rejoined the circle with the icon in hand.

Beatrice watched, fascinated. She glanced at Belle, who was furrowing her brow as the Memory touched Verena's hand and winced in pain.

"Victim's name? Verena. Attacker violent," Withersby murmured. "Towers, shouting from towers . . . It's so angry, it has followed us, waiting for us . . ."

It was a muezzin, Beatrice yearned to say. *It followed us here, here where everything changed, here where the dead so terribly outnumber you . . .*

Perhaps there was divine commonality in the air, bringing them together, for Miss Thompson began to recite a verse Beatrice recognized instantly. Rumi. Ibrahim and Ahmed had tears in their eyes as she spoke with clarion confidence, and so did a strapping young lad who was circling his fellows and touching their collars.

It seemed the new Heart was an amiable, ruddy-cheeked and bushy-haired man, the sort you instantly wanted to be your friend.

The Heart bowed his head and bestowed his gift. "Lovely verse, Miss Thompson."

"Thank you, Mr. Carroll," the Intuition replied. To Beatrice's surprise, he blushed.

In the tumult Beatrice hadn't noticed until that moment that the air near them was shining with a strange light and carrying a vague, familiar scent. The goddess was present, hidden from view, managing the situation. *That's* why they were paralyzed, she realized, because Persephone likely knew they would tell these poor sots to run for their bloody lives. She was ensuring that the new Guard learned the Grand Work in their own way, undisturbed.

The new Artist set the icon hanging from the side of the pew to be in Verena's line of sight, then moved with fluid grace to Alexi's side. Beatrice saw George gaping at her. She *was* beautiful.

"Pardon me," the Artist said with gentle deference, and in a French accent, no less. She lifted the Leader's hand, which cupped a ball of blue fire, and blew the flames toward the dove. The fire nestled into the heart of the bird, and the icon lit, luminous from the inside, becoming a magic talisman. The girl repositioned Verena's head, saying "Gaze on that, dear."

Verena's rolling eyes steadied now that she had a point upon which to focus her strength. Beatrice wanted to look at the icon, too. The Grand Work was affecting them in the way they'd always affected others. At least in part.

"Simply brilliant," said Withersby, giving the Artist a wide, appreciative smile. She was clearly flattered by his approval. Beatrice saw couples forming within their group, just as they had for her company. Only their Leader stood apart, not struck by anything or anyone besides his purpose.

The possessing spirit made Verena flail her limbs, refusing to go quietly into any good night. Alexi narrowed his eyes, undaunted by the challenge, and began to experiment with his new power. He pressed the fire closer, moving it in; then he withdrew, gauging what the spirit did in reaction.

He looked like an orchestra conductor, Beatrice decided, which made her wonder what the Grand Work sounded like to spirits. To the Guard it was always wonderful, and even now she could faintly hear the music of the stars playing in her ears, though the song was different than it had been when she directed it herself. How did the notes sound to spirits? Terrible, like death knells? Or sweet, seducing them toward Peace?

"Quietus," Alexi said. "Thus is our cantus. I assume it is in your minds as well as mine?"

A burst of song was affirmation; the air was thick with magic. Beatrice fought against those enthralling strains, fought to clear her mind of the cosmic lullaby of wind and stars, wanting to shout that Quietus wasn't strong enough. But she couldn't. He'd have to learn on his own. This spirit was the first one her Guard had battled, in a Cairo alley. They'd failed, and perhaps it had grown stronger for its success.

Verena shuddered and convulsed, causing more tears to fall among the women and the men's faces to harden. She screamed in pain as the spirit ripped free, which surprised them all, but Jane was immediately responsive with a healing hand. The specter careened loose.

Alexi swiped at it with an impressive arc of fire, but it eluded him and vanished. "Damn!" He bellowed and flung open the church door, rushing into the lane to chase the monstrosity, but it was gone. Beatrice felt a small flare of satisfaction, seeing that the new Guard had proven unable to destroy it, either.

Then Alexi reentered, and Beatrice well remembered the frustration, shame, and sense of failure evident on his face. She did not wish that on anyone. "I didn't choose a strong enough spell," he said.

"I daresay we'll have another chance with that one," commented his Intuition.

The Heart rallied them. "The lovely lady is alive," he said, staring down fondly at Verena. "That, at least, is cause for celebration. We have not failed. The offender is gone. The rest we must leave to God and pray she heals completely."

Everyone nodded save Alexi, who did not seem convinced. None of them could be sure if lasting wounds and scars were left by hauntings. Beatrice certainly felt she'd never be the same for her experiences. No one in this room ever would.

"As you were!" Withersby cried to the room, waving his arms like a ridiculous puppeteer. The former and present Guards stared at one another for a long, uncomfortable moment. Withersby waved his fingers again for good measure. Belle looked like she wanted to laugh. Or cry. Both, likely.

Alexi turned to stalk to the front of the small church, a tormented scowl upon his young face. The Heart was by his side, asking his Leader, "What occurred in the hour since we parted? I feel your dread weight; what loss have you suffered?"

The Intuition was close by, too, concerned, and the rest fell in behind him. As they did Beatrice heard Alexi reply, his voice hard, "No matter. Life is but meetings and partings." And then the new Guard were gone from the building.

Beatrice whirled to the corner where the goddess had been hiding, ready to scream, but all signs of her had vanished. Good God, did the Grand Work cut its way into the world so ruthlessly each and every time? Who had poor Alexi lost today?

Belle's voice caught her attention: "Now what?"

"Back to Athens with Verena, and we keep watch until her dark night has completely passed," Beatrice replied.

"But the new Guard—"

"Came from all over the city. The sacred space may be in the school, but their homes are elsewhere. They cannot have settled in so quickly. We were here first; we don't deserve to be shunted aside. Athens is our home, too, for now." Beatrice turned to Ibrahim ruefully. "Forgive me if I ever seemed like I doubted you. But what were we to do?"

"Indeed. Fate has us round the neck," Ibrahim agreed.

He didn't appear angry with her. Relief surged in her veins; the Grand Work had been trial by fire, and as Leader she was responsible for their successes and failures. Now, with all guidance removed, she didn't know what to expect or to think.

She didn't care about anything so much as Verena. That, and having a few choice words with the goddess, who was likely following her precious new pets, recalling Phoenix apologizing for their lack of courtesy. That they had been pawns of gods was never so evident. So too were this new crop.

Beatrice had to admit, if only to herself, that the new Guard were good, if young. Quite good.

CHAPTER
TWENTY-TWO

As Beatrice hoped, with the possessing spirit displaced, the crackling, invisible barrier to Athens vanished. Within the hour their patient lay comfortably convalescing in her upper-floor apartments, far from the comings and goings of any workers below. Ahmed and Ibrahim sat attendant at her side. Belle and George had run off to their café, the only ones who now had something in London to fall back on.

Beatrice was too full of raw emotion to sit still, so she stalked to the third-floor seal.

"Why did you leave me?" she cried out to the Phoenix entombed within. She had never felt an emptiness like she now suffered.

Blue fire coursed around her ankles, as if happy to see her, and Beatrice scowled, wondering if it was a trick. The fire, and Persephone, had been fickle. Did this little show of affection hope to keep her mollified?

"Some good you were out there on the bridge," she murmured, kicking at the flames with her boot. "Fair-weather fire."

"Our Lady, you owe us an apology," she growled through clenched teeth. But now that she was no longer Leader, would the goddess come to her?

The light did indeed change, a sign of her summoning, and Beatrice whirled. "Where were you when we needed you?!" she cried, glaring at the beautiful creature before her.

She didn't worry if she appeared raving; there were no workers here due to the lateness of the hour, and she wouldn't have cared if there were.

Persephone stared. "I . . . was visiting with the new Guard, as I always do."

"Are we not still your Guard? Are we not still in your damnable service?"

Persephone blinked. "You are still my beloveds, but you are no longer the Guard. It all happened so quickly. I did not think there could be two Guards, but I'd hoped—"

"So now we're dispensable. We abandoned our homes, our lives, followed you blindly here to be cast aside thus?" Beatrice shrieked. "What if Verena had died?"

"I would not have allowed that. I gave her the kiss of life."

"And a bloody lot of good that did her, lying there, alive but possessed by a fiend, only a shell of your light flickering within her."

"She did not die," Persephone repeated. "Danger surrounds the Work; there's no cure for—"

"You could have warned us that, should any of our Muses leave, what we once fought might take its place!"

Phoenix fire crackled around Beatrice's feet. Perhaps she was calling it forth with her righteous anger. The azure flames soothed her heart and mind. They stood upon his grave, and Beatrice now felt confident an echo of fire would always exist in her, as it would always exist at his tomb.

"I would never wish harm upon you," Persephone said. "I don't claim to understand all the particulars, how the Guard are chosen and when. That's up to the Muses and to Phoenix—"

"Have you ever asked? Have you ever thought beyond your own immediate fancy? Your whims?"

"There needed to be a changing," the goddess insisted. "Even if there's no precedent. None of this has happened before; never two Guards, never on one soil. I felt a need, a possibility, and I followed the Liminal order . . . I've not always been able to be on hand, coming and going as I must between worlds. The blood-letting distracts me—"

Beatrice would have none of her excuses. "Beloved Verena nearly died tonight, senselessly, away from her home. Why, if those poor young wretches are the chosen ones, why weren't they chosen in the first place? Why involve us at all?"

"Because it wasn't yet time, you were our transition . . ." was Persephone's reply. She looked regretful, but only a bit. Beatrice was convinced the goddess, regardless if she loved them or not, simply did not understand mortals.

"The Muses found you first, you who are of proper age. When Darkness moved against all Guard spirits to take them prisoner, things changed. Moving the phoenix fire here to London, things changed again. This new Guard . . . Guards are never so young. So many things weren't in place—"

Beatrice glared. "You've just fallen in love with a mortal boy, that's all. Nothing else mattered."

"It is true that I've fallen for a mortal boy," Persephone replied. "He is a magnificent, worthy young man."

Pacing the fiery seal, Beatrice threw her hands in the air. "You're unquestionably one of those divinities of old, prizing nothing but your lovelorn fate. Gods are petty creatures after all. It's clear to me now that no one more powerful is listening, nothing helping mankind. No one knows a damn thing about any greater plan. Being your 'chosen' simply means people I care about must suffer. If you had been honest about that from the first, I might have more respect for you now."

In the face of Beatrice's wounded fury, Persephone was calm. "I am a force, but not an omnipotent one. I told you what I was—"

"You never said you were an accomplice to murder," Beatrice spat. She was finished with the argument, not that it had done any good.

Storming past the goddess, she took refuge in her chamber on the uppermost floor. That small room housed all that was left of her identity, her shell of an existence. Beatrice collapsed upon her bed and wept, her world shattered. Being Leader had fed her adventuresome spirit, made her feel important, given her beautiful, extraordinary friends.

She had thrilled at living an unconventional life. Despite the difficulties, she had found welcome in the purpose the work had given her, the direction she'd once so craved.

A wave of grief threatened to drown her. Standing in the sacred space, basking in the Power and the Light was an experience that could never be replicated. The Grand Work had made them a family—the six of them truly loved one another. Beatrice was not fond of loss. She'd had enough, and she didn't want to be severed and lonely again. But she was no visionary, to see an alternate future.

"What are any of us now?" she exclaimed to the empty room.

Bright colors appeared at the foot of Beatrice's bed. "I told you, you are my beloveds," whispered Persephone. "You will always be my beloveds."

Beatrice scrambled back. "Get out of my room. I did not invite you. You have no use for us, and I have no use for you."

"I need you," Persephone replied. "There is work yet to be done."

"Get your precious new Guard to do it."

"Beatrice, I need you. I *will* need *you*. Specifically you. And I trust you. There is no more precious thing than trust," the goddess added.

They stared each other down. Beatrice's nostrils flared; her fists clenched in her bedclothes. "I don't trust you. At present, I'm inclined to hate you."

Persephone stared at her, her aura cycling colors. "I know. I wish you didn't."

"Why couldn't we speak to them? To our own fellows? It was as if we were physically gagged. What's the sense in that? How does that help any of us?"

"I couldn't risk having you frighten them," Persephone replied. "It was manipulative of me, I know. But at the moment none of you are fond of the Grand Work. While I cannot blame you, I couldn't have you turning them against their destiny on the very first day it was given, not when Verena's life was in the balance. I paid for it, though." She lifted her sleeve to show what looked like burn marks on her forearm. "All magic costs me these days."

"What, I should pity you your scars? What if Verena *yet* dies? She is not fully recovered! What scar will you show me then?"

Persephone rose and paced the room. "I'm doing the best I can with a life I didn't choose, either!" she cried, and Beatrice realized there was nothing as disturbing as a nervous deity. "Everything I attempt is to protect the Balance, the Muses, and Phoenix. To protect what remains of my beloved and the balance between worlds. The Whisper-world and the Liminal edge is making its own decisions, and I've no choice but to keep up with Prophecy as best I can. I struggle to understand my own part, to do my best when others have controlled and punished me for eternity."

That seemed true. If Beatrice held any hatred for the goddess, she hated Darkness more.

"You've every right to be angry," Persephone allowed. "The Grand Work places you at the threshold of life and death, endangering your lives and the lives of all those around you. But for all the Grand Work takes, it also gives. It saves the lives, hearts, and minds of many whom it touches. I owe you endless thanks for your service. I do love you—all of you—and I hope you know it. I'm fighting to make sure all of you will remain free, in this world and the next." She moved toward the door. "Now I'm going to see Verena."

Before Persephone could leave, Beatrice said, in a small voice, "Could the Grand Work not have *asked* us if we wanted this? Couldn't you ask for volunteers instead?"

Persephone stared at her. Hard. "If we did, what would you say?"

Beatrice wanted to denounce the Work, to say that she wanted nothing to do with it. But would she really have refused? Even knowing what she did?

The goddess shook her head when Beatrice scowled. "You were chosen because you'd say yes anyway." Then she passed through the door.

Beatrice gave chase, following the goddess as she glided down the hallway. If further apologies would be made, she wanted to hear them. Apparently knowing Verena's location without being told, Persephone turned and vanished through the correct door as if she were a ghost, and again Beatrice followed.

Perhaps the divinity wasn't lying when she said that her heart was still tied to them.

Inside, Verena was unconscious. Ibrahim stared at Persephone with steely defiance, a glare that screamed he'd known better, that he had warned everyone of this. His tortured expression mixed self-loathing and fury.

"You. You chose your precious English Guard," he growled. "You, the Muses, the fire, you chose them over us and left us defenseless. What could we have done to stop this?" He indicated Verena's limp body.

Persephone shook her head. "I did not choose them over you. But I had to be there for their annunciation—as I was for yours. This new Guard is charged with a grave responsibility that you were not."

Verena woke with a heartbreaking cry. It both gave Beatrice hope and filled her with fear.

"I want to go home," the girl begged in Arabic. Seeing Beatrice, she repeated the plea in English, perhaps forgetting, in her pain, that the Englishwoman understood Arabic.

"Please take me home," she said to Ibrahim and Ahmed, again in Arabic. Then she saw the goddess. If she was angry, she chose not to show it. In English this time, she said, "Now that you've no need for us, I'd like to go back. To Cairo."

"I want you comfortable and happy." The goddess glanced at Beatrice, who clenched her jaw. "I've work for some of you but not all. Cairo can have you back. I shall not be too covetous."

Looking at Ahmed, Ibrahim, and Verena, Persephone said, "Go in peace, and know that I am with you in spirit"—her voice faltered—"even when I fail you, as I've failed every Guard that has come before. I am sorry for your suffering, and I promise to give *everything* I have, the very last of me, to make it right." Her lovely face hard with conviction and desperation, she opened a trembling hand and summoned a portal to the Whisper-world. Vanishing through, she left them with a disturbing whisper. "All my blood. I'll spend all my blood until we're finally free."

Beatrice shuddered. Ahmed paced nearby, anxious like she'd never seen him. Ibrahim was staring at her. Despite the goddess's welcome apology, it seemed none of them had gleaned any answers. Dismissed or not, they still had no idea of their next move.

She left her friends in Verena's room and retreated to her own, calming herself with a cup of tea. There came a knock on her door and she called, "Yes?"

Ibrahim entered. Beatrice was glad she had composed herself, since he seemed to be completely under control and looked characteristically stoic. "As you heard," he began, "Verena wants to go home. I think she should do so as soon as possible, though I believe she should rest here a few more nights and regain some strength first."

His dark eyes were haunted as he continued. "It may mean life or death for her. It's all she'll speak of. Ahmed won't leave her side. He'll make the journey with her."

Beatrice didn't answer. After all, what was there to say?

Ibrahim stared out the window at the graying sky. "What do we do now?"

"The rest of you are free," Beatrice replied. "Myself, I'm not sure."

"Why do you say so?"

Beatrice sighed. "I vented my spleen upon our Lady before she came to Verena. When I did, she intimated that there was work yet to be done, and that I'm the one to do it."

"And . . . me?"

"I've no idea. Ask her yourself," Beatrice retorted. If they were no longer the Guard, she was no longer their Leader.

Ibrahim set his jaw; she regretted giving him cause for that.

"I'm sorry," she began. "You're the last person who should bear my frustrations. You know I've wrestled with our fate as you have."

Her heart dropped into her stomach. Would he want to stay and help, or would he return to Cairo with Ahmed and Verena?

She turned away to make another cup of tea, rejoicing in how that ritual masked every awkwardness.

Oh, God, she thought. *Stay, or ask me to come with you. I cannot ask you to remain, no matter how much I wish to.* She felt ashamed at her intense yearning, but there was nothing to be done for it. The company of Ibrahim Wasil-Tipton was something she craved. Whether he took an English name or not, whether he wore tunics or fine English suits, she craved his eloquent words, his weighty stare, his compelling presence. She had from the first.

Ibrahim was evaluating her. She felt his regard and worked to keep her face blank, kept her gaze fixed upon her cup and saucer.

"I . . . have not decided," he said quietly, then surprised her with, "What do you feel I should do?"

He was asking for her opinion? Dare she give it? Was it her
responsibility to knock down the walls he'd built up, to ask him to
stay with her? It wasn't, and so she continued their maddening
volley of detachment instead. "The great Ibrahim Wasil-Tipton is
deferring to my judgment?" Straightening her spine, she turned
and gave him a smirk. "Are you feeling quite well?"

Ibrahim eyed her. A corner of his mouth turned up, surprising
her, and they stood there in silence, smirking at each other. Beatrice
hoped he was as engaged by the game as she. Their relationship
always held a subtle dance of power.

"I'll tell you in the morning," he replied. Then he stepped forward, grabbed her hand in both of his, pressed it, and brought it
to his lips.

Proper or no, Beatrice rejoiced that she was not wearing gloves.
She could feel the exquisite touch of his full, perfect lips atop her
hand, and time stopped as his dark eyes rose to meet hers. Her
other hand, the one holding cup and saucer, began to tremble.

A sound escaped her that was part choke, part gasp, part cry of
exquisite bliss, a sound that revealed too much of her inner emotion. This moment held all that she had desired, made her struggle to maintain even a shred of composure. This glimpse behind
the mask of his stoic, impassive character was a moment of aching
intimacy that revealed so much more than words . . . She felt a
blush bloom on her cheeks like phoenix fire.

He lifted his mouth away but kept her hand in one of his. With
the other, he lifted away the still shaking cup and saucer and set it
gently aside, then took that trembling hand in his as well. "You
have been a very good Leader in the time allotted you, Miss Smith.
It has been strange, but a true honor, to serve at your side."

After that quiet compliment, he lowered her hands and walked
away. Beatrice was left thunderstruck, with the sound of her heart
pounding in her ears.

CHAPTER
TWENTY-THREE

THE CORE OF PHOENIX LAY LISTLESS IN ATHENS'S BRICKS, FIERY and formless. After a time, he allowed himself to trickle out and course across the foyer floor, pacing as he had in corporeal form when pondering a great problem, always in concentric circles.

He'd almost forgotten how it felt to press firm feet upon the Earth. Floating did not satisfy. Still, he floated around the marble floor, now and then pausing, a ghost of blue fire. He couldn't be too active, lest he wake up the young man to whom he was so tightly bound.

His goddess was right: There had never been a Leader quite so like Phoenix himself. Young Alexi Rychman was everything that Persephone had hoped, fiercely intelligent, with more raw promise and potential than they'd ever encountered before.

Being buried here in Athens had attuned him to new things. He knew that here, much would come to pass, Prophecy would be unveiled, and their great war would be wrought.

Surely Persephone did not know the extent of costs to come. If she did, she would not be so excited, so full of the life that had been missing from her for centuries. She had been a divinity since the beginning of time, and such was how she'd always see herself. But Phoenix knew she had to take mortal form or she was going to fall apart. There was no choice anymore.

If she took a mortal shape, she'd no longer be bound to shadow. But she would lose much by making this change. Perhaps he wouldn't tell her what she couldn't take with her. Perhaps it wasn't his duty to tell her. If he said nothing, it would still happen. She'd pass into her new world none the wiser.

And be gone forever. The lover he'd known, cherished, and trusted would have vanished. If he didn't tell her, he was no longer the god he claimed to be.

He'd have to reveal to her that she would remember nothing of this life. That she would, in effect, truly die in a way he doubted she could fathom. She wouldn't come into the mortal world full of power, knowledge, and glory. The girl in her vision was a stranger to them both.

Phoenix pledged that he in turn would lose himself, sink so deep into the farthest reaches of Alexi Rychman's mind that only his powerful fire would remain. They two ancients would offer up their gifts and let go entirely, allowing mortals to take their places and live reborn in the love that gods once knew.

BEATRICE ROSE WITH THE SUN AND NOTICED A NOTE ON THE floor. Probably slid under her door sometime during the night. Seeing the familiar hand, a blush burned her cheeks. She bit her lip and picked it up. His writing was impeccable in either the beautiful sweep of Arabic or the rougher alphabet of English.

Though the Grand Work had aged her, she was still a young woman. In this moment, her heart was as fragile, thrilled, and fanciful as that of any who would soon attend this academy.

I have decided to help Ahmed see Verena safely home. It is the only appropriate action, especially given our summary dismissal. I have no sense of the goddess needing me or the others again and I would like to help assure both their safety.

That said, I shall write you anon. After making sure our friends have all they need in Cairo, you and I shall speak

*of Egypt and of England. We shall come to an agreement on
what is to be done next.*

*Safe travels with the goddess, whatever madness she has
planned. Tell me if there is some way I may yet be of service.
And take care of yourself. I don't want anything to happen
to someone as important as you.*

Warmly,
Ibrahim

Beatrice's pulse raced as she read and reread the note. For a man
as stoic as Ibrahim, this was quite the change. *Warmly. As important
as you.* The gray sky over London now seemed as golden as Cairo.
If Ibrahim would yet agree to be the light of her life, she didn't care
which sky she spent it under.

ALEXI RYCHMAN STOOD IN HIS STUDY, CONTEMPLATING DARK
and dismal things. His grandmother's funeral had been hard on
him. She was the person for whom he'd strived. Now all he had to
replace her was supernatural madness.

A light across the room caught his gaze. In his doorway stood
their prophet, the angel of their annunciation, a breathtaking young
woman, impossibly beautiful, luminous with subtly shifting colors,
as if lit by a rotating prism. His heart leaped into his throat, and
he felt his command of the universe shatter.

"It's you," he breathed.

"I've been watching," she confessed shyly, immensely powerful and yet somehow eternally youthful, naive. "I shouldn't, but I
have."

"And you haven't made yourself known?" he asked, trying not
to sound hurt. He could muster no craft when he spoke with her,
no artifice or maturity; she drew from him raw, unfettered emotion, as if he'd known her all his life. There had been an immediate

intimacy when she first appeared and charmed her way into his heart by merely saying his name.

"I've been trying to be good," the goddess breathed. "And to get on with the next phase of our plan so that I may come to you, in form newly refreshed, to take up our destinies. But I'm a coward. I can't bear the idea that if something goes wrong, I may never see you again."

She grabbed him by the hand, which suddenly felt encased in a gentle, humming fire more potent than the flames he himself these days commanded. He was a careful youth, quiet, often brooding. But with this woman he felt alive, happy, and eager. With her, this supernatural calling seemed no curse but a blessing.

With a start he realized she'd led him into his bedroom. Heat flooded him at the idea of them in so intimate a space.

"I shouldn't do this," she continued, yearning clear in her voice.

Alexi's body nearly convulsed with desire. "Do what?" He meant to sound inviting but only sounded like an overwhelmed boy.

She sighed ruefully. "I must be going. We must begin. We must bring Prophecy to light. I've never done it before, you know."

Alexi trembled.

"Never taken a mortal body," she clarified. "We're long overdue for these bold and dire acts, you and I. I was just waiting for the right time. You. You're the right one. I choose you. Now, and in the future. I will choose you."

When she leaned in, it was as if a sunbeam broke upon Alexi's face. The soft, warm press of her lips against his sent crashing waves of pleasure across his body. Perhaps knowing it was his first kiss, she bestowed it tenderly. He was frozen, unable to take her in his arms as he wished. All he could do was drink in the sensation of her lips questing over his. They danced over and across his sharp cheekbones, and her murmur in his ear caused frissons down his body.

"Nothing is as exciting as a stolen kiss, is it?"

She drew back and blushed, an action Alexi found wondrous. She was impossibly feminine, an ageless, timeless girl. Her impish smile was inviting, her shifting and overpowering shades of beauty dizzying.

"Furtively given and taken, out of sight of watching eyes," she continued. "Illicitness is half the thrill of desire. Perhaps our situation in the future will be similar. Perhaps *you'll* steal *my* kisses next time. I shouldn't be here now, but I cannot help myself. You're so like him, you know."

"Who?" Alexi breathed, confused.

"Phoenix. My love of long ago. Before I was taken under." Her voice broke, and Alexi dared place his hand upon hers. "Your destined will love you as much as I do. She'll come with my heart."

"Love me?" Alexi stammered, reeling. "How can you say that? You don't even know me. You think you know my destiny, and that of my new friends, but do you know *me*?"

She traced a luminous finger down his cheek. "I have a way of knowing souls, Alexi Rychman. Yours is worthy and true. The Grand Work has its curses, but I promise you joy."

She touched his temple with a gentle finger. It was not the touch of passion for which he hoped. He wanted to take her in his arms, to be her conquering hero, but her fingertip on his temple held him still.

"What are you doing?" he asked.

The sudden sadness on her face doused his excitement. "I can't let you remember this. I want you to know what it's like to truly fall in love, like a mortal, with a mortal. Not like this. This isn't real. You're under my spell."

"No, please," he begged. He was not accustomed to knowing his desires, let alone articulating them. "Don't take these moments from me."

"In part they will live here." Her fingertips, glowing and prismatic, slid past his vest, inside his shirt and across the skin of his chest. He felt something flutter inside: a seething longing, a fierce strength. "Steel your heart until your destined beloved comes. When you're sure, you may unleash these floodgates upon her. But be patient. Be cautious. It will not be easy for any of us. Darkness will look to drive a wedge between."

Her eyes filled with silver tears.

"Eternity awaits, my love," she murmured. Then all the room was light. She was gone from his arms like a vanishing ghost.

Alexi returned to his senses. Hearing his sister calling his name, he descended the stairs and entered the parlor.

"What were you doing? I thought I heard voices," said Alexandra, shifting her wheelchair.

All he could remember was blinding white light. Nothing else. "Muttering to myself, as usual," he replied.

Turning to gaze out the window, he saw a host of flowers in the garden below. Had there always been so many? He felt three overwhelming sensations: loss, loneliness, and the belief that some-day, despite this hollow pain, he would be provided for. Guided by something beyond his control.

BEATRICE WAS STARING DREAMILY OUT HER WINDOW WHEN Persephone appeared at her side, a jolt of light, color, and the scent of flowers.

"Ah, *love!*" the goddess exclaimed, grabbing the young woman's hand and dragging her to her feet. "There is nothing so delicious as a man's first kiss!"

Though she felt the goddess's contagious, bubbling glee and wanted to give over to it, to share the bliss that had been Ibrahim's lips on her hand, Beatrice raised an eyebrow and muttered, "Having fun with your new pet, I take it? Isn't he a bit young for you? I doubt that's quite fair."

At this, Persephone sobered. "I was looking for the others.

Have Verena and the rest gone already? So swiftly departed for Egypt and home?"

For the first time in Beatrice's experience, the goddess was dressed not in robes but in the style of the day: wide skirts, capped sleeves, and tapered cuffs. The fabric was grandly, absurdly red. Playing at mortal, she clearly relished in the costuming, but the garish crimson silk made Beatrice wince.

"I am unsure; their boat may have already departed. It would be . . . too sentimental of me to have followed along."

The goddess looked at Beatrice more closely. "You seem nervous, but you're blushing. Wait! I know that look. I'm sure I'm wearing it, too."

Beatrice composed herself and countered, "Are you? Are we feeling the same thing? I worry still for Verena, about her health and her journey home, about Ahmed and Ibrahim, traveling with her. I'm heartbroken to see our coterie break apart, no thanks to you. Don't you have things to do in the Whisper-world? Like pour your blood onto some stones?" she chided bitterly.

The expression on the goddess's face changed to hurt in an instant, a terrible sight, and Beatrice felt an apology spring to her lips, but she bit it back, saying only, "I remain furious with this whole turn, my Lady."

Persephone nodded. "Of course. I reel from it just as you do. I declared a prophecy to the new Guard, and the words changed on my very lips! I'm not sure how in control of my destiny I am."

"How comforting," Beatrice muttered.

Regaining her earlier *joie de vivre*, the divinity said, "Let's see the boat off. I want to wave from the docks and send my love to those who cross the oceans!"

"But the train to the port—"

"Take my hand; we'll be there in the instant. I've enough magic to spare for such a moment as this."

Beatrice sighed. She could not refuse the goddess's enthusiasm—
or her own desire to drink in Ibrahim's visage once more.

The world spun, and Beatrice felt the roil of seasickness. She
closed her eyes, and when she opened them again, she stood at the
Southhampton docks. The goddess slid heaps of crimson silk out
onto the stones as if she were stepping down from a precipice.
Beatrice noticed her motions were slightly awkward, as if she were
stiff or in pain.

Ahmed was visible at the prow of the Peninsular steamer, and
his dark face lit with a smile upon seeing them as Persephone nearly
dragged Beatrice right to the dock edge. He ran along the rails,
shouting, "Oh, my Lady, you're here!" He seemed not to harbor
the anger of the rest of them did, which was odd, considering his
love for Verena, but then again, anger simply wasn't in him.

"Please," he called, heedless of the surrounding Londoners
who turned wary glances on him. "The visions keep coming. I've
seen betrayals—I don't know when they will take place, but I feel
in my heart that those who love you will betray you. They won't be
able to help it.

"Be careful," he continued. "Be wary of all. Betrayals will come
from close by, from within your coterie; they won't mean it, so be
wary. There is beauty ahead, but much pain beside."

Ibrahim appeared beside Ahmed at the rail. Beatrice's heart
skipped a beat. He did not notice her at first; he was eyeing Persephone and her costume.

Ahmed continued, "I know this defies Ibrahim's rational mind.
I've been driving him mad with it. Our powers gone, yet my visions
remain. I must be heard. The war in the ground. The dead have no
place to go. You can't close every door . . ." He clutched his cap in
his hand and ran his hand through his hair, disheveling it.

Persephone nodded. Her voice carried easily to her former Guard.
"You are heard and appreciated, Ahmed, though I do not yet see
what you see."

"Because you are too focused on what is directly in front of you. I, objective, can see further," Ahmed insisted.

"I do not doubt it and will make sure your words are recorded," the goddess assured him. "That is all I can do." She faced Ibrahim, who was standing more stiffly now, staring at Beatrice as if his eyes could burn holes in the dock.

The tension was palpable—delicious, Beatrice thought. She clenched her fists and saw that Ibrahim had also clenched his.

"Oh, for God's sake. Go kiss him, will you?" the goddess said with a chuckle. She batted an elegant hand. "The damned propriety of this age. Thank God we divinities aren't bound by such ridiculous constraints!" She moved away and stepped up on a small platform, where she began waving and blowing kisses to the departing passengers, leaving Beatrice blushing furiously.

She saw Ibrahim's lips curve; he was surely imagining what Persephone might have said to make the stoic Miss Smith lose her composure. He put his hand to his heart, still gazing at her. She couldn't breathe, could only look at him in return.

Her eyes welled with tears, and she was glad he was far enough away not to hear the little hitches of her breath. She placed her hand on her heart, too, and she hoped with every bit of that pounding instrument that their gestures signified a compact. A vow. For two such stubborn souls, this departure might have been the only thing that could have brought it out of them.

The ship shifted, moving into the current, and Ibrahim walked away, his elegant form, clad in a tunic and long coat, vanishing through a door. Beatrice supposed he did not think it practical to linger in aching sentiment. Surely it was only a matter of time before they could move forward, hopefully together. At last she let her tears fall, gasped for breath, and dabbed at her face with a handkerchief.

A bit of a crowd had formed around Persephone, watching her wave and send kisses. Beatrice laughed, saying quietly, knowing the goddess would hear, "You look as if you know and love every single one of us mortals."

"I do! In my way." She hopped down from her platform perch, wobbling a bit on landing. Making a face she said, "Shoes. Never have liked them."

She held out her arm and Beatrice took it. It was damnably impossible to stay angry with the creature.

"Now. What's to be done with you two?" the goddess asked. "Are you returning to Cairo, or is he coming back for you?"

"I . . . I don't know. It's yet to be determined." Beatrice felt a wave of trepidation. "I suppose it depends how long you're keeping me."

"Not too much longer, else I ruin everything. Come then. We'll have to buy you some beautiful stationery for love letters."

Beatrice made a tiny noise. "That's presumptuous!"

"One should always be writing love letters," the goddess declared. "One can never write enough of them."

The route they took back to Bloomsbury and Athens passed a small shop selling all things epistolary. Next door sat a jewelry shop. Persephone seemed unsurprised at this pairing, smiling when she saw it.

Drawing on a thin chain around her neck, the goddess showed Beatrice an elegant silver ring shaped like a feather.

"I'd like to do something with this," she said. "My tears worked very hard to craft it. I'll meet you out front in a bit." She entered the jewelry shop, opening the door as if she were a mortal woman.

After going into the stationer's, it wasn't long before Beatrice reemerged with a set that had her dreaming of better days and times. The idea that a composed man like Ibrahim might be more forthcoming in letters than in person, that the written word might better reveal a guarded heart, was a titillating new prospect.

Persephone was waiting on the pavement. Beatrice noticed the jeweler placing the lovely silver band in the window. The goddess showed Beatrice a new bronze locket she had procured.

"Talismans," she stated. "Can never have enough of these either. Love letters and talismans. Come, escort me to the grave of my love. There is much to be done."

Back at Athens, Beatrice and Persephone cordoned off the third floor foyer with velvet rope. While the goddess was masquerading as a mortal, it wouldn't do for any administrators, workmen, or teachers to see them while they went about their work.

The goddess bent and began murmuring, placing her new locket at the center of the seal. A bit of blue fire reached up to kiss her cheek, and Beatrice felt that phantom heat course through her body. She supposed it would always make her ache, like the smoke of opium did an addict.

"We must take every precaution," she heard the goddess say. "Your fire and my blood—precious alchemy. Together they will break down the walls, knit the worlds together, and set the army free." She lifted the locket, now awash with bluish flame, and hung it around her neck.

Her magical glamor faded and her garish crimson dress became her usual diaphanous robes, now laced with silken red patterns that Beatrice assumed corresponded to her wounds. Persephone fought showing her pain, but could not hold back a cough. Blood pooled at the corner of her mouth and as she dabbed at it with her sleeve, Beatrice saw the fabric turn to crimson silk, and understood what had seemed a garish costume. She felt a stab of empathy.

Persephone was sick, indeed; a consumptive goddess. She was, Beatrice thought mordantly, the very epitome of Victorian beauty. This was her age, after all. And this age would claim her.

Yet the sleeve of her divine robes took what was terrible and made it into something beautiful. Persephone tore free a long crimson strip and wound the lovely shimmering length around her neck. She turned to Beatrice with a grin, fluttering the accessory.

"I'll have to offer this to Alexi—a bit of flair, a spot of passion. I fear he wears too much black—he's so serious for such a young man! And you, I feared the same for you, but love quite becomes you, Beatrice. Go! Write your letter!"

She threw out her hand, and the Whisper-world opened, the portal edges sparking. A moment later she had vanished. Beatrice chuckled despite herself, unable to feel wholly lost when at last her heart's time was at hand.

PERSEPHONE FOUND AODHAN WAITING, DREAMY-EYED, AT THE Liminal edge. He bowed his head to her, and his gray face darkened in a blush.

"Cannot help it," he murmured. "My Jane, she has me in thrall, and I cannot stop watching. Her guardian, her champion—I shall be both.

"Her gift grows stronger by the day," he continued. "But I have to find ways to help her. They're so young, all of them. We weren't this young, were we?"

"You were not," Persephone agreed. "But everything has changed."

"How are they faring as a group? How is the Leader?"

It was her turn to blush, and Persephone fondled the crimson swath about her neck. "He's terribly serious. But my mortal self will find him delicious once she sees the passion within him." She shook her head and gathered herself. "But I dally foolishly. The Liminal is wise, and I am grateful we are here together, Aodhan. I will need your help."

"Anything, my Lady."

"There will come a time when the barrier between Whisper and mortal worlds will come undone. I believe I've routed the paths, by blood and fire, onto the very stones of Athens Academy. There we will fight, for there are enough Guard spirits to win."

Aodhan nodded. "I am eager to defy the will of Darkness at any opportunity."

"I will take a mortal body. Likely that body must enter this world to see the Guards' prison break open. But if something should happen . . ." She stared at the Liminal; lightning crackled across its surface, reminding her nothing was certain, that there were details she couldn't predict.

"Take this," she said, handing Aodhan the locket. "It is packed full of phoenix fire. I would a Leader wielded it, but I'm not sure whom I'll have to spare, should the Cairo Guard, fate forbid, get caught up by Darkness. Be my eyes, my assurance. I do hope Beatrice will help when it's time, but I don't know how much more I can ask of her. I know I ask too much from you. From all of you."

"The Grand Work is both too much and not enough, everything and nothing at once," Aodhan replied. "But I'm not sure any of us would trade it. Not even those imprisoned."

Persephone wrung her hands. "I will set them free."

"We'll make sure of it. I promise."

CHAPTER
TWENTY-FOUR

DURING THE VOYAGE, THOUGH THEY STILL SAW SPECTERS, THERE was no trouble. Until the day they were scheduled to dock in Alexandria: It was Ibrahim's turn for a vision.

Not a vision, a nightmare. An echo of his instinct remained—perhaps phantoms of their powers would live on in each of them—and the sense of inevitable doom seized him.

Many years in the future, he and Beatrice and stood side by side like husband and wife. While he had once chafed at the idea of allowing even a portion of his heart to belong to another, now he found himself unsettled by the thought of life without Beatrice Smith. Their time together had led him to discover that they truly complemented each other, not just as Leader and second, but in life, mind, and heart.

She took his hand; he cherished the sensation. Then she died.

Ibrahim's heart was sundered. A portal opened before them, and it whispered. The Whisper-world was aptly named, and it called for Beatrice by name.

Her beautiful colors had already turned to dull gray, and her piercing blue eyes were now a dull silver, though her lovely face had not much changed. That beautiful smile he had silently adored was at last his, and she gazed at him still with affection. But she was dead.

He would be the death of her. Could there be any other meaning? He brought ill luck, it would seem, to all his friends. He was a curse.

His cry woke Ahmed, and they both sat up, having fallen asleep in chairs in Verena's room. She had taken a turn for the worse, perhaps because the roll of the sea reminded her of the vicious pitch of the possessor she'd battled. She had told them nothing of her possession, but Ibrahim assumed it had been terrible.

Now the two found the goddess sitting at the head of Verena's bed, stroking her brow and murmuring that she was sorry. Perhaps their fear had summoned her, but seeing her genuine regret began to ease Ibrahim's anger toward her.

She evaluated his expression. "Nightmare or vision?"

"Both," Ibrahim replied.

"Do you want to tell me about it?"

Ibrahim sighed. "I doubt there is anything you can do. You've done quite enough."

She bit her lip and did not press him.

Ahmed, eyes wide, was in the throes of a vision of his own. When it had come upon him Ibrahim could not be sure; they had all been lost to their private nightmares.

"My Lady! I see a black-haired girl and fire. Furrowed ground, terrible, muddy—there's so much death, terrible noises, monsters, machines . . . all inevitable," he sobbed. "The girl says, as if she's speaking to me, 'We couldn't have stopped this. None of us could. All we can do is ease the pain. What little we can do, we must. To ease just an eddy of this ocean of pain . . .' Does this mean anything to you, my Lady?"

Persephone blinked as the Sufi leaned toward her. "Alas. I've no reference for it, dear Ahmed. My visions have been insular: of Alexi, of the woman I must become. Nothing epic and dreadful like that."

She frowned, placing her hand on her abdomen as if there was a terrible ache from deep within. "I wonder," she murmured, "if she could be of my lineage, that dark-haired girl. If a creature like me could bear a child. Not in this form; the rot of the Whisper-world has eaten me alive from the inside out."

Sadness overwhelmed Persephone, her colors dimming. "I couldn't dare hope—" She choked and shook her head. "No. I can't say I comprehend your visions. I'm sorry."

"Perhaps she is a child of the Guard," Ahmed said.

Persephone was further stricken. "None of the women have ever conceived. Their bodies are full—with a Muse, with fire; there's no room to spare. Perhaps the Muses even stop it, for the Guard live and work at the threshold of life and death, a dangerous place for a child. And it would change the priorities of the parent. One cannot be the servant of two masters."

Sensing Ahmed's disappointment, Ibrahim shuddered. While he couldn't disagree that such a policy was likely best for all involved, it was a further sacrifice, another forfeiture.

With a shred of hope, the goddess added, "I cannot say, but your case of limited service may be different. It is . . ."

"Unprecedented," Ibrahim finished for her. They all nodded, silent.

Ahmed smiled wearily. "You know, I wish you *were* omnipotent."

Persephone joined him in the smile. "So I could give you answers to all that troubles you? Ah, but that would be untrue to the Sufi heart, which craves the divine mystery of which we two are a part. All your poetry would be gone."

Ahmed sighed. "You are wise."

Verena woke with a tortured cry. Ibrahim stormed out of the room, unable to bear more sadness. His Intuition had done nothing to keep them from harm, and now he had even less power with which to work. His vision of Beatrice's death, a death that he felt certain his presence assured, refused to leave his mind's eye.

Leaving Ahmed and the goddess to deal with Verena, he fled

to his cramped quarters. At the small writing desk in the corner, his world went as gray as the Whisper-world. He had to write a letter he would forever regret, for it might keep alive the woman who had become his treasure.

IN THE DEEP PRESS OF THE WHISPER-WORLD, PERSEPHONE broke from an obligatory promenade, a ritual that surpassed unbearable since Darkness had destroyed the field she had created for her Guard. She no longer deigned to take his flesh-then-bone hand, but occasionally walked with him, if only to keep him from sensing that she was plotting.

He'd insisted on a journey round the stone tower that imprisoned her most beloved mortals.

"What if," Darkness growled, "I didn't let you go above anymore?"

"My answer remains, as always, the same. How ever would I heal?" was her reply. "Your hold over me would cease once there's nothing left to hold."

Quitting his company, she felt the cool stones of the Whisper-world warm beneath her feet as she fled. Each step left Darkness farther behind, each step brought her closer to her new dawn. Persephone felt the Gorgon following her.

Outside the vast chamber where the Liminal waited, the goddess turned and addressed the creature, saying, "You really should take over. You want it, I do not."

The Gorgon's eyes flashed bright green and hungry. "Gladly. I never understood why he wanted you, a simpering weakling."

Persephone shrugged. "Nor did I." It was good for the Gorgon to think her weak. To underestimate her. She didn't need to prove herself to anyone but her Guard and Phoenix.

She fled into the Liminal chamber knowing the Gorgon would not follow to such an unwelcome place.

Before Darkness had claimed her for a promenade, Persephone

had been at her task, anointing more stones with her blood and preparing the pins for the future battle between worlds. Her pain from this work grew steadily; at every door she felt beaten and ravaged. Upon the Liminal edge she let go of all façade, yearning for something to cleanse the terrible palette of death.

The Liminal gave her access to her desire, revealing the Rychman estate. She entered, gliding down an oddly silent hallway. Keeping her diaphanous cloak about her, she patrolled the house, unseen.

Alexandra was in the parlor, working on her embroidery, as had become her custom after her fall. Alexi was likely caught up in the long hours of his apprenticeship; she could feel nothing of the Pull that might draw him elsewhere. But where were their parents? The house looked oddly bare, with furnishings and decorative items missing.

To the study she went, knowing it was Alexi's favorite haunt; she could await him there. Spying a freshly inked letter drying upon the desk, the goddess could not resist reading it.

> *Alexi,*
> *There is no easy way to say this, but you are a sensible lad, so I'll be frank. There is something wrong with the house. Your mother cannot abide it. She is full of fanciful and ridiculous notions, as women often are, of hauntings and curses and such. She's grown distracted, and I can no longer delay in removing her from these premises.*
> *Since the day of the accident, all has changed—you, your sister, our home, even the city. . . .*
> *We leave this house to you. It was bought with your grandmother's money and she left her entire estate to you. Your mother says that woman cursed you, but I think it quite a blessing that she should have left you so well furnished for your future.*

*Mr. Absolom will look out for you, and he'll make sure you
have a proper job when you are ready, perhaps as an academic.*

*It would likely be best if you don't ask after us. It would only
upset your mother. We feel that it would be easier for you to
make a home without the presence of staff who think of you as a
child, so we have discharged the few we are not taking with us.
In their stead I have employed the Wentworths, a quiet,
unobtrusive couple who will think of you as their master.*

*I have left information about the solicitors retained to
handle your affairs on a second sheet. There is more than enough
there to see you into adulthood. You shall lack for nothing but
our presence. Take care, my boy; I know you will, as you've long
been independent. You are the master of all you survey.*

> *Sincerely,*
> *Alfred Rychman*

*P.S. We've left it to you to tell Alexandra. We couldn't take her
with us and we know you love her dearly. We've hired a maid
to look after her, though of course you may choose to put her
into a convalescent home should she prove a burden. Such is the
unfortunate lot for women who can't serve their born purpose.*

A silver tear splashed onto the paper just as a voice came from
the doorway. "It's you."

"Hello, Alexi," she said, allowing herself to revel in his presence a moment.

"It's you," he repeated. "What are you doing here? What are
you reading?"

She handed it over.

ALEXI COULDN'T BELIEVE WHAT HE READ. FINISHED, HE DROPPED
the letter and stared at the beautiful creature before him. Prismatic

and silent, she picked up the sheet of paper and set it upon the desk.

She reached out to touch his temple.

"What are you doing?" he asked hoarsely, ducking her hand and trying to keep hold of himself.

"Easing the pain," she said.

His heart spasmed, his fists clenched, his mind spun. Everything had gone wrong since he was chosen.

"Leave me alone! You must be the curse. Get out of my house!"

He stormed out of the building, tearing through the back garden and plunging into the line of brush and birch trees on the other side. Would he could escape his fate so easily. He didn't know where to begin, with anger, with terror, with indignation that his beloved sister was relegated to no more than a dismissive postscript?

Anger. Anger was the appropriate response for abandonment with so little courtesy or explanation. A personal encounter was too much to ask for, even from a father. He was left all alone with no more than a *Sincerely, Alfred Rychman*. If Germans really were so cold, he was glad to count himself an Englishman.

Sadness. This had happened because his parents were frightened. He thought of the things he and his Guard friends had seen thus far: poltergeists, séances gone awry, violent possessions, and swarms of seething spirits. Everyone should be frightened of what floated unseen upon this earth. But to those who did not see, perhaps *he* was the nightmare.

Anger returned, the violent pitch of his emotions making him sick to his stomach. He wished he owned reason and analytical prowess alone. Feelings he could do without.

Moving slowly back to the house, he entered the parlor, a respite of light and color. Hearing his step, Alexandra wheeled her wheelchair toward the door.

"What is it, Alexi? Why so weary?"

"Mum and Dad are gone," he said quietly.

His sister gasped. Following her gaze, Alexi turned and saw the goddess standing patiently behind him.

"Who . . . *what* are you?" Alexandra asked the goddesss breathlessly.

The divinity moved forward; Alexi tried to grab her, but she nimbly eluded him and glided to Alexandra's side.

"Stay away from my family," Alexi hissed, fighting back sudden tears. "You've done enough, thank you very much."

Alexandra began to panic. "Alexi, what is happening? Who is this?"

Placing a hand on Alexandra's head, the goddess looked at Alexi and said, "Let me help. Trust me, you'll thank me."

Before he could take more than a single step, Alexi saw a calm smile wash over his sister's face. A genuine smile.

"Mum and Dad are gone?" she said. "That's all right. It was always you and me anyway, wasn't it, Alexi? I'm not sure they ever wanted us. Now we can do whatever we please."

The prismatic goddess spoke calmly. "Tell your sister whatever you need to, to keep her safe and make your life easier." Alexi opened his mouth to admonish her, but the goddess held up a hand. "Later you can rail at me all you like and scream that I've ruined your life, but right now you'd best attend Alexandra. We must make sure she won't break from the strain. For some mortals, ignorance can be bliss. Your sister is one of those."

Alexi gulped. His mother's superstitions were right: He carried danger with him. His sister did not deserve such a fate, so he would assure her peace and safety, as best he could.

"Alexandra, I'm buying you a little cottage nearby. It will be far more peaceful than this dreary place. This house is cursed. *I'm* cursed," he added in a tone too tortured for a man so young.

"No," the prismatic goddess countered, speaking softly to Alexandra, her colorful hands lovingly stroking the young woman's head. "Your brother is an angel. A prophesied angel. But his work has its dangers, and he loves you so much that he needs you safe. Removed. Because he doesn't want you to be frightened of him. He doesn't want anyone to be frightened of him."

Her sparkling gaze pierced him to the core. Alexi choked and turned away, overcome.

"Yes, brother, of course. Do what you must," Alexandra said quietly, as if in a dream. "Just come visit, please."

Alexi's throat worked, painfully dry, and he stared at his one true friend in the world, the only remaining member of his family. "Of course, sister, of course."

Then he could bear no more. He left the room, nearly running.

Persephone bent, kissed the top of Alexandra's head, then brushed a hand over her wide eyes, closing them. The young woman fell asleep in her chair in the next breath. Holding her breath, the goddess silently exited the room, closing the doors behind her. She wasn't sure where Alexi had gone but was determined to find him.

In the hallway, she loosed the cough she'd been holding in, catching pulp and blood in a cupped hand. Her heart faltered. Even helping humans with simple tricks of grace and peace taxed her like never before. How much had she left to give? She might fall apart before all the doors were knit together.

Moving into the garden, she placed her sullied hand over a white rose and turned it red. Her hand was now clean.

His voice startled her. "I'm supposed to trust you because Prophecy is going to make all this better?" He was standing on the veranda, leaning against the bricks of the back wall, his dark coat, vest, and shirt all open and disheveled, as was the mop of black hair that Persephone's fingers itched to caress.

She cleared her throat and smiled, hoping her teeth were not stained with blood. "Yes. I'm going to make it better. I'm going to make it all up to you, Alexi, I promise. Though I will say this isn't my fault any more than it is yours."

"Then whose?"

"Whose fault is it when buildings topple, when quakes rattle the earth or storms fell trees? Is it the hand of the heavens or is it just the way of things? With as much as you've now seen that you cannot explain, and with the knowledge that I am a divinity without absolute power, what answer would you give?"

"I didn't choose—"

"No, you didn't. But you were noticed. When someone gains notice for greatness, sometimes that gives them choices. Sometimes it takes choices away."

He stared at her stonily. She glided up the walk and he followed; she gestured that they sit on a bench, and when he refused, she shrugged and took a seat, tucking her legs up and shifting so that she sat facing him. Her glowing robes gathered in layers, looking like the absurd poufs and skirts so fashionable in his century.

"I was noticed once," she said. "It got me stolen away to a place where I rot year after year. I didn't choose. So often we don't. Your Grand Work has its blessings and curses—"

"There are no blessings."

"No? What about those lives you've already saved? The glory that you feel in the Power and the Light? The true knowledge, in your very veins, that you work for heavenly good?" Persephone watched as Alexi's face twisted, a wordless admission that she was right.

"I'll come back," she promised after a long silent moment, rising. He allowed her to place a kiss on his cheek as she passed. She could see his pleasure, watched his teeth clench as he struggled not to reach out and take her in his arms. Pausing, she placed a sorcerous finger on his lips to prevent him from letting this encounter trouble him.

Slipping the crimson strip of fabric from her neck, she said,

"Take this. A spot of passionate color in what must feel like a life of utter darkness."

She wound the cloth dyed by her blood around his neck like a cravat. She finished the knot with a soft kiss that made Alexi gasp.

"That's *enough*," the voice of Phoenix warned in her ear. "You've done enough to this young man; leave him be, don't torture him with dalliances. Where you have riled him up, I must settle him down. Don't undo my Balance with games. What you're doing isn't fair."

She drew back, chastened; a wash of blue fire passed over both her and Alexi's face and Persephone walked away with a quiet, sincere apology to them both.

She moved once again into the house, leaving her love and his vessel staring out at the darkening garden, settled by Phoenix's safeguarding power.

In the study, the goddess glanced once more at Alfred Rychman's letter and grimaced, saddened.

Her head suddenly swam. A vision formed, a vision of this house. The ghostly girl, the woman, the mortal Persephone must become, sat at a harpsichord. Alexi stood at her side. The pair was striking and filled with love, but older than when she had first seen them.

As the woman's impossibly white hands played a tune, folded paper dropped from somewhere within the keyboard, landing on her boots. She plucked it up and opened it with a frown.

The goddess recognized the first page immediately; it was the note from Alexi's father. The second and third sheets were a missive in an even more familiar hand: Persephone's own.

The vision faded.

"Well, then . . ."

Persephone never argued with her visions. She plucked two blank sheets of paper from atop the blotter, took a fountain pen and ink, and sought an empty room in which to write. She would leave the letters to be found at the appropriate time. Words of hope, of praise, of thanksgiving.

She would, as promised, also record and include Ahmed's warnings of the war in the ground, to not close every door, to allow room for the dead. Whatever that meant. There were times when it was best to offer warnings. When mortals were cautioned, they kept better Guard.

Finishing the note and hiding it where her vision bid, she nearly ran into the portal she opened. There was nothing else she could do here, as Alexi's presence was too tempting for her to leave well enough alone.

CHAPTER TWENTY-FIVE

ALEXI WALKED SLOWLY TOWARD ATHENS ACADEMY AND HIS Guard meeting, his mind hazy and numb. He remembered that his sister had taken the news of their parents' departure surprisingly well. However, it felt as though part of his day had gone missing, and he couldn't determine why. Perhaps he had gotten so adept at blocking his feelings that his life simply happened? That certainly left a void, but emptiness was better than the alternative. How many years would it take before humanity escaped him altogether?

He also wondered when he'd taken to wearing a scarlet cravat. But he liked the look of it. As he wondered at this, the fire within him offered a reassurance that he was a good man, and all would eventually be well.

Coming upon a weeping Jane at the Athens portico, he realized he retained some human compassion. She looked up at him and blushed, then wept harder as he drew near and placed a firm hand upon her shoulder.

She fell into a stammering torrent of words, her accent heightened by anxiety. "I'm sorry, Alexi, to be seen like this, but I'm beside m'self. I've nowhere to go. Mum said I'm useless if I won't marry or take a job—but I can't marry!" She blushed more. "And the factories, ye can't just walk off the line if the Grand Work calls, so I've been kicked out. I know Elijah's magic was supposed to have taken hold and made us invisible, but Mum's stubborn, and I don't go unnoticed. I think it's my light. Too bright. I don't know what to—"

"Jane," Alexi interrupted with gentle firmness, "you and I will walk through Aldgate tomorrow and we shall find you a flat. Rebecca and I were just discussing how that area gets spiritually fitful, so having a Guard resident there would be a great asset. Would you mind Aldgate?"

Her red, tearstained face showed excitement for a moment before falling again into terror. "But I've no money."

"You leave money matters to Withersby and me, and I don't want to hear one more word about it," he commanded, proffering her his breast-pocket handkerchief. "Ever. You are provided for, Miss Connor, and that is all there is to say."

Her eyes had gone wide, and she was leaning on him a bit. He tried to exude the strength he felt was appropriate to his commission.

"Thank you, Alexi," she breathed. "I . . . knew you could help me."

"Of course," he said proudly. "Such is my job."

He offered Jane an arm as they ascended the steps to Athens. As he heaved open the great front door, he deigned to admit, "I've been similarly abandoned." The Irish girl turned in alarm, her warm heart ever ready to offer sympathy and mutual aid, so he quickly added, "Though not without recourse. Worry not a whit for me, Jane. But trust me. I have learned today that we, the Guard, are the only family we can rely on."

"Oh, aye, Alexi," Jane said. "That much seems true."

Her tears vanished. Her relief and gratitude made him realize that friends were indeed a blessing, and that helping them made his heart less heavy. He smiled—or gave the best approximation he could muster, and felt better than he had since the work began.

"While being Leader is my job, helping a friend is a pleasure.

Tomorrow, at the tower gates at eleven, we'll find you a home. Tonight, stay at Athens. There's room in the ladies' dormitory for now. But only until Rebecca takes over; then she'll have this place crawling with as many girls as families will allow."

Inside they were met by their fellows. Spectral matters were discussed, and they were renewed by the Power and the Light. It was an uneventful meeting, but the rejuvenation was necessary. He felt that the meditative ritual in the sacred space was going to be necessary every week, to recall them to their purpose, to remind them what was good in spite of all their youthful sacrifice. It filled him with great hope and alleviated the darkness within, much like the spot of crimson against his black attire.

Later, after a silent dinner with his uncomplaining sister and the small house staff, Alexi realized there was still something missing from his life, something unrealized. He was as empty as his vast estate, and he didn't know how to find peace. If he couldn't have peace, he grasped somewhere deep within for a bit of hope.

BEATRICE WAITED OUT THE PENINSULAR STEAMER'S JOURNEY IN anxious delirium, reliving Ibrahim's kiss upon her hand, the look in his eyes, the hand on his heart. Frequenting Café La Belle et La Bête, she found the friendship of Belle and George did her heart good, as did the knowledge that George continued to paint. His work was as beautiful as ever. For all the Grand Work had required in sacrifice, it had also brought her a treasure. Such friendship as the Cairo Guard shared was priceless.

"Have you heard from Ibrahim?" Belle asked casually, as she did every time they met.

"Belle, he can't send a letter from the ship. He has to dock before the mail can set sail again in return. Patience," Beatrice replied, as if their relationship was still all business. She wondered if Belle knew how her heart pounded at the sound of his name. If so, her friend never let on.

"George and I shall retire to the coast," the French girl announced. "Won't that be nice? We've been discussing it for some time. We're thinking Grimsby. But not yet. I've this odd feeling we're meant to stay here for a bit, to do something with this building. We feel it the same way we felt we were supposed to buy the place. What does the goddess have in store for you?"

"I've no idea," Beatrice said. "She means to take a mortal body, but she'd best stop dallying with her precious new Leader and do it already. If we're all headed for Darkness's dread prison, we'd better get her war well underway."

Maybe then they'd be free to live their lives—and afterlives—in peace.

WHEN A LETTER FROM IBRAHIM FINALLY ARRIVED, PRINTED IN the delicate script of the man who, in the murmurs of her midnight hours, she achingly called beloved, Beatrice felt like a giddy, anxious schoolgirl. She rushed to her room to drink in the message, but from the first lines, she knew it would not lead her to happiness.

Miss Smith,

I truly apologize for the delay in my missive. The words I must write are not easy to pen and I have waited to see if my mind might change. But I am resolute. You and I were thrust into a most unlikely partnership, and I maintain my respect for how you have handled yourself. I have valued your presence in my life more than I dare say.

Growing up with the knowledge I was left on a doorstep has made me care for people cautiously. Losing the father I so luckily gained made my fear of growing attached all the more ingrained. I hope you can understand this, and I hope you can therefore forgive the times I made our interactions difficult. I hope you can also comprehend that being abandoned by you

strikes me with great terror. I feel now, in writing this,
as though I am already a ghost, restless, gray and sad.

I saw my greatest nightmare with my own eyes. I lost you.
There is no other way to say it. As we came upon Cairo, so a
vision came upon me. I trust it, for Ahmed and Verena have
both confirmed that we have all retained echoes of our powers.
In my vision you took a fatal turn, and I somehow was
involved. It was when you took my hand that you died.

I cannot again go against what remains of my Intuition and
cast you unwittingly into harm's way; you are too valuable.
As much as I at first wished the fate of the Grand Work were
otherwise, I now wish this vision were untrue and that you
might join me in Cairo. But I'll not risk your life upon it.
I cannot. We must not be together. It seems the only way to keep
you safe.

Beatrice, you deserve a life full of light and glory. I'll not
have you turn Whisper-world gray before my eyes. Live well
and be well, Miss Smith. There are so many more words I want
to say but I dare not. I shall surely see you someday in some
Great Beyond.

> *Sincerely,*
> *Ibrahim Wasil-Tipton*

The letter fluttered to the ground, released by her trembling hands.

There it was. A kiss on the hand was all she would ever receive. Love would be denied her. Such was her fate.

Black clouds were rolling in, and with every crack of thunder that broke over London, so too did Beatrice break. The letter had not been entirely cold, but neither could she comfort herself with its passion. Ibrahim was a man of fact. If he had emotions, he buried them deep. His disturbing vision was the last thing they would share.

Her first sob carried with it all the grief she had held back when Jean had fallen to his death before her eyes. That was not the pain of true love but this . . . Beatrice didn't remember the last time she'd wailed, if indeed she ever had, collapsing in tears upon the center of her floor, but the recklessness of the storm inspired her own. Her world, which had gone Cairo golden when Ibrahim had kissed her hand, now went Whisper-world black.

She didn't care if anyone might hear her and was startled when she heard a timid knock. She muffled her cries, but the knock came again, followed by a male voice, slightly familiar.

"Terribly sorry. I know it might seem impertinent, but I was just seeing my dear friend to her new rooms here at Athens and in passing . . . I just have to ask, miss, if you are all right."

"Fine," Beatrice barked. Yet she stood and moved to the door, laying a hand upon the wood.

The man spoke gently. "If I'm not mistaken, that was the cry of a broken heart. You must forgive me, but hearts are my specialty. I just want you to know that you are not alone. No mortal is alone. Even if you can't see or feel them, there are angels all around."

The stranger on the other side of the door made her feel as though she were in a confessional, something doubly bizarre for an Anglican. Surprisingly, the intimate anonymity was soothing. Beatrice found herself confessing, "I . . . found out that someone I love cannot love me in return."

"Ah, how I understand you, miss" came the sad reply. "And there's hardly a pill more bitter. But God loves you, always."

"Are you a priest? If not, you should be. The church could use an advocate like you."

"Why, thank you, miss, and indeed I have chosen to serve the church. Michael Carroll, at your service. Should you ever need an ear or a reminder of angels, please think of me. Especially during the worst storms and the darkest nights of your soul. Rest well."

Beatrice shook her head and listened to his footfalls recede.

Michael Carroll? Of course his voice was familiar. He was the new Heart, and well had he been chosen. Though she no longer wielded her powers, and Michael wouldn't have known her as anything but some resident of the growing academy, she would have connected with him anywhere. The Grand Work refused to be ignored.

The storm rumbled, and she wondered what would follow in its watery wake.

CHAPTER
TWENTY-SIX

ALEXI RYCHMAN STARED OUT THE WINDOW OF HIS HOME AT the raging storm, master of a dark estate. Alexandra had been moved out to her own quarters, where she had a kind young maid who would be ever at her service, so this haunted house, though full of murmurs, strange tricks of the light, and endless shadows, was as empty and echoing as his soul.

The wind howled. He'd never seen weather like this; akin to the wrestling of gods. His mind raced and his heart pounded. Was their intended Prophecy afoot? He felt a moment of foolishness, thinking that inclement weather might have a whit to do with the supernatural. Then he felt the Pull, and the Grand Work dragged him out into the storm.

SHE HAD BLED PROFUSELY ONTO SEVERAL SEALS WITHOUT TAKING time to heal herself in the mortal world, despite the danger to her form. Only two barriers were left, then all would be ready to be kissed by fire when the moment was right—provided no forces from the Whisper-world disturbed them in the meantime.

Persephone's yearning for the mortal world was stronger than ever, but the end was too close to turn back now. Two more final bursts of her life force and she could finally make the change, become no longer broken or tied to Whisper-world prison.

One more.

At the last seal, Persephone cast aside the sharp thorn that she had used to reopen her tender wounds. Moaning in pain, she watched her blood drip onto the stones, a familiar ritual at this point.

"You're such a weakling," the Gorgon hissed, coming into view around the corner of a corridor.

Persephone heaved and expelled a mixture of blood, bile, and pomegranate to mask her purpose. She hoped she appeared to be having merely one of her fits, as she'd had for centuries.

"You're such a pest," the goddess countered, wiping her mouth with her begrimed robes.

"You know, he'd never know the difference if one day you just completely fell apart. Surely I could convince him of its inevitability. So why don't I help you? Allow me to put you out of your misery. You want to die; you've been trying to kill yourself for so long. Let me help."

As the Gorgon drew close, her head of snakes hissed and snapped. Two serpents stretched, long and limber, to wrap tightly around Persephone's wrists, breaking her delicate skin.

The goddess spat in the Gorgon's face. "Don't you dare touch me!"

Luce hissed in pain, scalded by the goddess. Her grip weakened and Persephone broke free, her forearms slippery with blood. The snakes' tongues lapped at her injuries, but Persephone batted them away.

The Gorgon growled and snapped long fingers. A command.

Behind her, the dog began to bark, countless red eyes blazing. It pounced, its body first one then a hundred mongrels, and Persephone screamed in pain and terror as a rain of teeth scored her flesh. Focusing her energy, the goddess created a slap of white light that threw the protean canine off and sent the snakes hissing and reeling backward.

She tried to flee, to move toward the beckoning Liminal light she spied down another corridor, but the Gorgon blocked her path, lashing out with all her fury, hatred, and jealousy. Those base emotions were magnified by the Whisper-world, giving monsters the upper hand. Serpents wrapped around Persephone, driving their fangs and forked tongues deep into her wounds, tasting how weak she was.

Persephone screamed in genuine agony and heard every restless ghost take up her cry. The very ground of the Whisper-world shuddered. Rocks began to fall, and the sound was deafening. The Groundskeeper would be appalled to see all his stonework and bone sculptures tumbling down, the poor wretch.

Struggling, Persephone tried to muster her strength. She had to get away, to complete the final phase of the plan. When the dog pounced again, she felt her consciousness slip and her light flicker, dangerously close to being put out for good.

This was *not* how she was supposed to end . . .

THE PULL BROUGHT ALEXI AND HIS GUARD TO A GRAND INN outside the city proper, a stone edifice ringed with lush rosebushes and a tended lawn. The storm was merciless, rain soaking them as they worked. Alexi wound fire around the irascible spirit of a man who'd died in one of London's last legal duels, his spirit holding on to bitter vengeance.

The sky was lit with a horde of luminous dead, all swaying, mouths open. Not that the Guard could hear their wailing cries, but the heavens seemed to take up the cause of unrest.

"Alexi," Rebecca called in alarm. Standing under a portico with an open notebook, she furiously scribbled down every particular of the situation, as was her custom.

"Yes?"

She pointed to the stone foundations lined with red rosebushes. "The roses."

"What about them?"

Her face was ashen. "They were white. When we arrived, these roses were all *white*."

Throwing a definitive punch of blue fire to stun the duelist's spirit into submission, Alexi bent to touch the deep crimson colored blossoms. They were wet. He brought his fingers to his nose, sniffed, and took a startled step back. The whole bed of roses was covered in blood.

Josephine, the Artist, cried out. "Is this a sign of Prophecy?"

Alexi set his jaw. "Everything in our age is a sign of Prophecy."

He touched his blue fire–kissed palm to the open bloom, and the crimson began to roll away as if repelled. Too oily to be human, the gore dripped to the earth, revealing still white petals.

"So shall we heal the world," Michael intoned, staring at the subtle miracle. "Through blood and fire."

"So long as the world is not *too* awash in blood," Alexi retorted. "Every power has its limits and we're ill equipped for a flood."

He glanced at the sky filled with clustered dead and wondered at the Guard's ability to maintain balance. With such omens, he couldn't be sure of long-term success, even though the duelist's spirit appeared mollified at long last.

With what energy he had left, he used his cerulean fire to kiss clean the sullied bushes.

Michael drew close. "'O day and night, but this is wondrous strange!'"

The quote echoed exactly Alexi's thoughts, so he responded in kind. "'And therefore as a stranger give it welcome. There are more things in heaven and earth, Horatio, than are dreamed of in your philosophy.'" Though he considered himself full of Horatio's rationality, Hamlet's line seemed fitting. The Grand Work forced him to be both skeptic and believer. The leading player in a drama with no end in sight.

He twisted a rose petal between his fingertips. "Perhaps the gods battle in some unseen place. If so, I wager the blood on these roses is hardly the half of it."

*   *   *

"*WHAT. IS. HAPPENING?*"

The walls of the Whisper-world, wet with blood and echoing with Persephone's agony, amplified Darkness's bellowing cry. Rocks, silt, and Whisper-world muck went flying.

A whistle ten times that of the largest steam train sounded, and the dog yelped and whined, withdrawing its teeth from the goddess's hair and flesh. Luce the Gorgon grumbled but called back her snakes.

Persephone collapsed onto the blood-drenched stones. Barely alive, she prayed she had enough strength to crawl to the Liminal edge and slip through.

"She was trying to kill herself again," Luce muttered to the regal, red-eyed shadows seething at the mouth of the corridor.

"No. She tried to kill me," Persephone gasped in rebuttal, her hands slipping in her own gore as she struggled to lift herself. It was the truth, and if she was to live, she needed his help.

Luce pouted as the shadows drew close. "You believe her?"

The Lord of Shadow stared at them, Luce standing upright, Persephone groaning in pain as she once more faltered to her knees upon the stones. "By the look of her. Yes. She could not have done this to herself."

Darkness's eyes, when he had them, regarded Persephone in horror. She must look a sight indeed. Luce began to creep backward, in obvious fear of Darkness's wrath. His bone fingers seized a cluster of her snakes and yanked. Hard. It was Luce's turn to shriek. Snakeskins, scales, and blackened blood slid down her face, her hair writhing and hissing.

The dog whimpered, its tails between its legs. Darkness whipped the shadows with a long, sharp lash that seared its chimerical hides.

While Darkness was administering these punishments, Persephone mustered all her strength and dignity and managed to stand upright before him, swaying and shaking.

"Th-thank you, my lord," she gasped, blood pouring from her wounds. "If you'll permit me . . ."

"*Go*," he said, his voice like gravel. His beautiful face—then skull, then face—was tortured.

"It will take . . . some time away this time. This is the worst it's ever—"

"I. Realize," he said.

She bowed her head and turned away, trying to move without collapsing.

This was the window of time she needed. He'd not come looking for a while. She would be a mortal woman come of age when he would think to call her back. The Gorgon unwittingly helped her plan.

Persephone stumbled away, supporting herself on the Whisperworld's gray walls.

The Liminal grew in her sight as she left Darkness behind. Blue fire surged forward, all that could be spared from the thick of a Guard fight; it came tearing up, wrapped blue cords around her, loving and trying to heal her. Phoenix come to help her failing body. She basked in his warmth.

One of Luce's snakes, sheared verily in half, slithered along at Persephone's feet. The head and first third of it were fleshy, the latter part torn and skeletal. It extended its bloody forked tongue at the flowers struggling to blossom at her feet.

"I'll see you again soon," the snake hissed. "And when I do, I'll finish what I started."

"I know you'll try, Luce," Persephone said. With a delirious surge, she struggled to the swirling, misty Liminal wall. Emboldened by the fire of her love and the sparking Liminal light, she cried, before tumbling through: "But I'll prove love's the greater power and settle the score."

* * *

WITH A HORRIBLE ROAR OF THUNDER, THE BLACK MAW OF A portal spat the goddess onto the foot of Beatrice's bed. Beatrice cried out in alarm at the sight of the dripping, gory mess. Persephone's bloodstained face was lovely as ever, but it was full of a ferocity Beatrice had never seen before.

She couldn't help but rush to the goddess's side, to ease her into a more comfortable position on the bed. Beatrice felt thick, warm blood course over her hands, and she bit back a gasp and stilled a disgusted shudder.

"No, no," Persephone protested. "I can't lie down. We've work to do and only a bit of—"

"My Lady, what happened? You're in dire need of attention, so I'll find that blonde, Jane, the Healer—"

"No, no, we've no time! I must offer my last energies to my new form, I can't afford to convalesce—"

"My Lady, you're half dead."

"I'll be better off if you *help* me!" The goddess had clearly come from a fight and was ready to begin another. "It's time," she continued, breathing deeply.

Moment by moment, the blood and gore seemed to vanish, the sickly sweet scent of sour pomegranate lessened. The mortal world did this creature such good.

"I need your help now and in the coming months. Will you come?" the goddess rasped. "I must speak to the point, Beatrice. Since you were so angry before, I need to know your choice now: Do you accept the dangers that may yet come if you follow and aid me?"

Beatrice was too moved by the terrible sight of her to refuse. "I accept."

Ibrahim had abandoned her, but the goddess needed her. The fire of purpose flowed through her veins.

"I understand now," Beatrice said sympathetically, "how you

can lose all sense of time. When you lose a person who had begun
to define you . . . you just float. Like a ghost."

The goddess nodded. While the blood on her gown had faded
and its torn layers had mended themselves, Persephone's lungs
still rattled. She frowned and placed a hand on Beatrice's blood-
soaked bedding, turning the duvet entirely into red silk. "I'd give
anything to spare you that hollow existence, Beatrice."

Beatrice shook her head. "The solution is not in your power,
and I'd not take such charity if it were. It would be wrong to make
someone love me who chose to forsake me with an unsubstanti-
ated explanation—"

"Ibrahim?" interrupted the goddess. "Why?"

"Something about a nightmare."

Persephone sighed. "He senses the danger you are about to
face. There *are* trials ahead. I dearly trust and truly need you, but
I also respect mortal choice. If you refuse me, I will try to make
do. If you choose to help me, your willing mortal choice will
strengthen and empower all that I ask."

Danger felt so much better than numbness. "You once told me
we were chosen because we would say yes," Beatrice stated. "What
do we do now?"

The goddess smiled, grateful. As she got to her feet, she swayed,
and Beatrice steadied her. "We must go. I'm sorry about the bedclothes. I know you hate that garish color of silk."

Beatrice couldn't help but chuckle at such a mundane concern.
"Lead on, my Lady."

Persephone opened her hands; Beatrice's stomach dropped and
her head spun in a dizzy whirl. Suddenly they stood on a precipice
high over a darkened London, lashed by a freezing wind. The
divinity's robes that had cleaned themselves were again bloodied
and dripping.

The goddess steadied Beatrice and herself on the great frame
of a wide void that looked out onto the mortal world.

"The Liminal edge must help me find the girl I'm to become in order to finally be done with this form. You, Beatrice, are one of few mortals ever to see this threshold, which has proved the doom and salvation of countless numbers of your kind. This is the place from which fate's greatest commissions are wrought."

A flicker of familiar blue fire coursed round the edge of the Liminal frame and kissed Persephone's cheek before the tendril floated to touch Beatrice's hand in deference.

"My love," Persephone murmured to the fire. She breathed a sigh of happiness. "Are you here to watch me find her?"

"Indeed," rumbled the voice of Phoenix. Beatrice marveled at it, the rich baritone that had so rarely brushed her ear. "I want to be with you when you go."

Persephone addressed the Liminal. "Tell me what you want. I shall go where you bid. Tell me what sacrifice I must give."

Beatrice shivered. What could such an awesome threshold ask? Hadn't this goddess, and everyone who suffered with the Grand Work, made sacrifice enough?

A torrent of images played over the great space like pictures cast upon a canvas, villages and towns along northeastern England. A clock high above them whirred. When the blur of images stilled, the barrel of numbers above hovered between 1875 and 1878.

The scene revealed a little girl, with white hair and skin and ice-pale eyes, alone in a brick courtyard, staring up at a ghost in Elizabethan garb. Perhaps all of seven years old, she spoke timidly: "Gregory, why do I see you and speak to you if others can't?"

"Because thou art special, my girl," the spirit replied.

"I'm not special. I am a . . . *freak*. That's what the novices say when they think I can't hear them."

"You mustn't listen."

"I can't help it. It hurts. I'm so scared. I see things. Terrible things I don't understand. Reverend Mother says I'm not to speak to any one of them."

"And thou shouldst not, dear girl. The world, I fear, shall not understand thee."

"It doesn't. But you do." The girl reached out her arms. Gregory, chuckling, tried and failed to enclose her in his incorporeal arms.

"I love you, Gregory, but I wish you could give me a real embrace. I want so badly to be touched," she said, displaying a quiet mournfulness far beyond her years.

"Someday, my girl, thou shalt gain a beloved. I swear this upon my buried bones."

The eerie girl looked at him from beneath her wide-brimmed hat and smiled a hopeful, lovely smile that could make flowers grow. The Liminal shifted, showing them the exterior of the convent before its vast surface went dark.

"I . . . I won't *take* a young woman's body," Persephone breathed, seeming to have gleaned more than Beatrice, who remained confused, "but be born again. Born as a timid girl who doesn't remember who she is. That's why I couldn't say 'I' when declaring Prophecy! She doesn't remember a thing. She's all alone with ghosts, never touched . . . How is the life of a mortal freak any different from my life now?" she cried, clenching her fists. "Why can't I simply take a mortal body as I am; blaze down upon the Earth in glory, without a further lifetime of trial?"

Beatrice watched her. This was clearly new and heartbreaking knowledge.

"It is as I feared," Phoenix murmured.

Persephone whirled, droplets of blood flying everywhere. "As you feared?"

"Yes, but you must make this change, beloved, or you'll end up with nothing. Choose life while you still can. Before you're all bled out and nothing is left. Go. You must, there's no turning back."

The goddess shook with terror. The Liminal registered and amplified her anxiety; its glassy portal shuddered and shed sparks at its edges. Lightning streaked across it, illuminating their surroundings, revealing pillars made of skulls marching deep into the Whisper-world. The shadows scurried and hissed. This was not a place Beatrice wanted to linger.

"I don't want to die!" Persephone cried. Her colors shifted and whirled, dizzying. Beatrice had never seen her so addled or un-hinged. It was terrifying.

"You won't die," Phoenix assured her. "You'll live on, you've seen—"

"But I won't remember. It will be as if I never existed."

"Tell me the alternative!" Phoenix bellowed and Beatrice winced, terrified by the sudden desperate tone of the Balance him-self. "Living like this? How long before you're nothing but rot, memory, and misery? How many times have we yearned for peace, since you first spilled your blood on these stones? First we must free our Guard, and then we can perhaps at last earn the Great Beyond!"

Persephone balled her fists, her prismatic eyes going onyx. Be-atrice's blood ran cold. This was not a look for a goddess of beauty, hope, and life; this was a harrowing look the Whisper-world had fashioned. Beatrice wanted to weep for this great decaying force that had been reduced to near madness, a husk of herself.

The shadows lengthened and more lightning forked across the Liminal. Its glassy surface practically went convex, as if reaching out for them. Behind them was a dank, dark labyrinth. Beatrice had stood in the shadow of death often enough to know it in her bones. Ahead, she saw possibility.

"My Lady, we must go," Beatrice pleaded. "If Darkness comes to this place—"

"Give me time," Persephone barked.

"You don't have it," Beatrice hissed. "Time isn't yours anymore. You're weak, and your immortality is fading." She dared grab hold of the goddess, squeezing her arms. "This is what you have pre-pared for, whether you knew everything or not."

Persephone seemed to come to her senses. Snapping from misery's stranglehold, the Whisper-world's poison, she importuned Phoenix, "What will it feel like?"

"I don't know," his fire replied. "It will feel . . . mortal. But your death won't be painful. Not like mine."

"I'm so sorry—"

"Stop. You've apologized for my death a million times. It's time to let go. We both must let go. Go unto the vessels awaiting us."

"I love you," she gasped.

Blue fire wrapped her tight. "So you do, and so you shall. And I shall love you in return. Eternity awaits."

Persephone turned to the Liminal edge once more, silver tears glistening. "Dear Liminal. Show me how to proceed. I know you require sacrifice, so tell me—"

"My Lady," Beatrice murmured in sad realization. "You *are* the sacrifice."

Persephone stood on the threshold, wavering. "Ah." She swallowed. "So I am."

The shadows nearly exploded around them. A roaring sound, rattling bones. A flash of red. Darkness was nearly upon them. They had to go.

"I beg you, Liminal, who needs me?" the goddess asked the portal in a small voice.

There was a sparking, answering light to counter the growing abyss.

"Now!" Beatrice cried, and grabbing hold of the divinity, she threw them both into the void.

CHAPTER
TWENTY-SEVEN

WITH A DEAFENING ROAR AND A CORUSCATION OF LIGHT, BEATRICE and Persephone found themselves lying on hard stone. They opened their eyes and struggled to their feet, gasping, for they were surrounded by fresh human blood. Beatrice had enough of the sight, smell, and feel of blood to last lifetimes. A shaking woman lay next to them.

"Oh my," Persephone breathed, looking down at the source. The divinity's fear seemed to vanish, replaced by the need to be luminous and strong for the woman before her. "Who did this to you, dear girl?" she asked. In the mortal world, the goddess was again clean, clad in swaths of red silk.

Before them lay a broken woman in a threadbare dress. She was young, redheaded and sickly pale. She stared up in wonder at the two women who had quite literally fallen from the sky to land beside her. The Liminal remained open; its light was strong at Beatrice's back. Its humming vibrations felt much the way phoenix fire once had in her veins.

Suddenly Beatrice felt a shock—the woman's position mirrored Jean's, lying in his own blood on the Cairo stones. A hand flew to her mouth and she turned away, unable to look.

"It was Bill," the woman said in a light Irish brogue. "He's in the drink again. I-I don't think he meant to push me." She took a shaking breath. "They all ran when I fell. I can't . . . feel my legs. But you're surely angels so I'm just fine now, come to carry me . . ."

Beatrice glanced up. They were in the courtyard of an old inn; three floors of whitewashed balconies rose above them. There was no one there; the doors were all closed and the shades drawn. An eerie, deadly hush had fallen.

Anger swelled in Beatrice's heart. Had this woman been left to die alone, abandoned by cowards who feared danger or the law? Not that women fared well under the law; abusers were the ones more often protected. Damn the miseries and injustices of the Whisper-world, there was plenty of that and more on Earth.

"We are here to help," the goddess stated. Persephone's anxiety, pain, and madness were entirely forgotten; all her attention was on the injured woman. Beatrice was oddly touched by this selflessness.

"Think of someplace important to you . . ." The goddess paused, kneeling at her side cycling colors, touching her cheek gently and in doing so, intuiting something. "*Iris.* You're Iris, aren't you? Lovely name."

The young woman nodded, grateful to be known.

"Someplace safe, think of it *now*," the goddess continued, scooping the young woman into her arms. An instant later, the Liminal blazed bright, and they were transported.

The sensation was again whirling and light-filled, but this time when they touched down, Beatrice was steady on her feet. They were in a stone room furnished only with a chair and a cot, upon which Persephone settled her burden.

She urged her patient back onto the pillows, imploring her to relax and lie still. The young woman obediently did so. Persephone's prismatic shifts of light grew more subtle, less manic. Iris's blood vanished.

"Tell me about this place," Persephone said, sitting on the edge of the bed and brushing the hair out of the young woman's face. "Tell me where we are and all about you."

The young woman glanced around the room, then down at her

body, now whole and unsoiled. She stared at the goddess and spoke softly, in awe. "M-my name is Iris Parker, and we're in the north of England, where my family landed after a failed time in Ireland. This is the convent where they sent me before I ran off and fell in with sinners. Oh, Holy Mother, I beg your forgiveness of all my sins!"

"You are forgiven everything, child," Persephone said, assuming the identity Iris needed her to be. "A child named for the rainbow. Beautiful Iris, God loves you."

Beatrice hung back in the shadows as Iris wept; the scene was too intimate to disrupt.

"No need to cry, unless it is for joy," Persephone said with a smile. "You've been chosen for a great task."

"I have?" the young woman asked.

"Yes, Iris. You shall bring something great into the world. I give my rainbow unto you, and all my colors together shall be a bright and brilliant white."

Iris seemed much younger than Beatrice, though they were about the same age. The responsibility of the Guard had put aeons between their hearts and minds. "Why me?" the redhead asked.

"Because when I asked, the heavens responded that you needed me," Persephone replied. "And I need you, too."

The goddess stood. Her light brightened, though it left Beatrice shrouded in shadow.

"You shall bear a child," Persephone said, and Iris's expression bloomed. Beatrice had only seen such transparent emotion on Ahmed's face, and she found herself caught off guard and inordinately touched by Iris's joy, as if a child were all she'd ever wanted. Perhaps by watching other people's emotions, she encountered her own.

Persephone continued. "A child like no other, she will offer hearts peace, and she will triumph against Darkness despite obstacles and iniquity. She escapes a prison of her soul to be reborn in love. She will make a life of pain into a life of love, a life that she was denied."

As she spoke, the goddess wept, glistening tears rolling down her cheek. She cupped her hand at her sternum, and Beatrice saw her palm glimmer silver as the tears pooled in her palm.

"Wh-what shall I call the child?" Iris breathed, not for a moment questioning her destiny. Beatrice wondered at that. Though perhaps if she'd had her own life so obviously saved, she wouldn't question fate, either.

The goddess blushed. "I ought to be more original, but I am too fond. Call her Persephone as . . . it is my favorite of all names. And now, dear girl, sleep. In the morning you will not be alone."

She opened her hand, revealing what her tears had made: a silver chain bearing a glorious phoenix pendant, wings boldly outstretched and fiery tail arched artfully. The silver talisman faintly glowed.

Persephone kissed Iris's forehead and clasped the pendant about her neck. As the girl's eyes closed in sleep, the goddess said to Beatrice, "I need you to listen very carefully to what I'm about to say. If you fail, perhaps all we've done will be for naught."

Beatrice stared. Fear of her own limitations seized her, and she echoed Iris: "Why me?"

The goddess returned her stare. "Why not you? Are you not capable of great things? Did you not think that, when you asked the heavens to clarify that most grand of all human questions, 'Why am I here, and what is my purpose,' that the heavens might actually respond?"

Beatrice swallowed. She had not. But she did not back down from the goddess's gaze.

Satisfied, Persephone continued. "I cannot be too careful. Darkness has sentinels and might take drastic measures when he realizes what I have done. It's why I've never done this before. I've been too scared about what it might unleash upon the earth."

Beatrice shivered. "What sorts of things?"

"Terrible things. Hounds of hell that your lot, thankfully, has had never to deal with—and that I pray he doesn't let loose. Horsemen, riding up from the river of Death itself. What you see as a violent storm, I see as dread horsemen seeking to drown souls in an undertow of misery."

"Do you mean all these things will pursue poor Iris Parker?"

Persephone shook her head. "Time in the Whisper-world is different. Darkness will not perceive my absence right away, nor will he pinpoint exactly where I have gone. Iris, and you, will be safe. Though I fear you'll be quite haunted."

"But when he realizes you've abandoned him—"

"Yes, Beatrice. Then, there will be war."

"War." Beatrice's already cold blood froze. "*War* is a good time to cast aside divinity and become mortal?" She checked on Iris, but the woman slumbered on, undisturbed at her raised voice.

"It's the only way, Beatrice. Phoenix was right. I cannot foil Darkness otherwise. A stranger can, so that stranger I shall become. I've been knitting the worlds, readying for the phoenix fire and the time when that eerie little girl we saw becomes a woman, ready to receive her fate."

Beatrice was amazed by the change in the goddess's demeanor. Her faltering youth and naive fear had evaporated, replaced by determination.

"For safety's sake," Persephone continued, "cover traces of the child's birth. Make sure that Iris Parker arrives at that convent in York, the one from the vision. The reverend mother there will know what to do, I'll make sure of it."

She displayed a different chain, a silver key sparkling in the moonlight. "From the Guard's sacred space, this key will reveal the terrain of the Whisper-world and the location of the Guards' prison. Conceal it in a false infant's grave next to the real grave of Iris Parker."

Beatrice started. "Grave?"

"You saw the girl I am to be, she appears an orphan. I do not think Iris survives the birth," Persephone said sadly. Moonlight surrounded Iris's sleeping head like a halo.

"You've saved her only to kill her?"

"You saw me ask the Liminal what mortal needed me most. Who am I to question?"

Beatrice couldn't find words. This work defied right and wrong, joy and sadness, life and death. She supposed that dying alone in a heap of blood and broken bones was far worse than dying as the mother of a prophecy. This way, Iris could perhaps go more directly to that heaven for which she pined, feeling like one of its angels.

"You must go now," Persephone said. "Take Iris someplace safe. You cannot stay here where the Liminal deposited us; Whisper-world agents may trace the scent of me."

The divinity's expression grew very sad, and her voice was hollow.

"I thought I could come to him now, matured," she murmured. "I thought I'd simply take a body, knowing who I am and what we're to do. Now I see the timing's off. In those first visions I just didn't see it or realize. I should have tried sooner."

She couldn't mask the pain in her voice, but steeling herself, Persephone continued: "I'm going to go appear to that reverend mother and proclaim that an odd child born like starlight and snow shall come into her care, and when she is a woman, she shall take her place at Athens. And I'll pray that she's loved by he who is meant to love her. I've prophecies to proclaim, and I must also . . . say good-bye."

Beatrice stepped toward the goddess. "Please, my lady. Be mindful of mortal time," she cautioned. "Remember you're not good at it."

"When it matters, I am." The goddess placed her hand on

Beatrice's shoulder, and Beatrice felt how it trembled. "Can I trust you to remain here and wait for me?"

Beatrice swallowed and nodded. She had little else to live for.

"I'll return before morning. Thank you. Thank you for pushing me out into this world. I needed it. I needed you."

Beatrice nodded again. It was nice to be thanked and needed. It eased the sting of the bittersweet wound that had defined her life. Thinking of Persephone, she wondered if the Grand Work would also define her death.

CHAPTER
TWENTY-EIGHT

PERSEPHONE STOOD OVER ALEXI'S SLEEPING FORM.

"This is the last time, Alexi," she whispered.

Phoenix fire responded to her presence, rising up from his host in protest. "I have warned you, take care with him. Remember he is but mortal youth. He doesn't react well to your mitigating his memories. I daresay you cause more pain than pleasure. We've a vested interest not to break him prematurely."

Persephone winced. "May I say good-bye in a dream, then?"

"Yes, just . . ." Phoenix hesitated as Beatrice had. The divinity realized she was losing trust.

"I'll return to you, and do what must be done . . ." the goddess promised.

ALEXI DREAMED THAT HE STOOD AT THE EDGE OF A MOOR AT twilight. At his side stood the goddess. His goddess. Heather rolled away from them in gently bending waves, rustling; while the flower was subtle-scented, in a mass their odor was powerful, yet pleasant. There was nothing in view save the field and her, all light and color and breathlessness. She wore a red silk gown. Her eyes seemed tired.

Stretching her limbs, she closed her eyes, breathed in the heather, and sighed.

Her colors were shifting more slowly than usual and her breathing was strained, Alexi realized. Could a goddess grow ill? Perhaps there was a limit to how long a being of light could live in a dark world for which she was not meant.

"Heather," she said at last. "It can grow in dim, gloomy climes; its loveliness refuses to submit to shadow. It is a flower that represents me well."

He stepped toward her, close enough to feel her shifting temperatures, warm then cool, depending on the color, and took her hand. He strained to stay sensible, was choked with fear of saying the wrong thing, even in a dream.

"This is the last time I can ever come to you, Alexi," she whispered, squeezing his hand, pressing it to her lips. "In person or in a dream, save for what your imagination may fashion."

"When you go," he murmured, "and take memories from me, please do me the courtesy of taking my heart as well. Cut it from me. It's a pointless instrument without you." He tried to suppress desperation and speak with the dispassion he retained in his day-to-day life, but such detachment was impossible around this being.

She shifted her head to look at him, smiling in that maddening way that combined love, pity, and sorrow. "You'll need your heart. For her. Her breath will whisper of me," the goddess said softly. "Her light will call down my strength. Her love will be boundless."

Alexi furrowed his brow. "But she will not be you? You are what I need."

"She will be what you need, and you what she needs. Shall you yet argue? You break my heart as you fight me, eroding my resolve to do what I must."

It would seem expressing his true feelings only made things worse. Choking back a torrent of declamations, he resolved to say nothing, withdrawing his hand from hers.

Her resulting chuckle was almost more maddening. "Oh, Alexi, look at you! Such impassioned intensity, my brooding, tormented hero. I daresay your enigmatic nature will make some young romantic fall quite helplessly in love with you."

Alexi frowned. When she giggled, his frown became a scowl.

"Have I offended you?" she breathed. "Oh, come now, such a face!"

"I'm practicing," he retorted. "For that brooding hero role you suggest."

She studied him for a moment before laughing, turning him to face her, running a hand through his mop of black hair. "There's hope for you yet."

"Well, I'd like to be fallen for helplessly, so I'll do whatever you suggest."

Persephone grinned. "You shall be successful."

Alexi grabbed the goddess by her arms.

"Promise me that when Prophecy comes, she won't be taken away. Promise me something that's mine, a haven I can rely on. I've been abandoned by my parents; my beloved grandmother is dead. Everyone looks to me for answers and asks something. Let me have something of my own. If she will be taken away, as you take yourself and these memories, I swear to you I'll go mad. Give me something I can *keep*."

"I have seen your future," the goddess replied. "I promise."

"So, why not tell me everything? If there is a plan, how are we to follow it if we do not know it?"

She fought back silver tears. "That is for you to learn. But be careful. I've been warned of betrayals, that mortal hearts are fallible. I dare not pin your hopes on anything that may yet change, not when your capacity for *choice* is what makes Prophecy come true. Divine machinations agree that two lonely mortals must find and love each other, on their own, or none of it will take."

"Why can't you just stay with me?" he asked plaintively, moving to embrace her, clutching her with tight, trembling desperation.

"Because this form is rotting, Alexi, I don't show you the damage and I won't, but I'm broken and I am at my last gasp. I am tied to the Whisper-world. I must break those bonds." She leaned over him. "You'll be wonderful. You'll have something wonderful. I promise. Now let me go."

"I love you. She'll love you. Let me go," Persephone whispered to the slumbering Alexi, extricating herself from his consciousness.

Now that she did not need to be strong for him anymore, her shoulders fell, and she wept.

"I need to change that letter."

Ascending the stairs, she wandered to the little room she had seen in her vision, withdrawing her and his parents' note from its hiding place, fumbling for a fountain pen. Her silver tears wiped clean the ink, and she began again, adjusting for new knowledge, speaking to the woman she would become as a stranger. Finished, she folded the sheets and wrote *The Rychmans* on the outside before tucking it back into its hiding place.

Returning to Alexi's bedroom, she gazed one last time upon him, trying to store his image in her memory, hoping her colorless form would know him when she saw him. As she stared, blue fire began to pour out of him, and Phoenix amassed himself before her.

"I'm scared to die, my love," she whispered.

The voice of Phoenix was choked. "Oh, love, I'm as scared and devastated as you. I lose *this* you. I'll never see you like this again." His fire raced over her, trying to seize her in the form he had first and always loved.

"When I return to him," the fire continued, "I will give over to him and fade to his background. I will defer to him, have no control. Without you to command me, I'm only the fire he wields, nothing more. Now we must trust two mortals full of Power and Light to find each other. Like you and I once did."

"I know that they must be left to it," she said, fear in her voice. "They are so beautiful, he and she."

"We are so beautiful, you and I," Phoenix declared.

For an endless time they stood, murmuring their love as a mantra to strengthen their resolve. Eternity awaited, perhaps Peace like they'd never known. Their aching good-bye would birth a new dawn.

A bright light suffused the room as the Liminal drew Persephone away. Knowing she was nearing the end, she nonetheless went willingly.

Phoenix sank back into Alexi and was erased until he and his beloved met again; when they would be called to be gods once more.

CHAPTER
TWENTY-NINE

PERSEPHONE'S LIGHT WOKE BEATRICE, WHO HAD SLUMPED against the stone wall. It was still dark. Iris Parker slept peacefully.

The goddess knelt and took Beatrice's hand, captured her gaze with those prismatic eyes and spoke with quiet urgency: "I pray that when all is said and done there may be no more need for a Guard, that the difficult questions of the Grand Work will never again plague mortals. In the meantime, remember its goodness, its beauty. Remember this in the future, when the most harrowing things are asked of you."

Beatrice shuddered, wondering what ominous things were yet to come. Persephone kissed her hands before releasing them. A complex torrent of emotions passed over the goddess's face, amplified by her youthful divinity.

"Remember blood and fire," she continued. "When you are called again, I hope you will choose to come and help. Our fates are tied, Leader." Her tears streamed so steadily she might have made many divine talismans had she caught them, but she let them roll away like tiny gems.

The goddess took a deep breath, wiped the silver from her eyes and straightened her shoulders. "I can't wait any longer else I'm truly a coward. To the undiscovered country!"

So, it came down to this instant, where things would change

forever. Beatrice held her breath. Persephone moved toward Iris Parker, her colors shifting less rapidly.

"Let it, at last, in ending, begin," she breathed.

The room blazed with crackling threads of light that Beatrice recognized from the Liminal threshold. The air was filled with the music of heaven, a celestial chorus. The light grew ever brighter until Beatrice had to close her eyes and look away.

"Oh! It *will* be beautiful," Persephone cried joyously. Then all was darkness and silence.

Beatrice opened her eyes. The room had filled with ghosts who gazed at Iris in awe, in seeming confirmation that she was now a new mother-to-be. The space grew chill from their presence, though they seemed harmless enough.

In any case, Beatrice thought, there was nothing she could do to deter them. Wide-eyed, she kept watch and pondered what she had witnessed until sleep eventually took her.

At dawn she awoke. The ghosts still surrounded Iris's bed; as Beatrice pulled a chair to the bedside, she batted her hands at them, to no effect. They remained enraptured by the lovely young woman who now carried within her an instrument of peace. Beatrice wondered at the fate of the child, who might not have any concept of who she was: the mortal child made from an immortal being.

Iris woke with a start. Beatrice placed her hand on the young woman's forehead. "Do not be afraid," she said.

"For you bring great tidings?"

Beatrice's lips thinned at the recited scripture. "Something like that. My name is Beatrice."

"You were one of the angels that saved me!"

Beatrice offered a partial smile and thought it best not to argue this.

After a long moment, Iris began to look around in amazement. Beatrice wondered what she saw, but the young woman's next words confirmed her suspicions. "Spirits! Like in the magazines!

I've had stories read to me whenever anyone might humor me. I've always wanted to see a ghost, like in those tales."

Beatrice herself wished she couldn't. Not when she could not do anything about them.

"You must stay here, Miss Parker, and rest. I must fetch us some things in London, as our fates are now entwined. I'll return to you soon." The room grew increasingly cold as more spirits appeared, floating peacefully, watching. Due to their deep reverence, Beatrice did not worry they would do harm to Iris while she was gone.

At the door, she turned. "If the spirits frighten you, hold to that pendant of yours. It is your guardian angel, the only power we have left."

"But we've all the power of heaven," Iris replied, beaming.

"Hold tight to that certainty, my dear." Beatrice wished she were as confident.

CHAPTER

THIRTY

"THERE YOU ARE!" BELLE CRIED IN RELIEF AS BEATRICE ENTERED La Belle et La Bête, closing the wide umbrella that had only partially shielded her against the insistent rain. Embracing her, she hurried Beatrice inside, took her accoutrements, and immediately fussed over some tea.

"I was very worried about you! I went to Athens, and you were nowhere to be found. It's been a week! What was I to think? Where were you?"

"The goddess whisked me away to the Whisper-world," Beatrice replied, adjusting the folds of her traveling skirt as she sat at the polished wooden bar. "When the Whisper-world spat me back out again, I was all the way in the north country."

Belle gaped. "What? The Whisper-world? Isn't that forbidden? Isn't that supposed to drive you mad, going in there as a mortal?"

"There is a Whisper-world threshold few mortals see, a terrible, awesome place. But the goddess protected me," Beatrice said. "I cannot stay here, but I wanted to gather my belongings and tell you and George what's gone on. A packed trunk sits in a waiting carriage, and I have a duty in the north, caring for a mother-to-be. Much is yet needed of me," Beatrice said into her cup of tea, which warmed her comfortingly. "No rest for the wicked."

"You're hardly wicked. What was it like there?"

"At the edge of the Whisper-world? It was like a proscenium arch, and I sensed that from it or through it all things may be possible—with sacrifice. That's the way of life we have come to understand, isn't it? Strange, awesome beauty; painful sacrifice. I saw visions of the future, watched as our Lady realized she won't come again to this Earth as herself. Her powers will pass on in some form, but she, no. Not as herself. It was . . . difficult. And now she's gone."

"What?" Belle murmured.

"The goddess is gone. A young woman will bear a mortal child—what's left of the goddess we knew. I must see that she ends up in York, and then I must leave her to her fate."

Belle blinked. "The goddess is gone? She made mention of turning a new leaf, of a new dawn, but . . ." Tears appeared in her eyes. "Is there anything I can do?"

"No. The seeds of Prophecy are already put into place. After this, even my role is limited. But first I must return to Iris Parker." Beatrice sighed. "Her mortal coil will also be sacrificed to the Grand Work. A Work that gives and takes life so freely . . ."

Belle shook her head, dismayed. "Would you like me to go with you?"

Beatrice smiled wanly. "You're a dear, Belle. But no, I need to be on my own. This is my cross to bear, and I am unfit for company. But I did want to tell you. I wanted someone to know . . ."

"Has Ibrahim—"

Something about saying his name, the expression on Beatrice's face must have told Belle all she needed to know.

Belle clutched her hand. "Being Leader is an oft lonely fate."

Beatrice did not argue.

"Poor Iris," Beatrice murmured, changing the subject away from the pain of unrequited love. "Full of loving faith. Such a joyous soul for such a hard life, she shames me with her fortitude, her bright kindness, her blind trust. I believe she knows she's going to die. Ghosts flocked to her immediately, knowing she holds something special. The spirits aren't malevolent, which is good, as I've no power to guard her. Nothing but a talisman the goddess left before she passed on. *In.* Passed in, rather. Into mortality."

Beatrice spoke as if to herself, in a reverie, but her glazed eyes eventually focused back on her friend. "So pray for me. For us. I don't know if I can trust in prayer, but I need *some* help as I take her to York. It's supposed to be far enough from London so that the child won't be caught up in the Grand Work but close enough for her to come here when she's a woman, ready to love and ready to take charge.

"Timid, though," Beatrice added with a shudder. "She looked too timid in the vision. I pray that once she comes into the Guard's care that she is bolstered, that those eerie eyes blaze with confident power. I'd hate to think that the fate of every Guard rests in trembling, ghost-pale hands. But nothing's certain. We can plant seeds but the rains still have to come. Prophecy must have room to grow."

"I cannot presume to understand a word of this," Belle said, "but I can most certainly pray for a joyous result after all our sacrifices. Though I'll be the first to say that my fate has been a blessing." Her smile indicated she thought of George. "But tell me of your heart before you go. How *are* you?"

"I'm fine," Beatrice replied.

Belle just looked at her. She refilled Beatrice's tea. She kept looking.

"I'm fine," Beatrice repeated. "Ibrahim is gone from my life. He wrote saying he would not be returning for me nor should I look for him in Cairo. What more is there to say?"

Belle leaned in across the bar. "Your countryman Dickens claims that 'life is full of meetings and partings.' Even the new Leader says so."

"And?"

"He leaves out reunions."

"Ibrahim is not coming back," Beatrice said sharply.

"Beatrice, you two are suited. Like it or not, you are. Elegant, stubborn, strong, and true. If he doesn't come back, you must go to Cairo, I don't care what he said."

"I'm not about to chase him! He clearly doesn't care for me, and I don't want to hear another word about it." Beatrice turned. "It's good to see you, Belle. I'll return once the child is born and poor Iris Parker's body is in the ground . . ." At this, Beatrice choked. She kissed Belle softly on the head, snatched her umbrella, and fled back out into the rain.

An onlooker would surmise Ibrahim was a young man in control of his destiny, a savvy traveler and son of the world. Inside, he was filled with fear and regrets that were eating him alive. He had two choices: Ignore the past year or embrace it as his defining hour and risk whatever was to come. Declare himself to a magnificent woman, despite his vision, and see what she would say.

He had an inkling that she cared. Surely he couldn't have imagined it. But likely she cared no longer, not the way he did. She was an Englishwoman, he an Egyptian, and they'd damnably never spoken about this sort of thing, so what did he truly know? To love or not to love. That was the question. Hamlet-like, perhaps. How English.

Ahmed and Verena's company was ever pleasant, but watching them grow joyfully closer was its own agony. They never made him feel unwelcome, but there were moments of awkward sadness. Verena once dared ask about Beatrice. When Ibrahim made no reply, neither Verena nor Ahmed spoke of her again. But the Leader was there, silently, in their hearts, as were Belle and George. Their beloved circle was broken but still part of them.

Ibrahim was there to celebrate when, beneath a particularly incredible moon, Verena agreed to be Ahmed's wife. When Ibrahim asked how they'd manage their different faiths, Ahmed pointedly reminded him that the Prophet said a man might marry any chaste woman "of the book"—and that the Abrahamic faiths included Jews and Christians. Abraham. *Ibrahim*. Perhaps his namesake was trying to tell him something.

"Besides," Ahmed exclaimed, "the Grand Work brings strangers together to weave new understandings. We each have personal truths: our loves, our respective faiths. But we also have the truth of our mutual love, born within the Power and the Light. It would be a shame and its own sin to deny that, would it not?"

Ibrahim couldn't help but agree, though he was uncomfortable with the way Ahmed eyed him. Ahmed didn't need a Muse to be powerful; he was naturally adept at penetrating the human heart. The man's own heart was twice the size of any regular mortal. They all were, in their way, still *more*.

Time passed, Ibrahim became numb; he did not allow himself to think of Beatrice. He was only jarred back into focus one evening when he and Ahmed stood on the balcony ledge of Ibrahim's rented rooms.

"Your vision," Ahmed said. "What you assume was Beatrice's death. We are not gods able to know the circumstances. You share little of your heart with me, but I read your eyes, the corners of your mouth, the tone of your voice . . . You're a different man without her. You grow increasingly like the ghosts we once fought—insubstantial yet bitter."

With a sigh, Ahmed continued, "The fact remains, you cannot take her hand in Cairo when she lives in England. And I do believe, no matter what you saw, that you should take her hand."

Ibrahim opened his mouth to protest, but Ahmed waved him to silence. Behind him, Verena appeared, carrying a tea tray, and the beautiful woman said boldly, "Staring down death made me discard subtlety. Go back for her, you lovely fool."

"I can't," Ibrahim choked out, as if the desert took hold of his throat. A painful, wrenching feeling. "The vision of Beatrice going gray in death . . . It is too terrible to tempt. I believe she's safer if I remain far away."

No more was said on the subject.

Some time later Ibrahim received a letter from Belle and George, sent via Ahmed. Belle began the note and wasted no time in getting to the point.

Mr. Wasil-Tipton,

I understand you wrote to our beloved Miss Smith and severed ties. While I think this cowardly, I trust you have reasons. Despite those, please understand what your prolonged absence has done. Beatrice is a ghost of what she once was. Her pride would never admit it, but as friend to both of you, it's time someone was honest. She needs her pillar, her second-in-command.

I believe it is proper to tell you this: Beatrice is currently engaged in the Grand Work. The goddess as we knew her is no more. Did you feel the storms in Cairo, or do you shun the traces of our power like you do our Leader?

The goddess will be born mortal. Ghosts swarm around her expectant mother, and Beatrice protects her. I asked if we could help, but she adamantly refused. I do not think she would refuse you.

Despite your vision, it is my instinct and perhaps my too-bold opinion that you do more harm than good by staying away. You could read to these ghosts, just as you did to Verena when our powers had gone. You could still be of service, keeping them civil and passive.

Could you not try to be our Leader's companion—in any and every way she needs? She will take no other.

Or are you truly as lost to us all as you would seem? We all love you,

Belle

Here the script changed:

This is George. Must I paint you a picture of what is required?
Don't be stupid. Hie thee back to England.

Ibrahim laughed. It felt so very good to laugh, to feel tears rimming his eyes in happy release. Was his beloved truly so struck by his absence? Knowing this did not solve his fear of harming her, but he rejoiced in a manner of exquisite pain.

Belle spoke truth; an echo of his previous power remained. Intuition flooded him. Assisting his Leader was the right thing to do. Fear had made him foolishly don a mantle of misery. He could help in Persephone's transformation, and having seen the danger in advance, perhaps he could keep his treasure safe. He would indeed be a coward not to return, bearing a brimming heart unto a worthy hand.

ONE BRIGHT MORNING, BELLE OPENED THE DOOR OF LA BELLE et La Bête to an insistent knock. She and George had spent a late night at the theater the night before, then treated themselves to a bottle of wine from the café's stores. She had not yet opened the café for business that day.

"Ibrahim!" she exclaimed, finding her former comrade on the doorstep. He was well appointed in a new suit coat and vest, looking every bit the Englishman as he'd looked the Egyptian in Cairo. She eyed him warily. "What are you doing here?"

"I was struck by your letter. I . . . I've come back."

Belle just stared, waiting for him to continue.

"I . . . am worried for Beatrice."

"You should be," Belle exclaimed, her French accent suited to scolding. "You should've seen her after your letter!" She gestured that he enter as a teapot began to scream behind the bar. "What are you going to do about it?"

"If her work is as you've said, then I agree that it remains my duty to offer assistance. I'll simply . . . be very careful." He added, as if to himself, "I won't ever take her hand. In my vision, I clutched her hand and she died."

Belle's eyes flashed. "You won't 'take her hand . . .' Metaphorically or literally? Vision or no, to base your future on that one detail is absurd."

Ibrahim couldn't hold Belle's gaze. He nodded. "Ahmed also reminded me that visions may have multiple truths and variable interpretations." He cleared his throat and admitted, "Truth be told, I am miserable without her."

"That's better." Belle brightened so swiftly the dizzying shift mirrored the goddess. "Tea?"

Ibrahim shook his head. "Women. You are enigmas."

"No, we're just always waiting for men to say the proper thing. Now and then you do. And upon such occasions, we rejoice." She slid a warm cup in a delicate saucer across the bar.

"What's all this racket before noon?" George called. His freckled face lit with happiness as he came into view upon the stairs. "Ho-ho, Ibrahim, my friend. You're back! Love it or hate it, the Grand Work can't keep us apart, even when we're done with it!" He bounded down the last few steps, pumped Ibrahim's hand with a hard, jovial shake, and gave him a strong pat on the back for good measure.

Belle pulled out a notebook and launched into particulars before Ibrahim could ask. "Beatrice spoke of a general route—convents, safe places for two women traveling without male company, ending inland at a Catholic convent in York. Can't be too many of those, so that narrows things down nicely." She scrawled names and locations.

"Did you . . . know I would come when you wrote?" Ibrahim was agog.

"I prayed desperately you would. I've never seen such hollow sadness on so regal a face."

"She was so visibly affected?" Ibrahim asked, trying to sound nonchalant.

Belle sighed, irritated. "Neither of you is capable of showing it when you're in the same room, but she's been heartbroken! Thorny and defensive . . ." Belle grinned. "If there's one thing I know, it's love in all its many colors. She's *deeply* in love."

George grinned goofily, as if this conversation were the best sport ever. Ibrahim pursed his lips, though his already careening sensibilities reeled anew. He tried to maintain his usual reserve; it would not do to come undone.

"The English think they invented civilization," Ibrahim muttered, "and the French think they invented love."

Belle and George laughed heartily and kissed each other.

Ibrahim cleared his throat again. He had long wondered that any human being could stand the idea of caring for someone so deeply, of needing someone, of wanting someone.

Apart from James Tipton, he had been an independent, solitary person with few meaningful connections—until the Grand Work. Now, a life alone would not satisfy. Not once one had the experience of being so peculiarly tied to other human souls. To such a soul as Beatrice Smith.

"My dear friend, has that golden skin of yours paled?" George laughed and then sobered, scowling, though his bright eyes still twinkled playfully. "I'm sorry. We should not be so sporting with you. This is a serious matter. The two of you." He crafted an exaggerated frown. "Such *serious* people—"

"The two of us nothing. I returned because I'm compelled to assist her work," Ibrahim barked. Defensive. Terrified. Goodness. They *were* suited.

"And so you shall," Belle said, producing a leather pocketbook full of bank notes from under the bar. "Take this. Use it for travel. Buy Beatrice something lovely. Give it to orphans." She tore her annotated paper from the notebook, placed it atop the pocketbook and said, "Here are the places she cited. Now, go on with you."

Ibrahim nodded. "Thank you both. I shall see you anon. Together we all shall celebrate the culmination of the Grand Work. Whatever our parts in it may be."

ONCE IBRAHIM HAD GONE, BELLE WAXED RHAPSODIC. "WHAT will their reunion be like—reserved or tender? Will they greet each other with civility or passion?"

George leaned upon the bar, grinning. "Passion? They don't know the meaning of the word."

"Oh, don't underestimate the stoic," Belle giggled. "Behind closed doors their kisses are often the most torrid!"

Clearing fallen window box petals from the street in front of the café, she was still imagining the possibilities when she saw an unlikely couple turn down the street. Recognizing them instantly, she hid behind the door. It had been many months since their paths had first crossed with any of the new Guard.

The lean, flaxen-haired youth with sharp features, was dressed finely to the point of gaudiness, while the olive-skinned, dark-haired girl beside him wore more sensible garb. One English, one French. How familiar. Belle wondered if it was a common pattern; the coupling of Memory, Artist, and disparate cultures.

The Artist's beauty outshone Memory's wealth; her youth was belied only by the two jarring shocks of white hair framing her face.

Memory looked around. Believing that he and the Artist were in no danger of being discovered, he closed the distance between them. His sharp features twisted into something devilish, rakish, and surprisingly attractive.

"At last, a moment away from our tedious lot," he exclaimed. "I now gaze upon the only thing that makes this bloody Work bearable."

"Why, Lord Withersby, you flatter me." The Artist giggled, her olive skin flushed. Belle decided to come out from behind the door to hear better, continuing to work with her broom while she eavesdropped.

"Flattery isn't always untrue. Come now, Josie—may I call you that?"

"Lord Withersby, you've been calling me Josie for months."

"Ah, so I've no manners. But, Josie, you're a balm to my misery. The six of us are to be joined for eternity, and I'd open my veins if not for you. Ruled by that brooding, insufferable Rychman? No title, no ancestral lands, yet he acts as if the heavens themselves opened to appoint him Leader."

"But, Elijah, the heavens did exactly that."

"Don't you play Rebecca and take his part! He doesn't have to be so haughty. I daresay he rubs it in, knowing I'd have twice his status were we not subject to this paranormal meddling!"

"His fine estate aside, a man's worth should be determined by his actions. By what he *does*." Josephine paused and raised an eyebrow as Elijah loosened his cuffs and waistcoat. "Or doesn't."

Josephine suddenly noticed Belle, and she and the Memory turned toward the door of the café. The Memory tipped his top hat.

"Good afternoon, mademoiselle, don't mind us, we're simply discussing the more tedious details of our Grand Work—we're spectral police, you see, keeping ghouls at bay by rites and rituals, with inexplicable fire, with music and all manner of incredible trickery." He smiled, believing he could reveal whatever he wished before wiping himself and his companion from her mind. Lifting his hand, his pale eyes sparkling with preternatural light, he tried to do just that.

Belle grinned, playing along, and allowed her eyes to glaze. Not that she could have retorted if she wanted; the goddess's protective spell yet held.

The Memory turned back to the Artist, his expression triumphant, but she stared up at the sign above her head. "La Belle et La Bête . . ."

The Memory began down the lane, his fine boots clipping against the stones. The Artist lingered.

Pretending to come back to herself, Belle resumed sweeping, then "noticed" the young woman in the street.

"*Bonjour*," she said. The other French girl lit up, and they exchanged a few pleasantries in their native language.

The Memory stopped and turned back, folding his arms. Josephine raised an eyebrow. "Since when is Lord Withersby so keen to return to his fellows? I thought you were taking me for refreshment."

"I had a place in mind," he replied.

When Josephine didn't move, Belle spoke in French. "Sometimes you don't know what you're looking for until you find it." She gestured down the stairs to the open door.

"Here, Lord Withersby," Josephine called. "Here."

When she entered, Lord Withersby, shrugging, traipsed after her. Cordial introductions were made as Belle seated them. Josephine looked about appreciatively at the work on the walls, products of George's brush.

"My resident artist," Belle said with a wink.

"Exquisite. Reminds me of someone." Josephine's dark eyes looked into her hazel ones.

"Funny that," Belle said, pouring some fine French wine. "Do you like the place?"

"I'm quite taken with it," Josephine breathed, lifting the stemware and swirling the deep red contents, breathing in the bouquet.

Abruptly Belle realized that this was a more fated encounter than she had at first suspected.

"Business is slow, you know. It's a bit out of the way," she said.

Elijah and Josephine replied in chorus, "I like that about the place."

"Pardon me," Belle said. "I shouldn't be so forward, but I sense you're a lovely young couple, well intentioned—"

Josephine blushed. "Oh, well, we're not a—"

"So I'll get to the point," Belle continued. "My partner and I have been planning to leave London for the coast. We're looking for someone to take over the café. Do think about it."

Either they were there because of Prophecy or they weren't. She left the pair with the bottle of wine, and cups of tea for good measure, and moved up the stairs, allowing them time with their thoughts. On the landing she found George, who'd been eavesdropping, too.

"Are we leaving?" he whispered. "Already?"

Belle shrugged. "We're on to Grimsby soon, and I think they should have the place. I may have lost my power, but I certainly haven't lost my instincts."

George poked his head around the balustrade to stare at the couple and shook his head.

"Poor sots," he whispered, turning back to her. "We had it easy, Belle, I see now. Those poor fools inherited the hard work for the rest of their bloody lives." He turned and went back up to his room.

Unable to resist, Belle continued to spy on the newcomers. She hardly knew them, but she loved this new couple like kin. They *were* kin. Sad that they couldn't know it.

The Memory was leaning over the table excitedly. "Let me buy this place for you, Josie. It's much better than that sordid flat of yours, and it will give us a safe place to occupy ourselves. I can't stand sitting about that *school*. I was meant for leisure, not labor! In the name of dear Saint George and whatever French saint you choose, grant me this safe harbor instead of that echoing institution. A Withersby simply doesn't know how to *exist* without a fine glass of wine. Come now, Josie—"

Josephine's laughter filled the room and Belle's heart. Elijah leaned close to her, trading his constant jokes for an earnest plea.

"Let me do something for you, Josie. Don't let the Withersby fortune languish without ever having done something decent. Perhaps you won't allow me to express my thoughts for you in any other way but material goods, but . . ."

In a tone heavy with anticipation, Josephine said, "Why? In what other ways would express your thoughts?"

The Memory leaned forward, reaching out a long-fingered hand and cupping the Artist's cheek. He kissed her, gently, tentatively. Belle felt that this moment had been brewing from the Grand Work's commission. She'd wanted George in the same way, from the very first.

The kiss deepened before Josephine broke away with a gasp. "We mustn't tell a soul about this!" she murmured. "Our stations, our work, it could never be—"

"What, caring for you must be as secret as the rest of my blasted fate?" The Memory scoffed. "Well, I couldn't tell my family, of course—"

Josephine gave him a sharp look. "I don't mean your family. I mean our motley circle. Poor Rebecca only has eyes for Alexi, Alexi only for himself and his work. Michael loves Rebecca, and Jane . . . Well, Jane baffles me. But we cannot be the lone pair—"

"The envy of all." Elijah chuckled.

"We mustn't drive such a wedge between us," Josephine said. "But you, Lord Withersby," she said, leaning close, "come from a class that is expert at keeping secrets."

"Just as you, my dear, are French. And I'll never let you forget it."

"Won't the others suspect, you buying me this place?"

Elijah shrugged. "I'll make Alexi pay half, like we did for Jane." He lifted his glass and said, "To La Belle et La Bête, our new home away from home!"

Belle went back downstairs, rounding the corner in time to see Elijah sweep Josephine into his arms and spin her about the floor.

"We'll take it!" he cried.

CHAPTER
THIRTY-ONE

IN TRUTH, BEATRICE WANTED TO BE FOUND. SHE WANTED TO feel she was joined with others in purpose, wanted to know her friends were interested in her safety. To her surprise, she missed the random, unannounced appearances of the goddess in all her mystery. She missed their maddening interplay.

Desired or not, however, no one was coming to find her, she knew, no herald or guardian angel. Life had moved on. Once Iris Parker gave birth and passed on, so would Beatrice, and her time doing the Grand Work would be entirely forgotten.

For the thousandth time, she debated rushing back to London, finding Alexi Rychman, and telling him exactly what would come to pass. But she knew that nothing was set in stone, that all the planning in the world couldn't make events take place as desired. And her tongue was yet shackled by the goddess's lingering magic.

What of her heart? Had she fallen in love of her own volition, or had that too been an act of magic? Leaders and seconds often did become lovers, she remembered. But she felt Ibrahim's loss more keenly now that her powers were gone and he was a world away.

She took some comfort from her task as she and Iris made their way, moving every few weeks, convent by convent, to York. Prophecy was progressing as well as it might. Beatrice was itching to leave their current place, afraid the concentration of ghosts, which grew with each passing day, would attract the wrong kind of attention.

"Good morning, Beatrice," Iris chirped as they took their tea and warm breakfast oats. "Are we relocating today?"

"If not today, tomorrow. We've grown weary of the ghosts of these walls, have we not? I daresay you're the spirit world's most popular mother."

"I wonder why that's so," Iris mused, then smiled. "No. I *know* why. It's because of my child, my Percy. Isn't that an endearing nickname for Persephone? I know it's a boy's name, but it will be special and unique, like her. My child will be a child of peace and love. She will be the sort of girl who sets souls at ease. That's why the spirits flock here."

"I believe you are correct," Beatrice replied. "Are you feeling well?"

"Oh, heavy and stiff, with pains here and there," Iris said cheerfully, adjusting her position against the headboard of her narrow bed. "She's healthy. I'd know if she wasn't. I'm sure the pain comes from being raised from the dead to bear her," Iris added, with a surprising matter-of-factness. "And I know, Beatrice, that my time is short."

Beatrice opened her mouth to protest, but Iris continued joyfully.

"No, it's all right, I was saved for this purpose. I'm utterly at peace, Beatrice Smith, so don't you cry over me. You may cry for yourself, certainly, for I see your heart is heavy. You may tell me your troubles if you've a mind."

Beatrice fought back astonishment at the other woman's perception. "No, you keep your lovely mind and heart focused on that baby. Give her your all energy, and fill her with love. She'll need all the love afforded her. It's a dark world into which she'll be born."

"She'll fill it with light," Iris promised.

"That she will. But she'll need your strength. She will likely be odd. Fragile."

"The meek shall inherit the earth."

"So they shall," Beatrice murmured. Privately, she wondered about the haunted. The dead, and those with hearts like her own. What would they inherit?

She kissed Iris on the forehead; she had grown genuinely fond of her in the weeks they'd spent together. Then she exited the room, envying such faith, trust, and joy.

THAT AFTERNOON, ONCE BEATRICE HAD HELPED BRAID IRIS'S hair and assisted her aching body into a flowing white shift, just as Beatrice was considering whether or not to set off or wait another day, there was a surprise as a sister came to their door. "There's a gentleman here to see you, Miss Smith. We aren't supposed to let men in, but he was so insistent, saying he's sought you for some time now, all down the English coast. He's just out in the hall, but, miss, he's a *foreigner!*"

Beatrice's heart convulsed in her chest, and she pushed past the girl almost without a word. At the last moment she said, "Thank you, Novice Clarence, I'll see him."

In the hall, she found Ibrahim in a fine long suit coat and waistcoat, a look he'd donned at times during their work in London, shifting fluidly between the diverse worlds to which he'd grown accustomed. Though she cared not a whit what he wore, she had to admit to herself that he looked unbearably dashing. Especially since he carried a large stack of books and magazines. Traveling with a library.

She made herself scowl, though she knew her eyes must glow. *He had come for her!*

"You may leave us, Novice Clarence. Mr. Wasil-Tipton is a colleague, and we've business matters." The novice bobbed her head and vanished.

Beatrice folded her arms and opened her mouth to speak, but Ibrahim set the reading materials on a nearby ledge and strode forward a few paces, forestalling her.

"I assume you received my letter. I maintain that I must keep my distance so that I will not endanger you, but I am here to help. It was wrong of me to abandon you with work to be done." He stopped, still some feet away, and smiled at her. "Powers or no, the power of the word remains. And I promise to be careful with it."

So, yet fearing he'd be the death of her, he was all business. Still, it was very good to see him.

She found herself replying with her customary curt and de-tached tone, the one that betrayed nothing of her heart. "I welcome your assistance. The haunting becomes unmanageable at times, and we must keep moving else the dead overrun the towns in which we stay. But come and meet her. By the end of the month we shall move west, into York, and await the final days there."

Beatrice took a step back, but Ibrahim did not move. They shared a long, aching moment of mutual regard.

"It is . . . good to see you," he murmured.

Beatrice felt her hard expression soften, her breath catch, and her color rise. "And you."

Ibrahim took up his stack of books and strode into the room. Iris was singing softly to herself, the remains of her breakfast set aside. At his entrance, her mouth fell open.

"You're one, too!" she cried, raising both Beatrice's and Ibra-him's eyebrows. "You, too, were saved from death to live a life of glory and service!" She smiled, radiant. "Don't be surprised, sir. I know things."

This effusive, unexpected greeting made Ibrahim chuckle, and Beatrice hurried to introduce them, thankful the dear girl hadn't batted an eyelash at the entrance of a *foreigner*. "Iris Parker, Mr. Ibrahim Wasil-Tipton."

"But you may call me Ibrahim, Miss Parker. You remind me of a friend of ours. Ahmed. He, too, is full of joy and mysterious knowledge."

The girl stared at him. Then she said, "Iris then, please. We must all be friends here—friends brought together by wondrous fate. And you have brought books! Oh, you must promise to read to me, Ibrahim. I adore being read to.

"I never learned to read," Iris explained. "The sisters tried during my first few years in the convent, but I could not manage it. Then I fell in with sinners and had no one to teach me. But now I've found saints."

Ibrahim looked unsure what to say and finally stammered, "I . . . I'm here to help. I understand you are plagued by spirits."

"Oh, they're no bother, really. I think they're here for the baby. Did Beatrice tell you? She's very special, the baby. Beatrice, too, of course, but the baby was heralded by our Lady. Where are you from? Do you have a Holy Mother in your land?"

Her innocent curiosity was irresistible. Ibrahim smiled. "I am from Egypt. But I do know of our Lady."

"Egypt?" Iris repeated, wide-eyed. "Have you come all that way to help me?"

"Yes," he said. "I think it might be best for you and the child not to be too long surrounded by the dead. They can be taxing. For that reason I've brought some . . . recommended reading." Stacking the books on the room's desk, he selected a thin periodical. "*Household Words*. Dickens." He turned to Beatrice. "Do you think ghosts like ghost stories?"

Beatrice laughed despite herself, fighting back tears. She felt like Elinor in Austen's *Sense and Sensibility* at the moment she had found out Edward was free for her to love. She wanted desperately to leave the room and sob with happiness. It was so good to see Ibrahim, to be near him. All felt right with the world. Prophecy was unfolding like a flower.

Then the ghosts swooped in.

Iris shuddered at the sudden chill. The horde surrounded the bed like nurses around the dying, only these were not administering aid. Iris tried to pretend she wasn't startled, but the pendant around her neck began to glow. Beatrice believed it was the goddess's power, trying to keep Iris safe. The ghosts were not ill-intentioned, but their energy was frantic and overwhelming.

Ibrahim nodded. "Well, I suppose it's time to try my hand," he said.

Before he could open the volume he already held, Beatrice said, "Do try Rumi, Ibrahim. I miss him as much as I miss our friends. As much as I miss Cairo."

"You miss Cairo?"

"Of course I do, that hasn't changed. I miss our home," she replied.

Ibrahim's face lit up as he exchanged Dickens for the poet and began to read. Warmth flooded through Beatrice as well; for a moment they both seemed caught by the idea of *their* home.

As Ibrahim spoke, the ghosts dispersed. Perhaps certain texts contained power of their own, or perhaps Ibrahim retained some of what he'd been. Either way, the reading was effective. It seemed to Beatrice that Iris breathed a bit easier.

"That was lovely!" the pregnant woman said. "Would you read some prayers to me? Do you believe in God, Mr. Wasil-Tip—*Ibrahim*? Do you mind?"

Ibrahim answered slowly. "In *God*? Let us say that Beatrice and I call ourselves people of spirit."

Finding a Christian Bible, he began reading various annunciations. From that he moved to the Quran, about which Iris showed intense curiosity. She listened in awe until she fell into a peaceful nap convinced that there were angels of all faiths, goodness of many shapes and beauties.

Once she was safely resting, Beatrice motioned Ibrahim out into the hallway. She had to know about the fullness of his intent.

"Do you plan to stay for the remainder of this duty?"

Ibrahim nodded. "I told you, I want to help."

Beatrice waited, her gaze daring him to say more.

He looked away. "Cairo was not the same without you. Still . . . I fear your life being cut short." He gestured to his head, then his heart. "I feel—"

"Ibrahim. It's been a harrowing, grim few months. I've seen wondrous, terrible things. The goddess's tasks nearly destroyed her. One day to the next, we're never guaranteed life. Tell me," she implored him, "Persephone once intimated something, and Iris just repeated it. The day James Tipton died, do you believe the Grand Work saved your life?"

"I know it did."

Beatrice nodded, feeling phantom blue flame caress her heart. "And for that gift, for the gift of your life, the Grand Work is worth all its sacrifices. But"—she trembled as she dared prompt— "can we not choose how far we allow such sacrifices to rule and inform our hearts?"

She waited for him to speak, to acknowledge his love for her. To grant that they were meant for each other. She waited for him to reveal what she hoped he felt in his heart, what it seemed like his journey here proved. But though he stared at her and she thought she glimpsed something simmering in his expression, he said nothing.

Beatrice straightened her shoulders and spine. "The sister at the door can direct you to an inn. Rest well tonight, and we'll begin the final leg of our journey on the morrow."

At the door of Iris's room, she paused and turned back. "It is . . . *very* good to see you, Ibrahim. Good day."

That was the best she could manage to his face, though in her heart she said a thousand things more.

CHAPTER
THIRTY-TWO

THE WEEKS THAT FOLLOWED WERE BOTH JOYOUS AND HEART-wrenching. Ibrahim, Beatrice, and Iris traveled together. The women stayed at convents; Ibrahim stayed at inns nearby. They did not speak again of feelings. At last they came to York and the Institute of the Blessed Virgin Mary. All was progressing according to divine decree. As one final assurance, they would not go to the Bar Convent until the very last moment, when Iris, obviously close to delivery, could not possibly be turned away.

Drawing near the place, intending to make arrangements for them all at the inn across the street, Beatrice caught a glimmer in the air, something only eyes accustomed to strange sights could see. It seemed there was a bit of Liminal shelter over those Georgian convent walls; a thin, sparkling parasol under which a strangely beautiful, colorless flower would magically grow.

Late that night, Ibrahim sat in the corner of Iris's room, reading aloud as he had every night since he'd joined them, both to entertain her and keep the ghosts at bay. Iris was a wonderful audience, laughing, sighing, and crying, and if Beatrice wasn't mistaken, Ibrahim thoroughly enjoyed her responses and occasional hypotheses. She yearned for him to turn that pleased gaze upon her, but their quiet amiability persisted.

Iris requested more of Mrs. Gaskell, having loved her ghost stories in magazines prior. They had nearly gone through Ibrahim's whole array of material and it was time for Gaskell's serialized

North and South. Written more than a decade prior, it showcased two very different worlds and stubborn persons.

There were moments when Ibrahim sat stiffly in one corner of the room and Beatrice stiffly in the other, Iris lying in rapture between them. During these periods Beatrice was struck on more than one level by the story, yearning for its two stubborn characters to give in to each other. Sitting opposite Ibrahim during the recitation became unbearable, a painful rapture where her whole body tensed as though one simple touch might entirely break her.

They neared the end of the tale. Ibrahim was reading the strained financial proposition from Margaret Hale upon John Thornton's mill, a conversation between two people who were desperately in love but who refused to show it.

" "Mr. Lennox drew me out a proposal," " Ibrahim read quietly. " "I wish he was here to explain it—showing that if you would take some money of mine, eighteen thousand and fifty-seven pounds, lying just at this moment unused in the bank, and bringing me in only two and a half percent—you could pay me much better interest and might go on working Marlborough Mills." Her voice had cleared itself and become more steady. Mr. Thornton did not speak, and Miss Hale went on looking for some paper on which were written down the proposals for security; for she was most anxious to have it all looked upon in the light of a mere business arrangement, in which the principal advantage would be on her side.' "

Beatrice stood, agitated. She could hear no more.

Ibrahim glanced up, so she blushingly gazed down at Iris, mopping her brow, relieved and satisfied that the young woman was sleeping comfortably. She hurried to inform him, "She's dreaming. I daresay she'd not want to miss the ending of the tale, and we're not far from that, are we?" Beatrice could not meet his eyes.

"We are not."

"Shall Mr. Thornton and Miss Hale end their stubborn charade or no?" Beatrice drew a pained breath. "I suppose we'll have to see tomorrow. The end must come, just as it must for the goddess's own tale. At least, our part of it. Soon the child will come, which will mark the finale of our duty."

Ibrahim laid the magazine aside, his face thoughtful. He said nothing, just took up his tea.

Too much to bear. Beatrice fled to her rooms, needing to cool her face and be alone. The sooner this business was done, the better. Ibrahim could go back to Cairo, for clearly he had not come to claim her. If he had, he'd have unclasped his heart at some point, rather than maintaining such maddening distance.

Was he so afraid, still, that he would be the death of her? Life and death were ever precarious where the Grand Work was concerned.

Pacing the room, she did not notice the door open or the figure standing tall in the doorway until a voice continued reading; "'While she sought for this paper, her very heart-pulse was arrested by the tone in which Mr. Thornton spoke. His voice was hoarse, and trembling with tender passion as he said, "Margaret!"'"

Beatrice turned to see Ibrahim standing on the threshold, a smoldering light in his eyes, magazine in hand. He stepped toward Beatrice as he kept reading. "'For an instant she looked up and then sought to veil her luminous eyes by dropping her forehead on her hands. Again, stepping nearer, he besought her with another tremulous eager call upon her name. "Margaret!"'"

Ibrahim drew nearer. She could feel the warm heat of him, could taste the scent of myrrh oil that faintly hung around him, delectable, could feel his breath on her cheek as he continued reading.

"'Still lower went the head; more closely hidden was the face, almost resting on the table before her. He came close to her. He knelt by her side, to bring his face to a level with her ear and whisper-

panted out the words: "Take care. If you do not speak I shall claim you as my own in some strange presumptuous way. Send me away at once if I must go . . .""" Here Ibrahim paused. He leaned in, his body brushing hers, and the final call was not Mr. Thornton's but his own.

"Beatrice . . ."

She turned her head, wondering if her eyes were luminous as Mrs. Gaskell had described. Her expression betrayed her anticipation, she was sure, for her body ached for his touch.

He lifted the magazine once more so that he might read it over her shoulder as he stood so unbearably close, his breath upon her ear. "'At that third call she turned her face, still covered with her small white hands, toward him, and laid it on his shoulder, hiding it even there; and it was too delicious to feel her soft cheek against his, for him to wish to see either deep blushes or loving eyes. He clasped her close. But they both kept silence.'"

Ibrahim dropped the magazine. He cupped her warm cheeks in his cool hands and pressed his lips gently but firmly to hers. The taste of tea, the smell of incense and priceless myrrh . . . The soft press of his lips grew hungrier. Their long fight against the magnetism that had been drawing them together from the first was at an end; they could not resist crashing greedily against each other.

They drew back to breathe deep, to shudder, but it was merely a pause in their mutual surrender.

"Mrs. Gaskell was a savant. Keep more silence with me," Beatrice whispered, then drew him into another kiss that sent them to the divan to press as close as layers of clothing would allow.

After a time during which sighs and soft gasps flew from Beatrice's lips, Ibrahim spoke softly into her ear.

"The man who raised me gave me every opportunity. He never forced me to be like him or his colleagues; he gave me fine, upstanding examples of men and women within my culture, both devout and secular, sent me to be educated in my native tongue and planned that I would live as my people do. And I resented them all because none of them were truly like me. Nothing was truly mine."

Beatrice opened her mouth to say, *then let me be yours*, but her damnable pride had her saying, "I've always wondered if you resent me."

"That's not what I'm trying to say, Beatrice," he corrected her. "I never thought I was meant for love, for passion. Certainly not with a woman like you." His breath was hot against her forehead. "Working with a woman like you, deferring to a woman like you—"

"You've never deferred to me a moment in your life," she exclaimed.

"*Wanting* a woman like you." He traced a fingertip from her throat to the edge of her bodice, and Beatrice shivered with desire. "Perhaps it's time for us both to defer to the higher calling."

"And what might that be?" she breathed.

"Passion. Will you be mine, Miss Smith? Would you make a home with me? All that should have kept us apart, the Grand Work erased. Culturally, religiously, ideologically—it literally gave me new life. Would you give me, at last, a place to belong and someone to belong to?"

This was everything she'd wanted. Dared she trust it? "You no longer think you'll be the death of me? Aren't you afraid to take my hand?"

He ran his fingers up her body and pulled her fully against him. "Does it look like I'm afraid to take your hand? The Grand Work may be the death of us all, but it already saved my life, saved me from a deadly house fire on the day we were called. It is as you said. If we're living on borrowed time, we might as well live fully."

"Finally we agree," she said, fully relaxing against him, feeling all the mortar of their stubborn walls turn to powder at their feet.

Physical vows were torturously slow and delicious in the making; gentle, sacred acts; delicate promises of the life they would yet share. For one night, the dread press of fate was abandoned for the duty of the heart.

CHAPTER
THIRTY-THREE

A STORM GATHERED, BLACK CLOUDS FORMING A RING AROUND the convent where Iris Parker would soon breathe her last. Above the convent itself, the sky was clear, but it shimmered with that particular light Beatrice had come to expect from the Liminal.

Iris knew it was time. She asked Beatrice to write a letter from her to her daughter. Words of faith and love—and some instruction for good measure. Beatrice held Iris's hand when that was finished, promising to do her best to see it was delivered. Ibrahim kissed Iris's brow and Beatrice's in turn, then left them to their silent vigil as they waited for the time to take Iris to the convent.

He had been quiet and gentle since his and Beatrice's passionate foray, but they'd spoken not a word about their future. Beatrice couldn't be troubled by it, not when Iris was her present concern and needed her aid.

At last the pains began, and they left the inn.

"There is something of safety about that place," Iris gasped between contractions. Beatrice nodded. "I believe our Lady offered it a particular benediction."

The swarming ghosts were agitated, billowing like sails in a squall. They hovered all around them as Beatrice led Iris to the convent door. She glanced at the carriage where she knew Ibrahim waited outside the convent walls with texts in hand. If she needed him, she'd call for him. But this was a woman's threshold.

Beatrice knocked boldly. Iris leaned upon her, gasping.

A young nun opened the door, her habit a dress of simple gray with a coif. Beatrice didn't wait upon niceties.

"Hello, I'm Beatrice. This is Iris, and she needs your help."

"You are the one whose coming was foretold," the sister murmured.

"Ah, it's good to be expected." Beatrice helped Iris into the plain foyer as the doorkeeper excused herself to summon the mother superior.

An older, plump, ruddy-cheeked woman, the picture of authoritarian kindness, was already rounding the corner. "So it is, so it is," she said.

The sisters provided Iris with a room and the assistance of those trained in such matters of the body. Beatrice was content that Iris was in good care. The general compassion and lack of prejudice was comforting and made her rethink her opinion of the Church. It had its flaws, as did every institution. But here, in this place, women's magic was rife. Though they'd hardly call it magic. It was faith, firmly wielded.

Iris shared passionate prayers with the sisters. No one bothered Beatrice, no one asked her relation, no one hurried her away; she took a chair in the corner, sitting with her hands clasped in anxiety. She wished Ibrahim could be there to read soothing things of beauty to her, but that would hardly have been proper. As unusual as this birth was, they couldn't attract any more undue attention.

After a time, when Iris's cries were too much to bear, Beatrice sought out the reverend mother in her office.

"She won't make it through the night," the nun said, looking at Beatrice with calm gravity. This, Beatrice thought, was the perfect hand to grow an odd child into a substantive woman.

"I know this because it was foretold to me by the Holy Mother herself, who came to me in a vision," Reverend Mother clarified. Beatrice recalled Persephone saying she'd paid a visit, and it was well regarded.

"Our Lady gave us the particulars of what is to come after," the Reverend Mother continued. "The burials, the protection of the child. We shall cover her traces as specified. It is uncommon, this night. Uncommon, this charge. But when the Lord decrees something and sends his messengers, so it shall be."

Beatrice gaped. How wondrous, when mortals could talk of such spectacular goings-on as simple fact, especially those not directly called into the service of the Grand Work. Goodness knows she had not gone so effortlessly into the good night of her own fate.

Closing her mouth, she composed herself and spoke plainly. "I'll not subject your sisters to such melancholy work. If you would kindly supply me with two shovels, my colleague and I shall make sure a site is ready." Beatrice pulled bank notes from her reticule. "This shall pay for headstones. Thank you. I do believe, as odd as this is, and odd as this child shall be, that you are doing good."

"I agree." She eyed Beatrice. "Don't speak as though you doubt, Miss Smith. Speak as though you know. If you're confident good shall win, it will. If you doubt it, it won't. Do not leave room for darkness, lest it wedge its way in."

"You are wise, Reverend Mother."

"No, not personally. I allow for higher truths to flow through me. I am a vessel. So I shall give this child what I can and see that she journeys where the Holy Mother commanded. I promise."

"Thank you," Beatrice said.

She exited the convent to find the storm still held back its fury. Good, for there was a grim business yet to be done. Once necessary supplies were brought to the carriage by obedient sisters, she joined Ibrahim inside.

Without a word between them, only an occasional bolstering nod, the two of them went to a small York graveyard. There they began to dig. The physical work felt good, exorcising demons of anxiety and uncertainty as well as the grief of pending loss, of such a sweet soul as Iris Parker. Soon there were two graves set aside from the rest of the graveyard.

Beatrice placed the letter from Iris and the key from the goddess in a metal container, which she closed firmly before setting it into a wooden box the size of a dead infant, provided without question by the sisters, who were unflinching about bringing life into the world or seeing it out.

Lowering the tiny coffin into the grave, she and Ibrahim buried the subterfuge, then took a moment to say many different prayers. It would be well that this ground was blessed with multiple wards against any evils, lest it become the wedge of which the reverend mother warned.

When Beatrice and Ibrahim returned to the convent, they were greeted by the scream of a newborn. Uncannily, almost immediately, it quieted.

Ibrahim waited respectfully in the reverend mother's office, as the mysterious chamber of childbirth was entirely off limits to him. Beatrice rushed to Iris's side, stroking her hair and trying to ignore the blood-soaked bedding and cloths that surrounded her. A broken body that had yet birthed a child was indeed a miracle; she tried to focus on miracles instead.

The attendant nun midwife cried out, when the child was wiped clean, "Why, the girl's a ghost!"

"Let me see her," Iris murmured, barely audible, her strength gone but tears of love in her eyes.

"Hush," the reverend mother said to the two sisters who anxiously whispered to each other that the child was a frightful omen. "This is a child of God, and she will be raised as ours. She is sacred to us, and I'll not hear one word against her."

"Thank you," Iris whispered, gazing at the precious bundle in her arms, the baby whose icy-blue eyes were staring intelligently up at her. Iris said to Beatrice, "She's very special. See how she doesn't cry? See how gentle and peaceful a soul she is?"

"Beautiful," Beatrice choked out.

A host of spirits hovered at the edges of the room, making the cool space even colder. Beatrice had never seen them so respectful, not even during Iris's pregnancy. They hung silent, watching, listening, perhaps worshipping. Neither Iris nor Beatrice acknowledged them, lest the nuns think their strange charge further cursed.

"Give her the pendant, Beatrice, and my letter, please."

"She will be provided for," the reverend mother said, seeing Beatrice struggling for composure.

"And so it is finished," Iris murmured. She kissed her daughter on the forehead; the baby's tiny arm reached out, pressing its small fist against Iris's cheek. "Good-bye, Percy. Always remember, no matter what, you are a child of Power and Light. Unique as you look, you'll likely not think yourself powerful, but you must have faith. I did, and you were my reward."

She closed her eyes and was gone. Simple. Peaceful. Beautiful, in a way. In that moment the storm broke and the rain came. So did Beatrice's tears.

The others left the room, but Beatrice, weeping, curled over Iris's body, doubled over her as if she might yet catch a bit of the young woman's effervescent, wonderful soul. A cool draft encompassed her, and she looked up to see Iris's spirit, luminous and radiant, hovering above her, a veritable angel, suffused with joy and life. The ghost stared at Beatrice and at the tiny, colorless baby still cradled in her mortal shell's dead arms, then blew them each a kiss. The room grew blindingly bright, and Iris vanished, just as the goddess had.

Beatrice lifted the newborn into her arms, surprised by Percy's preternatural quiet and her inquisitive, eerie eyes. But then again, the child was an older soul than any could possibly know. She hugged her tight, brushing away tears that had fallen into the baby's pearlescent hair.

"Persephone Parker. You'd best make things right, young lady. You've a lot of work to do, do you hear me? Grow up fast, my girl. Grow up fast."

The baby made no sound but stared at her almost as if she understood. If not now, she would someday. She *had* to.

Beatrice carried the baby into the reverend mother's office. Ibrahim stared at the infant in awe. Handing her to the reverend mother, Beatrice said, "I'll stay the night here, if I may."

The reverend mother nodded and scrutinized Beatrice, aware of her unease. "Of course. You needn't worry, Miss Smith." She stared down lovingly at Percy before reassuring Beatrice. "A wet nurse will be found for the child at once, and there will be a funeral mass for Iris in the morning. This is hardly the first orphan we've reared. All has been provided for."

"Thank you. God bless you." Turning to Ibrahim, she added, her voice shaking, "Tomorrow we are free."

Ibrahim said nothing, just pressed her hand in support and love. She waved him gently off, and he left. The reverend mother had Beatrice shown to a spare, clean room. Sleep, when it came, was heavy.

She woke to the cry of the novices. At first Beatrice was afraid something was wrong, that the baby was ill, that any number of strange phenomena, the aftershock of divine interferences, was taking hold of the convent. But no. Looking out her window at the bright dawn, at the storm clouds rolling away, Beatrice saw the gifts Iris Parker had left and her tears flowed anew.

In the sky were a hundred rainbows.

CHAPTER
THIRTY-FOUR

ALEXI SLEPT FITFULLY THROUGH THE TERRIBLE STORM. His fingers felt wet, as if still soiled by those bloody roses from months earlier, their grim oil impossible to wash away. Midway through the night, the wind of the Grand Work swept through his room, carrying the brief cry of a newborn and then a great and glorious peace. It was a dream so powerful that his hands and heart were cleansed.

Awaking with tears on his cheeks and his heart beating wildly, he strained his eyes against the bright morning light. Out his window he found multiple rainbows in the sky, an impossible act of nature but a beautiful omen.

Throwing back the covers, he found a talisman at the foot of his bed: a luminescent feather. He held it up to the light, and it reflected every color, as if the rainbows outside shone directly upon it. The goddess who had revealed herself to announce Prophecy came to mind, a goddess he'd kept close in hazy dreams.

"'From the flame of Phoenix, a feather did fall and Muses followed,'" he murmured. It was the mythology that bound them, words ingrained in his brain when he was first chosen by Phoenix.

Seizing a notebook from his bedside table, he began to write furiously. Something had been born today; his destiny was closer than ever. How long before it all reached fruition he could not know, but something of Prophecy had been completed. He wanted to tell the others, yet this joy felt so personal, so private that they couldn't possibly understand.

The feather in his pocket, Alexi was en route to a meeting when something glimmering caught his eye in the window of a small jewelry shop. He spotted an elegant silver ring in the shape of a simple feather wrapped into a circle. As he looked at it, a terrible pain seized his body and soul, an agony he'd never before felt. A field of heather, a phantom embrace, a hand being dragged from his. Something wonderful, stolen away, leaving a hollow in his heart.

Shaking, he had to steady himself with his hand upon the bricks of the shop. A concerned customer clutched her purchase tight as she hurried off the doorstep, murmuring to her top-hatted escort, "Why, that young man looks mad."

In his ear sounded a whisper, the voice of an old, familiar friend. Or lover.

"*I promise.*"

Whatever had lurched and ached within him lost its breath in a sudden rush of hope as his thoughts narrowed to that one word. Promise? His pain was supplanted by determination. By hope.

Straightening, he put himself to rights, smoothing his waistcoat, tightening his scarlet cravat. In a matter of minutes the ring had been purchased and placed on a chain and was hidden beneath Alexi's clothing. There it would lie against his heart for however long it took to find the mystery he hungered for.

Everything marched toward Prophecy.

"DID YOU SEE THE SKY?" BEATRICE ASKED IBRAHIM WHEN HE collected her from the convent.

He nodded, touching her arm. "I did—heralds of a new dawn, releasing us to our lives."

Freedom. Was it possible? A gnawing feeling had Beatrice

wondering what the goddess had meant by "blood and fire" in the
midst of her final instructions. Such intense words had her wondering if the Grand Work would yet call on her at some future
date.

As they walked out onto the road to town, where they supposed
they'd take a hired carriage onward, a familiar ripping sound made
them whirl. There stood an open vertical rectangle, through which
Beatrice could see her father's apartment building in Cairo.

"Home! Oh, Father . . ." Beatrice choked. It was only now
that she allowed herself to entertain how dearly she missed him.
How she missed the simple human interactions she'd known before being one of the Guard. Perhaps it was time to gather family
back again and cherish each and every moment.

Crackling threads of light coursed about the edge of the portal:
Liminal light.

Ibrahim asked warily, "Are you here to carry us home? Is this
the reward for a job well done?"

The edges sparked and flickered, but the Liminal wasn't one
for conversation.

Ibrahim approached and gingerly pushed the tips of his fingers
into the space. He said, "It feels like the air of home."

Beatrice chuckled. "Well, stepping through *would* beat weeks
on a steamer. See? You'll take my hand and we'll go home. A much
better vision. Not everything we fear comes to pass as we fear it."

The word "fear" seemed to shudder through him and he stepped
back. "Having escaped death, I do now fear it. I fear these thresh-
olds, Bea. I have been warned of them."

"A portal like this?"

"Well, no, not quite like this."

"Then shall you be ruled by fear? Or by your own decisions?"
she asked gently, but firmly. A quality she knew he admired.

He considered her a moment, Cairo waiting patiently before
them. "You know, one of the reasons I chafed against loving you

was that a few of my countrymen once chided me for living among English people. They would have shunned me for our relationship.

"Yet I think upon the benediction of Ahmed Basri's smile, and the encouragement of our friends. I am that which I choose, as simple or as complicated as I may be. No other opinion has a right to that choice. Indeed, Miss Smith. My choices shall not be ruled by fear."

When Ibrahim offered his hand, she took it. They smiled and stepped through, into warm golden light.

Once a dizziness had passed, it was as simple as if they'd walked between rooms, not across continents.

"Hello, Father," Beatrice said tentatively, whole worlds having passed since she'd last spoken those words, even if only one of them noticed.

Leonard Smith looked up from his clay fragments with a smile. The blue eyes she'd inherited sparkled. "Ah, Bea! Hello! Seems I haven't seen you in a while. School, wasn't it? Did it go well? Are you back, then?"

"Yes."

He stood, acknowledging the newcomer. "And who's this?"

Ibrahim stepped forward. "Ibrahim Wasil-Tipton, sir, at your service."

"Tipton. Tipton . . ." Mr. Smith's brow furrowed before he suddenly lit up. "Are you James Tipton's boy, then?"

"Yes, sir, I am."

"What a good man, Tipton! One of the best I knew at university! He spoke so fondly of you, said you were brilliant. I'm so sorry about what happened—he's sorely missed—but am grateful you're alive. Have you met my daughter, Beatrice? Bea, you remember my telling you about the good father from England? Why, this is James Tipton's boy, Ibrahim."

"Yes, Father," Beatrice replied patiently. "I brought him here to see you." The Grand Work had made some people lovers and some strangers. She was trying to bridge her world once more.

"Sit, both of you, I'll send for tea. I'm so glad you've come! Bea, the new dig, it's exquisite! I have to keep idiot tourists from tromping around in it, but the government's giving me permission to cordon it off."

"I look forward to seeing it."

"Oh, yes, do come," Mr. Smith enthused. His thoughts shifted visibly as if struggling to pierce the clouds of Belle's lingering magic. He turned to Ibrahim. "Pardon me, my boy, why are you here?"

"I've something to ask."

Her father seemed not to hear. "Good, good. I'm so glad you've met my daughter. I always meant to invite Tipton over, Bea, and then, you know, you just take life for granted . . ." His eyes watered. "Then it's gone. But I'm so glad you've met. Isn't that fortuitous? How did you meet, anyway?"

"On the street," Ibrahim replied.

Beatrice looked down to hide a helpless smile. Her mind replayed the first time she had seen him, when he'd turned the corner outside Abu Serga. When his eyes had met hers, her breath had caught and her heart had skipped multiple beats.

"You see, Mr. Smith," Ibrahim continued, "I'm here to ask for your daughter's hand. On that fateful day, my life changed. I could have died that day. Yet I lived. I was saved. I was visited by an angel."

Beatrice looked at him, shocked by his pronouncement and by the softness of his tone. She'd never heard him use that voice apart from that night in the inn, with Iris sleeping in the chamber across the hall.

"That angel was fated to be mine," Ibrahim continued. "Heaven sent, against all odds."

Beatrice smiled, suddenly realizing that he hadn't meant the goddess. He'd meant her. This was even lovelier than she'd imagined.

Her father blinked. The young lovers sat still and silent, terribly anxious. Guard magic could no longer simply influence people to do what they wanted, even though the traces of it remained. They did have to navigate permissions, proprieties, and barriers of the age. She stared at her father, hoping he could be as open and loving as his friend Tipton seemed to have been.

Mr. Smith jumped up. "Ho-ho, Bea! I can't think of a better man than Jim Tipton, so the boy he so dearly loved . . . Why, I daresay you couldn't do better! Tell me, son, do you have an interest in the digs, as your father did? Would you like to come along?" He clasped Ibrahim in an enthusiastic embrace.

Beatrice's hand flew to her mouth, grateful tears leaking from her eyes. Ibrahim tentatively returned the embrace, a bit shocked himself. Shrugging at Beatrice with an amazed little smile, he seemed moved to be so effortlessly called son again.

"I would like that, Mr. Smith. Very much."

"We'll all go! A family expedition to relish and cherish the exquisite riches of this marvelous land!" His excitement couldn't be contained; Beatrice felt that perhaps she should have simply trusted her father all along. He had raised her to be the woman who loved Ibrahim; why, then, wouldn't he feel the same? He threw wide the door and without a hint of propriety cried, "Scratch the tea. Champagne! There's going to be a wedding!"

THERE WAS INDEED.

The ceremony was simple but powerful. Beatrice had heard so many heralds and prophecies that all she wanted was a quiet, meaningful pledge. So under a golden Cairo sun, she and Ibrahim were wed, in a simple ceremony. Ahmed read a Rumi poem on marriage. Verena sat beside Mr. Smith, who looked on, proud.

Belle and George surprised them by turning up. Beatrice had

sent the pair an invitation but hadn't expected them to hop right on a steamer. Belle claimed she'd been packed for weeks and took full credit for their relationship.

For the first time since fire coursed in her veins, Beatrice felt a sense of contentment.

"Welcome home, Bea," Ibrahim said, whisking his bride into their new flat. She giggled and threw her arms around him, stunned to see tears in his eyes. "Thank you," he said quietly.

Beatrice cocked her head to the side, waiting for an explanation.

"For choosing to make this home. For wanting Cairo. For wanting me. You did not have to."

Beatrice smiled. "Ah, yes, you and your choices. Home sometimes chooses us, you know."

"We are so blessed," Ibrahim murmured. "To have done our parts and be rid of it all. To have the luxury of the home of our heart. I pray they all will find their way, the new Guard, everyone involved. I pray for a shining star. I pray their safe passages home."

"Ibrahim prays for the Guard at last? For our dear Lady made flesh?"

Ibrahim nodded. "Most heartily for her."

This time it was she who shuddered in fear. "Love, forgive me. Tasks may yet lie ahead of me. I'll know when, but I must always heed the call."

Ibrahim nodded. "And I shall help you always. No more regrets. I live on borrowed time, and every moment with you is a blessing to be cherished, not to be squandered in fear."

EPILOGUE

Autumn, 1888

BEATRICE AND IBRAHIM ENJOYED YEARS OF HAPPINESS, NEVER forgetting the forces that had drawn them together. Every now and then Beatrice caught a fleeting scent of flowers on the breeze or strains of faraway music, distant echoes of Percy Parker and Alexi Rychman. Each time, she wished them every blessing. They'd need them all.

One night, as she and Ibrahim sat, hands clasped, upon a divan beside a blazing hearth, there came a roaring sound, one not heard in years yet instantly familiar. Beatrice was surprised and yet not—all day she had known that something was going to happen, without knowing what that something was.

The huge black rectangle opened, revealing a dim, dank maw where figures floated down the gray length of a seemingly endless corridor. A man stood in shadow, just beyond the portal, with one faintly glowing hand raised. A familiar light . . . Was this someone waiting just for her?

The door had opened for some fell purpose.

The goddess's work. Suddenly everything fell into place.

Beatrice voiced her dread realization: "The Whisper-world . . . Oh, God. *I'm* the one to bring the fire, to knit the worlds. To free the Guard spirits. But from within." She felt a wave of anger swell within her. "How, if I've no power?"

A tiny lick of blue flame coursed around the edges of the portal. Familiar blue flame, an old friend coming to collect a promise she'd made to face dangers whenever they came. But this time she realized her entry into the Whisper-world would be more than that fleeting glimpse beside the goddess. She wasn't coming back. Not as she was, not to this world as she knew it. To do her job, she would have to pass. Like dear Iris.

Ibrahim knew this was his vision. "Eternity wouldn't be enough by your side," he declared. "No matter when this portal came for us, we'd want another day."

"It's not coming for you but for me," she hissed, her anger cresting anew.

"But you remember my vision. We are hand in hand. You've work to do, and I am your second. When I came for you in York, I made a pledge to never let you go. No matter the dangers, this vision be damned. Do you regret that I came for you?"

"No," she choked out.

"So we mustn't move forward in anger, as it is but duty that again comes for us," he continued. "Anger will chain us inside this drear place, and we must fight for a brighter dawn."

"But we could've done so much more."

"I daresay every living person feels the same, but to all there comes a time for something new. For our Lady, for us."

Beatrice took a deep breath and exhaled slowly. There was no sense in waiting; the door would not close on its own. She extended a hand to her beloved, grateful for his fortitude, for the choices that had made him her husband. He took it. Now, as they'd stepped from England to Cairo, so would they step . . .

"To the undiscovered country?"

Ibrahim offered her a rare gift: a sweet chuckle that held boyish excitement. Beatrice was bolstered by his strength.

"Eternity awaits," she murmured, stepping to the edge, then hesitating a final time. Juliet and Romeo, they were, uniting houses and taking a journey together. Unlike Juliet, however, Beatrice knew there was work to be done on the other side. Blood, fire, and a captive army.

Ibrahim squeezed her hand. "I love you, Bea. And I will be with you, now and for every adventure to come."

There was no promise she could believe save this one, not after all she had seen and done. Luckily, this was the only promise that mattered. They stepped forward into darkness and believed in the coming light.

Under attack by dark forces, England and
the US must survive a new threat.

THE ETERNA SOLUTION

LEANNA RENEE HIEBER

Having vanquished the demonic pretender to the British throne,
the now-united forces of the Eterna Commission and the Omega
Department reach America ready to take on a new menace.
But like the United States itself, this evil is rapidly spreading from sea
to shining sea. Will the new magic our heroes have discovered
be strong enough to defeat it?

"*Eterna and Omega* expands the hauntingly beautiful
world of Hieber's inventive gaslight fantasy series...."
—*RT Book Reviews* on *Eterna and Omega*

TOR
TOR-FORGE.COM